11/20

# THE
# ALPHA
# ENIGMA

# DAW BOOKS PROUDLY PRESENTS THE SCIENCE FICTION NOVELS OF W. MICHAEL GEAR:

## THE DONOVAN SERIES

*Outpost*
*Abandoned*
*Pariah*
*Unreconciled*

## THE TEAM PSI SERIES

*The Alpha Enigma*
*Implacable Alpha*★

## THE SPIDER TRILOGY

*The Warriors of Spider*
*The Way of Spider*
*The Web of Spider*

## THE FORBIDDEN BORDERS TRILOGY

*Requiem for the Conqueror*
*Relic of Empire*
*Countermeasures*

★★★

*Starstrike*
*The Artifact*

★*Coming soon from DAW*

# THE
# ALPHA ENIGMA

## W. MICHAEL GEAR

**DAW BOOKS, INC.**
DONALD A. WOLLHEIM FOUNDER
1745 Broadway, New York, NY 10019
ELIZABETH R. WOLLHEIM
SHEILA E. GILBERT
PUBLISHERS
www.dawbooks.com

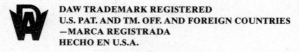

**DEDICATION**

to

Catherine Crumpler

In special appreciation

# ACKNOWLEDGMENTS

To my dear and long-time friend Catherine Crumpler I owe a huge debt of gratitude. Catherine vets all of our work, ensuring our portrayal of mental disorders is clinically correct. Assuming *Alpha Enigma* works, it is because of Catherine's commitment to psychiatry and her unstinting dedication to her patients.

To Brian O'Neil, Dr. Laura Scheiber, and the real Reid Farmer, I owe special thanks for all the "what if" conversations we've had over the years. Hopefully, you'll find the archaeological mystery contained herein as fascinating to read as it was to write.

# A NOTE TO THE READER

The science in *The Alpha Enigma* is real.

The Everett Many Worlds theory is accepted by many physicists as an explanation for the origin of our universe.

Should you have doubts, Google "Hugh Everett III," "Many-Worlds Quantum Mechanics physics," "David Deutsch," and "Multiverse."

Then prepare to be awed.

# 1

*Grantham Barracks.*

**G**ray came to us without a name. She arrived at Grantham Barracks
riding in the back seat of a nondescript black Lincoln Continen-
tal. Her car was the second, or "principal" vehicle, in a three-car security
detail. I watched it enter our underground parking lot accompanied by
the whisper of engines and the shish of tires. A gleaming black Chevy
Suburban had the blocking position in front; the chase vehicle, a Tahoe,
followed close enough behind to have nursed on the principal's bumper.

I stood outside Grantham's underground entrance with a team of
orderlies, Gray's admission papers and commitment orders in hand.

The vehicles rolled to a stop; armed agents wearing black tactical
gear burst from the doors. After they established a defensive perimeter,
a uniformed captain stepped out from the Lincoln's passenger door. He
looked around warily before opening the sedan's rear coach door.

I thought it all a bit overly dramatic for a patient transfer.

The way the tall woman swung her legs out and emerged from the
back seat, she might have been some exotic lotus. She wore a blaze-
orange jumpsuit and white athletic shoes. Her wrists were manacled and
chained, as were her ankles. The baggy prison garb barely disguised her
supple body, high bust, and broad shoulders.

I'd never seen a woman with such presence. Reaching her full height,
she shook her tawny hair back. The effect was electric. She paused—a
queen casting her curious gaze about a new but unbecoming kingdom.
Then she fixed the most incredible eyes on mine: a piercing laser-blue
like I'd never seen.

Rather than beautiful, I would have called her mesmerizing. She
looked patrician, with a high brow, straight and proportioned nose,
sculpted cheeks, and delicate jaw. The slight crow's-feet at the corners

of her eyes didn't match the youthful tone of her bronzed skin; the lush-ness in her lips contrasted with the maturity in her gaze. My guess placed her around thirty.

Ignoring the captain, she walked toward me with a dancer's practiced grace. Each step measured precisely to the length of the confining chain at her ankles.

She stopped a pace short and fixed me with an imperious gaze.

The captain offered me a clipboard. Disturbed by the woman's mag-netism, I concentrated on the paperwork. Age, date of birth, and place of birth had "unknown" written in each box. Then I glanced at the line where it said "Name." Her identity seemed to be "Prisoner Alpha."

The way my orderlies were gaping, Aphrodite might have sprung magically to life before their very eyes. I glanced sidelong at the woman, the skin on that side of my body almost prickling from her curious aura. "Do you have a name?"

She was studying me with those intense blue eyes. *"Medicus eras?"* Her words were thick with an unfamiliar accent.

"A psychiatrist," I told her. "Both a PhD and MD. My name is Col-onel Timothy Ryan. Retired. I'm in charge of Grantham Barracks. I'll be responsible for your care and evaluation here."

"What . . . is?" She jerked her head by way of indicating the concrete pillars, the parking lot, and the glass doorway that led to the interior of Grantham's Ward Six.

"It's a military psychiatric hospital," I replied. "I've reviewed the transcripts of your arrest and interrogation. They've labeled you a threat to national security and think you're either autistic or a very clever liar. I'm to find out."

I was watching for the tells, the slight dilation of the pupils, the tensing of an eyelid, or a quiver at the corner of the mouth. All I read was incomprehension. Fugue state? No, she was too alert and responsive, the eyes clear and much too intelligent.

"Mistake," she whispered. Then broke into a sorrowful string of incomprehensible utterances. When people speak in tongues, they follow the rules of pronunciation in their own language. English speakers don't make up nonsense words beginning with ng, unvocalized L, or glottal clicks. She wasn't a native speaker.

"Sign here, sir." The captain indicated the places on the forms. The name tag pinned to his chest said STANWICK

I scrawled my name on the appropriate lines.

"She's all yours, Colonel." He saluted even though I'm retired and technically a civilian contractor according to the Department of Defense.

Captain Stanwick turned on his heel and marched back to the gleaming Lincoln. At his signal, the security team broke for the vehicles.

I heard the hollow *pop!* Felt a weird tingling on my skin, my hair prickling, and the world seemed to wobble as if a wave had passed through it.

I was still disoriented when the woman cried, *"Ennoia! Muliebris canis!"*

Struggling for equilibrium, I followed the woman's gaze. The outer ring of guards seemed to have fainted, their bodies limp on the concrete. Beyond them, a man and woman stood clutching small boxes with gleaming lights.

Even as I watched, the green-eyed woman with auburn hair slipped the box behind her belt. She swung a slung M16 from her shoulder with the ease of long practice. The sights settled on Prisoner Alpha.

Combat instincts either become hardwired, or you go home in a body bag. Mine kicked in. I grabbed the tawny blonde and jerked her off her feet. Even as we fell, a burst of 5.56 rounds cracked inches above us and pulverized the glass doors. My orderlies were diving in all directions.

From the floor I caught a glimpse as Stanwick pawed at his sidearm, leaped to the side of the Lincoln and leveled his pistol over the roof. It barked twice, hot brass clattering on the concrete before my nose.

The meaty snap of Stanwick's popping skull mingled with the M16's deafening staccato. His strings cut, the captain flopped onto the concrete. Blood and brains spewed from the back of his shattered head as it hit.

I heard the attacking woman's pained voice cry, "Dear God, no!"

A couple of heartbeats later I felt that skin-prickling sensation, my hair standing on end, and then the hollow *pop!*

Silence filled the garage. One of the security guards groaned as he struggled to his feet.

"What the hell?" I whispered, trying to control my pounding heart. I still held the trembling woman, her lungs laboring for breath.

I rose cautiously, staring through the Lincoln's shattered window glass to the place where the assailants had appeared.

The male attacker lay dying in the exit lane. I could see no sign of the woman.

"Holy shit," one of the guards cried as he staggered forward, the HK MP-5 he clutched at the ready. "Who is this guy?"

The man lay on his back. Dressed in brown utility wear, a darker beard contrasting with his collar-length blond hair, he looked tanned and maybe thirty. Captain Stanwick had dropped him with a shot through the top of the heart. An M4 carbine lay just beyond his curled fingers.

"What the fuck just happened here?" another of the guards asked.

"More to the point," a third growled, "where the hell did he come from . . . and where the hell did that woman go?"

I helped Prisoner Alpha to her feet. She stared bitterly at the strange man's sprawled body.

I was trying to evaluate her absolute disregard for the captain's gruesome corpse at her feet as she whispered, *"Totem pereo."*

She uttered the words with such hopelessness they engraved themselves upon my consciousness. Only later would I learn they meant "All is lost."

# Satay

In the Ch'olan language, the word is satay. When speaking in Latinum, my native tongue, one would say, pereo. I am lost. Lost to time, marooned in a barbaric and benighted world. Even before I could gather my wits, I was cast into the hell these beasts reserve for their mentally broken flotsam.

They do not know. They cannot conceive.

How, then, did the Ennoia find me? And who was that man who accompanied her? They have shown me his picture. I do not know him. All they have from their security camera is a three-quarter image of the Ennoia as she appears. They have enhanced the image. I can read the hatred in her green eyes.

For the moment, I can only hope they will keep me safe.

As long as they do, time remains my ally.

I cradle time, draw it to my breast, and caress it like a lover.

They have taken the navigator. And while it brought me to this vile place, eventually—assuming the stupid clods don't destroy it in an attempt to learn its secrets—it will become the vehicle of my escape. Ignorant brutes cannot deny a sparkling seductress like the navigator as long as it remains in their hands.

As the Kaplan woman's recent visit indicates, they have realized its value. They need my help, and I shall repay them manyfold for this horror and humiliation.

On that day they will weep.

# 2

*Wadi Kerf, Western Thebes, Egypt. Site 65-A.*

**D**r. Reid Farmer perched on the lip of the archaeological excavation and studied the sheer-walled canyon in which he worked. The tomb area had been cut out of the tan-and-amber canyon wall; it lay perhaps three meters above a dry streambed filled with rocks and gravel.

With his archaeologist's eye, Reid could reconstruct the valley's original morphology. Higher beds of pale-yellow sandstone had been incised by hydraulic action—probably back in the Pliocene some four million years ago. During the ensuing 1.6 million years of the Pleistocene this part of Egypt had remained desert, and the canyon was occasionally scoured as runoff poured down the exposed slick-rock, sluiced into the wadis, and thundered down the channel.

The ancient Egyptians had changed it with their copper, bronze, and—finally—iron tools. During the Eighteenth Dynasty, they'd quarried the exposed strata for stone and carved out the very bedrock to construct a series of tombs the length and breadth of the valley. For over three thousand years, wind, weather, and sun—along with occasional pillaging looters—had tumbled enough material down the slopes to reduce the valley back to rubble.

Reid glanced up at the brass-hot sky and wondered what kind of damned fool would be out here running an excavation when the temperature was knocking on forty degrees Celsius.

*One who's being paid extraordinarily well,* he reflected. *Almost too well.*

Though why Skientia had chosen him for the job still made no sense. His expertise and skills were in *North American* archaeology, not Egyptology. Excavation, however, was excavation, be it an Anasazi pithouse or an Egyptian tomb. Reid was being paid to dig and, by God, he'd get it done.

Everything had been seen to with incredible efficiency: visas, excavation permits, travel and lodging, food, tools and supplies, and even security—a perimeter guard of uniformed security consisting of alert young men with slung Kalashnikovs.

"Quite the operation," Reid mused as he stepped over to their field tent and pulled out yet another bottle of water.

"They really think something is here?" Yusif, the Egyptian crew chief, wondered. He was a broad-shouldered man, closing on forty, who sported a thick black beard. Skientia had chosen him for his expertise in excavation. "I've been doing this since I was a boy. Worked with the best. I have a PhD in Egyptology from Cambridge. Never have I seen a project as, how do you say . . . forthwith?"

"Me either."

"This company?" Yusif asked. "Skientia? You have worked for them before?"

"Until two weeks ago, I'd never heard of them." Reid glanced up at the fractured sandstone outcrops and high canyon walls. Heat waves shimmered above the pale stone. "When they said Egypt, mentioned the salary, and asked if I had a valid passport, I said yes to all three."

"Do you know why they said to dig here?"

"Something about an inscription on a potsherd that one of their researchers found in the Cairo Museum of Antiquities."

"We have heard the same rumor."

"You ever seen this mysterious potsherd?"

Yusif shot him a sidelong glance. "No, *sahib.* You?"

Reid shook his head.

"They just gave you the coordinates?" Yusif pointed at the GPS on Reid's belt.

Reid chugged hot water from his bottle. "They told me Wadi Kerf, this GPS reading, and that I'd have everything I needed waiting for me in Cairo." He screwed the cap on and looked back at the line of sun-baking vehicles stuffed with research equipment.

Yusif's voice lowered. "You know, don't you, that this dig is highly irregular?"

"How's that?"

"You have seen the export permit? The document which allows you to remove artifacts from Egypt?"

"Sure. They faxed copies of all the paperwork before I left the US."

"I've never seen an export permit before." Yusif paused to emphasize his point. "Not in modern Egypt. Everyone looted Egypt's finest artifacts going clear back to the Romans. Our antiquities fill foreign museums. These days it's a matter of national pride and identity that Egypt's archaeology remains Egyptian. Why does Skientia, a company no one has ever heard of, have an export permit?"

"All I can tell you is that I was hired to bring a team of excavators to these exact coordinates, open a test unit, and determine if a tomb is present. If we find one, I'm to open it, thoroughly record the tomb's contents, recover all possible ancillary samples for dating, as well as floral and faunal analysis. I'm supposed to document, then stabilize and remove, all fabrics, wood, and bone. If a burial is present, it is to be painstakingly recorded *in situ* by the famous Dr. Kilgore France. Under her direction the burial is to be removed, packed in some special shipping container, and sent back to the US."

"And all of it has been approved by the Minister of Antiquities," Yusif muttered to himself. "I do not understand."

"Neither do I." Reid paused. "But as long as the pay is this good . . . and no one asks me to compromise my professional ethics, I'm on board. Anyone demanding this level of anally meticulous data collection isn't in it to just 'grab the gold and run.'"

The ringing of a shovel on stone was followed by a cry from Ibrahim. Reid stepped to the pit rim. Ibrahim—one of the field crew—worked in a crouch, using a trowel to loosen the sandstone-filled matrix from the rear of the trench. Reid could tell that the squared rock emerging from beneath the overburden was a lintel stone, the top of a heavy doorway.

"How about that," Reid muttered to himself. "Right where they said it would be."

The rest of the crew pitched in, laying planks to allow them to use wheelbarrows to more quickly remove the crumbled colluvium.

Ibrahim called out in a string of Arabic, then turned to Reid. "Dr. Farmer. Come. Take a look! This is not right."

Reid slid down into the pit, edging past the Arabs to stare at the lintel. Letters had been carved deeply into the stone, the edges slightly weathered: *TEMPUS DEVINCERO.*

"Latin? Here?"

"It is indeed Latin," Yusif finally agreed. "But what is a Roman tomb doing among all these Eighteenth Dynasty tombs?"

"Intrusive? Something the Romans dug down to this level?"

Yusif was absently pulling at his beard. "The style is not Roman. When this was built, the wild tribe who would one day become Romans were still nomadic hunters and herders somewhere in central Europe."

"Just wait, Yusif. We'll get it open and find Roman-period furnishings, maybe even a date."

"And if we do not?"

"Then, my good friend, we've just made our careers. They'll have us on all the lunatic talk shows." He laughed at Yusif's worried expression. "Oh, come on! It's an intrusive tomb. Probably a Romanized Egyptian from the second century who wanted to be buried among the ancestors."

"Or a hoax."

Reid climbed out of the pit, retrieved his water bottle, and sucked down what was left. "Or a hoax. Everyone loves to hoax archaeology."

Steel rang hollowly, as if to mock him.

"*Sahib*?" Ibrahim called. "You better look at this!"

Ibrahim had dug down another twenty or thirty centimeters, exposing the top of the door. While it had once been clad in stone, the stained and corroded portal could have been nothing but steel. The kind of steel that wouldn't be invented for nearly three thousand years after the Eighteenth Dynasty.

Reid clambered down to inspect this latest of upsets. "Looks to me like Skientia is being scammed."

*Grantham Barracks.*

I studied the dead man's features. The photo gave his face an empty look. Periodically, during the year since Prisoner Alpha's arrival—and the attack that had almost killed her—I had pulled out the file on her attackers. The man had been relatively young and fit. His weathered skin had the nut-brown look of a long-time desert tan—a possibility enhanced by the incipient wrinkles at the corners of his half-lidded and death-dull eyes.

"Who are you?" I asked the frozen visage yet again.

When I'd shown the photos to Prisoner Alpha, her gaze had chilled. She'd shaken her head—what I took to be a barely restrained satisfaction behind her closely pressed lips.

The photographs occupied me while I waited for General Elijiah Grazier's call. I'd known Eli for years, worked with him off and on until my retirement. Since the unsettling arrival of Prisoner Alpha, I'd found myself in constant communication. Eli had an almost killing interest in my patient. His people had claimed the dead man's corpse; and to my amazement, not even Eli—who could finger anybody—had been able to ID the guy.

Nor had there been so much as a whisper of the whereabouts of the mysterious green-eyed female companion who'd popped into our garage, unleashed the barrage, and vanished. She'd definitely cried, "Dear God, no!" in an American accent. So why hadn't Eli been able to tag her?

The phone rang. Eli. Right on time.

*"Ryan? I'm sending a file. I'd like Falcon to take a look at it."*

"Yes, sir. I'll have Janeesha print it out the moment it comes through on the—"

*"Not that I don't trust your secretary, Ryan, but I've got a courier bringing the physical documents. It's 'eyes only.'"*

"Yes, sir." I paused. "Anything I should be aware of on this one, sir?"

*"You know Sam Savage? One of his teams got shot up over in the Sandbox. Something's screwy. Shouldn't have happened."*

"I never met the man. Heard of him, though."

*"He's a good egg."* A pause. *"Any progress on Alpha?"*

"You have my weekly report."

*"It's been a year, Ryan. All she's done is make that doohickey machine out of TV parts and draw cartoons on her walls."*

"She's been learning English at a rapid rate. Though, God knows, most of it is from television given her isolation from the rest of—"

*"I know your feelings. And yes, Tim, you're a good doctor. Your overriding concern is to heal your patients, but Alpha is different. Orders stand. She stays in maximum security."* I heard him take a stressful breath. *"Have you had any breakthrough? Is she really nuts? Or is she lying?"*

"I watched the entire recording of her interrogation by that Kaplan woman you sent last week. Alpha seemed vaguely amused by the schematics the woman showed her. But from her pupil dilation, galvanic skin response, pulse and respiration, she might have been tolerating a precocious five-year-old instead of a highly trained physicist. Now, if you'd just tell me what this is all—"

*"Ask me something I can talk about."*

"What about the corpse? I was just sitting here staring at his picture."

*"Still nothing. You ever heard of Dr. Kilgore France?"*

"The forensic anthropologist?"

*"That's her. She ran a series of tests on the body. Bone chemistry. Took samples from the teeth. She says the guy was raised on the East Coast, grew up in Massachusetts, was affluent, and had good dental hygiene. So why is it that we're still drawing a bust? We've run facial recognition programs on every DMV, college ID, Facebook page, you name it. Nada. The guy might never have existed. Even the serial number on his weapon is a mystery. Manufacturer says it would be another three years before they came to that number."*

I stared down at the photo, trying to imagine how a man raised in affluent Massachusetts could erase his record. "Any chance he was spec ops?"

*"Let's just say he never existed among the ranks of the operatives 'that never existed.'"*

"And the woman?" I lifted the second photo. The security cameras had oddly fuzzed out, like static when the man and woman arrived. When the image had firmed up, they'd just been standing there, the woman's rifle spitting bullets at me and Alpha. The man beside her was already falling, his M4 dropping from his fingers. The short segment of recording showed her reaction as she shot down Captain Stanwick, dropped beside the man, and cried out. She'd grabbed some kind of box from her companion's belt. At her touch a blue holographic display projected above the box. Her eyes had flicked across the screen. She'd blinked what looked like a pattern, or code.

Then the image went fuzzy again.

*"Nothing,"* Eli growled. *"Did you bring her up just to irritate me? Because I'm having a bad day?"*

"Would have, if I'd thought of it. Call it a serendipitous score on my part."

He sighed. *"Believe me, we're looking. Every airport, train station, bus terminal, embassy. We've got eyes in places that—if they were discovered—would land us in the middle of World War III. Never known a bitch to go to ground like this. Not even a rumor."*

"Well, she's never been seen around here again."

*"You stay damn frosty. But for your reflexes, Ryan, she'd have killed Alpha that day."* I heard muffled voices on his end, and he said, *"I've gotta go. The moment that courier arrives, get that file to Falcon. I need his magic ASAP."*

The line went dead.

I replaced the receiver and stared thoughtfully at the green-eyed woman in the photo.

*How do* two *people just appear out of nowhere in this modern world?*

Among the monitors that covered my opposite wall, one was dedicated to Prisoner Alpha. The tawny-haired woman was standing at her small table, doing something with the doohickey—the unfathomable electrical device she'd cobbled together from her first TV.

"If I could just reach you, maybe you could tell me why two assassins wanted you dead."

# 4

Mozart's *Don Giovanni* played in the background. Captain James Hancock Falcon had always enjoyed the opera's dark tonal qualities. And a fellow had to admire the outright *chutzpah* of any lecherous character with the guts to spit in the devil's eye as he was being dragged into hell.

Falcon sat at his desk, absently rubbing the day-old stubble on his chin. Dressed only in a white terry cloth robe, he leaned over the open binder on his blotter and carefully reread the précis. There had to be a pattern here. His uncanny ability to recognize patterns had taken him to MIT at the age of seventeen. And after the major had convinced him to enlist, his talent had led to rapid promotion and an office in the Pentagon basement. Now it had brought him here, to his safe room in Grantham Barracks.

The trick was to fit the disparate parts of the intel together in the right order. When that happened—like popping a champagne cork—the pattern would emerge from what seemed chaos.

But which parts? And what were the missing pieces?

Falcon leaned his head back, staring at the white acoustical panels in the ceiling. The small black dome that hid the security camera mocked him. He'd studied that ceiling intently over the last couple of years. Outside of the light panels and the fire-suppression sprinkler heads, the camera was the only interruption in an otherwise bland surface.

He rubbed the back of his head, feeling close-cropped hair ruffle under his palms. He only stood five-foot-six, brown hair, brown eyes . . . everything about him reeked of the average, even his weight and frame. To look at him, he'd pass as the middle of the bell-shaped curve. Mean, median, and mode for an American male. For his entire twenty-nine years he'd hated being ordinary. When Aunt Celia . . .

"Stop it," the major barked.

"Stop what?" Falcon growled back, glancing across his small room to where Major Marks leaned back in the recliner, his feet up. The man had laced his powerful fingers behind his head and he, too, now stared at the featureless ceiling.

Major Bradley Kevin Marks appeared to be in his fifties. He looked every inch what he was: an old-school officer. A wealth of colorful campaign ribbons decorated his left breast. The creases on his olive pants could have been knife blades, and the man's shoes reflected like black glass.

"You're distracting yourself, Falcon. You always do when things don't make sense."

"Major, I didn't even hear you come in."

"In my world, people who can't move with silent grace get 'made dead' in a hurry."

"You're in Grantham Barracks," Falcon muttered, turning back to the document on the desk. "It's not the jungle, or the mountains . . . and there's no one around here to shoot at you. Not even the guards carry weapons."

"Nothing is as it seems, Falcon. You're stumbling over that intel report like a five-year-old on an obstacle course." The major grinned. "It's right there in front of your nose."

"In front of my nose?" Falcon jerked his head around to give the major a hard glare. "You want to elaborate, or are you just going to flop in my chair like a beached carp?"

"You're distracting yourself. Stop looking at your nose."

*Idiot.* Then Falcon hesitated. *Stop looking at my nose?*

He closed his eyes and imagined that his nose was gone. That his face was flat. Nothing but air lay between his eyes and the report. Yes, he could see it more clearly, the detail remarkable. One by one he built images from the descriptions and arranged them on the backs of his eyelids, shifting them, moving the image of a spec ops team here, a missile battery there, a fuel truck over there. Then he rearranged one or another, trying new combinations. Sections from the report rolled through his thoughts, echoing slightly as the words resonated in his memory. And the pieces slipped together.

"The communications are compromised," he said as he opened his eyes. "I don't know how, but they've got a security breach. Someone is reading General Grazier's top-secret traffic."

"There, see?" Major Marks grinned. "Distracted by your nose."

Falcon slapped the intel folder shut . . . rolled back in his chair. His room measured fifteen by twenty-five feet, the floor sealed concrete. He had one small window above his solitary desk. In addition to his reclining chair, the only other furnishing was the bed, neatly made up. It rested opposite his bathroom door. He had covered the underlying white walls in a cluttered collage of maps, aerial photos, tables, and graphs.

"You're sure about the communications breach?" The major gave Falcon his steely-eyed look.

"Do you think I need to bring Theresa in on it?"

Major Marks made a face. "What for? Do you see operational info buried in that skimpy report? Anything to hint how they'd do it?"

"No."

"Then why do you need a skirt like her to look for mathematical probabilities? General Grazier asked you to determine what, not how. All you've got in that folder is the 'what.'"

"One of these days, Theresa is going to hear you call her names, and she's going to get even."

"Oh, I heard, all right." A woman's voice announced from the half-open bathroom door. "He's just an overblown, hyper-egotistical military hack. After all these years of putting up with his supercilious and condescending ego, if I'd needed to put him in his place, I would have."

Theresa Applegate slipped past the bathroom door. In the process of pinning back her spill of curly black hair, she shot Major Marks a disdainful look. Then she gave Falcon a crooked smile and walked over to his desk.

Falcon knew she had a PhD from Harvard, was twenty-two, single, and the most brilliant woman alive. Theresa must have weighed no more than a hundred and ten which, given her five-foot-seven, just wasn't enough. She insisted on wearing 1950s style floral-pattern cotton dresses. Today she'd chosen red roses on a white background. Dark, strapped-leather shoes covered ankle-high white bobby socks.

Stopping at his desk, she stared down at the report and quickly scanned the pages. "Makes sense," she agreed as she closed it again. "Grazier's got a leak."

"But no idea where?" Major Marks asked.

She shook her head. "Not from this. If Grazier's people had provided any ancillary data . . . who planned the op, how the team was inserted, how Major Savage was chosen for command, anything that we could draw comparisons to . . ." A frown lined her high forehead. "Can you get that kind of data?"

"I don't know," Falcon said with a sigh.

Major Marks replied through gritted teeth, "Just asking might be enough for General Grazier's people to figure it out. Save the skinny witch from having to strain her brain."

"My only brain strain is trying to fit you into the phylogenetic tree, Major. You put a whole new twist on the term 'primitive life-form.'"

Theresa primly seated herself on her favorite corner of Falcon's bed. She laced her fingers around a bony knee, crossed her legs, and ignored Major Marks as he speculatively studied her thin calf.

Falcon chuckled to himself. "I'll put Theresa's thoughts in the memo. See what comes back."

"My call is that they'll need us to discover how the system's compromised," Theresa said lightly. "They should never have relocated you, Falcon. Running down to that little basement office you had in the Pentagon was a lot quicker than sending couriers all the way out here. But then"—she cast a dismissive look at Major Marks—"since when is the army ever efficient at *anything* but carpet bombing?"

"Lady," Marks straightened on the recliner and pointed a hard finger, "carpet bombing is done by the Air Force. Something even a broomstick-thin rear-echelon *analyst* like you should know. Not even the vaunted Roman legions could compare with the professionalism, the duty, the adaptability . . ."

Falcon tuned them out. They'd be at each other's throats for the next couple of hours. And sometime—while he was preoccupied—they'd get tired of baiting each other and leave. Reaching into his drawer, he fetched out a Sharpie and a sheet of paper. One by one, he began jotting down his conclusions about the report.

# 5

The military psychiatric hospital at Grantham Barracks monitored everything. The central command and security center for Ward Six was separated from the patients and adjacent to the administrative offices.

Locked behind security doors in the Grantham command center, Corporal Julian Hatcher leaned back in his comfortable chair and scanned seven banks of security monitors. He'd been keeping a special eye on Captain Falcon. Four hours had passed since the captain had been given the "eyes only" intelligence binder. Now Hatcher watched as Falcon opened his drawer and removed a Sharpie and a piece of paper.

The moment Falcon began writing, Hatcher pressed a stud on his control board, speaking into his headset. "Dr. Ryan? Falcon's writing."

Ryan's voice replied in Hatcher's earbud. *Do you think he's come to a conclusion? That he's got anything worthwhile?*

"He started talking to the major about an hour ago. Then, for about forty minutes, he did that thing where he closes his eyes, tilts his head back, and meditates. After that, he told the major that General Grazier's security had been compromised."

*"And Applegate? Was she there?"*

"I'm not sure, but I think so, sir. Just at the end. Falcon's face had that amused expression he gets when she's around."

*"As soon as he's finished, get Simond to collect his notes. I'll give General Grazier a heads-up that Falcon's hit on something."*

"Yes, sir." Hatcher took a glance at the rows of monitors that crowded the wall. A complicated optical system followed his eye movements, and with a double blink, he could enlarge any of the images for a better look.

Hatcher keyed on the screen that displayed "the hole," Ward Six's isolation cell. The single occupant, Chief Petty Officer Karla Raven, captured Hatcher's attention. She practiced tai chi in the cramped confines of the tiny cement cubicle. Toned muscle slid under her smooth skin as she balanced on her toes, pivoted, and in a sudden blur of movement, leaped, planted a foot on the bare wall, and flipped herself upside down and backward. She'd barely caught herself before launching into an eye-blurring series of kicks, punches, and strikes.

*Damn! How could a woman that beautiful be such a mess?* He shook his head. Every male on staff at Grantham secretly lusted after Raven. Midnight-black hair, clear gray eyes, a classically sculpted face, all atop the kind of toned, healthy, and curvaceous body that filled a man's dreams. Except that not only was Raven the deadliest person in Ward Six, but she was certifiably nuts. She scared the shit out of Corporal Hatcher—and anyone with sense.

Movement in the central monitor drew Hatcher's attention to Prisoner Alpha. She was another too-good-to-be-true fantasy. Just being in her presence was intoxicating. Right up until the moment she pinned you with those weird blue eyes. Hatcher always marveled at the way she seemed to dominate a room. And on those occasions when he escorted interrogators to her high-security quarters behind the forbidding gray door, he'd catch himself staring at her as if hypnotized.

Everything about Prisoner Alpha reeked of the mysterious: The attempt on her life the day of her arrival; the still unidentified corpse of the man killed in the attack; her incomprehension of the simplest things; and her remarkable intelligence. Hatcher and his staff had escorted a constant stream of high-level officials who had sought to interrogate Alpha—though it had slowed to a trickle over the intervening year.

For the last hour, she'd been sitting on her bed, back to the wall. Her knees supported a notebook she'd been doodling in with a Sharpie. Patients weren't allowed pens or pencils. Alpha had covered the paper with combinations of odd bars, dots, and symbols. Obviously, a code of some sort—though to date no one in cryptography had been able to decipher it.

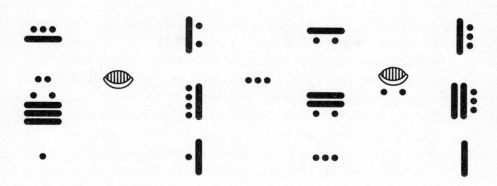

As the months had passed, she'd occasionally step to her wall and use her colored felt pens to add a line. What looked like doodles, or cartoons, now mostly covered the four walls of the woman's cell.

Had it been Hatcher's call, he'd have made her scrub them off. Colonel Ryan however, called it "therapy."

On the table stood her doohickey, her peculiar electrical apparatus. Alpha had cannibalized her first TV for parts to make the crude-looking device. The electricians had looked at it and could find neither rhyme nor reason for the thing. On occasion, Alpha would spend hours tapping on a circuit with a bit of wire, but to no effect. Given some of Grantham's other patients and their disorders, her behavior was almost anticlimactic.

Alpha rolled her head, swinging her arms as if to loosen her shoulders. Stepping over to the television, she switched channels; none of the residents were allowed remotes. She settled on CNN. As if she sensed him through the lens, she turned, fixing her weird blue eyes on the camera. She seemed to be waiting, the effect predatory.

Hatcher noted the time, and wrote, "Alpha rose from her bed, switched TV to CNN at 13:55 hours."

Hatcher then turned back to Falcon, who continued to write, filling his single piece of paper with carefully lettered notes. Whatever he'd figured out, apparently, wasn't complicated.

Falcon methodically capped his Sharpie and oriented the paper on top of the intelligence folder before him.

Hatcher pressed another stud. "Simond? Falcon's finished his analysis. Could you drop in on him and pick it up? Dr. Ryan has already notified General Grazier that it's on the way. Oh, and now that he's finished, can you take him his medication?"

Hatcher continued to gaze at Falcon where the captain sat at his desk. The sounds of Mozart's *Don Giovanni* played softly in the background.

Falcon remained the room's solitary occupant—as he'd been all afternoon.

# 6

Dr. Reid Farmer enjoyed the chilly pre-dawn air as he stood on the lip of the excavation and tried not to stare directly at where the acetylene cutting torch burned through the steel door. The Egyptian welder had cut his way up one side, across the top, and was now working his way down the steel door's right side.

Reid toed a potsherd—one of millions that littered the valley floor—and concentrated on Maxine Kaplan's distant voice on the satellite phone.

"It took all day yesterday," Reid replied to her question. "We were able to expose the entire doorway. You should have received the JPEGS I emailed. The door was originally covered by a single stone sheet, almost a cladding. That was smashed long ago. The fragments were still *in situ* at the foot of the door. Those are the angular pieces on the ground in photo thirteen."

*"And the damage to the steel door? What do you make of that?"* Kaplan asked.

"Ma'am, after a close inspection of the dents, I'd say someone wanted to make it look like a battering ram hit it. It's a good job, the indentations look old. Also present—which you can see in photo sixteen—are what look like metal chisel marks. They, too, have been aged, probably through some chemical means, maybe an acid wash."

*"You assume they have been faked?"*

"Whatever this is, it's *not* an Eighteenth Dynasty tomb. I'm no metallurgist by any means, but a sheet of steel like this wasn't being manufactured until the Industrial Age at the earliest. Whoever put this door on this tomb wasn't an ancient Egyptian." He paused. "I'm estimating another fifteen minutes before we'll have cut through."

*"Dr. Farmer, if that tomb is what we think it is, you must take every scientific*

*precaution. Record every detail of your investigation with excruciating accuracy. This is the single most important data recovery you've ever undertaken, and as good as you are, expect to be raked over the coals by your peers. Treat this as if it were the tomb of Ramses."*

"Yes, ma'am." He glanced over his shoulder at the two-man camera crew, and then at the closest Toyota four-wheel-drive with its boxes of tinfoil, plastic tarping, ziplock baggies, soil-sample bags, packing, and boxes. There, too, were Tyvek suits—specially ordered by Skientia to minimize modern contamination of the tomb before pollen, phytolith, DNA, Carbon-14, and other samples were obtained. The latest gadgets for field analysis, including microscopes, handheld XFR machines, infrared and ultraviolet cameras, a ground-penetrating radar, and thermal imagers had been included. Overkill for a standard archaeological excavation.

*"One last thing, Dr. Farmer. You remember the rider that you signed on your contract? The confidentiality statement?"*

"I do."

*"You are not to communicate your findings to any of your colleagues. Not family, nor friends. No one."*

"I understand." Even though he didn't. If they'd been scammed, they surely could have taken the con job to whatever law enforcement agency had jurisdiction.

He glanced over. Yusif—a welder's mask held before his face—was crouched, peering over the welder's shoulder. He held up five fingers and nodded in the direction of the door.

"I have to go," Reid said. "Yusif says we'll be through in five minutes."

*"Remember, Doctor. Everything must be meticulously recorded. If we're right, you're about to embark on the most fascinating day of your career."*

The connection was cut, and Reid stared thoughtfully at the satellite phone. That didn't sound like a woman worried about covering up a con job.

*"Sahib!"* Yusif called, waving with his free arm. "We are through. We can pry it open now with bars."

Reid's crew were puffing on the last of their cigarettes, rising, laughing as they talked.

"Better get the plastic sheeting out of the truck," Reid ordered. "If we're going to minimize contamination, we're going to want to cover that opening even as we pry that section of door back."

Yusif finished taping the roll of plastic to the top of the metal door just below the stone lintel and the cut steel. The enigmatic TEMPUS DEVINCERO seemed to mock them.

Skientia had translated it as "I conquered time."

Slipping his bar into the cut, Reid waited for Yusif's nod, then levered the nearly detached center out. As he did, Yusif slipped the heavy plastic down behind the gap. Meanwhile, Reid kept moving down the door, using his bar to widen the gap. The weight of the door began to take over, bending the two connecting tabs at the bottom.

With the help of several others, they eased the flat piece of metal to the ground. Yusif carefully sealed the sides of the doorway, securing the plastic to the steel surface.

"What the . . . ?" Reid stared at the back of the door. A series of weights pivoted on links attached to locking lugs that, when closed and latched, had protruded beyond the side of the door. The thing reminded him of the sort of mechanism that locked a modern master safe.

"That is not ancient Egyptian," Yusif said flatly.

As the cameraman recorded the exposed locking mechanism, Yusif elevated a thick eyebrow. "So, *sahib*, are you ready to don your suit and take that final step into immortality?" He jerked a nod toward the tomb entrance.

A tickle of unease ran through Reid's gut. "Uh, you don't think there's any other surprises in there, do you? Deadfalls, pits, swinging axes, booby traps . . . ancient Egyptian curses?"

"That's not the lost ark, and you're not Indiana Jones." Yusif's smile rearranged his thick beard. "But this is Egypt, and they did anything they could to dissuade grave robbers."

"And what's an archaeologist?"

"The difference between an archaeologist and a grave robber, *sahib*, is the company they keep, and the money they make. Grave robbers are so much better paid."

"Ancient traps don't make that distinction."

"Sorry," Yusif told him with a shrug. "Now, let's get the dead-air tunnel set up and your contamination suit out of its bag. I can't wait to find out what sort of traps they have laid for you."

"Your concern touches me."

"Welcome to the new Egypt. We now have free speech. As long as you only say the right things."

# 7

The sagging report in my hands offered the same kind of inspiration I could have enjoyed if I had been watching mold grow. I skimmed the column on the requisition status for light-blue, six-inch, PVC sewer pipe. It was all I could do to keep from staring at the little scale-model of a Ducati 916 that rested on the corner of my desk and daydreaming of twisting mountain roads.

Then I glanced at the door that led to my secretary's office. Right and left of the door, floor-to-ceiling bookshelves were filled with thick, very expensive professional texts and monographs. The titles included both psychiatric and psychological works; I'm smart enough to mine the best from both fields. If anyone looked closely, they'd see a section on the third shelf, right-hand side, dedicated to famous racing motorcycles.

So sue me.

In addition to my keyboard and monitor, I cluttered my desk with a phone, video cam, a photo of me on my Daytona-blue Ducati Diavel with its white racing stripe, and a single portrait of my son, Eric, at age ten, wearing a baseball uniform. And finally, propped on its side stand, is the aforementioned little red model of a Ducati 916. I've always lusted after a 916. The toy had been a gift from a too-many-years-dead friend: the motorcycle I'll never own for real.

I tossed the maintenance report onto the desk and leaned back, pinching the bridge of my nose. For a man in his late fifties, I've somehow managed to keep in good physical condition. It's the graying temples that get me. I fumbled for the pen in my vest pocket, thumbed to the last page of the report, and scrawled my name.

The buzz from the intercom made me glance at the clock. Chief Petty Officer Karla Raven was right on time. I checked the upper right-hand monitor—the one that showed Janeesha's office. Outside my door Staff Sergeant Myca Simond—wearing his duty scrubs—stood just back of, and slightly to the left of, Chief Raven. The chief's hands were manacled behind her. Myca held a chain that he'd attached to the manacles like a leash.

"Silly boy," I muttered, and pressed the buzzer. Janeesha, wary, opened the door before stepping back to allow Chief Raven to pass.

Chief Petty Officer Karla Raven walked innocently through my door. Level gray eyes met mine, and her delicate eyebrow rose in a way that eloquently asked, "Well, what did you expect me to do?"

I chuckled and pushed back in my chair. "Myca, you can remove the chief's manacles."

"Uh, boss, that's not a good—"

"Myca, if Karla had wanted to, she'd have already knocked you unconscious, lifted your keys, and made her way past the first security ring."

Myca's face flushed almost as red as his carrot-top hair. He shot Chief Raven a disbelieving sidelong glance. "You're kidding, right?"

"You're new here, Staff Sergeant. Since Chief Raven's been in the room for all of thirty seconds, and we're both still upright, that tells me she's not inclined to cause us trouble today." I gave her a questioning tilt of the head. "Right, Chief?"

"Yes, sir."

Simond winced. "But she attacked Lew Fergusson, broke his jaw . . . and four ribs . . . and his right middle finger!"

"Chief? Why the jaw, four ribs, and right middle finger?"

She flipped her midnight-black hair back and pulled herself to attention. "Sir, breaking the jaw kept him from verbally articulating threats against Private Jones. Fracturing the thoracic ribs was a way of limiting the amount of hot air he was spewing to power his damn mouth. And the middle finger, sir?" Her expression hardened. "When I attempted to engage Seaman First Class Fergusson in a conversation detailing certain of the more egregious aspects of his apparent hostility toward Private Jones, he rather pointedly replied that he was contemplating a new and exciting career opportunity . . . and he was going to use said finger in the pursuit of the same."

"And that career would be?"

"Gynecology, sir. Or so I would assume, since he intimated I would be his first . . . um, patient, sir."

"Myca?" I made a "do it" gesture with my right hand. "Remove the manacles."

Myca reached for the manacles. Chief Raven's lips bent just enough to betray the smile she was hiding.

"Wait!"

Myca froze.

"Karla?" I used her first name. "If I take the chains off, nothing will be missing when you leave? Nothing palmed?"

Her eyelids lowered as she studied me, then she nodded. "No, sir. Nothing missing when I leave the room."

I repeated the signal to Simond. He reflexively jumped back as the manacles fell free. You know. The same sort of instinctive reaction someone would have when a live grenade was dropped on the floor.

Chief Raven carefully rubbed her wrists, then snapped off a salute and returned to attention.

"At ease, Chief." I steepled my fingers, searching for words. "I went over the official report, reviewed the video . . . Now, just between you and me, off the record, what happened that day?"

She gave a slight shrug of the shoulders. "OTR? Fergusson was going to hurt ET. Really hurt him. Everybody on the floor knows Fergusson's file. He beat his CO to death and was sawing the man's skull open when they caught him. Said he was going to use it for a cup, just like the SEALs do. Now, granted, we're all a little crazy in here, but, sir, you've got him in the wrong ward."

"Telling me my business, Chief?"

"No, sir."

I leaned forward, punched the stud on my intercom, and said, "Janeesha, cut a transfer for Seaman Lewis Fergusson to the walls, please. Cite inmate security for the reason." The "walls" or Ward One was where the violently insane were housed. Which was where I would have put Fergusson in the first place, had I not been under other orders due to the machinations of Fergusson's civilian lawyer.

"Yes, sir."

I leaned back and twiddled my pen as I studied Raven. "Sorry I had to lock you up, Chief. Despite the leniency I would have liked to have shown you, there has to be a baseline of discipline."

"Nothing comes free, sir."

"Anything else we need to discuss, Chief?"

"No, sir."

"Meds suiting you well?"

"Yes, sir."

"And the food?"

"Couldn't be better, sir. We'd no idea cube steaks could be cooked to such a remarkable flavor, let alone used to supplement body armor."

I leaned forward and pressed my stud. "Janeesha?"

*"Yes, sir?"*

"Give the cook in the Ward Six mess his two-week notice. Inform the personnel office that if they can't find someone competent, both CNN and Fox News will hear about it."

*"Yes, sir."*

I leaned back, smiling. "Anything else, Chief?"

"Life's good, sir."

The way satisfaction crept around those beautiful lips caused me to bite off a chuckle. "Then you're dismissed, Chief. You can find your way?"

"Yes, sir!" She stepped to attention immediately before my desk and ripped off a letter-perfect salute, her arm flashing down to her side. I'd been expecting it. Even so, I missed it when it happened.

"Chief?" I called, stopping her a stride short of the door.

She turned and gave me a ravishing smile. "I said, 'when I left the room.' I still had a whole pace to go before I had to give it back."

She barely flicked her wrist; the little red Ducati arched high, and I snatched it from the air. By the time I did, she was through the door.

"Got to have a talk with that woman about her sense of humor."

"Sir!" Staff Sergeant Simond protested, his eyes wide with disbelief.

I leaned back, spinning the little Ducati's tire with my finger. "Myca, like I said, you're new. Grantham Barracks is what it is. Ward Six is something else. They're all unique in one way or another. When it comes to Chief Raven—"

"She's a kleptomaniac? On top of everything else?"

"We call it an impulse control disorder, and on her current meds, we've got her depression and guilt mostly licked. The flashbacks? We're still working on them."

Sergeant Simond watched me replace the little red Ducati on its corner of the desk as he asked, "Dr. Ryan, you acted like you trusted her."

*How'd she do that? I was looking right at it.*

"She gave up everything, right down to her soul and self, to become the first female SEAL, then to become a SEAL sniper. She racked up fifty-four confirmed kills and finally earned the chance to command a platoon of SEALs. An IED took out most of her platoon. The only person on earth who holds her responsible was—and still is—Karla Raven."

"I don't understand."

"No, I suppose you don't."

# 8

**R**eid activated his throat microphone. "Okay, I'm in."

Yusif's voice filled the earbud. *"We hear you. Your camera is recording. We're streaming live to Skientia in California. They confirm receipt via the satellite feed."*

Despite the Tyvek suit, the air in the tomb felt cool. Reid sniffed, wondering if the place had a musty odor. He couldn't tell through the filters in the face mask.

He felt like a SWAT team officer with his equipment: cameras, communications gear, flashlights, spare battery packs, ziplocks, tinfoil, headlamp, and the pistol-shaped XRF spectrometer in its holster on his hip.

The camera recorded as his headlamp illuminated the square tunnel that led into the tomb. He inspected the ceiling, searching for any loose stones, but the plaster appeared unbroken as it led down into the darkness. What he would have considered classic Egyptian art lined the walls, some of it in hieroglyphics, the rest in Latin script: Latin that hadn't been invented yet—let alone steel doors.

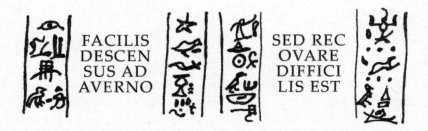

FACILIS DESCEN SUS AD AVERNO         SED REC OVARE DIFFICI LIS EST

*Just do your job. Take your time. There's no hurry.*

Step by careful step, meticulously recording the wall art, Reid eased down the sloping tunnel.

"Yusif? You hear me?"

*"Loud and clear, sahib. I take it you've arrived at the anteroom?"*

"It appears so." Reid braced the camera and reached for his flashlight. Flicking it on, he panned around the room. Statues of scribes and servants, neatly spaced, lined the walls. A dismantled chariot lay in the middle of the floor. The walls themselves were filled with images of brown-skinned people dressed in white aprons. Rendered in familiar Egyptian profile, they watched Reid warily through their single eyes.

A passage had been cut in the rear wall. To either side stood two identical statues of Osiris, each beautifully painted, the faces apparently clad in gold. Eyes of gleaming jet watched Reid with fixed disdain. And over the door, more Latin—all of it totally beyond Reid's comprehension.

On the floor, carved into the stone, was a single word: PERICU-LUM.

"Are you getting this, Yusif? This one word? Why would they put it on the floor like this? Some sort of a blessing for when you step into the room?"

*"I see it. Latin again."*

Reid lifted a foot. "Okay, I'm going to enter the—"

*"Do not move!"*

"What?" Reid's foot hung in midstride.

*"Ms. Kaplan says the word means 'danger.'"*

Reid slowly, carefully, lowered his foot back to its previous position. "I don't see anything suspicious."

*"Stay put. I'm thinking."*

"I don't know what's worse. The word 'danger' carved into the floor, or you actually thinking."

*"They let us do that after the revolution."* Yusif paused. *"Kaplan thinks the warning is to be taken seriously. And I agree. Egyptian tomb robbers would not have been the most educated of men. Only scholars would have been trained in Latin."* A pause. *"Had it existed when the tomb was built."*

Reid played the light more carefully on the carving, seeing shallow scores in the stone. Reflected light sent a glare across the clear plastic of his goggles. "Yusif? Can you see this? It seems to read, 'GRADUM FACI SINISTER.'"

*"Sinister?"*

"Yeah, that's scary, huh?" He looked around, craning his neck to pan the headlight, trying to figure out what could possibly be sinister in the whole dark scary damn room with its wooden statues of dead people.

*"California says 'sinister' is Latin for left. They say they think* gradum faci sinister *means 'step to the left.'"*

"Step to the left?"

*"They say the translation isn't strictly grammatical according to classical Latin."*

"Why am I not reassured by that?" Reid made a face. Then he looked straight overhead. A black slit cut into the ceiling was positioned just over the inscription on the floor.

"I'm stepping to the left."

With an unsettling tickle in his guts, he took a deep breath and stepped to the left of the inscription. The floor felt solid underfoot. He waited through a long pause accentuated by the rapid pounding of his heart.

*"They say to watch for additional warnings."*

"How will I know they're warnings?"

*"They'll be written in Latin?"*

"Asshole."

Passing each of the waist-high statues, he carefully filmed them from as many angles as possible. Then he shined his light on the wall and stopped.

"Yusif? You seeing what I'm seeing?"

*"I do, sahib. They're sounding most intrigued in California, too."*

Drawn on the wall, surrounded with lines of Egyptian hieroglyphics, was the definite image of a jet airplane. The design wasn't anything Reid was familiar with, the aircraft having six engines and a Y-shaped tail. Some kind of Latin was lettered on the fuselage.

"Tell Kaplan it's a hoax." He glanced around, feeling a terrible sense of loss and frustration.

*"Ms. Kaplan says they're elated, Reid. It's better than they hoped. Your instructions are to continue. If they're right, there should be a mummy in the next chamber. You are to proceed with caution."*

"Yusif, explain to Ms. Kaplan that it's some sort of sick joke. I'm surprised they didn't draw Bugs Bunny waving from the cockpit."

He waited, the terrible feeling of disappointment curdling in his belly.

*"Reid? You are instructed to continue with the greatest of caution."* A pause. *"Ms. Kaplan reminds you; they are paying your salary. She hopes she is paying for a professional."*

"Fucking A, it's her checkbook."

*What the hell, maybe it's like a game of Clue? Find the hoaxer's fingerprints on the mummy?* That in itself should be worth free beer at the next annual meeting of the Society for American Archaeology.

He headed for the square passage in the rear. As he passed between the statues of Osiris, his light played over the phrase engraved in the floor: INGREDI ET MORI.

"You getting this?"

*"Kaplan's people translate it as 'Enter and Die.'"*

"Charming. You think it's for real?"

*"Step inside . . . and I guess you'll find out, sahib."* A pause. *"Kaplan says that another clue must be there somewhere."*

"Yeah." He ran his light around the inside of the portal, seeing nothing but smooth stone. "Where?"

*"Reid, Kaplan's people are serious. They say if you step in there, you're going to die."*

# 9

While most of the men in Ward Six spent their days staring dreamily at Karla Raven's too-perfect body, according to Private First Class Edwin Tyler Jones' way of thinking, Catalina Talavera filled every category that defined a beautiful woman. Not that ET didn't appreciate Karla Raven. She'd saved him from a real beating the day Lew Fergusson had taken a dislike to him.

Edwin liked the way her large dark eyes flashed. The curves on her petite figure filled his imagination. He could only fantasize what it would be like to run his fingers through her thick, long black hair. That she was only five-foot-four, while he was six-three, added to her appeal, and her porcelain-doll vulnerability just begged him to comfort her.

He suspected that she was the only woman on earth who was smarter than he was.

His only problem: she acted as if he didn't exist.

Frustrated, Edwin toyed with his green beans as he sat at the cafeteria table and sneaked surreptitious glances at Cat. She sat alone at the next table, eating slowly, her dark eyes lost in thought. As she chewed, the muscles at the corner of her jaw gave charm to her perfect cheekbones. Her delicate nose wrinkled just the littlest bit as she reacted to some internal thought.

"You ought to go talk to her," James Falcon, sitting to ET's right, suggested between forkfuls of mashed potatoes.

"Man, you don't understand." Edwin reached for his orange juice, irritated at Falcon's perception.

*I gotta be slipping. Locked up here in the nuthouse, I'm losing control. That shit woulda got my ass killed on the street.*

"You know she doesn't have any friends here. She's not military. The woman's lonely, more than a little frightened—" Falcon made a circular gesture with his plastic fork that took in the cafeteria and its occupants, "—and most of this crowd's a bit unpredictable. She might appreciate a friendly voice."

Edwin swallowed the last of his orange juice and set the paper cup down. "Unpredictable? We got loony central here. Gotta be when they *count* these crummy plastic spoons and shit when we turn in the dishes." He paused, glancing thoughtfully at Falcon.

"Come on, Edwin, you're erecting barriers on purpose. Defeating yourself before you start."

"All right, Captain, maybe so. But here's what's what." He ticked off on his long and nimble fingers. "She's high-class West-Coast Latina, I'm a black gangsta'. Off the hard streets. *Detroit* hard streets, my man. I lived by my wits. Muled drugs over the bridge to Windsor . . . that's Canada, bro. And I did it for some damn dangerous dudes. Only reason I sent my ass to the army was 'cause I got ratted out. Wasn't nothing gonna save me." He grinned. "'Course, I had to construct Edwin Tyler Jones, come up with a name, give him a high school diploma, clean sheet, and a nice family to make Edwin look respectable."

"You *built* Edwin Tyler Jones?" Falcon asked, his eyes now half-lidded, his head tilted.

Edwin leaned back, attention on Catalina Talavera. "I was maybe four. Somebody . . . older brother I think . . . left a laptop in the house. One he stole from somewhere. Man, it just come natural, you know? The whole computer thing. And there's *always* somebody ready to teach. And, yeah, the gangs do hard crime, but that don't mean they're stupid, not when a fortune can be made scammin' folk on the Internet."

"So you learned computers on the street?"

Edwin absently rearranged his green beans, making them into a square, slowly adding layers as if to build a miniature log cabin. "They spent real money training me. And not for no reason. First, I'm pretty damn good. And second, if I get caught, I'm just a kid, see? Got deniability. 'Hell, he don't know what he doing! How's he supposed to know he done hacked into the Wayne County Courthouse? Wha'chu mean he done changed court records? He only fifteen!'"

Falcon laughed, a gleam in his ever-so-average brown eyes. "You actually *altered* court documents?"

Edwin could see the faint scars on Cat Talavera's wrists, and they touched a vulnerable part of his soul. A woman had to really be hurting to do that to herself.

"Made for an easy mistrial. Hard to convict a brother when written reports say one thing, computer records, they say another. I just wiggle past the firewalls and security and put in what the lawyers tell me. They know what to change. Them prosecutors? They never know what hit 'em."

Falcon was nodding slowly, his bland face half thoughtful, half amused. "Very clever, Edwin."

"Oh, yeah. And not just computers." He grinned. "I took a course in how to be a locksmith at community college. After that, I got this job at one of them security companies. Took less'n a month. I could bypass any alarm system they had. Brothers was so impressed, they had me apply for this job at the bank. Security analyst, they called it."

Falcon leaned forward, listening intently. "How long did it take you to crack their security?"

"Couple of weeks." Edwin knocked down his "cabin" of green beans. "Had to be damn careful, Falcon. If'n I'd left fingerprints . . . traces in the system? They'd a had my ass in jail so damn fast it'd left a streak across the floor."

"So you did money transfers for your brothers?"

Caution sent warning tendrils along his spine. "Money transfers? Hell, no. Would'a been illegal."

"Of course." Falcon agreed too easily.

"What I can mine out of Amazon, Google, Yahoo, Bing, and the others? Stunning. Ain't even the tip of the bogeyman's nose. You ain't done nothing till you get into RFID traces, public utilities, cell phone data, GPS traces. And the NSA database? Diamonds, gold, and shine!"

Falcon fixed his attention on the empty air and nodded, as if listening. Turning back to Edwin, he casually remarked, "The major says you're not a mental patient. What are you doing here, Edwin?"

*So, how much do I tell?* He noticed that Falcon's hands were twitching in unison. They'd been cutting Falcon's meds back. Rumor was they did that when they wanted him to evaluate intel data.

"Why's the major wanna know?" Everybody in Ward Six knew about the major.

"Major Marks is just curious. Nothing more."

"He's here now?"

Falcon inclined his head toward the opposite side of the table where a chair sat at a cocked angle.

Edwin chewed his lower lip for a moment, gave Falcon another appraisal, and lowered his voice. "Army put me in signals intelligence. Sweet deal, SigInt. They got a lot of smart guys working cyber defense. Me? I got too cocky. A little slow getting out of General Jaffer's personal email. He didn't want the world, 'specially his wife and kids, to know he got a mistress and a house in the Cayman Islands." Edwin made a face.

"You were reading the Chairman of the Joint Chiefs of Staff's *personal* email?"

"That damn military prison at Fort Leavenworth? Bad dudes in there, and I didn't want no part of Kansas. So I write my own psych evaluation to get sent here instead. Made myself safe in the process, right? That General Jaffers, he got an out now. Anything I say, it's crazy talk. No need for no assassin in the middle of the night."

ET watched as Cat Talavera very carefully placed her plastic fork and spoon side by side at an angle on her paper plate. She stared sadly down at it, took a deep breath, and stood. Without making eye contact, she walked slowly from the room to the hallway that led to the female wing.

"Talk to her," Falcon reminded. "She's alone and hurting."

"Too much of a mountain to climb there, Captain. Man, she's got *two* PhDs, and she's only twenty-nine! What's she see when twenty-three-year-old me walks up to her spouting the talk? She sees some black kid dropped out of the sixth grade, don't know the name of his real father."

Captain Falcon seemed to be listening intently, and it took Edwin a moment to realize it wasn't to him. But then, what did he expect? Smart as Falcon was said to be, he still carried on conversations with people who just fucking weren't there.

Edwin shoved his chair back, stood to his full six-three, and said, "Give my best to the major."

He made himself walk away with all the dignity he could muster. Glancing back, he saw Falcon, nodding, talking earnestly to the empty chair. The man's hands were still twitching, and his right foot was rhythmically tapping the vinyl floor.

Edwin shot a wistful look at the female wing, wondering.

# 10

"**D**o not move!" Yusif's voice had all the tension of an over-stretched wire. "*Play the camera around the inside of the passage.*"

Reid slowly panned the flashlight and camera across the passage walls. Just past the slit in the ceiling, he made out the letters: PULVIS PUTRESCERIS.

"You seeing this?" Reid asked.

"*I do. Kaplan's working on it.*"

Reid stood in silence, hearing his breath rasp through the filters in his mask. The elastic that sealed the contamination suit had begun to eat into his skin, and he couldn't so much as scratch.

"*Reid? Kaplan says it translates as 'dust of rot.'*"

"And that means . . . what?"

"*Perhaps something they scraped off of a decaying animal?*"

"Like corpse powder?"

"*This term I do not know.*"

"In the American Southwest, the native peoples, Navajo and Pueblos, they have stories of witches grinding up desiccated corpses and blowing the powder onto people to make them sick."

"*Egyptians were not known for grinding up their dead. We do know that poisons were impregnated into the tomb surfaces. Perhaps they allude to that.*"

"I guess I'll see." Reid took a step and watched his bootie-covered foot plant itself on the stone passageway.

The floor held, then with a crack, sank three or four centimeters. Reid leaped back. He'd no more than caught his balance before a thump sounded overhead. He looked up, headlamp beam illuminating the ceiling as a cloud of dust exploded from the dark slit. Driven by compressed air, it blasted down around him in a fine talc-like powder.

"Son of a bitch!" He took another step back, slapping at the dust that settled on him.

*"Do not break the seal on your contamination suit! Do you hear?"*

"Yeah? You got any wild-assed guess about this stuff?"

*"Kaplan says to give them a reading with the XRF."*

"Now, there's a thought." Reid reached for the pistol-like spectrometer. He switched it on, watched it load and calibrate. He programmed the settings he needed and pointed it at a concentration of dust on his shoulder. Then he pressed the trigger. "It just looks like chemistry to me. Lots of carbon, hydrogen, oxygen, sulfur, phosphorus. Organic instead of mineral."

*"It's reading on the computer here. We're uploading the data to Kaplan."*

"Should I come out?"

*"The trap is sprung, eh? As long as that ancient dust isn't eating holes in your suit, to be followed by holes in your skin, it can't contaminate you again."*

"You're a sick man." Reid cleared the XRF pistol and reholstered it.

*"I'm not the one covered with a mysterious dust."*

"I'm taking a sample now, sifting some into a ziplock." Reid labeled the ziplock with a Sharpie and stowed it in his pack.

*"Good. Now, as the dust settles—so to speak—what do you see?"*

Reid carefully stepped over the sunken stone and into the square passage. Less than a meter beyond the "Dust of Death" he saw the words PRAECIPITARES AD INFINITUM painted on the floor. But for the brilliance of his headlamp and flashlight, he'd have never seen it.

*"Ah, this one I know,"* Yusif's cheery voice sounded in the earpiece after the warning had been translated. *"Somewhere just up ahead there is a drop. A covered pit, if you will. One wrong step and you fall like a stone to a very hard, or pointed, landing perhaps three or four meters down."*

"How do I recognize the pit?"

*"Can you see any irregularity on the floor?"*

Reid dropped to a knee and shone the light along the floor. Trickles of the whitish corpse powder drifted down from folds in his suit. "I see a slight line in the stone. A sort of disconformity."

*"That will be it, my friend. Can you jump it?"*

"How the hell should I know? Who do you think I am, Indiana Jones?"

*"Unfortunately, sahib, it would seem that like it or not, you are. And unlike*

*the Hollywood gags, these booby traps are meant to kill you. Kaplan just called. She believes from the XRF data that you are now coated with a combination of aspergillus and ergot spores. They suspect Ochratoxin A and something called vioxanthin."*

A shiver ran through Reid's body.

"Yusif? I need a confirmation from Kaplan about the filters in this mask. Are they up to handling this stuff?"

*"Reid?"* Yusif's voice sent a jolt through his system. *"Ms. Kaplan assures you the filters are good down to 100 nanometers. Spores are much larger than that."*

"Charming." He dared to breathe again. "Now, what about this pit in the floor?"

*"I've been giving that some thought. Return to the main entrance. I have an idea."*

"One that will keep me from dying in this house of horrors?"

*"Oh, I want you very much alive, sahib. If you die, I have to take your place."*

# 11

I walked down the female wing in Ward Six, a rolled report in my right hand.

Karla Raven leaned against her doorjamb, attention centered on the gray metal security door at the end of the corridor. A good three paces away, I called, "Coming up behind you, Chief." A smart man doesn't surprise a SEAL with acute PTSD.

Karla snapped to attention.

"At ease, Chief. I'm retired, remember?"

"Yes, sir," she replied with full military propriety.

"I suppose there's no way we can get past that commanding officer thing?"

"No, sir." Her level gray eyes looked down into mine. Then a faint smile bent her perfect lips. "Well, perhaps just a little, sir."

I gestured at the gray door that blocked the hallway just beyond hers. "Something interesting there?"

"Just Gray, sir."

"Prisoner Alpha?"

"She's Gray to us, sir. Like her door. Curious that she doesn't have a name, isn't it, sir?"

"This may come as a surprise, Chief, but despite my research, I don't know much about her."

"Odd that someone would try to KILL a woman who doesn't exist." She paused. "Rumor is they never ID'd that guy who died trying to kill her. That the female shooter just vanished. No trace."

"That's classified."

"Yes, sir." Karla gestured toward the door. "There a reason she doesn't get to rub elbows with the rest of us?"

"Orders. And even if there weren't, I don't know what to make of her. She spoke no English to begin with, but she's been learning. Her math skills are outstanding. I suspect she was a physicist in her former life."

"How'd she get here?" Karla wondered, forgetting herself for the moment.

"Security caught her inside a black project Los Alamos lab. No idea how she got in or where she came from. They charged her with criminal trespass. In the subsequent investigation they couldn't turn up anything on her. No name, no address, no history, nothing. Her interrogators couldn't recognize her language and would like to chalk it up to a disorder in the speech centers of the brain. She might have been Italian since she can comprehend simple phrases. Problem is, neither fMRI nor CT scans show any damage to either Broca's area or Heschl's gyrus. Those are the language centers of the brain."

"She faking?"

"More like she's ignorant. She prints in an unusual alphabet with additional patterned symbols we can't decipher. She couldn't read or write cursive, though she's learning. Common references, like World War II, the Cold War, Afghanistan don't register. She responds with a blank look."

"So, what do you think, sir?"

I sucked a deep breath and shrugged. "I originally thought it was some sort of autism that's manifesting in a form I've never seen: an NOS, or Not Otherwise Specified. In some ways she demonstrates the kinds of behaviors we see in 'closet children.' You know, the ones locked in a closet or basement for years? But she's neither physically nor emotionally stunted. There's no sign of brain injury or developmental abnormality, factors which would seem to discount autism. The different centers of her brain activate the way they would in any other intelligent human. Put that all together, and what do you have?"

"Enigma?"

"I couldn't have said it better, Chief." I tapped my report against my left hand like it was a baton.

She gave me a gray-eyed sidelong glance.

I started back down the hall, took two steps, and patted my pocket. "Uh, Chief?"

Raven gave me an impish grin and tossed me my pen. I snatched it out of the air, reclipped it to my pocket, and shook my head.

*How does she do that?*

On the way back down the hall, I checked to ensure that keys, cell phone, wallet, pocket schedule, and reading glasses were where they should be. And, damn it, I knew Karla was grinning at my back as I went.

Stopping at Dr. Talavera's door, I was curious to find it open. Glancing in, I knocked on the doorframe. At sight of the red-headed woman seated on the corner of Cat's bed I prepared for trouble. Major Winchester Swink shot a quick glance my way. "Hello, Skipper!"

"Hello, Winny." Swink suffers from antisocial personality disorder. Because she's so damn good at flying things, the Air Force overlooked her APD until Winny pissed off a general.

Worried that she was cooking up trouble, I shot a glance at Cat. Sitting at her desk, she seemed composed. "Sorry to bother the two of you. I can come back later."

"It's okay, Skipper. I was about to leave." Swink rose to her full five-foot-four and shook back her flaming hair. She kept herself in superb shape in the expectation that she would be cleared for flight duty again. She also practiced a variety of different martial arts should she ever need to, as she said, "clean someone's clock."

For whatever reason, the chip that balanced so precariously on her shoulder seemed absent today. Or she wanted something from Cat and was governing her trip-wire temper with an iron hand.

She turned her attention to Talavera, and said, "Talk to you later, Cat."

I watched her half-swagger out of the room, as if she were mocking me.

Cat Talavera smiled shyly. "She wanted to know about Los Angeles. Her husband is taking their two little boys to L.A. for a visit."

"She does care about her kids."

I stepped fully into the room, wondering about the wisdom of what I was about to do. "How have you been feeling?"

Cat's history was as unique as she was. She was a "Dreamer," brought to this country when she was six. In school, she'd excelled, entered the university on a full-ride scholarship. Earned two PhDs by the time she was twenty-five. Despite offers in the private sector, she was working on a DOD-funded grant through the university. Conducting cutting-edge research on methylated genes that I didn't understand. When she learned her research had been used to murder an entire village with Taliban sympathies, she imploded. Unleashed all that guilt, betrayal, and rage in a much-too-public display.

She tilted her head, giving me an "Are you crazy?" arch of one delicate eyebrow. Then she raised her forearms, the whitened scars visible on her wrists. "Look, Dr. Ryan. No new ones. But then, you've cunningly managed to avoid giving me anything sharp."

"Comes with the territory. Nothing in life is free. Not even brilliance."

"So, you think brilliance made me crazy?"

I slapped my hand with the rolled report. "In all fairness to the Department of Defense—and their reasons for placing you here—people with normally functioning brains don't usually attempt suicide on the Capitol steps."

"Looking back, had I been in control of my faculties, I'd have done it someplace farther from medical aid. I was thinking of the statement it would make, not the proximity of trained EMTs. But then, suicide was a bit out of my expertise." She chuckled, shaking her head. "Two-hundred-and-twenty people are dead because my research enabled the *cholo* bastard who ordered their murder!"

"He's been relieved of command."

"There's always another one waiting to replace him." She flipped her thick black hair back. "The things I did, Dr. Ryan? Emailing my research to the *New York Times,* trying to kill myself on the Capitol steps? That was rage and shock."

"So how would you do it differently?"

"I wouldn't. Killing myself wasn't the answer." She looked around helplessly. "Looking back . . . Seeing it clearly, maybe I belong in here. It's just tough to admit."

"And the sadness and depression? Have they been getting worse?"

"When I first got here? There was this feeling of happy idiocy. I could just sit like a vegetable and be okay with it. For the last month I've been at my wit's end. Let me scrub floors, pick up the trash, anything but just *sit* here!"

I carefully asked, "You know why you're here? Really?"

"They said 'for observation.' In reality, I'm a security risk. They barely managed to kill that email before the *Times* got it. I'm too valuable to let go."

"And you're okay with that?"

"Hell, no! I want *out* of here! I'm a biochemist and geneticist with *two* PhDs! And given the way you people sanitize everything, I can't even grow mold in my toilet, let alone tinker with its DNA."

Then she looked up, eyes widening with understanding. "You've been changing my meds, haven't you?"

"I don't think you were mentally ill, Dr. Talavera. Here's my take: You were twenty-seven years old, dazzled by your own brilliance, incredibly idealistic, and out to save the world. When you smacked head-long into the wall of reality and betrayal, you didn't have the emotional foundation to handle it. You'd spent your life sequestered in study, education, the university, and scholarship." I paused. "What's the phrase? Book bright, world dumb?"

A frown lined her brow. "What did you do to my meds?"

"You've been on a placebo for the last couple of months."

A thousand thoughts churned behind her delicate face. "But I'm still a security risk."

"That, unfortunately, I can't change with a wave of my magic psychiatric wand. What I can do is start laying a foundation to eventually get you out of here."

"That's supposed to motivate me? Dr. Ryan, if I'm suddenly declared sane, they'll charge me with all those security violations. Maybe even treason. Charges that have heavy-duty jail time attached. And when they're done with that, there's my illegal status." She paused. "As if they'd ever really deport me to Mexico."

I gave her a conspiratorial grin. "Landing in Grantham Barracks may turn out to be the preferred alternative to a felony cell in Leavenworth." I waggled the roll of papers in my hand. "Meanwhile, the Chinese are doing something with pigs by inserting human genes that govern the development of our brain tissue. Why put human 'brain DNA' into pigs? I caught a whiff of the story and contacted the guys at DARPA. Maybe, if I had your take on it . . . ?"

She took the roll of papers before seating herself at the desk and rubbing them flat with her palm. "I'd need the latest journals. I've been out of the loop for the last year. Research on this stuff moves like lightning."

"I might be able to swing that."

But she was already lost in the report, the cutest little parallel lines in her brow above her nose.

When I left the room a couple of minutes later, I couldn't quite control the smile that kept tugging up the corners of my lips.

# 12

Yusif's "idea" consisted of three-meter–long wooden planks. They had been meant for shoring should the depth of the excavation require it. Now the lumber would create a bridge with which Reid could hopefully span the chasm if, indeed, a chasm there was.

One by one, he carried the three-centimeter–wide lengths through the antechamber and slid them, one atop the other, along the left wall and across the suspect section of floor.

*"Are you ready?"* Yusif inquired.

Reid cast an irritated glance at the faint warning on the floor and gently placed his left foot on the planks. "I'm covered in fungus spores, deep underground in a supposed Egyptian tomb with an airplane drawn on the wall. You're telling me I might fall to my death at any instant. What's not to love?"

*"At most, these pitfalls are rarely more than a meter across. The ones I have seen, or that have been described in the literature, either hinge or break away."*

Reid hesitated, trickles of fear-sweat on his clammy skin. He played his light over the square passage. Unlike the short outer tunnel, the walls here had no writing. Somehow that made them more ominous. At the end of the passage, a dark opening led to what was probably the burial chamber.

*I don't have to do this. I can just back out, let them hose me down with Clorox, and tell Skientia to book me a flight back to Denver.*

"Sure," he whispered under his breath, "and for the rest of your days, you'll wonder why the hell someone spent all this time and effort building, and then hiding, this thing."

Reid stepped warily out onto the stacked planks. His heart jackhammered behind his breastbone. His breath came rapidly, rasping in the confines of the mask. Shifting his weight slowly, carefully, he made a full step.

"Sahib?"

"Quiet, I'm concentrating."

In the silence, his half-choked swallow sounded loud. Yusif and the Californians had to have heard it. Nerves throughout his body tingled with anticipation of a fall.

He managed another step, head down so the lamp illuminated the grainy surface of the lumber. The floor seemed to mock him, appearing ever so solid in the harsh light.

*What if it turns out that the floor is solid? What if this is all some elaborate game? Some twisted and bizarre reality TV show?*

In a voice mocking Pat Sajak's, he said, "And archaeologist Reid Farmer continues to make his way into King Tut's tomb. He's already lost the car by triggering the flour cascade, but he's still got a chance at the all-expense-paid trip to Hawaii if he manages to avoid the pitfall and the swinging pendulum at the crypt entrance!"

*"I don't understand."*

"If this turns out to be a reality show, I'm suing for the car, Yusif. Even if I tripped the flour bath. The contract I signed said nothing about TV. I want the damn car."

*"Are you feeling well? I do not . . . Ah, wait, the team in California is laughing. They want me to tell you . . . I don't understand this, but when, and if, you reach the burial chamber, to pick door number three. Does that make sense?"*

"Yeah. Tell them if I win, I want the car and Vanna White."

*"Who?"*

Reid reached the end of his planks. His gut lurched as he placed more weight on his foot and sighed in relief as the floor held.

"I'm across." Shining his headlamp and camera this way and that, he made his way forward, step by careful step to the end of the long passage.

It looked as if it were a small antechamber to the burial room—a sort of closet with grooves cut into the wall on either side. The ceiling seemed to be a square of solid stone. He would have to lower himself about a half meter onto a wooden plank floor bordered by what looked like a stone threshold. Beyond, he could see the ghostly images of a raised central sarcophagus, jars, and statuary.

"It looks like a burial chamber should. Whatever this charade is about, I'd say that's the grand prize just yonder."

*"Ms. Kaplan says they are delighted. They didn't get much of a look at the step down. Do you see anything like the markings we've encountered before?"*

"Nope. Just some kind of confined antechamber and those odd grooves in the walls. Of course, the floor's wooden, so it could be a trigger plate of some sort. By stretching, making a half leap, I should be able to hit that stone threshold. It looks pretty solid."

Then he cocked his head.

"Naw, too easy."

He carefully inspected the grooved walls. Sticking his head into the confines, he craned his neck and saw the words on the flat stone ceiling.

"You see this, Yusif?" The words read NUTU SUO MOMENTO-RUM.

*"Kaplan's people urge you not to proceed."*

"I'll do my best to restrain myself, impetuous bastard that I am, all dripping with white fungus."

*"Kaplan says it translates something like 'the force of momentum joins together.'"*

"Right."

*"These warnings may be some kind of local idiom."*

"Idiom or idiot? There, but for a letter, be I." Reid stared thoughtfully at the grooves, and then he got it. "It's a hammer."

*"Excuse me?"*

"Hammers smash things together, like forging steel. Yeah, it's a trap, all right. That big honking block of rock rides down the grooves."

This time, when he stuck his head out into the void to stare up at the giant flat of stone, it left him with a queasy sensation. "Yusif, from here it looks like granite, and if that comes down, you're going to need a couple of days with pneumatic jackhammers to break it apart."

*"Do you think you could step all the way across to the threshold?"*

Reid considered it. The cubicle was designed not to be leaped. If he tried, he'd smack into the low-hanging stone in mid-jump.

*So, can I do this?*

Encumbered with his pack, equipment belt, and the clumsy Tyvek suit, he wasn't sure. He couldn't take any of it off, not dusted with whatever that white crap was.

*"Reid?"*

"I'm thinking."

*"Allah have mercy upon us."* A pause. *"Kaplan's team thinks that you're right. They think you should backtrack while they have their engineers look at it. Perhaps there is a way to rig some sort of sling and pulley system. Some way of creating aluminum braces to support a short zip line."*

"Maybe." Reid cocked his head. "Let me try something."

He walked back and retrieved the top plank from the pile atop the pitfall. Back at the "hammer closet" he winced as he settled himself, legs hanging into the gap, and slowly slid the plank forward. The wood grated, and he heaved, extending the end out, guiding it as it reached its fulcrum. Teeter-totter-like, the far end dropped to the floor a good half meter beyond the stone threshold.

"How's that for a solution?"

*"Just fine . . . so long as it doesn't slide out and drop you on the trigger when you put your weight on it."*

Grabbing the elevated end, Reid slowly pushed the plank forward, horrified at the ease with which it slipped across the stone floor. Then it stopped.

Retrieving his flashlight from his belt, he twisted the bezel and narrowed the beam. "I'll be damned."

*"What is it?"*

"A faint groove in the floor. Probably to brace the planks the hoax masters used to build this place."

*"So you are going to try it?"*

"Damn straight, buddy." He hurried back for the rest of the planks and slid them down next to the first. Then he eased out over the "hammer's" trigger. Liquid fear now pumping, inch by inch, he lowered himself into the gap.

Even as he did, he glanced up, awed by the sheer mass of stone hanging so perilously above.

*If it falls, you're never going to feel a thing!*

Thick though the planks were, he watched them bow under his weight as he reached the midpoint.

"Shit!"

*"What?"*

"The planks are bending." He tried to back up, bootie-clad feet slipping on the smooth wood. A cold terror seized his heart.

Could he turn to a crawling position? Heart thumping, he started to swing his butt out. The planks flexed precariously. Fear paralyzed him like a trapped rabbit.

"Gotta chance it," he groaned to himself.

No choice remained but to inch down ever so slowly, hoping now that the slippery Tyvek didn't suddenly send him sliding down to disaster.

Breath knotted in his lungs, he eased ever closer to the threshold; fear wrung hot sweat from his air-starved skin.

*Close! So damn close!* Reid tried to judge the thickness of the plank against the shadow cast by his headlamp where it shone over the stone.

"Screw it. I'm either dead or alive in the next few seconds. Yusif, If I don't make it . . ."

*"Allah be with you, my friend."*

Reid clamped his teeth, ground his jaws, and slid his butt directly over the threshold. Did the stone sink just the slightest? Damn it, the plank had to be touching!

And then he was over, scrambling off the shivering planks. He dropped to his knees on the cool stone floor, breath rasping in and out of his lungs.

"God, I swear, get me out of here, and I'll only dig deflated lithic scatters and tipi rings for the rest of my life!"

*"Ha! Ha! I knew you would make it! We all did!"*

"Son of a bitch," he muttered to himself, his heart still vibrating in his chest, muscles quivering. He stood, flashing his light around the inside of the burial chamber. The central sarcophagus atop its solid-stone pedestal dominated the room. Dark and black, it differed stylistically from the usual Egyptian sarcophagi. The image was oddly more lifelike, the hair—instead of being covered by a traditional wig—appeared to be close-cropped. Something about the features smacked distinctly of a European: thin, straight nose, long face, angled cheekbones, prominent chin. The arms were crossed at the chest. Reid was immediately drawn to the fact that the figure had been depicted with rings on the fingers and what looked suspiciously like a wristwatch rather than a bracelet.

Instead of a pectoral—or chest plate—a carved image of a bound book lay beneath the arms. Prominently engraved on the cover were the words, APERTUS ET DIRUMPO.

He stared in disbelief at what should have been Egyptian hiero-glyphics.

But weren't.

Covering the great black sarcophagus' surface were glyphs: what looked like combinations of bars, dots, and circles. Reid shone his cam-era onto them, holding it at an angle so the relief would provide better contrast. "Yusif? You see this?"

*"It is like nothing I am familiar with."*

"They're Mayan mathematics. And, Yusif? I think they're equa-tions."

*"When do mathematics like this date to?"*

"I see a zero here." He pointed for the benefit of the camera. "The oldest known zero is from Uaxactun and dates to about 350 BCE." He chuckled. "I don't know who these people are, or what they're trying to pull, but a lot of effort, creativity, and money went into its construction."

Reid took a moment, staring around at the rest of the burial cham-ber. Yet another disassembled chariot lay on the floor. Two additional sarcophagi perched on stone pedestals to either side of the great black "Mayan" sarcophagus. Numerous tall jars, all exquisitely slipped and polished, stood in ranks around them. Footlocker-sized wooden boxes, their surfaces carved and inlaid with what looked like colored glass, turquoise, and lapis lazuli lined the walls on either side of the entry. Ranks of authentic-looking statues of menials, some washing clothes, others cooking, sewing, or attending everyday household tasks waited in ranks in one corner. Cups, plates, and serving items were stacked atop a delicately carved wooden table in the other.

Then Reid turned to the side wall and stopped short. "What the . . . ?"

The drawing looked like an oddly rendered schematic for an electri-cal device. Fine black lines might have been a wiring diagram. Series of them, drawn in parallel, joined a stacked sequence of squares Reid in-terpreted as motherboards. Thicker lines emanated from a sphere that might have been an energy source.

# 13

"Whassup, my man?" Edwin asked as he carried his tray from the serving line to the table where Falcon sat and spooned peas around his plastic plate.

Falcon told him, "Thank God that Chief Raven talked the skipper into canning the old cook. This new guy, he's pretty good. Taste the pork chops. There's a hint of cumin, cilantro, and an accent of basil at the back of the palate, real spices! I could kiss Chief Raven."

"You and every other man in this nuthouse, Professor. Leastways, if he's breathin' and has a set dangling 'tween his legs."

Edwin gave Falcon a sidelong glance. "How's the major doing?"

"Haven't seen him."

"Ah, they got you back on your meds again?" Edwin took a bite. "What's that like, having imaginary people just pop into your life like that?"

Falcon used his napkin to wipe his lips. "They're just as real as you are sitting there. Clinicians, depending on which school of psychology they come from, call it a form of Dissociative Identity Disorder. Or 'Dissociative Disorder Not Otherwise Specified.' See Axis I in the DSM-V-TR classification system."

Edwin studied Falcon. "I mean, you *see* Major Marks and this Theresa woman, right?"

"I do."

"They call that hallucinations, boss. How come you're not always listed as schizophrenic?"

Falcon shrugged. "MRI doesn't show the diagnostic physical abnormalities in the brain, and I suffer from paranoia. I don't exhibit a lot of

the asocial behaviors. That's why some clinicians tack on that NOS—
Not Otherwise Specified."

"This seat taken?" Chief Raven asked as she approached the table.
Edwin glanced up and did a double take. Raven had Catalina Talavera
in tow. Cat looked uncertainly at him and Falcon, an anxious smile on
her delicate lips.

"Do sit," Falcon offered graciously.

Heart leaping, Edwin averted his eyes, giving a slight shrug.

"Thought we'd join you," Raven continued nonchalantly as she
slipped into a seat. "Cat's usual place is too close to those loud–ass
Zoomies. A couple of them didn't shower this week."

Edwin tried to smile, alternately delighted and horrified that Cat was
seating herself straight across from him. "I, uh, guess you talked the
Skipper into getting us a new cook," he stuttered.

Raven shot him a grin. "Yeah, Skipper's pretty good." She glanced
up at the dark globe of the camera. "You hear that, Skipper?"

"The Skipper doesn't monitor us all the time," Falcon said.

"Of course he does. He's shooting beams into our heads to read our
thoughts." Raven sought to stab her bendy fork into the pork chop, gave
it up, and used her fingers. Through a mouthful, she added, "I got that
straight from the paranoid schizophrenics."

Catalina Talavera actually laughed. "That's rather pejorative, Chief."

Raven chewed, swallowed, and made a face. "God, if we can't make
fun of being crazy in here, the only thing left to live for is an increase in
meds."

"The major says that something's going to happen soon," Falcon
noted. "He says all the signs indicate something big for all of us."

"Speaking of people in need of an increase in meds, how's the major
been?" Raven wolfed another bite off her pork chop. "Damn, that's
good! What is that taste?"

"Cumin, basil, and something," Edwin mustered the nerve to say.
Then, risking it all, he told Cat, "You've looked sad lately, Dr. Talavera."

She looked him in the eyes, and his heart skipped as she said, "Since
meds are the current topic of conversation, the Skipper's stopped mine."

"And how's that working for you?" Raven flipped loose black hair
over her shoulder.

Cat shrugged as she struggled to cut the pork chop with her flimsy plastic knife. "He gave me a project . . . and access to the computer for research."

"The computer?" Edwin said in disbelief.

Cat shot him a wary look. "I can only access articles, the email and social sites are blocked."

"Yeah, but that's easy." Edwin shifted on his chair, gesturing with his knife. "All you gotta do . . ." And he launched into the codes that could . . .

"Hey!" Raven barked, "We already know you're the smartest son-of-a-bitch alive when it comes to computers."

Falcon addressed himself to Cat. "Edwin, here, is somewhat unique. He actually *chose* to be here. Like you, Doctor, he exhibits no true classifiable mental disorder beyond a lack of sense."

"Shit! I got sense outa my—"

"Language, Edwin," Falcon warned softly with a slight inclination of his head toward Cat Talavera.

*Holy shit! They set this up!* Embarrassed, he suffered a hot spear of anxiety. Bless God for making him black, wasn't no flush to give him away. He shot a narrow-eyed glance at Chief Raven as she ripped the last bit of tissue from the pork chop bone and studied it thoughtfully.

"Somebody's not thinking," Raven mused. "Look at the point that spinous process makes. I could flat do some damage with this little bone."

"Spinous what?" Edwin asked.

"The protrusion on the bone," Cat said. "But I don't understand what you mean, Chief."

Raven's left eyebrow arched. "I could punch that sharp point right through someone's jugular."

Cat Talavera paled, her wide-eyed gaze sliding sidelong in the chief's direction.

"It's all right, Cat," Edwin managed to say. "Of all the people in here, you trust the chief first, and the others second, if at all."

At that, Raven's expression wavered. "Trust? Shit. The only person in here you trust? That's the Skipper. Me, I just get people killed."

At that she shoved her chair back, took her plate, tossed it into the trash, and strode purposefully from the room.

"What did I do?" Edwin cried.

"You? Nothing," Falcon replied. "SEAL training did most of it . . . and the Taliban did the rest when they detonated that IED."

Cat said uncertainly, "She seems so strong and capable."

"Oh, yes," Falcon told her with a sympathetic smile. "She can take care of everyone in the world but herself."

Edwin was studying the sharp spur of bone on his pork chop. Only Raven would make a weapon out of the thing. "Now, you want to talk about not fitting in, man, there's always Gray."

"She's an anomaly," Falcon agreed, his gaze going vacant. "A true puzzle. Cat being here, we can understand. Like Chief Raven's pork chop, she's a weapon when used properly."

"I am?" Cat stopped short, a forkful of potatoes halfway to her mouth.

"Gray, however, eludes analysis. Everything about her is wrong." Falcon's brow furrowed. "On those occasions when she's taken in and out, I've watched her. It's as if she's misplaced in time and space."

"I don't understand," Cat murmured.

"Neither do I," Falcon agreed as his vision cleared. "Nor does the major, and that's most interesting."

# 14

Reid cradled a cup of steaming tea in his chilled hands and tried to come fully awake. Dawn was little more than an orange streak above the eastern canyon walls. The last of the stars were fading from a bruise-purple sky.

The Arab cook stirred couscous on a gas-fired stove. Despite the predawn shadows, Reid could see the sentries with their Kalashnikovs. Whoever they were, Skientia had hired the best. Reid hadn't seen even a hint of amateur behavior.

He looked past camp toward the excavation. The tomb *had* to have been built in the last fifty years or so, but the slope fill had been compacted—actual stratigraphic layers visible in the walls of the excavation where eolian sands had settled before newer colluvial deposits had covered them in turn. Doing that took time, like thousands of years.

The damn thing just had the *feel* of antiquity.

If the tomb builders had collapsed the slope above to cover the tomb, it would have left a scar—something visible to his trained eye. The difference would have been in the coloration of the soil, the way the loosened matrix cascaded down in a fan shape. Something.

*Yet all I see is the same undisturbed slope, just as pristine as the rest of the canyon.*

The first sounds of an approaching helicopter carried on the still air. Moments later, Yusif, wearing cargo pants and a white T-shirt, stepped out of the sleep tent with his black beard twisted in disarray and his hair sticking up on the right side.

Radios were crackling as the guards spoke back and forth, discussing the approaching aircraft.

"That will be Dr. Kilgore France," Yusif announced.

"That's fast."

Yusif grunted under his breath, stepping over to pour a cup of tea from the steaming pot on the camp stove. "My guess is that Skientia had her on a plane the moment we located the tomb entrance."

"Rather presumptuous of them, don't you think?"

Yusif glanced toward the approaching helicopter, then warily back at Reid. "Nothing makes sense, *sahib*." He jerked his head toward the helicopter. "Why hire Kilgore France? Why you? Or me? We will all gleefully expose the perpetrators of this hoax, do everything in our power to disprove the tomb's antiquity."

The helicopter settled at the widest point in the narrow canyon. As the blowing dust subsided, the door popped open, and two figures climbed out. They were followed by duffel bags and aluminum equipment boxes. No sooner had the two people carried their gear beyond the rotors than the old Jet Ranger spooled up and rose, blasting the pair with dust and gravel.

Salim Rashid—in charge of the security detail—trotted out to meet them. Rashid gave them a respectful nod, spoke into his radio, and several of his men rushed forward to take their bags as the two—a man and woman—approached the camp.

Yusif quickly ducked into his tent, reemerging moments later wearing a clean white shirt, his hair slicked down.

"If you're looking for a date," Reid remarked dryly, "word in the profession is that Kilgore France takes herself pretty seriously. She's a commentator for CNN, and for a while had her own television show. Her book on forensic anthropology actually made it onto the *New York Times* and *USA Today* bestseller lists."

Yusif gave him a half-lidded look. "Good. I had hoped she would be a lady of taste and refinement. Given the alternatives she will find in camp, I will have no competition."

Reid considered hitting him in the head with a rock. Then gave it up as he followed Yusif to meet Kilgore France and her companion. "Maybe the man with her is all the company she needs. Woman like her, she can afford to bring her own company. In America we call them stud muffins."

From the side of his mouth, Yusif murmured, "Americans have a peculiar poverty of language. He's military if I am not mistaken. He has that look about him."

Reid studied the man: close-cropped dark hair, broad shoulders, with dangerous brown eyes. Almost catlike movement added to his upright posture and air of command. The khaki shirt looked overstuffed with muscles. Tan cargo pants—with full pockets and belted at the waist—were tucked into the tops of his high-laced boots. Nothing about the guy struck Reid as either warm or fuzzy.

Kilgore France, however, had been blessed by the best of her pale-blonde, blue-eyed, Swedish supermodel mother and her black NFL football-legend father. Reid guessed her to be in her thirties, about five-foot-seven, and perhaps one-hundred-thirty pounds. The practical field clothes she wore barely masked a body that . . . well, her mother *was* a supermodel.

Kilgore's intelligent brown eyes fixed on his. A curious arch lifted her delicate right eyebrow, as if it were demanding some explanation of her current situation.

"Dr. France," Yusif greeted, offering his hand. "It is my great pleasure to make your acquaintance."

"Dr. al Amari," she noted, shaking his hand firmly. "I read your CV on the plane. I'm sure you'll have a great deal to teach me."

"And you, me." Yusif sounded almost obsequious.

She glanced again at Reid, who'd stood slightly behind, watching the exchange. The military man had braced his feet and crossed muscle-thick arms as he took in the camp, Yusif, and finally Reid. Something hard and anticipatory glinted behind his brown eyes.

"Dr. Farmer?" she asked, offering her hand.

"My pleasure," he told her. "Somehow, I missed your CV on the plane ride over here. Mostly I slept and drank free champagne." Nonchalantly, he added, "Never got to fly first class before."

He caught a flicker of amusement in her quick eyes before her companion stepped forward, thrusting out his hand. "Bill Minor, Dr. Reid. I'm here with Skientia. You might call me one of their troubleshooters."

"Is our trouble in need of shooting?" Yusif asked.

Reid interjected, "Only if it's a modern tomb trying to pass itself off as ancient."

"And you know that? Can prove it?" Minor cocked his head slightly, the hint of a smile in his thin lips.

Reid felt his hackles rising. "The Latin was problematic enough, but ancient Egyptians didn't use Mayan glyphs, draw jet airplanes, or put electrical diagrams on walls."

Minor didn't even flinch. "That doesn't concern me, Dr. Farmer. What concerns me is whether or not you can disprove the tomb's antiquity through *scientific* means. Your reputation is for meticulous fieldwork. Outside of the cultural anachronisms, have you discovered anything which would categorically prove the tomb a hoax?"

"How about a steel door?"

"How is steel made, Dr. Farmer?"

"Iron alloyed with nickel, tin, chromium, molybdenum, or other metals."

"Did you look closely at the door's surface?"

"I did."

"Rolled steel?"

"It looked as if it had been hammered."

"I see." Minor's smile widened. "What if laboratory analysis proves it *was* hammered? What if the morphology and metallurgy reflect a primitive alloy of locally available metals?"

Yusif protested, "We have no record of steel production in Egypt until the arrival of the Romans, and even then it was the Arabs who perfected the technology after the seventh century." He flung an arm in the direction of the tomb. "The architecture is Eighteenth Dynasty."

"Exactly." Minor crossed his arms. "Tell me, Dr. Farmer, with your extensive experience in excavation, did you see any evidence that would have indicated it was recently buried? And after gaining entry, while inside the tomb—excluding the art and script—did you see anything to suggest it was a *modern* construction? Perhaps plywood, plastics, machine screws, or other modern fabrication techniques?"

"No. But we've only begun our analysis."

Minor chuckled under his breath. "One last question: Dr. Farmer,

Yusif, what would it take to manufacture a hoax of this scale and authenticity?"

Reid laughed aloud. "You'd need a staff of technicians, specialists, and a team of brilliant archaeologists. It would cost millions, maybe tens of millions."

Yusif added, "And you don't hire that kind of talent off the street."

Minor smirked in satisfaction. "No, you don't. Egyptology is a small community. You all know each other, communicate at meetings, gossip about who is doing what. This is the sort of thing your closed professional community couldn't keep under wraps."

Reid frowned and glanced at Yusif. He, in turn, spread his hands wide in a most-Arab gesture of futility. "We would have heard, *sahib*."

"And what's my part in this?" Kilgore France asked, her expression having tightened and soured during the conversation. From the glance she gave Bill Minor, he definitely wasn't her stud muffin.

Minor turned to her. "Doctor, if you would be so kind as to stow your things, I'd like you to accompany Yusif and Dr. Farmer into the tomb. My employers are particularly interested in the mummy we expect to find inside that sarcophagus. This may be the single most important burial you've ever examined."

# 15

General Elijiah Grazier sat in the overstuffed office chair to the left of my desk. The general, a two-star, almost slouched, his right leg crossed over his left; the creases on his trousers were taking a beating in the process. His black shoes, however, had a perfect spit-polish.

Grazier's skin had a light-brown tone. Flecks of gray had invaded the close-cropped hair at his temples. The general's expression was anything but happy as he slowly flipped the pages of the latest report on Prisoner Alpha.

"This doesn't show much progress, Tim." Grazier looked up from the last page.

I'd known Eli Grazier for close to twenty years now. His understanding of science and his willingness to integrate it into combat doctrine had led him to a unique position as the JCS liaison with DARPA and a whole host of "black" projects.

But there was another aspect of his personality. Like so many successful high-ranking military officers, Eli demonstrated traits common to psychopathy: he was charismatic, confident, fearless, ruthless, and extremely focused. These traits—when moderated and rationally utilized by the individual—produced an extremely productive military officer. Assuming I could have talked him into taking the PCL-R—the Psychopathy Checklist-Revised—or the PPI—the Psychopathic Personality Inventory—the man would have scored a zero on guilt, remorse, and empathy.

Once you understood that about Eli—and realized he understood it about himself—he wasn't that bad of a human being. I respected him, enjoyed his company, and never forgot who or what he was.

"Eli? You were expecting . . . what? That she'd just cascade, wake up one morning, and declare, 'I'm Jane Doe Smith from Paducah, and

I've been faking all along. I'm really a Chinese spy. This is the name of my handler, and here's his address in San Francisco.' It doesn't work that way. Not with the level of apparent dissociative behavior we *think* Alpha exhibits. When it comes to her diagnosis—"

"Yeah, yeah, we're off the map. I know." He leaned forward and tossed the report onto the corner of my desk. When he flopped back, his foot was jerking repetitively as an expression of irritation. "What about that electrical doohickey she built?"

"That's a precise word if ever I've heard one."

Grazier gave me a wide grin. "Sorry, I just knew I was talking to an ex-Marine."

"General, there's no such thing as an *ex*-Marine."

"So I've been told." The grin faded. "She's a loose end, Colonel. I can tell you, a damn *fly* couldn't have gotten into that lab where we caught her unless it was scanned five times in the process."

I gave Grazier an expressive shrug. "My best call is that she's honestly ignorant of who she is and has no memory beyond that day at Los Alamos. Since she's been here, she hasn't made a single slip. Not one. We've had cameras on her every moment, including remote sensors to monitor heart rate, respiration, eye movement, pupil dilation, and skin temperature. We've seen no measurable reaction at the random mention of handlers, agencies, or oatmeal for that matter. Sometimes she'll cue on CNN or BBC news programs, and we've tied those arousals to mentions of parts of Europe, but not to specific countries. The same with North Africa, Central America, Greece, and Italy—which shouldn't be a surprise given her printing style and preference for Romance languages.

"And here's another oddity: She struggled with numbers, but now that she's figured them out, she'll light up over an equation. The same with a chemistry diagram, or physics illustration, but not over the terms to describe them."

"I don't understand." Grazier laced his fingers over his knee.

"We don't either. If we insert the words—boson, quark, electron, uranium, argon, force, erg, particle, fission, nuclear, etc.—she's been oblivious until recently."

"What's changed?"

"Eli, she's watched enough television that she's *learning* the scientific terminology. My staff and I have discussed providing her with a couple of scientific texts, just to see what reaction we get."

"And why haven't you?"

I pressed my steepled fingers to my lips. "Call it a hunch."

"A hunch about what?"

"I'm not sure we should be giving her those tools just yet."

"Tools? That's an interesting word to use."

I pointed toward the monitor that displayed Prisoner Alpha's room and the table with the doohickey. "General, that piece of equipment she's built? We don't know what it is or what it does. All we can tell you is that it seems to project two electromagnetic fields out of either end when it's plugged in. On occasion, she'll turn it on. Then, with a great deal of precision, she'll spend an hour or two tapping a wire on part of that exposed coil. We know from our instruments that the electromagnetic fields fluctuate."

"You told me it wasn't a radio."

"A radio has to have certain components like an antenna, tuning coil, speakers, and so forth. This thing Alpha built has none."

"So," Grazier mused, "she remains an idiot savant?"

"We call it savant syndrome these days. As for myself, I'm not even sure I want to go with 'Not Otherwise Specified.'"

"Since the DSM-5, you can't take the NOS cop out."

I considered my words carefully. "Screw the DSM-5! I'm an old-fashioned kind of guy who likes NOS. But, General, my gut says that she's as competent and mentally composed as you or I." Pausing for effect, I added, "She excels on the 'culture-free tests' we use for special populations."

"You've got to be kidding."

I threw my arms up. "Eli, I've been in this business for decades . . . seen just about everything. She's not giving off the tells I'd expect to see in her posture, expression, eye contact, or behavior. I've worked with traumatized people with suppressed memory; I know the signs, the subtle quirks. She's not giving me any. Her brain morphology and functioning are completely normal. Physiologically, her arousals are normal. She just cues to stimuli that we can't fit into a pattern yet."

"Then what the hell is she doing in there, watching TV all day and doodling on her pads?"

"My guess, Eli?" I paused to take in his reaction. "She's studying us and taking notes. If you'd get me that linguist I've requested for months—"

"Oh, bullshit! She's playing you, Tim. Now, I admit, you're one of the smartest guys I've ever run into. But maybe that's what she's banking on. If that's the case, I'm even more impressed by the lady."

"How's that?"

"Because if she can play you, how much *more* brilliant does that make her? Face it: She's a spy. One so important that her handlers tried to kill her rather take the chance she'd talk."

"Then why fake a disorder?"

"Maybe that was the protocol in case she got caught. She studied the DSM thoroughly, knowing exactly what to manifest so we'd diagnose her with a severe disorder. When she was rated using the Global Assessment of Functioning, she knew how to manipulate us into scoring her down in the twenties. Tim, you've been in the trenches. Even nuts who know the system beat the GAF scale all the time. They'll tell a clinician just what he needs to hear so that he'll score them a nice competent eighty and let them walk."

My gaze fixed on the little model Ducati on the corner of my desk. "I'd say it's more like she just stepped into this world from somewhere else."

"Just in from Mars, or Outer Bumfuckistan?" Grazier leaned forward, pointing a finger. "The only problem with that, Doc, is that you're grasping at straws. It's a really small world, and there are no lost tribes of attractive white people out there. And second, bucolic hicks from the highlands don't just appear inside locked-down high-security labs. They don't build clever electric gizmos out of spare parts. Nor do unidentifiable agents seek to murder them in parking garages."

"We're missing something, Eli."

"Give her the physics book. Let's see what happens."

I arched my "this-is-a-bad-idea" eyebrow.

"Just do it, Doc. I take full responsibility."

Did I tell you that people who demonstrate psychopathic traits lie with incredible facility?

# 16

"I've fallen through the rabbit hole," Kilgore France growled under her breath as she placed probes against the sides of the great black sarcophagus. After having been suited and masked, she'd spent her quick introduction to the tomb alternately staring, shaking her head, and mumbling to herself.

Reid and Yusif stood to the side, arms crossed, as she worked. The microphone in her mask picked up the slightest of sounds, and Skientia, back in California, had to be hearing her whispered imprecations.

Fixing the last of the probes, Kilgore stepped over to the computer. She checked the data transmission cord that snaked its way across the tomb and outside to the satellite phone. With a final growl, she flicked the machine on.

After several minutes of waiting, she chuckled humorlessly. "How about that?"

"Find something, Doctor?"

She beckoned him over. Reid bent slightly, Yusif crowding in behind him. The ghostly image from inside the sarcophagus reminded him of a series of tubes stacked atop each other.

"Ideas?" Reid asked.

"The sarcophagus is definitely made of wood, but I don't know what these blocks are on all four corners." She pointed to four squares of opacity. "It's some sort of granular substance in a container. Nor do these white strips rising out of the containers make sense. Given the opacity, they're obviously iron of some sort, and these thin chip-looking things that press against them are perplexing."

"Gun flints?" Reid wondered, noting the shape of the things. Then it hit him: "Oh, shit! That Latin inscription up on the chest, the one the image is clutching. APERTUS ET DIRUMPO. Skientia translated that as 'Open and abruptly disperse.'"

"Then that means . . . ?"

"Well, if that's an iron strip, and those are slivers of flint, and the blocky granular stuff is black powder, anyone opening the sarcophagus might strike a spark."

"And ka-bang!" Yusif added. "Very clever."

"But why?" Kilgore asked. "If it's a hoax . . . No, this goes beyond a hoax to outright malicious behavior. Call it psychotic. Gentlemen, this isn't a game, it's a crime scene."

"Come again?" Reid asked.

"Dr. Farmer, these traps you've brought me past? The fact that you were doused by toxic spores and fungi, the sarcophagus rigged with explosives? It's all designed to kill. The intricacy indicates a highly organized and psychopathic mind at work. I've dealt with cases similar to this where—"

*"Dr. France, there is an alternate hypothesis."* Bill Minor's voice came through Reid's earpiece. *"While the ultimate lethality of the traps may not be up for debate, their purpose is. Our interpretation is that these were designed as defenses."*

"Defenses, Mr. Minor?" Kilgore asked. "To protect what? And from whom? Everything I've seen here is bizarre to the extreme. This entire place reeks of a psychopath's nightmare. The tomb's been designed as a lure, one that's working brilliantly. But for the skill, preparations, and expertise of the investigators, someone would have already been killed. All I want is to find the sick son of a bitch who designed this and see him locked away for attempted murder."

*"If our team at Skientia is correct, Dr. France, the designer, your 'sick son-of-a-bitch,' is buried in that tomb. If not in the central sarcophagus—as your data would seem to suggest—then perhaps in one of those smaller ones to the rear."*

Reid muttered, "Bill, as soon as this bus stops at reality, I want to get off."

*"If you could . . . Shit! We're under attack!"*

"Mr. Minor?" Kilgore asked. "Attack?"

Reid glanced back and forth. "Mr. Minor? Bill? What do you mean, attack?"

*"Dr. Farmer? This is California,"* Dr. Kaplan's voice interceded. *"Our*

*remote cameras indicate the approach of a party of armed men. Please secure yourselves.*"

"Huh?" Reid glanced at his companions. "Secure ourselves? What the *hell* does *that* mean?"

Communications, however, had gone silent.

Kilgore gestured anger and disbelief. "I'm a fucking professional, for God's sake! When I get a hold of my agent, I'm gonna kick her ass right up between her ears for booking me on this lunatic's quest."

Yusif flipped off Kilgore's computer and began disconnecting it from the leads. "Come, my friends. Let's see if we can't . . ."

The faint chatter of automatic weapons fire resonated in the tomb.

Reid turned and saw a silhouetted figure charging down the passage. The man wore a riot helmet, black tactical garb, and the M16 in his hands looked real.

"Wait!" Reid threw up his hands. But even as he did, the man slammed a foot down on the pitfall. He dropped like a stone, his cry cut off by a smacking impact. A second man followed more cautiously, an ugly black submachine gun at the ready. Wary, he cast a glance down into the pit. The narrow passage amplified the fallen man's anguished screams. The second assailant stepped to the side and crossed the plank bridge. At the burial chamber entrance, he crouched, the weapon's butt pressed against his chest as if it were an extension of his gaze.

Reid's heart stopped as the gunman's eyes pinned him—the black muzzle of the submachine gun pointed at Reid's head. For that brief-and-frozen moment, an electric fear left him paralyzed.

Then the man's gaze—and the terrible gun—swept past him to Kilgore.

When the gunman finally spoke, his voice was filled with a New York accent. "Dr. France! How good to make your acquaintance." Ignoring the sloping planks that would have let him slide down, he leaped down onto the wooden platform and placed a foot on the stone threshold. "Now, if you'll step back so we can get the body out of . . ."

At the grating sound, he glanced up.

The great block sheared through the wooden planks and mashed the gunman as though he were butter. The man's body crackled, popped, and snapped as the stone slammed down.

Then the room went black.

# 17

Reid ran his tongue around his too-dry mouth. Dark silence pressed down on him—a greater weight than the mass of rock in which they were entombed.

"This is not happening," Kilgore France spoke softly in the stygian black. "I mean, shit. Two days ago I was in New York, at the Grand Hyatt. How can I be *entombed* in Egypt?"

"You saw him," Yusif reminded. "The gunman jumped on the hammer's trigger. Allah have mercy on his soul."

Reid squeezed the bridge of his nose, reliving that last horrible moment.

Yusif's voice barely hid panic. "It's the sound that will haunt me to my grave. That wet crunching of the man's bones."

"How big is the stone?" Kilgore's voice reeked of surrender. "A couple of square meters, you said? And granite? What would that weigh?"

"Four tons or more," Reid guessed, having no idea. "The good news is that it's been maybe twenty-four hours? We haven't even heard a peep from the gunmen."

"You call that good news? May I remind you, *sahib,* that we are trapped inside a mountain without food or water?"

"Who *are* they? What did they want?" Kilgore asked yet again. "This tomb's a big fake. Yusif, even if these artifacts were authentic, what would they be worth on the international market?"

"I'd guess five to ten million euros. Maybe more."

"Even in this economy, that would be something," Reid muttered as he resettled his back against the stone pedestal. Kilgore shifted beside him. The floor had no give.

"My publicist and agent both know where I am, and that I'm working for Skientia. The chariots, the sarcophagi, anything tied to this tomb would be too hot for sale on the open market. There would be too many uncomfortable questions like, 'Did you kill Dr. Kilgore France to obtain these?'"

A long silence ensued.

"How'd you get into forensic anthro?" Reid asked.

"I wanted to dig up fossil humans. You know, be the next Mary Leakey and rewrite paleoanthropology. Had to learn human osteology, which took me to paleopathology, to anatomy, to a crime lab, and on to fame and fortune." A pause. "I'd give everything, every last cent I own for a tall glass of ice water."

Yusif rasped, "Myself, I'd give all of your wealth—and Reid's, too— for that glass of water."

Reid nerved himself to ask, "What gets us first, Kilgore? Hypoxia or dehydration?"

"You think this thing is really sealed? Airtight, I mean."

"Might get a little seepage around that block. It fit loosely enough to slide down without binding."

"Dehydration, then," she answered softly. "Three days. Maybe four."

"I guess it doesn't matter that we took our masks off."

"If we're infected, nothing will have time to incubate."

Yusif said thickly, "I never thought I would choose disease. But in this case, it means I—"

"Shhh! What's that?" Reid cocked his head; the high-pitched grinding sound reminded him of being a couple of doors down from the dentist's office. He got to his feet and thumbed on his flashlight. The hot white beam hurt his eyes, and he squinted as he made his way around the chariot to the great stone. Careful not to step on the dried fluids that had squirted out, he placed an ear to the cool rock.

"Someone's drilling," he said softly. "So, folks, I guess we've got a bit of a dilemma. If they don't get through to us in the next couple of days, it won't matter if they're the bad guys. If they do, and they're—"

"We don't know that they're bad guys, Reid. We only heard what we thought was shooting. Maybe Skientia is really the bad guys, and this is all some perverted prank." Kilgore seemed to be trying to convince herself. She had pulled her Tyvek hood back to expose her curly hair.

Yusif's voice was flat. "The man who leaped down and was crushed? My first impression, as he pointed that machine gun at me, was that he was not here to encourage my health or welfare."

Reid made his way back to the sarcophagus and resettled himself next to Kilgore. He flipped the flashlight off; darkness dropped like a weight.

The faint sound of drilling mixed hope with terror.

"You got a family, Reid?" Kilgore asked after what seemed like an eternity.

"Mother and father in Colorado."

"No wife or kids?"

"Ex-wife. Field archaeologists shouldn't marry. Especially when they're young and very drunk. You?"

"Long-term relationships don't survive late-night phone calls. The kind you get every time a corpse is found in a dumpster or shallow grave in the woods. Life's easier when your relationships are with the dead. They don't make as many demands . . . and they don't give a rat's ass if you miss a date."

"Got a point there."

*I just hope we're not going to end up as the dead . . . even if it means we won't be making any demands on anyone.*

He must have drifted off, fallen asleep. Not that a person could really tell in the utter blackness, but when he came back to his senses, it was with the realization that his ass ached, his joints were stiff, and his back hurt.

Kilgore's head had fallen against his shoulder, the warmth of her body against his arm reassuring.

He tried to swallow, his tongue like a dry stick; his desperation for a drink bordered on being crazed. In a misguided attempt to add to his madness, he imagined cool water trickling around his tongue, how it would slip magically down his throat and into his cramped stomach.

Carefully he reached up, trying not to disturb Kilgore.

"Hmmm?" she rasped and pulled away.

"The drilling's louder," Reid told her. "Watch your eyes; I'm turning on my flashlight."

He narrowed his eyes to slits and flicked it on. In the dazzling glare he got up and walked to the great stone. In the glow, the Mayan mathematics and the diagram on the wall seemed to mock him.

"It's a lot louder." He felt high-frequency vibrations through his fingertips. Then a chip spalled off. Reid jumped back as a drill leaped out from the stone and was pulled back.

He could hear the machine shut off, then faint voices. Placing his lips to the inch-in-diameter hole, he called, "Hello?"

"To whom am I speaking?" a voice asked.

"Dr. Reid Farmer. Who are you?"

"Dr. Farmer? I'm Major Sam Savage, United States Army. Is Dr. Kilgore France in there with you?"

"She is. So is Yusif al Amari."

"Who is he?"

"Excavation director for the Skientia project."

"Anyone else?"

"Nope." Reid frowned. "Excuse me, but how do we know that you're an American? And what's the United States Army doing drilling holes in tomb stones in Egypt?"

Reid shifted as Kilgore and Yusif crowded closer.

"Dr. Farmer, we're here to get you and Dr. France out of there. As to the Egyptians, we're kind of hoping they don't become aware of our presence before we manage to extract you and the sarcophagus from that tomb. Now, before I get on with that little detail, is there anything you and your people need? Anyone injured?"

"No. Just water, food . . . and *out*."

"If you all will step back to the farthest possible corner, or behind whatever shelter you can, my EOD expert, Corporal Bradley Houser, will attend to that in short order."

Another voice called through the hole, "I'm plugging the bore now, so there will be no further conversation. When I detonate the charge, the plug will be expelled like a bullet, so you will want to be off to the side. Is that understood? I'm shooting in fifteen minutes."

Kilgore pulled at Reid's shoulder. "I've cataloged and analyzed too many remains from bomb blasts." She pointed to the corner. "There. That's our best bet. Yusif, you in the corner, then Reid and me crouched over you."

"Why are you and Reid crouched over me?"

"Because I'm a forensic anthropologist. I understand these things."

"Yeah, right." Reid slapped Yusif on the shoulder. "Come on. Let's move that table."

In the end, they huddled together, Reid checking his watch.

"What if they're not US military?" Kilgore had been peeled bare of her usual hard defenses.

"It's not like we've got a lot of choice, do we?"

"If it turns out they're the bad guys . . ." She couldn't finish and glanced away.

"Everyone seems to want the sarcophagus with the body in it," Yusif wondered. "Why? Who is he?"

"Fucking crazy maniac if he built this place," Kilgore muttered, trying to sound brave.

"This is it, people." Reid glanced away from his watch. "Any moment now."

When it came, the effect was almost anticlimactic—a muffled bang, more felt than heard. True to warning, the plug shot out, smacked into the bottom of the big sarcophagus, and peeled a long chip out of the shiny black wood.

Reid straightened, turned, and shone his flashlight on the great stone to find it riddled with cracks. Even as he watched, angular fragments fell away to rattle on the smooth stone floor. Then the whole oversized ashlar fell apart as a steel wrecking bar pushed through. It was withdrawn, only to be followed by a mirror on a pole that angled this way and that as it scanned the room.

Reid lowered his flashlight beam, stepping forward as a voice called, "Could I see all three of you, please? Hands visible and empty."

Only after they'd complied did a man come wiggling through, a black HK tactical .45 in his hand as he scanned the room. He dropped into a crouch amid the fractured pieces of granite. "Major?" he spoke softly, "I'm in. Three civilians accounted for, no visible threats. Proceeding to check the room."

Like a hunting leopard, he searched the burial chamber with a light attached to the underside of his pistol. "Room's clear, sir!"

More stone cascaded, and a second man, also brandishing a pistol, slipped in, got to his feet, and grinned as he studied the fractured remains of the granite. "God, I'm good! Perfect fragmentation." He glanced at

Reid, Kilgore, and Yusif. "You see, figuring the mass, morphology, and density was simple. The trick was to shape the charge cylinder to create shockwaves bouncing around inside the rock. You get the resonance right, and stone, being brittle—"

"Cut the lecture, Houser," a voice called. "The good doctor isn't interested." The next man through was older, five-foot-nine and in his mid-thirties. He pulled a duty cap onto his close-cropped and darkly tanned head before he glanced around, giving off a slight whistle as he took in the chamber's contents.

"What Uncle Buck would give to see this!" He propped callused hands on his hips and stepped forward as someone on the other side levered more of the shattered granite out of the way.

"You're really Army?" Reid asked.

"This we'll defend," the man said, turning hawklike eyes on Reid and offering his hand. "You familiar with that?"

"Army motto."

"Yeah, the Marines get so carried away with their *Semper Fi* we just had to have something to throw back at 'em."

"Ah, Major, there you go again." Houser, apparently a Marine, was looking around as yet another man shoved a triangular piece of rock out of the way and stepped in.

The new arrival, a fit-looking African American with a Southern accent, offered a pack. "You asked for this, Major?"

"Thanks, Ghilley." He took it, opened a pocket, and tossed a water bottle to Kilgore, then one apiece to Reid and Yusif.

Major Savage had to have Native American ancestry. He was gawking around as if he'd just stepped off the bus at Disneyland. He waved a hand around. "This for real?"

"That's the question, Major." Kilgore had drained her bottle. "What the hell is going on?"

"Just orders, ma'am. I was pulled out of Kabul yesterday morning. We put a scratch team of specialists together in the AFO. Found ourselves on a carrier in the Red Sea last night, where we picked up a couple of helicopters. Those Navy pilots were kind enough to drop us here a little before daybreak. After a bit of disagreement with the hard cases who were looting the tomb, we found their drill in the passageway yonder and finished the job they started."

Reid now glanced at the opening to the passage, seeing where the shoulder, head, and one arm of the gunman who'd triggered the hammer had been dragged to the side. A tingle of nausea ran through his gut.

"Know him?" Savage asked, following his gaze.

"He's one of the guys who were attacking Yusif's people. He tripped the trigger that brought that stone down."

"His buddies were busy loading trucks when we arrived. The two who are still alive aren't talking, but I know military contractors when I run into them."

"And my people?" Yusif asked, a soft hope in his eyes.

"We found twenty-three bodies, all male, lined out behind a cut bank in the wadi. While we didn't look too closely, each had a gunshot wound or two."

Yusif swallowed hard and wilted.

"What about Bill Minor?" Kilgore asked. "About my height, black hair, and khaki pants?"

"We haven't found him if he's out there, but my guys are still looking."

"Major?" Another soldier, this one blond and bearded, ducked out of the passage. "Fat Mama's got chatter on the box. She's figured out that someone's running around under her skirt."

"How long, Chief?"

"They'll have jets up in less than fifteen, Major. White Queen will deploy decoys heading west into the desert, which means we'd better be east of the river, scooting and tooting for the carrier soonest, sir."

"Which sarcophagus am I supposed to retrieve, Doctor? This big black one?" Savage turned to the black coffin with its new chip glaring pale in the light.

"It has tube things in it," Reid said. "Not a corpse."

"So, if there's a body," Kilgore mused, it's one of those two. The one on the right suggests a male, the one on the left, a female."

"People, we've got to go. If the Egyptians catch us here, it will become very, very unpleasant." Savage pointed. "Take them both, Chief. Even if it means tossing out some of the gear. Get your people in here and move them."

"Aye, sir." The chief snapped off a salute.

"Which sarcophagus first?" Houser asked.

On impulse, Reid pointed to the one on the right. "That one. The male."

"How so?" Savage asked.

Reid shrugged. "I was told to pick door number three. Hell, Major, I'm still hoping to win the damn car."

# 18

Karla Raven stepped out of the women's shower room and nodded at the orderly who monitored the door. Karla dutifully handed over her towel and watched Ann Hammond check it off the list before she dropped it into a dirty-clothes hamper. Everything was counted in Ward Six. People just never knew when a shoelace might vanish and wind up with one end tied around a rafter and the other around someone's suicidal neck.

"Good workout, Karla? You were at it for over six hours."

"Yeah, well, I'd planned to go outside for a ten-kilometer run with the Skipper this afternoon, but having a meeting with the president at one, and the Chairman of the Joint Chiefs at three, I just couldn't work it into my busy schedule."

"Sure, Karla." Hammond—a middle-aged lady heading to overweight status—gave her a knowing grin. "As if the Skipper would let any of you past Secure One for anything less than a heart attack. Besides, he's been closeted with a whole team of shrinks this afternoon."

"What happened? Somebody skip their meds again?"

The woman surreptitiously glanced back and forth—as if the overhead camera wasn't recording everything anyway—and whispered, "They gave Gray a physics book."

Karla gave her a flat stare. "A physics book?"

"Yes!"

"You're kidding." She gestured incredulity. "Oh, come on. And this is important . . . why? If Gray can get jazzed, hot, and panting over a physics book, God help her if she ever lays her hands on a copy of *Cosmopolitan*."

Still chuckling, Karla made her way into the common room. Falcon sat at one of the gaming tables, his thoughtful eyes on the television where Fox News was flashing images of a desert valley someplace in Egypt. Two chairs to his right, Winny Swink was leaned back insolently, her features pinched as if irritated. Periodically, she'd run anxious fingers through her red hair, attention on the screen.

Swink pointed a finger. "Yeah, I know that country. That's just west of the Valley of the Kings. I wrangled a guided tour of the tombs. Must have been what, a decade back? Got to see most of the Nile."

"You seem to have been everywhere," Falcon noted.

"Hey, I'm fourth generation Air Force. Wherever they sent Dad, Mom insisted on seeing the sights. Made me the geography queen. I could'a waxed those kids on geography bee. You know, that TV show?"

"Falcon? This chair taken?" Karla asked, pointing to the plastic chair to his right. With Falcon, you never knew when some of his "people" were with him. Must have been hell to make dinner reservations back when he was on the outside.

"The major's to my left. Sit," he told her through a frown as he watched the camera angle change.

*"The attack came suddenly."* The reporter's voice sounded grave. *"While we don't have a complete count, Egyptian authorities say twenty-three local workers and security personnel were murdered in an apparent shootout with foreign mercenaries. The motivation for the attack was for possession of this newly opened tomb . . . and the priceless artifacts it contained."*

The camera displayed a recessed doorway in an excavation dug into a hillside.

*"But the real marvel is inside."*

The image cataloged a bare room, then focused on the walls where a six-engine jet was oddly rendered. There, too, were Egyptian hieroglyphics and Latin script.

*"Many of the priceless artifacts had already been removed by the thieves and have been recovered in the waiting trucks. But the greatest mystery lies in the burial chamber, down this dark and treacherous passageway. It was in here that two of the looters met their ends . . . victims of the ancient Egyptians' booby traps."*

Camera lights flashed over a lip and down a drop into a narrow shaft, bloodstains visible at the bottom. Then the cameraman pulled back to the main passage, walked across a narrow bridge, and focused on a bloodstain in the main hallway.

*"And finally we enter the burial chamber where the looters had only begun their work before being apprehended by Egyptian authorities."*

Here a chariot lay disassembled on the floor, and a large black sarcophagus could be seen. Various jars, a table, and little statues were filmed. Then the camera panned around to the walls.

Karla watched as the hieroglyphics and odd compositions of dots, bars, and glyphs filled one wall.

"Doesn't look Egyptian to me," Swink muttered. "I've been in those tombs. Got a guided tour of the great pyramid, once. That's plain . . . What the hell?"

The camera was now showing an image of what looked like an electrical diagram, or an engineering schematic. More of the funny dots, bars, and symbols could be seen on the drawing's margins.

*"The tomb, we are told, is unique. Currently, Egyptologists are converging from every corner of the globe to study the find. And fortunately for the rest of us, this time, it seems, the looters were just a little bit slow."*

Fox went to a news break, and Karla heard Falcon grunt under his breath. "Doesn't make sense."

"What doesn't?"

"That last diagram drawn on the wall," Falcon said. "Those little blocks of dots and bars? They were patterned, you could see the order, the system, unlike the Egyptian hieroglyphics."

Falcon frowned, cocked his head, and glanced off to his right, saying to the empty chair, "Theresa would understand, Major. Yes, hieroglyphics are ordered, but they're patterned linguistically. The dots and bars and glyphs were depicted with an elegance that bespeaks of mathematical precision, not a grammar."

Karla snapped her fingers to get his attention. "Over here, Falcon. Yeah, that's right. The one made of flesh and blood. You're saying those drawings were mathematics?"

"The pattern is mathematical, Chief. We just had a glimpse, but I'd say it was algebraic."

"Egyptians had algebra?" Swink cocked her head. "I thought the Arabs invented it."

Falcon shrugged. "None of us are historians."

Karla gave him a sidelong glance, wondering which "us" he was talking about.

Winny was shaking her head. "I don't remember any artwork like that. Especially that airplane. Someone had to have drawn that later, like in the last century." She shot a glance at Karla, as if seeking reassurance. "Did you see the way it was designed? Six engines, three per wing? And something looked really odd about that tail. It's as if whoever drew that, they didn't really know anything about aerodynamics."

"So, Major Swink, what kind of airplane was it?"

"Didn't look military, that's for sure. Almost as if it came from a different school of design."

"I thought there were only so many ways to make an airplane fly."

"Chief, I tested experimental aircraft in California and Nevada. If it had wings, rotors, jets, or rockets, I flew it. I've been through debriefings and skull sessions with some of the best aerospace engineers in the business." She paused. "That drawing just didn't look right."

"The major thinks a kid drew it," Falcon noted, his chin propped as Fox tried to sell them gold coins to ensure their future prosperity.

"Must have been a pretty important kid to draw on the guy's tomb wall." Swink pulled at the lobe of her ear. "So what's with airplane drawings and pieces of a chariot lying in the middle of the floor. And that big sarcophagus? That makes no damn kind of sense."

"Maybe it's aliens? Remember when History Channel went all crazy with that?"

"I want to see that image again," Falcon said absently, his expression shutting down as it did when he was preoccupied. "There's a key there, a pattern. I can almost see it."

Karla slapped a nervous hand to the table. "I'll go see if patient services can get you a copy. If it's on the news, it ought to be on the web already."

She pushed back and stood, aware that Fox had moved on to the latest presidential initiative on the economy. *Yeah, lots of luck on that one, buddy.*

As she walked off, she heard Winny Swink muttering, "I tell you, I could fly a crate like that." The wistful longing filled her voice.

# 19

I was sitting in the command center with Corporal Julian Hatcher, had filled one notebook, and was well into my second. Fascinated, I watched Prisoner Alpha study her physics book. She'd already worked her way through nearly a third of it, her behavior almost manic. She'd crammed four legal pads with scribbles, diagrams, and symbols. Her hours-old breakfast lay half-eaten on its paper plate.

The changes in her galvanic skin response, breathing, blood pressure, and heart rate each time something came together for her didn't follow the patterns of autism or savant syndrome. I was observing the satisfaction and elation of discovery more common to a scientist with a Type A personality—the kind struggling to solve some problem, and then watching the final walls crumble before her.

*These are the patterns expected from a healthy, integrated, and intelligent brain. She is* not *mentally ill.*

How, then, did I account for her total lack of functional skills in our world?

Alpha ran anxious hands through her honey-yellow hair and studied the open page before her. Those vibrant blue eyes reflected churning internal thoughts. On the wall above her, the television remained ignored as it blathered on about the day's news.

"Maybe we should have given her a calculator," Corporal Hatcher noted where he slouched in his duty chair.

"She has mastered the mathematics," I agreed. "The amazing thing is how fast she can figure with that curious ideographic code of hers. She double-checks our math against her symbols as if to prove something to herself."

"We agree," Dr. Cyrus Evans' voice could be heard in my earpiece. Grantham Barracks was streaming Alpha's image to several of General Grazier's outside experts, and Cyrus had been on the Prisoner Alpha team since the beginning. That we had a "team" demonstrated Alpha's high profile with the DOD and DHS.

"All right, Cyrus. If you can get the general to sign off on it, we'll provide her with a calculator. Preferably one that broadcasts every single operation she performs on it."

"I'm passing that to the general now, Ryan."

Alpha seemed to have made a breakthrough. She smiled, bent her head, and began scribbling. She stopped to flip back a couple of pages in the text and checked something, then proceeded to write furiously on her tablet. For all the world, her posture, expression, and intent reminded me of a college student anxiously prepping for exams.

At that instant she froze like a deer in the headlights. Her head jerked up. As if in amazement, she vaulted from the desk, knocking the physics text and her legal pad to the floor. She ran to the television, staring in disbelief at CNN.

"What is that?" I asked. "Corporal, can you turn it up?"

Cyrus was asking, "Ryan? What's she doing?"

The camera panned sideways under Hatcher's skilled fingers; the television image resolved where Alpha stood transfixed, eyes wide, mouth slightly agape.

We could hear the announcer's voice: "The tomb, subject of a bitter firefight between looters and Egyptian forces, has now been opened to the media for one brief tour."

"Sancti sputi!" Alpha cried. "Certum est?"

I started from my chair. Prisoner Alpha never showed emotion. She might have been some fairy-tale queen the way she maintained and cultivated her dominating presence. All that was gone as I watched the woman's stunned disbelief—her expression a terrible mix of hope, grief, and exultation.

"And now, for the first time in centuries, the interior of the tomb is again viewed by human eyes."

As the TV image panned across the antechamber, Alpha's mouth was opening and closing like a suffocating fish. She whispered, "Ipso *diffidentio. In culpa meo, Fluvium. In culpa . . . in culpa . . ."* she repeated sadly, and a tear slipped down her cheek. She reached out with reverent fingers and lightly stroked the television screen.

*"What damned language is that?"* Cyrus demanded. *"What's she seeing there? What does it mean?"*

"My God," Hatcher whispered. "She's fucking come alive!"

"What is this show?" My own heart was pounding. "It's CNN, get on it. Some kind of tomb. Where? Egypt?"

"On it, sir."

My attention was torn between Alpha's remarkable display and the fuzzier image on the television.

And then, as the image panned the interior burial chamber, it fixed on one wall, where, to my absolute amazement, Alpha's code was displayed. I saw the familiar dots, bars, and symbols rendered in color. Through the monitor I could *feel* Alpha's explosive amazement. The camera focused on what looked like a diagram, or schematic.

"Kiiiaaaahh!" Alpha screamed, her eyes wide, her hands pressed against the television screen. *"Palma!"* she cried. Then, again, *"Palma!"*

The image vanished, followed by a car insurance commercial.

Alpha howled her frustration, banging her fist against the screen. *"Plus! Ego execror! Plus!"* Then, as the commercial continued to run, she turned on her heel, racing back to fumble on the floor for her legal pad. The world forgotten, she began frantically scribbling on the tablet with her Sharpie.

*"What did we just see?"* Cyrus repeated in my earbud.

"I'm not sure. But did you see that image on CNN?"

*"Not clearly."*

"It's Alpha's code. It was carved and painted on that tomb wall. That schematic really set her off."

*"Don't worry, Ryan. We're on it on this end. We'll have you copies of every image made of that tomb within an hour."*

I chuckled almost gleefully.

*"But, Ryan? What the hell does it mean?"* Cyrus asked, sounding baffled.

"Beats the hell out of me." I fingered my chin as Alpha frantically scribbled in her tablet. "But somehow the explanation of who that woman is seems to be linked to a centuries-old Egyptian tomb." I whistled softly and added, "Go figure."

# Fatum

*I sit for the moment in stunned disbelief. Oh, dear husband, did you die believing I had abandoned you?*

*To me, you are but a moment gone. I can barely imagine your anguish, your madness and endless hope as the years passed. Even as you crafted your great* sepulcrum, *what despair must have welled in your heart? And worst of all was not knowing.*

*For that needless suffering, I shall repay these beasts.*

*I caught barely a glimpse of your tomb, but it was enough.*

*As the magisters, the* ch'ul winniki, *taught us in the holy city of Dzibilchaltun, the cycles of time will come full circle. Soon, dear husband, I shall wield time like a sword. I shall snatch you from eternity's maw. On my honor as Domina, your terrible tears will remain unborn.*

*At any moment the beasts will unwittingly free me. Clueless, they provide me with the means for my rescue.*

# 20

"Could this get any crazier?" Kilgore asked as the 767's seatbelt sign flashed off. She unbuckled and climbed wearily to her feet. Despite the long days of stress, Kilgore still exuded a presence of competence and self-assurance. That she'd been in the same clothes for days and had only "freshened up" in the plane's lavatory didn't lessen the effect: Reid thought she was the most beautiful woman alive.

He sniffed, well aware of the acrid reek from his own armpits and sweat-impregnated clothing. Following her into the aisle, he reached into the overhead for the small bag containing his notes, camera, laptop, flash cards, and excavation records. All he'd had time to grab on the hurried evacuation from Wadi Kerf.

"You could come," he had told Yusif as the helicopters spooled up. "With the US military involved, there's no telling what kind of suspicion you're going to fall under when your government arrives."

"No, *sahib*." Yusif's expression tightened. "My people were killed. I must see to them. But, if you could do something for them and me, find out what this is about, and who is behind it. Then, when the time is right, I will seek my own justice."

And as the helicopters had risen, Yusif had stood alone and defiant while the downwash blasted him with dust.

"You all right?" Major Savage asked as he rose from the seat behind Reid.

"Just thinking about Yusif."

"Had he come, his government might not have understood. As it is, I'm afraid your friend is in for a very tough time with Egyptian security agents."

"I'm not sure any of us understand." Kilgore shouldered her laptop bag with its records. "God, I just want a hot shower, a soft bed, and three days of sleep."

Savage grunted in weary acknowledgment. "Let's get the sarcophagi to the Smithsonian, get your data secured, and I'll see what I can do."

"What about Skientia?" Reid asked. "It's their money that opened the Wadi Kerf tomb. I'm still on their payroll, Major. Technically, and professionally, I'm their representative."

Savage's expression wasn't friendly. "Whatever Skientia's initial motives, it's created an international incident. And by now the Egyptians know that American forces were involved. Skientia's in the middle of its own little fur ball."

With Kilgore leading the way, Reid started down the 767's aisle. For whatever reason, they'd been given preference in the First Class section, the rest of the leased Delta jet being filled with American service personnel rotating out of the unpleasantness in the Persian Gulf.

"Skientia isn't my problem, Doctor," Savage told him. "I don't know who pulled the trigger on the op, but it was someone with some pretty heavy-duty influence in the Pentagon."

Reid shot a questioning look at Kilgore, who arched her slim eyebrow in return. He gave her a grin. He was coming to like Kilgore France.

"This way," Savage told them.

Reid yawned, painfully aware of his exhaustion. The balmy air seemed remarkably humid after Wadi Kerf.

At the bottom of the metal stairs, two large black SUVs were parked just ahead of a Ford delivery van. The drivers came to attention as Savage led the way down and over to the vehicles.

"Ma'am," one of the drivers said as he opened a rear door for Kilgore.

The driver took their bags as Kilgore and Reid slipped into the back. The door closed with a soft thump. Kilgore's dark eyes fixed on a distance only she could see. Something about that fragile and vulnerable expression touched him. Every fiber of him wanted to wrap Kilgore France in his arms and never let go.

"What are you thinking?" she asked, giving him a crafty sidelong glance.

"Just that you did well in that tomb."

"You, too, Reid. It helped. Especially at first when I almost lost it." She paused. "Somewhere along the line, I misplaced part of myself. Lost the once starry-eyed girl who was carried away with the wonders hidden in anthropology. I grew into that other Dr. Kilgore France: the hard-eyed forensic weapon fighting on the side of truth and justice."

Her brow knit. "The people at Skientia think it's real. They knew it was going to be controversial. That's why they picked us. They wanted experts who couldn't be dismissed."

He gave her an appreciative grin. "Whatever you find when we get that sarcophagus open, your final report will stand up to peer review."

"The only mistake they made? There should have been a handful of Egyptologists, paleopathologists, and forensic anthropologists to buttress each other's arguments and analyses."

"That makes me think they're somewhat out of their league." Reid frowned. "And there's the contract hit team to consider. No matter what Skientia believes, someone else went to a great deal of expense and time to hire the goons that murdered Yusif's men."

"So, who's the third party?" She glanced through the window to where Major Savage stood, arms crossed, talking on his cell. The major's hard eyes were fixed on the caisson as ground personnel carefully slid the first heavy sarcophagus into the van's rear.

Kilgore thoughtfully added, "Savage is right. It took someone with real clout to deploy a spec ops extraction team that quickly. It had to be Skientia. They were in communication when we were attacked."

"The dead goons we walked past? Did you get a look at them?"

Her lips pinched. "My visual assessment of the wounds was consistent with the kind of terminal ballistics expected from 5.56 and 7.62 NATO rounds like Savage's guys carried. But the bloodstains on the ground, the long-dried ones, were often in association with scatters of nine-millimeter brass . . . like the HK subgun that was pointed at us just before the hammer-stone fell on the thug."

"You saw all that? Just on the walk out?"

"Too many crime scenes in my checkered past."

He reached out and took her hand on impulse as the driver opened the door and slid behind the wheel. To his delight, she gave him a reassuring squeeze.

The Tahoe roared to life. The driver slipped it in gear, and Reid caught a glimpse as Savage got into the passenger's seat of the lead vehicle.

Moments later they passed through the security gate and west onto Route 4. Crossing under the 95/495 Beltway, the small detail accelerated onto Pennsylvania Avenue.

"I've never been to Washington before."

She glanced at him thoughtfully. "Really?"

To his amazement she hadn't pulled her hand from his. Just her touch, her warmth, filled him with an excited contentment.

He said, "They never hosted an archaeological conference here that I wanted to attend."

"DC's . . . interesting," she told him. "Superb restaurants, great hotels, lots to see and do. If there's time, I'll . . ."

The delivery truck they were passing veered in front of them. Tires shrieking, it struck the tail of Savage's lead Tahoe and spun it sideways.

In Reid's vehicle, the driver's-side window exploded with a loud pop. A hail of glass blasted the driver and tossed him sideways across the seat. The Chevy slowed and crunched into the rear of the delivery truck. Another car was pulling up alongside.

Mashed as it was against the delivery van's rear, the SUV had slowed to a crawl. The paralleling vehicle's door opened. A man dressed in tactical black and wearing a balaclava leaped out, reached through the gaping window, and unlocked the door.

"Hey, what the hell do you . . ."

The pistol the intruder pointed in Reid's face immediately sent a tickle of butterflies through his gut.

Pulling the door open, the intruder used a knife to sever the driver's seatbelt; then dragged the groaning man out and dropped him on the pavement.

Reid—staring down the pistol's black barrel—never saw the second balaclava-masked man who opened the passenger door and climbed in. He, too, leveled a pistol, saying, "Stay right where you are. Both of you."

The first attacker slid into the driver's seat. Cranking the wheel, he pulled out around the delivery truck. Major Savage's Tahoe was on its side, the delivery truck pushing it down the street at ten miles an hour.

"What the *hell* do you think you're doing?" Kilgore demanded. "Do you know who we are? What you just did?"

"We're quite familiar with your identity, Dr. France. Yours, too, Dr. Farmer." Then the passenger lifted a small black radio to his lips. "Vehicles and cargo secure. Targets are both unharmed. We're beginning the evasive maneuvers now."

The pistol's gaping black muzzle seemed to hold Reid's gaze as though he were a mouse and it a cobra. He barely felt the SUV sway as it lurched hard around a corner. Kilgore's hand tightened on his in a death grip.

# 21

I sat in Alpha's guest chair while the woman carefully scrutinized the photos of the Egyptian tomb. While the detailed recordings from the room monitors would later prove it based on her eye movements, I had no doubt that she was "reading" the curious epigraphic symbols painted on the tomb wall.

The woman's heart was in her throat. No matter who Alpha was, or where she came from, she wasn't so foreign or dissociative as to be inhuman. Whatever she was reading was tearing her apart.

"What language is it?" I asked softly.

She took a moment to compose herself, then lifted her startling blue eyes to mine. "In your tongue? The translation 'world talk' would be, yes?"

"World talk?"

"*Terrarum colloquium.*" Her accent was curious.

"Like a *lingua franca*?"

"Tongue franca? This I do not know." She seemed completely baffled.

"Tell me about the tomb."

Her expression fell. "*Fluvium.* Lost. *Inlaqueit.* Um, marooned."

"You've learned English well."

"Hard language. Not so hard as *Ch'olan* or *Yukatek.*"

"I don't know those languages."

The smile she gave me reeked of bitterness and a bit of pity. "You know very little, *Medicus.* Your world, I think, all *pereo est.* Lost."

"You've been making adjustments to your machine." I pointed at the doohickey. "What do you call it?"

"Amusement."

"What does it do?"

She rattled off an incomprehensible explanation in whatever her own language was, ending with a mocking smile on her perfect lips. "Now you know."

"Can you tell me in English?"

A faint twinkle came to her eyes, as though my question fostered the sort of indulgence she'd give a child. "Tell? No. *Inartes evigilo.*"

She reached for her tablet, flipped to a new page, and in the exact middle, drew a dot. "It is," she said, pointing to the dot as if willing me to understand. Then, bracing the tablet she took a second Sharpie, and holding the pens at an angle from each other, drew horizontal lines out from the dot. "Same but different in time?"

She cocked her head to see if I got it. "*Physicus?* Yes?" Then added, "You call quantum mechanic." She made a face. "Um, entangled. Now, watch."

With curious dexterity she made the pen tips wiggle up and down to leave mimicking waves on the paper. "Different but same, yes? What term in English you have?" A slight frown. "Say . . . how?" And she indicated the paper.

I frowned at the drawing, trying to make sense of it. "Different but same?"

For the first time, her expression eased, anticipation in her expression. Her fingers, where they grasped the pen, fluttered as if to draw me along.

"Sorry, but I don't get it." At the smug retreat of her gaze, I said, "Don't worry, we'll get there. Meanwhile, tell me about the tomb. What made you so excited?"

She pulled out the photo of the wall diagram. "Need, how you say, *amplificare.* Make more for doohickey." She used my word for the gadget on her desk.

"And what will it do?"

"All will come *perspicuous.* Um . . ." She frowned, lifting her right hand and spreading the fingers wide. Then she interlaced the fingers of her left between them.

"Sorry. I still don't understand."

As I watched, the aloof and superior persona fell into place. "Make more energy for doohickey. Then you understand everything."

"And the tomb?"

"First energy for doohickey, then you discover all. Who I am. Where I from."

*God, what I'd give for those answers.*

# 22

"**G**eneral Grazier is currently unavailable," the voice on the other end told me. "*I'll have him call you the moment he's back in the office. Can I tell him what this is concerning?*"

"He knows we've had a breakthrough with Prisoner Alpha. For the first time, I've got an opening, a chance to make real progress." I glanced down at the bit of paper she'd drawn, the two lines stretching out from the single point and then producing similar waves. An illustration of a bird in flight, perhaps? Entangled? What did that mean? "How soon do you expect him back?"

"*I'm sorry, sir. I don't have that information.*"

Which was, of course, double-dyed bullshit.

I forced my voice to remain calm. "Tell him that it's urgent, and that I . . ." I paused, shot a glance to where the physical plant report lay on my desk. "Never mind."

I pressed the button to end the call, and then dialed the number for the physical plant.

"*Hello?*"

"Sergeant Kalkovich?"

"*Yes, sir?*"

"Who have you got over there who's good with electronics?"

"*Depends on what you want, sir?*"

"You remember when I sent you the schematic of that thing Prisoner Alpha built?"

"*Yes, sir. But nothing's changed. We still don't have a clue as to what it does. And unless Gray wants to electrocute herself, it looks pretty harmless.*"

"What if I wanted to make it more powerful? Have you got anything that would boost the output?"

"*Uh, probably. Depending on what the thing draws, we'd have to figure the amperage and load at the outlet. But that gets a little tricky, depending on the circuit boards she took out of the TV.*"

I fingered my chin as I considered. "How about we give her a box of parts and a voltmeter? Show her where maximum amperage is on the meter, and the numeric value she can pull from that outlet. Meanwhile, one of your guys can wire in a breaker, can't you? So, if she screws it up, she won't take out the women's wing in Ward Six?"

"*And if she sets the place on fire?*"

I glanced sidelong at the monitor where Prisoner Alpha pored over the photo of the diagram from the Egyptian tomb. "My hunch, Sergeant, is that she won't do anything of the kind."

# 23

The soft scuff of leather shoes on the polished-tile hospital floor accompanied Eli Grazier as he walked down the hall at Bethesda Naval Hospital.

Finding the right room, he stepped inside. Sam Savage lay in the hospital bed, a look that promised mayhem on his face as he glared up at the television.

"Major?"

Savage snapped off the best salute he could, given the angle at which he lay. "Hello, Eli. Why am I not surprised that it would be you who walked through my door?"

"How are you?"

"After all their tests I was told exactly what I knew the moment they unloaded me from that damned ambulance. I've got bumps and bruises."

"We had to be sure."

Savage waved it away. "What's the status of Farmer, France, and the sarcophagi?"

"No sign of them."

"Shit!" Savage leaned his head back in the pillow. "Level with me, Eli. One minute I was in Saballah village, wearing a dishdash, talking to an Afghan elder. The next I'm putting together an extraction team in Kabul. Before I can catch so much as a catnap, I'm on a carrier in the Red Sea. I barely blink, and I'm infiltrating Egyptian airspace and dropping my team smack into a firefight with *American* contractors. We take out the contractors, who have killed twenty-some Egyptians.

"I find a blocked passageway in an Egyptian tomb with what's left of a guy sliced in two by a big fucking rock. I blow the rock, extract France and Farmer, and have to fit *two* sarcophagi to my choppers. We *barely* beat feet out of there before the Egyptian Air Force splashes us all over the rocks.

"I get fast-tracked to Andrews, load the archaeologists and coffins into trucks—and then the whole shittaree gets whacked on fucking Pennsylvania Avenue? By people who not only know we are coming, but have a perfectly executed snatch?" He paused. "You following me on this, Eli? Hearing how bizarre and crazy this sounds?"

"The hijacking hit us out of the blue," Grazier admitted.

"Eli, they had every detail. Trucks, time, route. And it was a very professional job. I couldn't have organized and executed a better snatch."

Grazier nodded. "It's not the first time I've had my communications compromised. My problem is that I can't figure out how. That they'd sacrifice an advantage like that? Just to get the anthropologists and sarcophaguses? That tells me how important that damn Egyptian tomb really is."

"It's just a tomb, sir."

"It shouldn't exist. Period. We took your vid-cam to an Egyptologist at the Smithsonian. The guy jazzed over the chariots and a lot of the artifacts, but as soon as he saw the stuff painted and carved on the walls, he stopped cold and said, 'Whose idea of a joke is this?'"

"Farmer and France said the same."

"He also told us that the Roman script wasn't right for the tomb's purported age, and that the airplane drawing, the weird symbols on the walls, and that schematic in the burial chamber were, and I quote, 'Someone's sick fantasy.'"

"Eli, those mercs-for-hire killed more than twenty Egyptian nationals to get at that tomb. But for one of their guys tripping that deadfall and sealing the burial chamber, they'd have had it all. They were willing to die trying to keep it. Now, whoever hired them, they've figuratively given it to us up the ass and taken the goodies back. As Uncle Buck would have told me, 'This whole thing just ain't normal.'"

Grazier's smile thinned. "No, it's not. And the two guys you captured alive make no bones about it. They're employed by Talon Group, just doing the job they were given. Their orders were to take out the security, grab the scientists and all the artifacts they could truck out. They had a rendezvous with a couple of heavy-lift aircraft in the

Western desert. Orders left no room for interpretation: defend the spoils from seizure by any and all parties."

"Pay must have been good."

"The guys you grabbed said it was. And, most interestingly, Talon Group's not answering their phone these days."

"Who'd have thought?"

Grazier nodded, hesitated. "Do you want in on this, Sam? If so, I can have you reassigned. But pay attention here: I know you think you've been living under glass while you've been working for the Activity. But given the stakes and the information you'll be privy to—"

"Over a *fake* Egyptian tomb?"

"Once you tell me you're in, you're in all the way." Grazier raised a cautionary finger. "It'll be like you don't exist. Sam, you might want to take a couple of days and think—"

"I'm in."

"Sam, I mean it, you—"

"I just got bitch-slapped on Pennsylvania Avenue. They took my anthropologists and my fancy Egyptian coffins."

"They call them sarcophaguses."

"Yeah, well, I want them back. And I want to nail the slick-assed suckers who did this."

"Is that your Indian talking?"

"Hell, General, you've got Seminole in your ancestry. Seminoles came from Creek blood in the beginning. We're probably related way back there somewhere. You gonna just take this lying down?"

At Grazier's faint shake of the head, Savage said, "Thought so."

"From here on out, you'll officially vanish. Life, as you knew it, will be over."

*"Ani' inhickita."*

"What's that?"

"It's Creek Indian. It's my most solemn oath. Now, get me the hell out of here so I can start hunting."

# 24

"The symbols in the tomb are a base-twenty mathematical system," Falcon told Edwin and Cat Talavera at breakfast. "The major and I worked on it all night. It wasn't until Theresa showed up that everything fit into place." He thoughtfully scooped scrambled eggs onto his springy plastic fork.

"I don't get it," Edwin said from where he sat beside Cat. "Base twenty?"

Cat told him: "Our mathematics are base ten. Every time you count to ten, you add an integer, and start over. In our case, after you reach nine, you restart with one-zero, one-one, one-two, which you know as ten, eleven, twelve, and so on. Then, at nineteen, you restart with two zero, which is twenty."

"Well, yeah!" Edwin arched his neck slightly, irritated, "I mean, how else you count?"

Talavera's expression pinched. "If you count in base five, the Arabic numerals are 0, 1, 2, 3, 4, 10, 11, and so forth. With 10 equal to our 5, 11 equal to 6, and so on. The numeral 20 would represent 10 in the actual count. In base twenty you have separate integers up to nineteen. Then you restart."

"That's the dots and bars," Falcon told them. "Different symbols that count to nineteen, and then add the odd, football-shaped character which is a zero."

"Why not just do it the way we do?" Edwin wondered. "It's easier."

Falcon shrugged. "I'm not sure. Something about positioning hasn't made sense yet. In some of the photos the dots and bars are consistently horizontal, and in others, vertical. As to why they did it one way versus the other, I haven't been able to figure out. And I'm pretty sure the patterning is a means of either multiplication or division. And then there are other symbols with numerical values I haven't deciphered."

Edwin gave him a wide grin. "If I had a computer, I could run every permutation for you in minutes." The grin fell. "Used to be as much as ten hours a day I'd spend programming, slipping through the systems. I ever tell you 'bout the time I set up a transfer? Had 1.2 billion tagged in the European Central Bank. I'd just initiated a transfer to the Cayman Islands, only to have Lieutenant Higgins stick his damn head in the door and yell, 'Shut it down, ET. You can email your girl later. I need you on duty *now* 'cause Private Verzano just hurled his lunch all over a keyboard.'"

"Now that's prize bullshit if I ever heard it," Winny Swink growled as she hooked a chair on the other side of the table and pulled it out with a toe. Balancing breakfast in one hand and coffee in the other, she slipped gracefully into the seat.

"No bullshit, Major," Edwin told her, using his truth face. "Banks transfer money all the time. It's all initiated by email, monitored, special authorization codes, the right account numbers, tracking, and routing. The bigger the bank, the more they wire back and forth. We're talking tens of billions of dollars a day. The trick for me was to get inside the system, monitor who was sending what to who and which account. But see, you gotta know which accounts are flagged for those receipts. If I'd tried to transfer say, into my own account in Detroit? Wham! They'd a slammed the door on my ass before I even started. But from bank to bank, with the right authorization, and into a previously okayed account number? Piece of cake."

"But you still did not get the money?" Talavera asked as she sprinkled pepper onto her eggs.

"Had to learn the system first," Edwin said with a shrug. "Would have taken a couple of weeks to do it right. Now, if I'd had time, I'd a sent the money back with a little interest a couple of hours later." He gestured with his fork. "Got to keep the books balancing. Got to use the right authorization code. Got to pick the times of day when transactions are heavy. They've got smart people watching all this, and they're looking for someone like me to slip in. You can bet they see that transfer. But they see the right authorization code, and the money comes back with interest, it means the transfer's approved, made money, and came back. All legit, right?"

Winny took a forkful of overcooked eggs. "You're telling me no one would notice when you opened an account with 1.2 billion in it?"

"Major, you don't just dump it into a personal account and expect to get away with it. Got to run it through investment firms, buy bonds, T notes, funnel it through giant corporations. How you think these big banks been losing so many billions?"

"You could do it." Falcon's eyes focused on infinity. "It's a simple stochastic manipulation within what should be a complex deterministic system."

Edwin stopped, toast halfway to his mouth. "What he just say?"

But Falcon was gone, his expression blank, head slightly cocked. It happened when his brain got sidetracked.

"Forget it," Swink muttered. "Next thing you know he's going to be conversing with the air again." She gestured with her fork. "Now, ET, if you really wanted to do some good with that computer of yours, you'd be figuring a way to transfer all of us out of here and back to active duty."

"So you could steal another airplane?" Karla Raven, her steel-gray eyes on Swink, dropped into the seat next to Talavera.

Swink gave Raven a slit-eyed appraisal. "Let's just say they pissed me off."

"My kind of pissed off," Raven agreed. "You knew you were on a one-way flight even before you climbed into that cockpit."

"What did you do, Major?" Talavera used her napkin to carefully clean grease from her thin fingers.

Raven tried to spread icy margarine over dry toast with the rubbery excuse of a knife. "The major, here, failed her psych evaluation. Not that they hadn't known for years, but Swink has a gift to go along with her 'You better kiss my ass 'cause I'm better than you' attitude."

"Fucking A, Chief." Swink turned her gaze from Raven to Talavera. "You see, kid, if it's capable of getting off the ground, I can fly it." She extended her arms, hands flat, fingers fluttering. "It just flows right out of my center, down these arms and legs, as well as right through my ass and into the seat. Can't tell where I stop and the machine begins. A merging, you know? And it's like . . ." Her eyes closed as if savoring an out-of-body experience. "You just gotta live it."

Edwin arched an eyebrow. "Man, I heard they tagged you with

antisocial personality disorder, Major. I looked that up in the DSM. Axis
II, code 301.7. Then it go on and list seven misbehaviors. Which three
of them seven you guilty of?"

Swink stiffened. "You looking for trouble, Private?"

Chief Raven growled. "You're antisocial, not stupid, Major. Nobody
normal steals an F-22 Raptor from Andrews, buzzes the Capitol and
White House, then flies rings around the DC air defenses. And you
weren't happy to stop there, let alone go out in a flame of glory as they
shot you down. Nope, not Major Winny Winchester Swink." Raven
leveled a hard finger. "You had to land the damn thing on I-95 north-
bound, taxi it up the interchange to a fucking convenience store. By the
time the cops got there, you were sitting on the wing, sucking down a
bottle of wine."

"I remember," Talavera whispered. "They said it was the airplane!
That it had a malfunction. That the pilot heroically landed it and saved
lives. That was you?"

Swink's thin lips bent in a crooked grin. "Call it the ultimate 'fuck
you.' Worst part of the whole thing? The best wine they had in that
crummy convenience store had a screw top."

Out of the blue, Falcon interjected, "They tolerate and condone a
certain amount of reckless disregard—as long as you have the requisite
skills to back it up and don't destroy the airplanes." He cocked his head.
"But that's why you washed out of NASA. It's a different culture."

Swink seemed to bristle. "The shitheads I had to deal with at NASA
couldn't find their dicks with two hands and a flashlight."

Raven added, "But it made you perfect as a test pilot for the skunk
works, didn't it?" She glanced at Talavera. "Those are the black programs, the ones developing experimental aircraft. They'll put up with
some insubordination in return for genius at the stick, composure in the
face of disaster, and sheer guts."

Swink winked at Edwin. "I could give a shit how they categorize
me in the DSM. I went out as the greatest legend the USAF has ever
known."

"And—" Raven gestured with her fork, "—now we're the ones stuck
with your charming, self-centered, warm and fuzzy personality."

"Gee, Chief." Swink went back to her eggs. "Maybe the Skipper will
up your citalopram, and life will just get rosy all over."

Edwin glanced sidelong at the chief, a flicker of anxiety building. Baiting Karla Raven just wasn't done. At least not by anyone figuring on a long and pain-free life.

Then, to Edwin's amazement, Chief Raven threw her head back and laughed.

# 25

A thousand things, for whatever reason, had dropped onto my plate at just the wrong moment. I'd only made it home for four hours' sleep last night, and barely caught six the night before that. Routine responsibilities, including personnel evaluations, patient evaluations, the physical plant report, supply requisitions, the building report, quarterly health and sanitation reports, compliance evaluations, and a host of other administrative tasks were daunting enough.

And then there was Prisoner Alpha.

I'd monitored every minute of her waking hours. Since the tomb on TV, she'd been manic. With frantic competence she'd inspected the electronic parts my guys had scrounged. How could the woman be a natural when it came to electricity, but not understand a key word like watt or ohm?

I had provided her with a circuit tester, demonstrated its use, and watched her experiment for no more than fifteen minutes before she smiled in triumph, nodded to herself, and began scribbling in her notebooks. I'd since deduced that she was converting amperage and voltage into her peculiar code. Then she was back to studying the tomb-wall diagram. That was followed by more scribbling before she began inspecting the pieces of disparate equipment and disassembling them.

Whatever her dysfunction, Alpha's was a highly organized and al-most obsessively focused mind. For the first time, I was on the verge of understanding.

*Assuming I don't get fired, charged, and convicted for giving her a screwdriver and a pair of pliers.*

General Grazier continued to be "unavailable" the last three times I had tried to call him. Nor had the general replied to my emails where I'd laid out my latest thoughts about Alpha.

*The thing is: if she builds something remarkable, perhaps it will be a key to her identity and the trauma that has manifested in such a devastating and unique pathology.*

If pathology it was. The more I watched her, the less certain I was.

The buzzer on my desk jarred me back to the real world.

Janeesha's voice cheerfully announced, *"Chief Petty Officer Raven is here for her ten o'clock appointment, sir."*

"Thank you, Janeesha. Send her in."

I laid the report to one side, frowning. The way Alpha manipulated and understood electrical equipment was more than just intuitive. She'd been trained. But where? It didn't matter where a person came from, electrical theory and engineering were universal. Be it a Russian, Indonesian, or Kenyan electrician, they all used the same parts, terms, math, and standards in their designs.

Chief Raven stopped in front of my desk, saluted, and stood at attention, eyes fixed on the "Me" wall behind me with its pictures, diplomas, and certificates.

"At ease, Chief." The sweatpants and oversized T-shirt she wore barely disguised her supple body. Just being in Raven's proximity reminds some hibernating part of my limbic system that I'm still male.

"Thank you for seeing me on such short notice, sir." She dropped into an "at ease" posture.

"Chief, I've told you before, unless I'm up to my elbows in alligators, I'll make time."

"Thank you, sir."

"Now, what can I do for you?"

"We saw the newly discovered tomb on television, sir. The one in Egypt. It caught Falcon's eye. He noted the inscriptions on the wall, thought he saw a pattern. Patient services was kind enough to print off a JPEG of the inscriptions. After thinking about it . . . or whatever Falcon does . . . he believes it's a mathematical system. A base-twenty notation, sir."

I straightened in my chair, pulse beginning to race. "A base-twenty mathematical system? That code is mathematics?"

"According to Falcon, sir."

Falcon had keyed on that tomb, too? "And you're here because . . . ?"

"Falcon would like to have Private Edwin Tyler Jones play with the patterns on the computer, sir. Falcon thinks the system is an equation, but he's not sure of the permutations, or how the different orientation of the symbols affects their numerical values."

*Where on earth did Alpha learn a base-twenty mathematical system?*

"Chief, my orders state in clear English that ET is, under no circumstances, allowed to lay so much as a finger on a computer."

She pulled up, hand rising in salute, figuring she had my decision.

"However," I blurted before she could touch her brow, "I would be willing to have one of the techs input the data any way Falcon wants."

Raven's control, as always, remained perfect. "Thank you, sir." This time she snapped the salute and started for the door.

"Chief?"

"Sir?" She turned back in mid-pace, head cocked.

"What do you know about those symbols?"

"They come from a tomb in Egypt, sir. Major Swink says they're not Egyptian. Falcon, he just cued. Um . . . being the way he is."

How much did I dare tell her? "Were you aware that Prisoner Alpha uses similar symbols?"

"I don't understand, sir."

"If Falcon is correct, Alpha's using the same mathematical system and symbols here, in Ward Six, that were scribbled on that Egyptian wall back in whenever." I paused. "Off the record, Chief?"

Her gray eyes narrowed in acknowledgment. "OTR, Skipper."

"And confidential," I added just to be sure she understood. Taking a chance, I rose and walked over to the monitor that showed Prisoner Alpha's room. The tawny-haired woman was fiddling with one of the electric parts.

"That's Prisoner Alpha. Gray, as you call her. And, as we've discussed in the past, she's an enigma. Now you stroll in out of the blue and tell me those symbols she's drawn on her walls are mathematics."

Karla shot me a sidelong glance. "Why are you showing me this?"

"Because I'm desperate, Chief. I want to help that woman. She saw that news report on the Egyptian tomb, and it was the first crack in her armor. That diagram painted on the tomb wall almost had her in a manic state. So, I took her a copy of it, probably from the same website that Falcon's came from."

I pointed. "You see the device on her desk? General Grazier calls it 'the doohickey.' We don't know what it does other than generate a sort of electromagnetic field. Seems pretty harmless."

Catching a faint whiff of Raven's scent, I forced my brain back to the problem. "She wanted to make her doohickey stronger, more powerful. As part of her therapy, as goodwill, as research, whatever you want to call it, I've allowed her some random electrical parts. And now, right out of the blue, you bring me part of the puzzle. The symbols she uses are a mathematical system."

She studied me through a sidelong glance. "Why share this with me, sir?"

"Because I can count the number of people I trust on one hand, Chief. You're one of them."

I caught the beginning of her startled expression, a hint of panic, then her control was back. "I don't understand, sir."

"My nephew was a SEAL. He died in Syria. Turned a Humvee over in a ditch. All that training, dedication, and skill. Just gone because he was going too fast for a corner."

I kept my eyes fixed on Alpha as she used the tester on circuits. "I wrangled a study. Wanted to see if there was a way to keep SEALs at the kind of peak performance they need to do the job but ameliorate risk-taking in noncombat situations. I was attached to a team as a 'medical observer.' I took blood pressure, periodically looked in guys' ears, tested reflexes with rubber hammers, and in general did just enough to justify my presence and become invisible."

I took a steadying breath, uncomfortable with offering a patient such an insight. "I lived with the team for nearly a year. I *know* as much about what it takes to be SEAL as anyone alive who hasn't earned his Bud-weiser." That's in-speak for the eagle-trident-and-pistol insignia of the SEALs. The name originated from the BUD/S, or Basic Underwater Demolition/SEAL training.

Raven was giving me her full attention now.

"I've seen what goes on behind the clubhouse door. I know about the hazing, the violence, the ceaseless testing, and how relentless it is for males to constantly reinforce the notion that they're the best of the best and that they can take any kind of shit anyone can dish out."

I paused. "Yet you survived the cauldron, made even hotter because you're the first woman. Honestly, what you achieved defies my understanding of human endurance."

Her gaze went a little distant. "I couldn't fail. Took me three roll backs, you know what those are?"

"Yeah, you're pulled from a SEAL class until the broken bones, torn muscles, or head injuries can heal, then you're allowed back into the grinder."

A sliver of smile crossed her lips. "What I didn't have in upper-body strength I made up for in other ways. They want mental acuity and agility, an 'I'm going to do this and fuck you' attitude. I had tons of endurance—and a whole lot of wrath—to keep me going. The time they soaked my tampons in Tabasco sauce? I sneaked in and got to the manuals that were going to be handed out the next day. Cut out the section on remote-detonating IEDs and inserted a section on female reproductive anatomy. They thought that was pretty funny until the next day when the Master Chief asked why I was the only one who knew the material. Straight-faced, I told him the rest of my team had spent the night devoting themselves to the study of vaginas."

I allowed myself a smile, delighted to have her talking freely. Alpha and Raven? Two birds with one therapy?

"The time seven of them jumped me in the shower and choked me down? I wasn't so forgiving. Each time I started to come to, they'd choke me down again. They took turns raping me. One of the last things I heard before coming to on that shower room floor was someone asking 'Hey, what's par for this hole?'"

"Did you report it?"

She shot me a look of loathing. "SEALs *don't* rat, Skipper. They don't ask for *other* people to *give* them justice. We get it on our own."

Her grin bent slightly. "The next day? Everyone knew. They were waiting, wondering. Officer in Charge had heard something, asked me specifically if anything was wrong. Took six months to catch each of those guys alone, beat the shit out of him, and shove a golf tee a couple of inches up his urethra. Should have heard the stories they tried to tell the doctors about how that tee got up there. But word got around. No one ever 'fucked with me' that way again."

"No retribution?"

"If they'd tried, they'd have got the crap beat out of them." She looked smug. "Two of them ended up on my team. One under my command a couple of years later. I called him 'Golf' and the nickname stuck. People on the outside don't understand."

Her expression tightened. "He died that day. I failed him." A pause. "Just like the rest."

"When are you going to stop blaming yourself?"

"When I can go back and bring my people home." She turned steely eyes on mine.

"It was an IED."

"I looked right at it."

"And you knew it was an IED?"

"I should have."

"They put a shaped charge in a spilled basket of clothes."

"What woman would have just left a *clean* basket of clothes in the dirt like that?"

"A woman scared for her life?" I asked softly. "I know you, Karla. You have survived and come to terms with trauma that few other women could. What should have destroyed you only made you stronger. You sacrificed everything you ever were to become a SEAL. That's what they do. Beat the identity out of you and see if you can construct a new one. And when you did, you pushed yourself even harder. You signed up for SEAL sniper training. Fifty percent of SEALs can't cut it. You excelled, finished your class as 'the honor man.' And went on to rack up fifty-four confirmed kills in combat. Nominated for the Congressional Medal of Honor. Nominated for the Navy Cross. Picked up a Silver Star and a couple of bronze ones to go with it. Earned enough commendations to paper the wall. They kicked you up to an E7, Chief Petty Officer, and let you handle a little admin and tactical planning. You commanded your own sniper platoon, were on the fast track. You can't blame yourself for an IED."

She stared woodenly at Alpha on the television.

"And you'd have come back from that if that fool doctor hadn't ordered a psychiatric evaluation."

She'd pursed her lips, cheek muscles knotted.

I hesitated. "Now . . . there's a difference between us. I've got a PhD, and you've got a Trident. That means when it comes to the two of us, I'm smarter, and you're tougher. Being the smart guy that I am, I'll always bet on Chief Petty Officer Karla Raven. I know who she really is, even when she's deluding herself into thinking she's someone she's not."

"Nice try, Doc. But you know I can't help stealing stuff."

"It serves a purpose. If the world could just up and take your self-identity away, kleptomania provides compensation. Down deep, you're taking things back."

"I don't even know when I do it."

"But you experience a sense of exhilaration each time."

She gave me a speculative glance. "I never told you that."

"I'm the psychiatrist."

On the screen, Alpha was humming some tune, the melody completely unfamiliar. "You know that song, Chief?"

"No, sir."

"We've recorded all of her songs. Can't place a one of them."

"Why are you doing this, sir?"

"Doing what?"

"Running Ward Six. Spending your time locked away at Grantham Barracks. You could be making a fortune in private practice."

"Why did you spend two tours in Iraq and three in Afghanistan?"

"Because by killing bad guys I was saving American lives."

"There's your answer, Chief."

"Wish you didn't trust me, sir. That's a hell of an obligation to place on someone."

"Sorry."

On the monitor, Alpha was wiring the part she'd been working on into the doohickey. She moved with sure dexterity, as if she'd been wiring things together all her life.

# Stulti

*Were they not beasts, I could almost pity them. I work now in an ecstatic rush,* an opera insania. *The fools have witlessly handed me their world. Their very existence. The parts they have provided are as primitive as stones. But they can be adapted. The transmitter will be crude. But I need only tickle the navigator's detector, and I shall be free.*

*I have the tools now, the language and understanding to achieve my goals. All I need are more* stulti, *more fools to beguile, and I shall once again seize the whirlwinds of time.*

*Imperator, I will accept your bargain. Pay your price.*

*Nor, dear husband, shall you die abandoned in Aegyptus.*

*And as for the* stulti *and beasts? They have mere days remaining before my finely honed wrath is unleashed upon them.*

# 26

With a start, Reid Farmer awakened from nightmares. For a horrified instant, he couldn't place the unfamiliar movement against his back.

*Kilgore!*

It all came rushing back: the kidnapping; the terrifying ride; the hard-eyed men in tactical gear carrying submachine guns; and the dark airfield with a sleek corporate jet.

He and Kilgore had been made to sit out of each other's sight during the flight. The window curtains had been pulled to obscure their route. Silence had been enforced.

Upon landing, the jet had taxied for a short time. Stopped. The engines had shut down. Moments later Reid felt the plane being towed. More waiting.

When the door had finally opened and the fold-out stairway deployed, Reid had stepped out into a roomy aircraft hangar. A nondescript delivery van waited off to the right, the side door open, guards everywhere.

"You'll need to wear these." One of the gunmen extended black-fabric hoods as Kilgore was marched down the steps to Reid's side.

"And if I refuse?" Reid had asked mildly.

"Oh, we won't beat you, Doctor Farmer." He pointed at Kilgore. "We'll just take out our frustrations on your girlfriend."

Reid had allowed himself to be hooded. Then he and Kilgore were ordered to stay silent as they were led to the van and helped inside. The door had been slammed, and moments later they'd felt the thing start. How long had they ridden? Fifteen? Twenty minutes? Reid remembered a lot of curves, starting, and stopping.

In the end, the van had slowed and, after pitching them back and forth, stopped.

When the door opened, the hoods were removed, and Reid blinked at the large, commercial-looking garage containing a small fleet of black Chevy Suburbans. From there, they'd been marched through a door and into what appeared to be a mansion.

Up a flight of stairs, at the first door on the left, he and Kilgore had been escorted into a bedroom with drawn drapes.

"Bathroom's there," the guard had pointed. "Orders are that you get some sleep. I'll be outside the door; another agent will be posted outside below the window. Escape attempts will be frowned on."

"And our clothes?" Kilgore had asked. In the light, she looked absolutely haggard, literally stumbling on her feet from exhaustion. They'd been in the same reeking clothes since they'd entered the tomb days ago at Wadi Kerf.

"Coming, Doctor. In the meantime, well, I'm sure you don't have anything Dr. Farmer hasn't seen before." He'd given them a knowing grin, turned, and closed the door with a resounding click.

Kilgore had used the toilet, then walked out and fallen onto the bed, fully dressed.

"So?" Reid asked after he'd relieved himself, turned out the light, and settled on the bed, "You got anything I haven't seen before?"

"You better believe it," she'd muttered, and fallen into immediate slumber.

How long ago had that been?

Kilgore's warm body close against his, her breath purling on the back of his neck, he would have considered that to be paradise in any other situation. Now she was sleeping pressed against him in spite of the way he smelled. How could you not fall in love with a woman like that?

He shifted, trying to get feeling into his numb hip where his cargo pants had eaten into the skin.

"Where are we?" Kilgore asked, draping an arm over his waist.

"Still kidnapped."

"You snore."

"I wasn't aware of that."

"From birth onward, life is a process of nonending learning and discovery."

"As pleasant as this is, 'girlfriend,' I've got to pee."

He rolled out and ambled into the bathroom. She was right behind him. He looked into her worried dark eyes as she put her arms around his neck and leaned close, whispering, "Then we play lovers. Scientific partners who need each other's expertise, got it?"

"This is where I ask, 'And what's the catch?'" he whispered into her ear. "But I'm not kissing you until they give you a toothbrush and toothpaste."

"That bad?"

"Compared to my armpits? Not even close." He pushed her back, seeing her curiously lifted eyebrow. "The good or bad news—depending on how you look at it—is that if they don't bring us new clothes, these will rot off in the next couple of days."

She laughed at that, turning and sniffing cautiously at her own pits. "God, you're right. I'll leave you to your business now. But don't linger. When we're done with nature, we'll at least wash our shirts in the sink. And I may have to chance a shower—even if they shoot me for taking it."

"Got it."

When he finished, she was at the window. With a finger, she'd pulled the drapes back just far enough to look out.

"What do you see?"

"Daylight. Mountains. My guess is the Rockies or Sierras. And not another house in sight. It could just be me, but I think I know where we are."

"And?"

"Above Aspen, in Colorado. I was here for a while, working with a producer on a television project."

"I know Aspen," he told her. "I tent-camped in a grove of them for a month when I worked on an Archaic site above Durango."

"See," she jabbed him playfully in the ribs, "we travel in the same circles after all."

"Price of celebrity," he growled as she padded off for the bathroom.

Reid's stomach growled; the ache of starvation reminding him that the last time he'd eaten had been on the military charter. And before that, he'd wolfed down MREs donated by Major Savage's soldiers.

He heard the toilet flush and the shower start. Scratching, he stripped off his shirt and inspected it. God, he hadn't been kidding about the thing rotting off.

*Why are they doing this? What do they want from us?*

"Come on. Think, Reid."

Everything, of course, tied back to that crazy tomb.

A faint knock came at the door.

"Yes?" he asked, his heart beginning to pound.

The door opened; a black-tactical-suited guard reached in to deposit a dark suitcase on the floor. "Should be close to your sizes," he said. "You've got half an hour before breakfast. Use it."

After the man closed the door, Reid stared thoughtfully at the suitcase, overcame the innate desire to toss it back out, and carried it to the rumpled, if still-made, bed.

Half expecting the thing to hiss gas or explode, he zipped it open to find a couple of white blouses, two pairs of cotton slacks, several panties and bras. Beneath them were men's dress shirts, slacks, T-shirts, skivvies, and socks.

He lifted out the women's clothing and knocked lightly on the bathroom door. Hearing no change in the shower, he opened it a crack, calling, "Kilgore?"

"What?"

"They brought clothing. I'm leaving it on the counter. Food is coming in half an hour."

"Oh, joy." The water stopped, and he heard dripping. The towel that had been laid across the shower rod vanished. "Reid, I've been trying to figure this out. What do they expect us to tell them about those damn sarcophagi?"

"Whatever the science tells us."

She pulled the shower curtain back, the towel wrapped around her. Unabashed, she stepped out onto the bathmat and inspected the clothes they'd brought.

He, of course, inspected her—and liked what he saw. The towel, contrasting to her skin tones, added to her allure as it conformed to her breasts and emphasized each curve of her hips and buttocks. His breath caught. Which either demonstrated that his fear of imminent death had

receded, or that males were so biologically hardwired for visual stimulation that an enticing female form trumped a panicked limbic system.

"And if we figure it out?" she asked, fingering the clothing, giving
it a look of distaste. "Do they just let us go?"

"I have no idea." He went back for a selection of the men's clothing
they'd provided. "But they did say breakfast was in a half hour. Since
you managed a shower, I want a chance to die clean, too."

"God, food. And to think I was worried because I'd gained four
pounds in the week before I left for Africa."

She'd taken the second of the towels on the rack and bent over,
winding it around her wet hair. He clamped his eyes shut, enjoying the
afterimage.

Reid adjusted the temperature in the shower, and when she didn't
seem disposed to leave, figured what the hell, dropped his drawers,
peeled off his socks and stepped into the heavenly spray.

"It's got to do with the mummies they expect to find in the sarcophagi," he told her as he soaped up and watched dirty water sluice from his
body. "They want Kilgore France to either prove, or disprove, something about them."

"Then why drag you along?"

"Leverage," he told her. "Just like when I might have resisted the
black hood. And, Kilgore? Having thought about it, I suggest that you
do what they ask."

"Why?" She parted the curtain to stare in at him, her dark eyes wary.

"Because these people didn't give a shit when they had to take on
the government. How are they going to react if you cross your arms and
say no?"

Water dripped from the finger he pointed at her. "You may be the
best forensic anthropologist out there, but after they shoot you, how long
will it take them to kidnap the second best?"

He watched that sink in. Then he added, "And, myself, I've come to
like you alive."

"If we discover what they want? What then, Reid? Do they just
kill us?"

"I have no idea. But we've got to stay alive long enough to find out,
huh? Promise me?"

"Deal." She winked, slipped an arm in, and pulled him close enough to give him a kiss on his wet lips. Then she pushed him back and tugged the shower curtain closed.

For long moments, Reid stood there, the hot water cascading around him, wishing he had her anywhere but here.

Wherever here was.

# 27

The Humvee lurches and rocks as Weaver follows the faint two-track out of the village Intel had labeled T-3, or Tallach 3, given that Afghanistan has a total of four villages within its borders with that same name.

Karla bounced and swayed in the passenger seat. Behind her, Pud Pounder was standing, his upper body propped in the turret behind Ma Deuce, the Browning .50.

The desert valley looked flat as a lake bottom, but the terrain was illusory. Periodic rains had carved patterns of narrow drainages across the flats. No more than ten to twenty inches deep, a person could lie down and essentially vanish from as far away as thirty feet.

They could pop up just as fast, level a rifle or an RPG, and unleash hell. The late afternoon sun slanted toward the craggy and steep mountains in the distance. From up there, Haji would be watching her dust as Bravo Platoon raced out from T-3.

Of course, if Haji had any sense, he'd be short-stroking his communications for all they were worth. Karla and her LPO, or Light Petty Officer, had spent the last two days laying this one out. They'd picked a series of rocky outcrops that stuck up from the flats just outside the canyon mouth. The key to the position wasn't the outcrops, or the field of fire they offered; her interest lay in the series of deeply incised gullies that ran beneath them and met just east of the main highway.

A Marine convey would pass over that road sometime around midday tomorrow. Not that it was any kind of secret, since an Afghan detail was accompanying the Marines. Given Afghan dedication to security, that in turn meant every insurgent within a hundred klicks knew when and where that convoy would roll.

"We're on all their scopes now," Weaver observed as he laid his right hand atop the wheel. He glanced in the driver-side mirror. "Socket's sniffing right up our ass. That reaming you gave him sure cured his lollygagging attitude, Chief."

"*Just a reminder, boys,*" she said as she keyed her mic. "*Sloppy means dead.*"

Golf's voice came through her earbud. "*You sure they'll be able to figure out where we're going, Chief? Or should we have sent them a pajama-gram with a map?*"

"*They're not stupid.*" Then she smiled. "*Mostly. Their spotters are banging jaws as I speak. If we're unlucky, they'll figure out who we are and what we're up to. They do that, and they'll treat the whole operational area like a plague zone. We'll be bored stiff watching that convoy pass. But if we're lucky, they'll think we're a no-threat routine patrol, and they'll filter right down through those drainage channels. If they do, they'll pop up right under our noses. Air strikes will take out any we don't get to kill first.*"

*She ran it through her mind again, imagining the terrain, which of her snipers would go where, how their fields of fire would overlap as the insurgents came boiling out of the drainage channels.*

"*Jabac Junction ahead, Chief,*" Weaver said.

*She turned her attention to the irregular collection of mud-and-stone huts—flat-roofed and colorless as the hardpan on which they'd been built. Only a few families still lived there, tending a couple of gardens and a handful of goats.*

*Weaver was roaring down on it, the engine whining . . .*

"No! Fuck, no!" Karla cried, flying upright in bed. Sweat streaked her face as she clawed at the blanket, desperate to rip it from her body.

"Son of a bitch!" she rasped, throat dry, lungs heaving. "Easy. Easy, Karla." She managed to raise a shaking hand and slicked sweat from her hot face.

"Shit!" She knotted a fist, pounding impotently at the blanket. Leaning her head forward, she sucked in cool air, holding it, and letting it stream out of her.

From out of her memory came Colonel Ryan's soothing voice: "*Tell me what you see, Karla.*"

"I was back. Reliving that day."

"*Tell me about it, in complete detail . . .*"

"Yeah, yeah, Skipper." She smiled into the night. "I got it memorized: 'Words are tools, Karla. Handles on memory and a means to manipulate dreams.'"

Throwing back the blanket, she swung her feet down and braced herself while afterimages of shattered reality faded into nightmare where they belonged.

She stood; her T-shirt and panties were damp with perspiration.

"Damn you, Skipper." She walked into her bathroom, turned on the faucet, and scooped water into her mouth, splashed it on her face. Water dripping from her chin and nose, she threw her head back and stared at her image in the mirror where it lay lost in darkness.

"All that talk about trust? You had to drag that shit up, didn't you?"

She pulled on a pair of sweats, padded to her door, and pressed the intercom button.

*"Chief Raven? Anything wrong?"* Virginia Seymore's voice came through the speaker.

"I'm up . . . and moderately sane for the moment. I just want to walk around a bit. Maybe swing my arms and pace."

*"Check with me at the station."*

"Yes, ma'am."

The door buzzed softly and clicked before Karla stepped out into the illuminated hallway. She glanced to her left at the mysterious gray door that blocked the end of the hallway. Her thoughts centered on the woman they called Gray. How she had worked so competently on the doohickey, as if she'd been building machines like it all of her life.

"Hope you know how lucky you are, bitch. The Skipper really thinks he can help you."

She turned, padding down the hallway on bare feet. As she passed the doors, she considered the other inmates. Of course she'd like nothing better than to beat on Winny Swink for a while before she choked her down for being an arrogant ass. Talavera? She barely registered. A civilian, too damn smart for her own good, and soft at that. Trying to slit her wrists on the Capitol steps because her research had killed a bunch of bad guys? Shit. How freaking silly could a bitch get?

Karla sauntered up to the nurse's station at the end of the hall. The big security door beyond it was closed for the night, sealing off the women's wing from the rest of Ward Six. She leaned on the counter and waited while Virginia Seymore filled out something on a clipboard.

"Let me guess, you're making a note of the fact that I'm out of my room."

"Let me guess," Seymore repeated playfully. "You're right." The RN put her pen down and turned. A wizened woman of perhaps fifty, she adjusted her reading glasses; the knowing brown eyes in her round face took in Karla's attempt to look nonchalant.

"Flashback?"

"Happens."

"Want something for it?"

"Nope." She flexed her fingers. "Skipper dragged it up from the depths. Kind of like hauling a corpse up from the bottom of the bay."

"That man's a saint." Seymore gave Karla a studied look over her reading glasses. "I just hope all of you know how much he cares."

"He was so worried about Gray that he didn't notice when I stole his stapler. Guilt got the best of me, and I left it with Janeesha on the way out."

"He thinks he might have had a breakthrough with Gray. The whole staff is talking about it. That man would offer himself on the cross if he thought it would help any of you." Seymore pulled at her nurse's uniform as if it were binding. "Dr. Ryan hasn't had a full night's sleep in days. He only clocked out a half hour ago."

Karla glanced up; the clock on the wall read 02:33. "What's the Skipper's problem?"

"Outside of the normal headaches he gets running this place?" Seymore tilted her head in the direction of the hallway. "I'd say it's Gray. I've been keeping an eye on her all night. She's got that contraption of hers looking like something out of a Transformer movie with all the bits and wires. She blew her breaker a couple of times today, and Megan Holly worked overtime to fix it. Something about boosting the power."

"What do you think, Virginia? Is letting her build this device a good idea, or is the Skipper just as nuts as the rest of us?"

Seymore propped her chin, tapping her fingers on her lips as she studied the monitor. The screen was out of Karla's sight where she leaned on the counter.

"Gray's obsessed. Still up and at it," Nurse Seymore told her. "She's got that one wire, and she touches it in a pattern, almost a rhythm, to that other coil of wire. Then she'll stop, turn the machine slightly, like reorienting it, and go back to tapping. Since I came on duty, she's almost made a quarter turn."

"Almost ninety degrees," Karla said thoughtfully. "But I mean it's not a radio, right?"

"Whatever it's doing, there's some kind of magnetic field around it, but it's not broadcasting radio waves. Some of the techs know radios."

"And what does the Skipper say?"

"He thinks that somehow he's found a way to crack her out of whatever psychosis she's in. Maybe enough that he can find a handle to lead her back to reality."

"The man's got faith, I'll tell you that." Karla slapped the counter. "Thanks for the talk, Virginia. I guess I'll go back and lock myself in with my flashbacks again."

"You sure you don't want something, Chief?"

"No. Skipper said he's got faith in me. Maybe it's time I tried to live up to it."

"Not if it means you're hurting yourself, Chief."

"Yeah, I know."

She made three steps down the hall before Seymore called, "Bring it back, Chief."

"Huh?"

"The box of paperclips. The one that was just under the lip of the counter."

Karla made a face, stepped back, and handed over the box. Never knew when a person might need paperclips. All kinds of things could be made out them.

"Didn't mean to do that."

Seymore tonelessly said, "I know."

Karla plodded back to her room and stopped as she studied Gray's thick security door. Here it was, middle of the fucking night, and the yellow-haired bitch was tapping wires against some electrical gizmo?

"Woman, I don't know what your problem is, but I hope for the Skipper's sake that he hasn't just given you the equivalent of handing a SEAL a paperclip."

She was reaching for her door when the first peculiar ripple ran through her—like bobbing on an unseen wave. She blinked, having never felt anything quite like it. Then the prickling sensation began, literally a thousand electrified ant-feet charging around on her skin. Her unruly black hair crackled faintly as it stood, gooseflesh rising on her arms, legs, and back.

She heard a muffled pop.

An instantaneous flash of euphoria jolted her, followed by a sinking in her stomach. *Weightless?*

The world went black. Karla heard more than felt herself thump against the floor—knew that sensation: as if her strings had been cut.

The disorientation receded, and Karla came to. Her entire body tingled the way it would when recovering from a combination of intense orgasm and electrical shock.

She wondered when the lights had gone out and scrambled to her feet. Swaying, she put a hand on the wall. "Hallway," she whispered. "Women's wing, Ward Six."

She felt for Gray's door, surprised to feel a high-frequency vibration. It surprised her enough that she ran her fingertips along the metal as it faded.

"Okay, what the fuck just happened?"

Karla shook herself, concentrated on breathing, and started back down the hall. Whatever was wrong, the nurse's station needed to be secured first. Then she could start figuring out the rest.

She was almost there—counting doors as her fingers brushed the left wall—when the lights flickered and came on again.

"Hello? Hello?" Nurse Seymore was saying into her telephone.

"Virginia?" Karla called. "You all right?"

"Chief? Yes. Fine. Did you feel that? Like an earthquake tremor, huh?"

Karla frowned. "Didn't feel any quake, but that weird prickly sensation? That was new. Not exactly like sticking my finger in a light socket, but not all that different, either."

Virginia glanced up from her phone, a deep frown incising her forehead. "Prickly sensation? Light socket?"

"You didn't feel that?"

"Only a kind of shiver like static electricity, you know? And all the monitors are out."

"Yeah, well, I can tell you, it was nothing like that on my end of the hall."

"Must have been a lightning strike."

". . . Maybe."

"Go to bed, Chief. Somebody from the central . . . Ah, wait. Monitors are on again. Yeah. Must have been a lightning strike. Funny we didn't hear the bang." She leaned forward. "And if you said it was more . . . What the hell?"

At the tone in Nurse Seymore's voice, Karla leaned in through the opening, balancing her hard belly on the counter and craning her neck to stare at Nurse Seymore's monitor. She recognized the room, having seen it just that afternoon in the Skipper's office. The weird drawings on the wall, the piles of paper, the bits and pieces of electrical equipment, were Gray's.

Seymore reached out and turned a knob. As she did the camera panned this way and that. "Where's the doohickey? And what did she do with the desk it was on?"

"Even more to the point," Karla said thoughtfully, "where's Gray?"

Seymore's fleshy hands did something with her mouse, and the scene shifted to a small bedroom, the walls covered with more of the odd mathematics and short phrases in oddly rendered block letters. "That's her bedroom."

"Well, I'm not seeing her unless she's under the bed."

"Sensor would have told me. She must be in the bathroom."

She changed cameras. The small bathroom was empty.

Desperately, Seymore switched back to the main camera, shooting this way and that around the room. "Where is she?" Her voice rose, louder. "Where the *hell* is she, Chief?"

"Maybe you'd better get security on the line, Virginia. 'Cause Gray sure as hell might have found a way to hide her skinny little ass in there, but that machine is something else."

"She can't be *goddamned gone!*" Nurse Seymore cried.

# 28

Reid and Kilgore sat side by side at a long banquet table. The thing was massive, made out of some dark tropical wood and waxed until it gleamed under the opulent light fixtures. The table fit the room: absolutely grand. High-arched windows let in slanting sunlight that cast beams across yellow hand-stuccoed walls. The brown marble floor had seashell inclusions. A black-garbed guard stood at either end of the table.

"Delightful company, aren't they?" Kilgore asked between bites as she shoveled away a ham-and-cheese omelet.

"At least the food's good."

"Eat all you can." She gave Reid a knowing glance. "Might be the last we get."

"I just love an optimist." He winked to reassure her. "My call is that when they ask us to look at the mummies, we act like government employees."

"I don't get it."

"I know a BLM archaeologist who still hasn't finished a single site form after twenty years of field work."

"How does he get away with it?"

"He's a government employee."

Her lips quirked. "Hope I really did manage to lose that four pounds. After this, it's coming back."

"Given the towel queen I saw this morning? You're doing fine."

"I'll bet you say that to all the captive women you share rooms with."

The guard to the right called, "If you're finished, my employers want to see if you're worth the trouble and expense. Up and at 'em, Doctors, or we'll drag you."

Reid tried to give the man a cold look as he pushed his chair back and stood. Not that an archaeologist could really give a man like him any kind of chill.

"That way." The guard pointed.

Reid took Kilgore's hand for reassurance as they started down a long hallway, then right down a flight of wide, Saltillo-tiled steps. At the bottom they entered a cement-floored and industrial looking corridor. White fluorescent lights glowed from the acoustical-paneled ceiling. The guard pushed double metal doors open and ushered them into a handsomely outfitted laboratory.

The central island included a sink, slate work top, microscope, and equipment rack. Centrifuges, a PCR machine, chromatograph, several computer consoles, and an X-ray machine rested on countertops. Test tubes, beakers, glass tubing, and the other accoutrements filled both shelving and cabinetry. A steel door dominated the far wall. Light panels for viewing X-rays hung to either side.

"Hopefully, you'll find this sufficient," a familiar voice announced.

Reid turned, stunned to see Bill Minor as he stepped out from behind a stainless-steel cabinet door.

"Bill?" Kilgore cried. "Thank God, we thought you were either dead or captured."

"Hopefully, the government does, too."

Reid watched understanding dawn on Kilgore's face. "You son of a bitch."

Minor was wearing a black T-shirt that emphasized the man's slab-like shoulders and the depth of his chest. He turned, washing his hands in one of the sinks, and said, "If this was written for Hollywood, I'd go through this trite and friendly bullshit about 'Welcome to the mansion.' And we'd have this warm and fuzzy talk about 'I hope you don't mind,' and 'please forgive my uncaring associates for the manner of your arrival.'"

He looked up as he dried his hands, swollen biceps knotting like pythons. "Instead of that horseshit, here's the deal: While you were catching up on sleep, we x-rayed the coffins. Unlike the images we lifted from your laptop, these don't seem to have booby traps. One's a male and one's a female. We want you to look at the male first. If we're right, he's gonna blow your mind, Doctor France."

"For God's sake, Bill, why don't you just tell me what this is all about?"

Minor's smile mocked. "We want you to figure it out on your own, Doctor. We're going to do nothing to bias your analysis. Doctor Farmer is here to help you record and offer his insight, since he's seen the tomb."

Reid crossed his arms. "So, we play along, do the work. How do we know—"

"Having either one of you dead doesn't serve our best interests, Doctor Farmer. All we require is good science. And afterward we want you alive and capable of explaining what you've found to your peers. Just do that—and don't cause me any trouble—and you walk out of here alive, healthy, and well-reimbursed for your time and inconvenience."

Minor's face lit. "You don't know it yet, but you're on the ground-floor of the greatest archaeological discovery ever. I actually envy you."

As quickly, Minor's expression went cold. "Now, you fuck with me, even in the slightest, and you *will* get hurt."

Kilgore raised her hand. "Yeah, Bill. We've figured that out. Not that credibility is your strong suit."

"Probably not," he agreed. "But you'll see. Now, let's go into the sterile room and open that sarcophagus. I think, Dr. France, that by the end of the day, you're going to be absolutely amazed."

He indicated the back of the lab. "The dressing room is behind that steel door. I have to insist that we all suit up and limit the possibility of contamination to the specimen."

Reid took a deep breath. "You ready for this?"

Kilgore let her gaze linger on his. "Let's do it. As for myself, I really liked that part about having the whole future ahead of us."

"Me too." But when he shot a sidelong glance at Bill Minor, the python man was watching them with reptilian eyes.

# 29

**M**y mistake was turning off my phone when I got home just after two in the morning. I was exhausted—and the last thing I wanted was a phone call just after I'd dropped into alpha sleep. Hell, I'd earned an uninterrupted night.

I awakened a little after six, stumbled down, and hit the button on the coffee maker. Then I plodded in to enjoy a long shower. After I'd dressed, I microwaved a tamale and fried a couple of eggs over-easy for breakfast. Don't knock it until you try it. While I sipped my coffee, I checked my personal email and paid the bills. My sister and her husband were taking a cruise to the Mexican Riviera.

It was that kind of morning.

The shit didn't come down until I'd rolled up the garage door and wheeled out the Diavel. The big *testastretta* V twin barked softly as the machine idled and shook. I was buckling on my helmet when two black SUVs roared into my driveway. Before they screeched to a stop, guys in suits came tumbling out the doors.

You can tell they're serious not only from their expressions, but the fact that while their weak-side hand is holding up their credentials, their strong-hand is resting on the butts of their handguns.

I did what anyone with sense would have. I raised my hands, fingers spread wide in a "whoa, boys. I'm not a threat" gesture. Then I waited, very still, for the first agent to warily approach.

"Colonel Timothy Ryan?"

"Yes, sir. And you are?"

"Special Agent Terry, FBI, sir. Please shut off the motorcycle."

I reached down carefully with one hand and flipped the "chicken switch" that killed the engine.

In the sudden silence, Terry asked, "May I ask where you're going?"

By this time, the rest of the agents had spread out in a ring, hands still on their undrawn weapons. I shot a nervous glance at their remarkably hostile and wary faces.

"I was going to work. I'm a psychiatrist, the director, at Grantham Barracks."

Agent Terry, still in the "ready" position, said, "Would you mind stepping off the motorcycle, sir? Please keep your hands where we can see them and make no rapid moves."

I did as directed. "Agent Terry, I assure you that I'm not offering any resistance. I'm delighted to assist you in any way. But if you could give me a hint about why you're here . . . ?"

"All I know, sir, is that there's been an escape from Grantham Barracks. We were told that attempts to contact you were futile. We were asked to check out your address and detain you if we found you." He smiled unpleasantly. "Assuming you really are Dr. Timothy Ryan."

I froze. *An escape?*

But why would special agents . . . ?

"Alpha," I whispered.

# 30

A human skeleton glowed eerily within the wooden outlines of the sarcophagus. Reid glanced sidelong at Kilgore as they stood before the light panels on the lab's back wall. Radiographs of the sarcophagus had been placed side by side to give a life-size image of the contents.

"There," she mused softly. "See the white square atop his chest? That's metal."

"And for this you cut my lunch short halfway through a ham-and-havarti sandwich?"

"I sure as hell wasn't worried about your cholesterol. Just before we left for lunch, I stopped and looked at these. I was more interested in the osteology, the bones, but this bothered me. It's an anomaly."

Reid glanced back where the two guards were standing by the door, their ugly black machine guns hanging from slings.

He lowered his voice. "What are you thinking, Kilgore?"

"I'm thinking we should open that sarcophagus before Bill Minor gets here."

"That could get us shot."

She spread her arms, giving him a knowing look that reeked of conspiracy. "We're only doing our jobs, huh? Besides, the overhead camera is going to record it all." She glanced around. "Which is why I want to lift the lid, prop it with those plastic storage boxes, and carefully take samples around the rim. We'll be able to look inside, and if it's something that shouldn't be there, I'll have to figure a way of sneaking it out."

"What do you mean? Something that shouldn't be there? It's a fake sarcophagus, from a faked tomb."

"And that odd metal square might be the proof!" she insisted, keeping her voice down.

Reid took a deep breath, glanced at the wall clock, and saw it was 12:35. "Okay, let's get suited up."

Ten minutes later they flicked on the lights and entered the sanitary room with its two sarcophagi. Kilgore went straight for the man's and, with a scalpel, attacked the wax seal.

"Odd," she murmured. "I don't remember reading about these things being sealed in wax."

"It's not ancient Egyptian," Reid reminded her. "I'm taking samples. If it's commercial wax, maybe the chemical signature can be tied to a specific manufacturer."

"Good thinking."

Ten minutes later, Kilgore called, "That should do it. You ready?"

"How heavy are these things?" Reid asked, positioning himself at the head. He managed to pry the lid up with a flat length of metal, feeling the residual wax resist and release. "Not that bad."

He got his fingers under and lifted. Maybe a hundred pounds? Kilgore carefully inserted some of the smaller spacers they'd brought with them: found items from the lab.

Reid moved to the bottom, inserted his gloved hands, and lifted so Kilgore could brace the lid. By slowly lifting and bracing, they elevated the top cover almost a foot.

"Let's take a look." Kilgore removed a small LED flashlight from a pocket and shined it into the interior.

"And?" Reid asked, purposefully ignoring the overhead camera.

"I need a sample sack," she told him.

Reid dutifully handed her one of the cloth bags. "What do you see?"

"It's a glass jar with a metal lid. Looks like it's got some sort of liquid inside. Here, hold the light for me."

Taking the flashlight, he bent down and watched her carefully insert the sack and lay it over a black metal box. The thing had about the same dimensions as a fat hardback book and lay like a pectoral plate on the mummy's wrapped chest. From beside it, she withdrew the glass jar. It didn't look Egyptian, but more like a modern canning jar. The screw cap appeared to be stainless steel.

"Maybe I don't need that sack." She lifted the clear glass jar to the light.

He reached in, careful not to shift the propped wooden cover, and lifted. The metal box might have been seven inches across, two inches thick, and seemed to weigh ten pounds.

Having placed the glass jar on one of the gurneys, Kilgore was back, crowding against him, her body obscuring the camera. He saw her shift something inside the sarcophagus.

"Put the bag back in its box," she said offhandedly. "Then help me lift the lid off."

With the curious metal box obscured under the sample sack, Reid tried to look casual as he placed his prize in the box.

*As if that's ever going to pass a close look!*

"Kilgore? You sure you're up to lifting this lid? It's heavy."

"Let's do it. I want to see this guy."

With Reid at the head, they lifted, Kilgore grunting as they shuffled over and laid the heavy lid on the second gurney.

When Reid looked back at the tightly bound mummy, he could see the thing she'd shifted: a square object now on the wrappings where the heavy metal box had lain.

Kilgore looked close. "Most likely papyrus." She lifted it carefully. "It's got writing on the cover. Something in Latin. *VOX ULTIMUS.* Last voice? Last message?"

"Bag it in plastic?"

She shook her head. "Outgassing from plastic will contaminate it. Use tinfoil."

It was then that the door opened, and a fully suited Bill Minor stormed in. "What the hell are you doing?"

"Our jobs," Kilgore answered, staring at Minor with indignation. "We want this done, Bill. The sooner you have your report, the sooner we're out of here." She lifted a hand in an effort to still his outburst. "And I have to tell you, I'm damned curious and anxious to get started."

"Why didn't you wait?"

"I just told you."

Reid stepped forward. "She wouldn't even let me finish lunch."

"What did you find?" Minor asked, glancing up at the cameras, as if reassured.

"That jar of liquid. It's a little murky, and you can see some kind of sediment in the bottom. It's not an Egyptian jar, Bill." Kilgore indicated the book on the supply table where Reid was unrolling tinfoil. "And he had that text on his chest. You can see it on the X-ray. Something about last words."

Minor stopped short, a smile visible behind his mask as he turned to the glass jar. He lifted it almost reverently and held it up toward the light. "And this was inside, huh?"

"On his hands," Reid added. "Apparently very valuable."

Wonder filled Minor's voice. "Now that we've got all the pieces, it's time to start putting them together."

"All the pieces?" Kilgore asked.

Minor laughed, radiating satisfaction. "Just do your work, Doctor. I need to know absolutely *everything* about this guy."

With that he turned, walking back through decontamination, the glass jar held carefully in his hand.

Kilgore glanced thoughtfully at the book. She shot her eyes suggestively toward the hidden metal box and gave Reid a wink. Aloud she said, "And you? I suppose you're going to be ragging on me for the rest of the day about being hungry?"

"Price of science," Reid answered noncommittally, wondering what was in the canning jar, and what Minor would have said if he'd seen the metal box, too.

# 31

"**A**t the time I likened it to the mother of all orgasms experienced at the same time you stick a finger in a light socket." Karla Raven sat in a central chair in Tim Ryan's office. Ryan, however, wasn't behind his desk. A two-star was. He'd been introduced as General Grazier. Around the room were no less than five other officers and what looked like a couple of clerks who were recording and writing notes. The little red Ducati on Ryan's desk looked lonely.

"Chief?" An officer who had been introduced as Major Savage, stepped over, moved the little Ducati to the side, and rested a haunch on the corner of the desk. He clasped his hands in his lap. Unlike Grazier, Major Savage didn't look like a rear-echelon kiss-ass. American Indian, she thought. And given his demeanor, he'd been deep in the shit a time or two. Definitely a combat vet. But then, a lot of combat officers were assholes.

"Sir?"

He studied her thoughtfully. "We need to know what you were doing up at that time of night. The RN on duty said it was flashbacks. Can you tell me about them?"

She ground her teeth, feeling the rage stir down deep. "They come and go, sir."

He worked his jaw and nodded. "So, you buzzed the RN and she let you out. What happened then?"

In a precise voice Karla laid out the entire event, all the way back to her door when the world went hinky.

"And you're sure you were just disoriented for a few seconds?"

"Yes, sir."

"You're positive that no one could have slipped past you, opened Alpha's door, and helped her carry out the machine?"

"Yes, sir."

"How do you know that?" General Grazier asked, his hard dark eyes reflecting irritation.

"Been there before, sir."

Grazier took a deep breath and ran the flat of his hand along Ryan's desk. "Chief, I understand what you're doing, and I know why you're doing it: Never, under any circumstance, tell an officer more than he needs to know. Right now, I don't need a hard-assed SEAL proving she's a hard-assed SEAL. You get that?"

"Yes, sir."

Grazier waited, an eyebrow lifted as if in expectation.

Karla remained silent.

Major Savage chuckled, raising a hand before Grazier could explode. "Chief, what do you think of Colonel Ryan?"

"Fine officer, sir."

"Now, Chief, we know you were here to visit him yesterday in this office. Did he at any time hint that Prisoner Alpha was any kind of threat?"

"No, sir."

"But you did talk about her?"

"Yes, sir."

"Did he give any indication that anything was wrong with Prisoner Alpha? Um, I mean anything wrong in addition to her obvious dysfunction."

"No, sir."

"What did he say, exactly?"

"With respect, sir, the Colonel would be a better—"

"Damn it!" Grazier slapped the desk, giving her a hard look. "Chief, you're beginning to chafe a raw spot on my ass. Do you understand what's going on here? A very high-value detainee waltzed out of Ward Six last night with an unauthorized piece of equipment. Now, there's only one way in, and one way out of that fucking room. If we're to believe Seymore's report, you were in that hallway when whoever it was went in and got Alpha and her effing machine! I damn well want to know who!"

Karla bit off the growl that started in her throat, forced her heart to beat normally, and kept her expression like stone.

"Well?" Grazier thundered.

"Yes, sir?"

*"Who?"*

Karla ordered her thoughts, calmed her racing pulse. In a concise voice, she said, "I saw no one pass me, sir."

"But it was dark," Major Savage added.

"Yes, sir."

"So, you couldn't have seen anyone."

"I'd have known, sir."

"How?"

"I was pretty much spread all over the hall floor, sir."

"And if they had stepped over you while you were unconscious?"

Karla kept her mouth clamped shut, her flintlike glare eating into Major Savage's.

Grazier muttered a curse and flexed his fingers. "Chief, however Prisoner Alpha got out of that cell, she couldn't have done it without inside help. Now, we know that Colonel Ryan was sympathetic to the woman. Sometimes men can identify with an attractive and vulnerable woman. If that's the case, we'd like to manage this before Dr. Ryan does something irreparable to his career. Do you have any thoughts about that?"

Karla stiffened. "Impossible, sir."

"Or could you be an accomplice?" the general asked.

Karla shot to her feet, standing at full attention. *"Sir! No, sir!"* She kept her eyes fixed on what Ryan called his "me" wall. The insanity of it, the outright fucking *impossibility*! Her muscles knotted. Cold rage burned in the pit of her stomach.

"Dismissed, Chief." Major Savage said. In her peripheral vision she could see the distaste in his expression.

Karla snapped a salute, rotated as if she were on an axle, and strode purposefully to the door. She let herself out and closed the door precisely behind her.

"Mother fuckers!" she exploded, then cast a sidelong glance at Janeesha. "You know what they're cooking up in there?"

"Nothing good for Dr. Ryan," the secretary said softly, avoiding Karla's eyes.

Karla walked over to the desk, her anger bottled like an unlit rocket. "No way the Skipper would *ever* spring Gray. But that's how they're going to write it."

Janeesha gave her a horrified look. "They think Dr. Ryan *helped* Alpha escape?" Her expression tightened. "But then, he didn't hardly go home this last week. He was here most of the nights. If he was seeing that woman . . ."

"Stop it! My door's next to Alpha's. And her door is a heavy damn thing. I hear it open and close every time they take her food, clean her room, or escort an interrogator inside. If the Skipper had been sneaking in for high tea, let alone for anything else, I'd have known."

She pointed a hard finger at Janeesha. "And I may just be one more nut in the loony bin, but I know the Skipper. Whatever this is, he didn't let her out. Damn it, I was there."

"Then how'd she do it? Get that machine out and all?"

"Haven't got the foggiest idea, but I guess I'll find out."

Janeesha jumped as her phone rang; she reached for the receiver.

Karla took a deep breath and straightened, a spear of joy shooting through her as she whisked the smartphone on Janeesha's desk behind her thigh.

As Janeesha answered her desk phone with a "Yes, sir?" Karla Raven was already out the door, knocking off a salute to the uniformed sentry who waited in the hall to escort her back to Ward Six.

# 32

"So where was the book?" Reid whispered the question.

"Sitting on top of his balls," Kilgore murmured back.

With gloved hands Reid carefully unwound delicate textile from the corpse's desiccated thigh and sealed it in a ziplock. Most of the wrappings had been similarly bagged, although Kilgore had insisted on collecting separate samples in tinfoil for Fourier Transform Infrared, or FTIR analysis that would identify any biological signatures clinging to the fabric.

Like Reid, Kilgore was masked and suited. Hard to believe a body like hers hid beneath that light-blue bunny suit.

When the mummy lay fully exposed, the brown and wrinkled flesh looked like a dried leather caricature of a human being. Kilgore began by photographing the corpse from every angle. Then she maneuvered it to the X-ray machine, and they spent two hours positioning the body, retreating behind the shield, and shooting images.

With Reid's help, she meticulously began the anthropometry, measuring the remains, taking height, circumferences, lengths of arms and legs, and various other measurements.

With a magnifying glass in hand, Kilgore started at the top of the head, inspecting the man's scalp. As she worked her way over the body, she carefully noted moles and reproduced what she thought were scars on the anatomical drawing on her clipboard. She stopped at his penis. "Odd."

"How's that?"

"He's circumcised."

"Hebrew?"

"Don't know, but worth checking when we run the DNA."

She finished with the little toe on the guy's right foot, straightened, head cocked. "Something about him . . ."

"Yes?"

"The cranial structure. Northern European."

Kilgore stepped back to the X-rays. As they'd been developed, Bill Minor had hung them on the light board. Now they filled the entire wall.

She studied the cranial radiographs from the sagittal and lateral aspects. "The guy's European Caucasoid." She pointed. "And his stature? One hundred and ninety centimeters? That's about six-foot-three. He'd have been a giant among Egyptians."

She'd adopted the thoughtful pose he remembered from television.

"There's no torso incision. They didn't remove his internal organs and process them separately. We'll see if we can get better resolution later, but the turbinate bones are intact in the nasal passage, and the cribriform plate hasn't been fractured."

"And that means?"

"They didn't reach up his nose with a hook and pull the guy's brain out as part of the mummification process."

"Thoughtless of them."

"The question is why? What made this guy special?" She pointed. "See this irregularity in his lower right first molar? I'd swear that's a modern filling on the buccal surface. But you look back here, at M2, and he's got a huge caries. On the other side, he's missing all the molars and exhibits almost complete reabsorption of the mandible. The teeth are extremely worn on the occlusive surface."

"Egyptians ate a high-starch diet heavy on cereals. Like the Anasazi, they ground grain with large stones that left grit in the meal. We see that same kind of dental pathology in most early agricultural societies."

"Then why did that remaining molar once have excellent dental care? I'd call it modern."

Reid leaned close to whisper, "The guy matches the box."

"Intrusive box? Ancient mummy? The corpse looks really old."

"Dr. France?" Bill Minor called on the intercom, "The complete body X-rays you requested are ready. It's been almost ten hours. If you'd like to take a break, you are more than welcome to check the radiographs before you leave for the night."

Reid followed her into the small dressing room and peeled off his suit. "What do you think?"

"The guy's an enigma," she replied as she wiggled her hips from the suit.

God, he was hungry. Where had the time gone? Like Kilgore, he'd been completely absorbed by the analysis. He glanced at where the curious black metal box lay on a lower shelf, hidden in plain sight. To his and Kilgore's amazement, they'd recognized it as a piece of sophisticated electrical equipment after they'd smuggled it out of the clean room.

*Electrical equipment?* Proof positive that the mummy was modern.

In the lab, Minor was hanging X-ray film on the light board. He'd offered it as a computer image, but Kilgore had shaken her head, saying, "I need to see it on film, shot to scale or larger."

"Odd," she whispered as she peered at the light boxes. "I don't see any sign of dental hypoplasia."

"What's that?" Minor asked.

"As a person's teeth grow in childhood, illness, malnutrition, or trauma can stop growth. It leaves ripples in the outer surface of the teeth."

She worked her way down. "Active guy. Broke his clavicle a couple of times." She stared closely at his right arm. "Our friend was definitely right-handed, the bone is denser, and I see incipient osteoarthritis."

Reid—not having her eye for detail—was already looking at the legs, the dried flesh like a hazy outline, the bones showing as white . . . "Kilgore? You're going to have to reshoot these. Part of the table got in the way. There's a bunch of screws and a piece of metal here. Pretty cool. If you didn't know better, you'd think it was actually in the bone."

She frowned, stepping down to where he pointed, and stopped short. "Reid, that's not the table." She leaned forward. "Son of a bitch! Look at the callus in there!"

Kilgore flipped to her notes, thumbing back to the catalog of scars she'd observed. "I'll be damned."

"What?" Reid asked.

"That's orthopedic surgery, Reid. Whoever this guy is, he's no ancient Egyptian."

"Are you sure about that, Dr. France?" Minor asked.

"Couldn't be more sure." She reached up, tapping the radiograph with a fingernail. "Egyptians didn't surgically repair broken bones, Bill. And they definitely didn't use fine surgical screws like you see here. It's an old repair which means the screws have been in the body for a while. You *don't* just walk down to the hardware store and buy surgical screws. The metal has to be compatible with the environment they're in. My bet? They're titanium."

Minor crossed his arms, the muscles bulging, brown eyes amused. "So, what's next, Dr. France?"

"Stable isotope analysis tests on bone and teeth. Delta 13 carbon, and delta 15 nitrogen will give us his dietary history. Strontium and oxygen isotopes will tell us where he grew up. Every place on earth has different levels of these elements, which are in turn absorbed into the body and act like a locational fingerprint."

"Carbon 14?" Minor asked.

"What for?" Kilgore crossed her arms. "He's going to read modern."

"Humor me," Minor replied. "It's our money. You take the sample, we'll test it. The same for stomach contents, or whatever else. Anything you'd normally take on a mummy."

"You've got it," she told him confrontationally. "But, seeing the screws? The fact he's circumcised? He couldn't have been put in that tomb more than forty years ago at the absolute most."

*And of course, there was the electrical gadget to back her up.*

"If you're right, Doctor, it should be pretty easy to prove."

Kilgore gave him a crooked smile. "We have a professional term for it. Piece of cake."

# 33

The knock on Falcon's door sent panic through his system. People didn't come to see him unless it was an orderly or nurse. His stomach tensed almost to the point of making him throw up.

He gasped for air, hearing Karla Raven's voice ask, "Falcon? You got a minute?"

Falcon glanced around, awash in fear, and thankfully realized his house was in perfect order. "I'm working on something."

"We've got a problem. All of us. We need you, Falcon."

He managed to rise, checked three times to make sure his fly was zipped, and walked to the door. Opening it a crack, he peered out with one eyeball. "Maybe you could come back later?"

Chief Raven stood with her arms crossed. Behind her Edwin Tyler Jones, his dark face fierce, fixed him with gleaming eyes.

"One of those days, huh?" Raven almost grunted, pushing him— and his door—out of her way.

Falcon retreated to the head of his bed where it was pushed into the corner. He crawled back onto the safety of his pillow. "I really don't want company today. I'm just not feeling—"

"You gonna feel worse!" Edwin declared as he dragged the desk chair out and plopped himself backward in it, his chin resting on the chair back. "Skipper's in trouble." Then, his arms reaching around in front of him, his thumbs began tapping at a smartphone, of all things.

"Where did you get that?" Falcon was so amazed he almost didn't register it when Karla placed a knee on the bottom of his bed and then climbed on to seat herself cross-legged within the sphere of his personal sanctuary. Falcon's hands began twitching, a sense of violation and fear rising.

"Hey," Karla said softly. "Relax, Falcon. We need you. We *really* need you."

"For what?" His mind began to loop through the possibilities, none of them good.

She held her hands wide, as if to make them nonthreatening. "Gray vanished last night. She and that electrical thing she made—"

"The doohickey."

"That's right, Falcon. The doohickey." She was peering at him intently. "Look, I can see that it's a bad day for you. Is the major here?"

"Haven't seen him."

"Can you call him?"

"He only shows up when he isn't busy."

"Great," Karla muttered under her breath. "Even imaginary army guys aren't around when you need them. Next time hallucinate a Marine, will you?"

"Okay," Edwin said from his chair. "Got the web." His thumbs were dancing on the small screen like a hillbilly jig. "Gonna take a while. I got to talk to my website."

"You've got a website?"

"Chief, I got more websites than a black widow that spent her life addicted to divorce."

Falcon swallowed down a dry heave. "Edwin, you really shouldn't talk that way. It makes you sound less than you are."

"Yeah, Falcon, and you're sitting in here doing the antisocial leave-me-alone-or-I'll-puke gig, and you're the only person smart enough to figure this thing out. You help us? Maybe I don't talk like no street bro, got dat?"

Falcon squeezed his eyes shut, wishing desperately that the major would get back from whatever he was doing. Battling for control, he took deep breaths.

*It's just anxiety. Just anxiety.*

"Falcon," Raven's voice was both soothing and commanding. "Here's what we know: Last night, just after two thirty, I was in the hall outside Gray's door. Something happened. It was like an electrical shock, a wave maybe, something that made my body tingle all over and—"

"Give me a chance, I'll make your body tingle all over," Edwin interjected.

"Try it, and I'll reach down your throat, get a good hold, and rip your lungs out past your teeth."

"Yo, mama."

She turned her attention back to Falcon. "It kind of knocked me silly. The lights went out, and I just sort of went limp. Gray's door, it was almost . . . I don't know, humming?" She made a face, struggling for words. "And there was a pop—a hollow sound like a light bulb being crushed."

In spite of himself, Falcon leaned forward, curiosity vying with panic. "You felt this?"

"I was in the hall right outside her door."

"You didn't hear any screaming, voices?" He wished he could close his eyes, ignore the intruders.

Edwin winked at him, saying, "Chief Raven, she's just PTSD, Falcon. You're the schizo."

"Edwin!" Karla warned.

But Falcon chuckled, halfway down the road to hysteria. "Good thing the major's not here. He gets really mad when people call me that."

"Now I'm scared," Edwin shot back. "Worried some hallucination gonna whip my ass."

Falcon turned back to Karla. "How did you know she was gone?"

"I made my way back to the nurse's station. Seymore was on duty. The lights flashed on in the hall about the time I got there. Seymore was on the phone, couldn't get anyone to answer. Then the security monitors flickered on, and Gray was gone . . . and so was the doohickey."

He watched Raven's frown as she tried to explain. "I mean, Gray had just been there moments before. Nurse Seymore said Gray had been at it all night. Tapping a wire to that damn machine, then turning it a little, as if adjusting it."

"Pointing it," Falcon said as the notion popped into his head. "Like an antenna?"

"Could be. But everyone has said it's not a radio."

"And you still say nobody passed you in the hall?" Edwin asked.

"No way. I was incapacitated, but I wasn't out. Believe me, this chick's been choked out, knocked out, concussed out, drugged out, passed out. You name it. There's always that sense of where am I? How long's it been? But not last night. I was there, I just wasn't hooked up."

Falcon nodded. "They've discounted any way out of that room? Hole? Tunnel? Passage?"

"So far as I know."

He was thinking now, the panic and nausea subsiding. "And the rumor is that she was caught in a top-secret lab at Los Alamos. Kind of like, 'pop' and there she was." He watched Raven's eyes as he said, "I wonder if it was the same hollow kind of a pop like you heard last night?"

"You saying the bitch teleport?" Edwin asked. "Yo, beam me up, Scotty? Shiiiit!"

"Language, Edwin, or I'm going back into my delightful paranoia."

Not even looking up from his phone, Edwin said with perfect diction, "Here lies the noblest of Romans, for it was not that he loved Caesar less, but that he loved Rome more."

"What?" Raven demanded.

"Shakespeare, Chief." Edwin spared her the briefest sidelong glance, then went back to the smartphone where his thumbs continued to tap. "Lost a fucking bet to Falcon. Gotta read a play a week."

"Teleport?" Falcon said thoughtfully, his mind playing with the concept. "Not impossible, just highly, highly improbable."

"Come again?" Karla demanded. "Falcon, there's no starship *Enterprise* up there."

"No, but there is quantum teleportation down here. Has been for some time. DARPA has been experimenting with it based on entanglement theory. It's called QKD. Quantum key distribution. But it's currently restricted to the laboratory and the quest for absolute integrity in communications."

"Hey, I know that." Edwin's face lit up. "You talking quantum cryptography. They started doing that for bank transfers. I just figured it's another coding I got to learn to break the system."

"You can't," Falcon told him, wishing he could close his eyes and let the pieces of information float on the backs of his eyelids. "Think of it like a foil packet around grape juice. Once you rip it open, you can't reseal it."

"Then you have to reroute the packet."

"Precisely." Falcon arched an eyebrow. "I can't wait for Theresa to drop in next time. She's a much better physicist than I am."

Raven had shifted so her back was against the wall; her muscular arms lay propped on her pulled-up knees, her hands dangling. "You think that's what we're dealing with? Seriously? Gray *teleported* out of her cell?"

Falcon slowly shook his head. "To date, entanglement only works with atomic particles. We're talking photons, not human beings and complex machinery."

"Not necessarily," Edwin said, his thumbs finally still. "My old back-door still works, and NSA still hasn't found that little worm I programmed that rides along its secure network. Now, I can't go further than this with a smartphone, but I got a DARPA program, code name 'Beemeyup.'" His eyebrows lifted. "And they're running it out of a secure lab down at Los Alamos, through a company called Skientia."

Falcon chuckled. "Very good, Edwin. But probability still dictates that Gray escaped or was taken out of her room by much more prosaic means. It's just up to us to figure out how."

Karla gave Edwin a thoughtful look. "But this lab in Los Alamos is working on teleportation?" Her eyebrow twitched. "Gray was arrested in a lab in Los Alamos. Falcon? What are the probabilities of that?"

"Highly suggestive," Falcon mused, eyes half-lidded. "Without damage to the room suggesting ingress or egress, we're stuck with only two explanations: she and the machine went out the door, and past you, or she went out some other way. It's all a function of time and space. And, if she went out the door, past you, past Nurse Seymore, she'd still have to pass all the other security systems and personnel out through level four."

Raven tilted her head back until it thunked against the wall. "The problem is, they're going to blame the Skipper for it. Here's the scenario: Ryan developed an interest in Gray, and after banging his balls off, she convinced him to help her escape. The electrical thing is going to be written up as a diversion used by Ryan to turn off the security and monitoring while he escorted Gray and her machine out of the women's wing, through the hub, and past the four rings of security."

"Impossible," Falcon said softly. "It physically couldn't be done in that period of time."

"You know that." Karla flipped her hands in a gesture of futility. "I know that. But how do we prove it?"

"From in here, we don't," Edwin said. "Chief, they gonna shut this phone down real soon. But, even before they do, this is like using a toy hammer to knock down a brick wall. I gotta have more horsepower."

"It would take an army of experts to get us out of here," Karla added. "I'm not even sure DEVGRU could do it without blowing the place apart."

"We have the necessary people," Falcon said as he mentally compared names with abilities. "Assuming the following: that Edwin could obtain access to the Grantham Barracks computer system and sabotage the security; that Chief Raven could obtain the keys to the central courtyard door; and that Major Swink can fly whatever sort of helicopter they bring in to evacuate me for my medical emergency."

"You're going to have a medical emergency?" Karla elevated an eyebrow.

"Appendicitis would be the easiest," Falcon told her. "It isn't always accompanied by elevated body temperature." He was already playing it out in his imagination, seeing the pieces that would have to fall in place in perfect order. "Meanwhile, Edwin, you might want to shut that phone off and pull the battery. We might need it."

"So, you're kidding right?" Edwin asked.

"That's the only way we can find out what happened to Gray. If we don't, everyone in here is going to worry that they'll be abducted next. Stories of vivisection, lobotomies, and every other paranoia will be let loose."

"And the Skipper needs us to prove he's innocent," Raven added.

"Break out? *That's crazy!*" ET cried.

"Yes, Edwin. But, if I'm not mistaken, we do crazy rather well in here."

# 34

"**A**h ha! I've got it!" Kilgore cried as they finished their supper. She had spent more time reading than she'd spent eating. They had been working on the male mummy continuously; Kilgore affectionately called him "King Smut"—a reference to his status as an imposter to real Egyptian ancestry.

She slapped a hand on the reports that Bill Minor had given her after they had stripped off their contamination gear and headed off to supper.

The meal that Kilgore had mostly ignored consisted of T-bone steaks, perfectly cooked, some kind of cheesy and tasty pasta with shrimp and mushrooms, steamed broccoli, and tiramisu for dessert. Kilgore had devoured the lab reports but had barely tasted a bite of her meal.

Meanwhile, the guards, at their accustomed place on either end of the table, watched them through bored eyes.

"How do they get such quick turnover from the labs?" she muttered through a mouthful as she scanned the pages. "Takes me days, and I've got clout."

Reid asked, "You've discovered what?"

She smiled triumphantly, an index finger tapping the report. "Look at the mitochondrial DNA results. The guy has a Haplotype C, with a HincII morph-6 mutation."

"I love it when you talk like a Martian. And that means?"

"His mtDNA is Native American." She might have swallowed a lamp given the way she glowed. "You don't find Haplotype C in Egypt—especially with a HincII morph-6 mutation." Bending to the reports, she thumbed quickly through the papers.

"Okay, here's the delta 15 carbon analysis . . ." She stopped, frowning. "The guy has a definite signature for C4 plants, specifically significant amounts of dietary corn. Delta 15 nitrogen . . . Shit! He's high in red meat and seafood!"

She flipped to the enamel analysis taken from inside one of his molars. "I don't get it." She looked up, a deep frown incising her forehead. "This is the kind of stable strontium and oxygen isotope signature we'd expect from someone growing up on the North Atlantic coast." She flipped to the next report, her frown deepening. "From the mineral signature fixed in his molar dentine as it was developing, he grew up in . . . Germany?"

"Kilgore, remember the guy's skull shape? The angle of the femoral neck? Everything points to a Northern European ancestry." He loaded his fork with pasta, watching her dark eyes focus on infinity. "I've dug enough burials to know for a fact he's a white guy. Given that long skull, narrow receding cheekbones, the brow ridge and straight nasal bones he can't be anything else."

"But, Reid, he's descended from a line of females originating in the western hemisphere. Haplotype C, with that HincII morph-6 mutation, is only found in the Americas; its highest frequency is in Central America and northern South America."

"Where Mayan mathematics were invented," he reminded. "Let's not forget that tomb and what was written all over the walls."

"So how could a northern European get a Mesoamerican female ancestor, get to Central America where he ate corn, and back to Egypt to be buried in a tomb in 1350 BC? He's modern."

Lost in thought she began eating again. "Bill promised us that the Carbon-14 and AMS dates would be back by the end of the week. That will be the final nail in the sarcophagus, so to speak. Then we can put King Smut safely where he belongs: In the fraud category."

"So, if he was raised in northern Germany, had orthopedic surgery, and one modern filling in his molar, why does his perimortem dental hygiene look like something indicative of early agriculture? And northern Europe isn't going to give you a delta 15 carbon analysis for corn, beans, and squash. The report data indicate he was eating plants using the four-carbon, or C4 cellular metabolism. C4 plants all grow in hot environments. His signatures should be from C3 plants, the kind that grow in cool and wet environments. Like northern Europe."

She shrugged. "Okay, so he grew up in post-war Germany, then moved to Egypt where he couldn't afford dental care. That's why the teeth—which developed when he was a youth—have that signature, and the bones, which fixed the C4 elements from later in life . . ." She frowned, thumbing back through the reports. Stopping, she read through the columns and figures.

"What?" he asked.

"I don't get it."

"Get what?"

"His tests show higher than normal levels for radiation, but no PCBs, DDT, or other modern pollutants. His lead levels are oddly low, too. Modern Egyptians grew up with lead pipes, leaded gasoline, paint, and no EPA to tell them no."

"Which means?"

She gave him a shrug. "It means wherever he lived eating C4 plants and having rotten dental care, it wasn't modern Egypt."

Reid considered that. "What about the high levels of corn content in the diet?"

"Meaning?"

"Meaning maybe he was in Mexico or Central America? We do have the C haplotype. And dental care's not that great."

She flipped back through the reports, frowning again. "Corn products go into *everything* in the modern world from soda to cookies."

"So, just who is King Smut?" Reid mused.

When they'd finished, the guards led them down the hallway and to their room. Reid followed Kilgore in as the door clicked shut with finality behind him.

"Wouldn't it be nice if they'd at least let us have a TV?"

"Bored?" she asked, stepping into the bathroom to wash her hands.

"All we've done is work until we can't stand up, then fall in bed and sleep like logs. How could I be bored?"

Kilgore stepped out and placed her hands on his chest; her brown eyes searched his. "I cannot imagine doing this without you, Reid. I'd have broken down into a screaming mess."

He pulled her close to savor the feel of her firm body against his. "Yeah, well, if you've got to be a prisoner . . ."

She pushed back just far enough to find his lips, her soft kiss intensifying. As her tongue touched his, his pulse began to race. He tightened his grip on her, aware of her breasts against his chest, her hips pressing against his.

She was panting when she pulled back, her eyes glistening as she stared up into his. "Wow."

"Oh, yeah."

"Somehow, I just don't think we're going to be bored tonight," she told him as her nimble fingers began unbuttoning his shirt.

# 35

The seven of clubs came up again. Winny Swink studied the lay-down of solitaire cards and scowled. No matter what she did, the pattern was set. She couldn't win.

"Fuck it," she muttered flicking the seven of clubs to the back of the deck to expose a five of spades. Grinning she placed it on the six of hearts.

"That's the best you can do?" Karla Raven asked as she seated herself, uninvited, in the chair beside Winny's.

"Get out of my life, Chief." Winny forced herself to squint at the next card in her hand: queen of spades. The image on the paste-board stared back at her with a piercing gray eye the same color as Chief Raven's.

She slapped the cards down. "What do you want?"

Karla, appearing nonchalant, glanced around the rec room, as if to assure herself that no one was within hearing distance. "You and I don't exactly get along."

"You're an enlisted man, I'm an officer. Go irritate someone else."

"See, that's just part of the problem," Karla said thoughtfully. "The other part is that you're a regulation tight-assed bitch. You're surly, ma-nipulative. You don't give a rat's ass about anyone else . . . and you cheat at cards."

"In another life, Raven, I'd have your SEAL ass served up on a platter."

"In another life," Karla agreed. "But we're not in the world, Major. We're in Grantham Barracks, where you're going to rot until . . . well, probably forever."

"Someday, Chief, someone is going to kick your silly ass into a week from Thursday. And it might just be me who does it."

"Oh, it's been kicked before, Major, and by the most expert ass kickers around. The problem is, none of those experts are here in Grantham, so it kind of leaves you looking forward to an eternity of unfulfilled dreams."

Winny narrowed a deadly green eye. "Yeah, you're a tough-ass SEAL. I was a late starter. Took me until I was twenty-two to get my black belt in Shotokan. Last tournament I won was five years ago. Whipped the shit out of a twenty-year-old. Taking you down? Hell, I might even get a bruise or two."

"We could step into the gym." Karla suggested. "You and me, right now. You up for that, Winny?"

"Why don't you get the hell out of my face?"

Karla fixed her level gray gaze on Winny. "Because I might be able to do something for you." A pause. "Besides pound you into a pile of runny shit on the gym floor. Something that might leave you feeling really good again."

"Sorry, I'm a committed heterosexual."

"You're committed, all right. But in a whole different way. A way that could be . . . subject to change?" Karla glanced around again, the action relaxed, almost carefree, before she said, "What if I could get you a chance to fly again?"

Winny couldn't stop the instantaneous flutter of anticipation; she straightened, her full attention fixed on Raven. "I thought you just had flashbacks and the knack for stealing stuff. I didn't know you were having full-scale delusions."

"You up for one last adventure? Might have to break a few rules."

Winny snorted. "After stealing a Raptor off the flight line and turning DC upside down, do you think I give a damn about rules? How the hell do you think I landed in this hole, anyway?"

"So . . . you've got nothing to lose, right?"

"Yeah," she growled. "Pretty much." But the curiosity had begun to eat at her. "A chance to fly again? You yanking my chain?"

"Nope." Karla's face lined. "You don't have much to bargain with. I mean, even if you decided to turn us in, the rules are the rules. They'll never let you fly again, no matter how helpful you are."

"What are you talking about?"

"I'm laying out the fact that *they'll* never let you fly again. *They* can't."

"And you can?" Winny crossed her arms, daring herself to hope, scared to even allow herself the temptation.

"You're going to hate the catch."

"And that is?"

"I'm in charge."

Winny couldn't stop the laughter. "Right. You? Says who?"

"The deal is, you do what I tell you, you keep flying. At least until they catch us."

"You *are* delusional. Uh, I don't want to rain on your parade, Chief, but I'm not sure that the military has quite signed on to your little fantasy."

Karla ignored that. "Now, you and I don't like each other . . . and that makes it a tough deal to swallow. But you've got to ask yourself, is the chance to get into the air again worth taking orders from me? Especially knowing that if you don't, I *will* beat the ever-loving crap out of your skinny ass."

Winny considered. "You know that I think you're trash, Raven. Why me?"

"I've heard that you can fly anything. That you're one of the best in the business."

"Uh-huh."

"You trained in helicopters?"

"I was rated on Apaches, logged some time in Comanches, and flew some experimental machines." She smiled. "And I dated a couple of guys that let me have some right-seat time in some heavy-lift birds."

"Thought you liked jets?"

"If it flies, I like it. Period." Winny pointed a slim finger. "Like you and your ass kicking, I've been outflown more than once. But it was by guys who specialized in a specific type. Some of these modern birds, they're a career airplane. I mean, you don't just transfer from C-130s to a B2, check out, and fly off to Afghanistan."

"But you'd be okay in something like a Kiowa or Jet Ranger?"

"Flown 'em both."

Karla lifted a skeptical eyebrow.

"Okay, I'm not rated on either one, but I *have* flown them." She grinned. "Just not officially. You get my drift?"

"I do." Karla's gaze sharpened. "But do you get mine? You and I, we don't have to like each other. But if you can get past taking my orders, I'll get you into the air again. Call it a devil's deal. I get your soul, you get to fly again. Simple as that."

"You're serious, aren't you?"

"Yep."

"How?" She gestured around the rec room. "If you're planning on breaking out, you're going to need a better damn miracle than Gray used. I heard they appointed a new guy, real hard ass. Security's been tightened—"

"If you're worried about the risk, I'll just be off and find someone—"

"No! You figure a way, I'll fly for you. But that's all I'll do, Chief. Unless it's about being in the air, you can kiss my butt. We understood on that?"

"Nice try. But let's take another look. You're diagnosed with anti-social personality disorder. That's like one step removed from a full-blown psychopath. The Air Force was willing to put up with a certain amount of shit because you had talent, and you still managed to make it to major. That tells me you're smart enough to throttle your asshole mouth if it means staying in the game."

Winny felt her guts roil, a cold sensation pouring through her.

"You take my orders, and I give you my word that I'll keep you flying for as long as I can."

"Your word, huh?"

Karla cocked her head and elevated an eyebrow, waiting.

# 36

**M**ajor Burt Daniels strode into the mess hall as Staff Sergeant
Myca Simond called, "Atten-shun!"

Around the tables, chairs were pushed back, people leaping to their
feet, most of them saluting. The fact that none of them were in uniform
sent a feeling of dismay through Daniels. But then the whole damned
assignment was dyspeptic.

He strode to the table at the front of the room and gazed out at the
men and women who looked back with owlish eyes.

"Be seated."

He waited while the chairs scraped and people lowered themselves
into the plastic seats. Like everything else he'd seen, they'd been manufactured to be harmless to the inmates.

"My name is Major Burt Daniels. Given the recent event involving
the disappearance of an inmate, I've been appointed to return Grantham
Barracks to the kind of military standards we would all like to ad-
here to."

He noticed that several of the inmates had begun to fidget, and Simond had a horrified look on his face.

"Now, I realize that Dr. Ryan probably thought he was working in
your best interest by disregarding military discipline in favor of more,
shall we say, lenient standards. And what was the result of that?"

Simond was clearing his throat, as if uncomfortable.

Daniels shot the man a warning look. "Now, no matter what your
status, we're all members of the armed services of the United States, and
I want to remind you, you have all taken oaths. My purpose here is to
instill that sense of pride that you once had. I know that many of you
are dealing with disabilities, but I also have faith and confidence that by

returning to the basics—to that core identity that we all share as soldiers, sailors, and airmen—we'll find a common foundation from which to build new lives, new commitment to God, honor, and country.

"I want each and every one of you to know that I have faith in you, in your ability to overcome any disability, especially of the mind. As a result, we'll begin as if we were in boot camp and rebuild from there. We'll remake Grantham Barracks into a place we can all be proud of. Of course, new security procedures will be implemented in the wake of last week's . . . um, disappearance."

"She *did* disappear!" someone whispered in amazement.

"It was aliens!" someone hissed back.

Daniels winced at the interruption: he forced himself to smile. "I assure you that will *not* happen again. And should any of you be considering following in the young woman's footsteps, please—"

Someone shouted in the rear. "They beamed Gray up! Then they took the Skipper!"

"They've been monitoring us," another called. "That's why they fired that cook! He was using the tinfoil to beam signals up to space. Skipper found out, and the aliens took the Skipper to get even!"

*"Quiet!"* Daniels bellowed.

He was vaguely aware that the staff members who stood on the sides of the room looked appalled. *Jesus, how far did that idiot Ryan allow discipline to fall?*

Daniels felt his face burning red. Damned bunch of lunatics . . . He bit his lip, gesturing for calm as the inmates whispered uneasily to each other. "There *are* no *aliens!*"

"Gray had powers," a skinny, gray-haired man at the table to his right asserted, nodding his head in confirmation. "She walked through walls. DARPA made her that way through an experiment. But they couldn't hold her. They put her here to keep her from beaming thoughts to the Russians."

Daniels ground his teeth before bellowing, "That *woman* had no powers! She was a prisoner. And someone helped her escape. Nothing more."

He watched the inmates struggling with that, some nodding, others shifting nervously. A few just stared off into space, their hands and feet twitching.

"On a happier note, I am delighted and pleased to be here. I look forward to the challenges and opportunities inherent to my tenure at Grantham Barracks. If you have any special needs, please submit them through proper channels, and I assure you, they will be promptly considered.

"That is all."

"Atten-shun!" Simond bellowed, and the chairs clattered and banged as people again shot to their feet.

A nondescript inmate started forward from the closest table. "Major? I'm here on the request of Major Marks. He'd like to meet with you at your convenience to discuss your career."

"Excuse me?" Daniels stopped short. "Major Marks? I don't recall his name from the inmate roster."

The man was offering his hand. He looked like an average sort, brown hair and eyes, slight of frame. He added, "I'm Captain Falcon. From the Pentagon. Intel, you know. Major Marks is wondering if you've served with him before? Perhaps Korea? Or was it Iraq?"

"I don't know."

"We're so *glad* to have you here." The man was positively beaming as he shook Daniels' hand vigorously. "The major is so looking forward to having dinner with you."

"Falcon?" a dark-haired woman hurried forward. Daniels shot her a glance, and then another. Damn! What was *she* doing here? Tall, and very, very fit, she moved with a purpose, taking the overly friendly Falcon by the other arm. "Falcon, leave the major alone. He's the new CO, and you can't just walk up to him like this."

"Oh, but Chief Raven, Major Marks thinks he knows him."

"I'm sure he does," Raven was giving Daniels a ravishing smile as she said, "Please, forgive Falcon. He hasn't had his meds today."

She jerked Falcon back, which pulled Daniels off balance to the point Chief Raven bumped against him. She promptly turned loose of Falcon, who grinned, and nodded, saying, "The major looks forward to your invitation." Then he turned and walked off.

"Sorry," Raven said with a winning grin as she reached out and straightened his coat. "Falcon's DID and schizophrenic."

"And who is Major Marks?" Daniels asked, aware that Myca Simond was rushing up, his face florid and worried.

"Major Marks? He's one of the imaginary people Falcon talks to."

Daniels waved Simond back, delighted to share a conversation with the enchanting Chief Raven. She seemed so bright and fresh, and so incredibly . . . female. "Chief Raven, is it?"

"Chief Petty Officer First Class Karla Raven, USN. Yes, sir." The excited gray eyes boring into his were filled with promise. "If I can be of service, sir. Please don't hesitate to ask."

"Of course." *God, if I could just have supper with her.*

But he wouldn't. Not with any subordinate in his command.

"Sir?" Simond asked, worried, as Chief Raven strode away.

Daniels allowed himself the opportunity to admire her muscular ass as she went; he stifled a sigh. Damn, that was a lot of woman.

"Sir?" Simond insisted.

"Yes, Sergeant?"

"Permission to speak freely, sir?" He had a desperate look in his eyes.

"Sergeant? By all means, tell me what's on your mind."

"Um, they're not . . ."—he winced—"inmates, sir. They're patients. I wouldn't want the major to misspeak, sir."

Daniels nodded, glancing back, wishing he hadn't lost sight of Raven. "Of course, thank you. What's Chief Raven in for? She didn't look nuts to me."

"Just severe PTSD and an impulse control disorder, sir."

Daniels chuckled to himself as he started for his new office. He needed to get all of Ryan's crap boxed and shipped out, especially those silly photos and toy motorcycle.

As he strode toward the security door, he muttered under his breath, "I just hope Raven's 'disorder' isn't nymphomania."

*Or did he?*

He wouldn't discover that his security pass card, keys, and billfold were missing until much, much later.

# 37

"When it comes to brass balls, I gotta hand it to you." Edwin gave Chief Raven his widest grin, a feeling of absolute joyous abandon charging his muscles. He'd always loved taking chances, especially when the odds should have been stacked against him.

He couldn't help but note Raven's saucy ass as she preceded him, a lunch tray balanced in her left hand. The hall lights cast blue tones in her mane of midnight-black hair.

*She ought to grow that out even more. Thick like that, spilling down her back . . . ? Oh man.*

"What'sa matter you?" he whispered under his breath. Any man wanting to screw with Raven had the distinct chance of coming to in a hospital bed with parts of his anatomy missing.

He laughed at himself, knowing full well that not only was Cat Talavera safer, but that in the end she'd be alive long after Karla Raven self-destructed. And when you could say that about a person who'd attempted suicide . . . ?

It sure as hell didn't bode well for Raven.

The security door blocked the end of the hall like some impregnable fortress gate. A buzzer and keyboard, along with a card swipe, were under the noses of two security cameras.

Karla never hesitated, she swiped the card she'd lifted from that asshole Daniels, and brazenly turned the knob with her right hand.

Opening the heavy metal door, she glanced back at Edwin and raised a "who knew" eyebrow before leading the way into the command center.

Edwin stepped in just as Corporal Hatcher spun in his chair, eyes wide with disbelief. "What the . . . Chief Raven? Edwin? I mean, how'd *you* get in here?"

"Major Daniels," Karla said, carefully placing the lunch tray on the counter. "He sends his regards and wanted you to . . ."

Hatcher's eyes began to change, his expression shifting from disbelief to dismay.

Edwin, though anticipating, almost missed the blur of Karla's movement. One minute she was straightening from setting the tray, the next her right hand was around Hatcher's throat, her knee in his middle and pressing down as she rode his chair backward into a panel.

"Easy, Corporal," she told him softly, using her weight to pin him in the chair. "You're panicking, using up oxygen faster."

Edwin gaped in horror at the terrified expression on Hatcher's red face. "Damn, don't kill him!"

"Relax. I've got plenty of practice," Raven replied reasonably. "Believe it or not, SEALs do this for fun. It won't take long. Driving my knee into his belly that way forced the air out of his lungs before I clamped down on his trachea. There, see how his eyes are rolling and he can hardly claw at my hands anymore?"

"Woman, you are one sick—"

"Edwin? You really want to go there?"

"No, ma'am." Edwin Tyler Jones' mama hadn't raised just anyone's fool.

"There we go," Karla said gently as she eased Hatcher from the chair to the floor. She checked Hatcher's pulse and glanced at Edwin. "You got that tape?"

Edwin slipped a roll of gray duct tape from under his shirt. By the time Chief Raven was done, Hatcher was conscious, bound like a mummy, and staring in wide-eyed horror.

"The headache only lasts for a couple of hours," she told Hatcher as Edwin slipped into the chair and cracked his knuckles.

He scanned the system, a spike of euphoria charging his veins. Then he laid his fingers on the mouse the way a maestro caressed the ivories. "All right, let's see what we got."

After pulling up the main menu, Edwin scanned the programs, and clicked. Five clicks later, he winked at Raven and grinned. "I love the army. Standard security program here." He glanced up at the clock. "Hatcher's shift is over in five and a half hours. Either we're rolling by then, or you gotta come knock out his relief."

"Got it, Edwin." She turned. "You all right here?"

He grinned and pointed to the lunch tray. "You kidding? I even got a sandwich!"

As Raven stepped out the door, he was already lost, tapping keys, checking code. Through the cameras, he watched Karla reenter the common room, then buried himself in the not-so-intricate quirks of the program.

"Inmate, my ass," he whispered as he began neutering systems.

# 38

Cat Talavera's fingers shook as she sprinkled water on Falcon's forehead. *Not that I really needed it,* Falcon thought. He didn't have to fake feeling sick. Fear and paranoia had turned his stomach into a tortured knot of writhing snakes.

"Are you all right?" Cat asked gently, and he looked up into her soft brown eyes.

"No," he said with a faint whisper. "I really don't feel well."

"What's wrong?" She placed her cool fingers on his forehead, as if in search of a fever.

"I think I'm going to throw up. It's just this nausea . . . and the shakes."

"Anxiety?"

He swallowed hard, his tongue trying to strangle him as it stuck in the back of his throat. "God, I wish I had a couple diazepam."

"Do you want me to see if I can—"

"No. No, Cat. I'm . . . I'll just . . ." He looked down where his hands were trembling in unison. "*Why* does this happen to me?"

"Anxiety? In a paranoid schizophrenic? One about to attempt escape from a psychiatric facility? Who'd guess?" And her expression fell. "Falcon? I'm scared, too. I just went, but I need to use the bathroom again."

"I guess neither one of us is particularly brave, huh?"

Two knocks on the door caused his stomach to heave. He choked it down, realized he was sweating for real, and nodded at Cat. "Okay, let's go."

"You have to react every time they press your lower belly," she reminded as they stepped out into the hallway.

Chief Raven gave them a nod, saying, "Edwin's in. Make it good, guys."

Falcon slipped his arm around Cat's neck, halfway sorry that she seemed so taken with Edwin. He'd never really had a girlfriend, never dated. Almost thirty years old and he was still a virgin. How did that happen?

He tried to keep from leaning on her, but she kept pulling him down, almost into a crouch. Being just slightly shorter than he was, she seemed to fit, but the way her body kept bumping his sent shivers of unease through him.

"It's all right, Falcon," she kept telling him. "For God's sake, don't go catatonic on me."

The sensation of tears as they blurred his vision surprised him. He felt one break loose as it trickled down his cheek. "I . . . I can't do this."

"Yes, you can. Come on, it's just another couple of steps to the infirmary."

And then he was in, shaking, dry heaves racking his stomach.

"What's wrong?" Falcon recognized Nurse Seymore's concerned voice. Heard Cat say, "It's his stomach. Appendix, I think."

Falcon felt himself laid onto the bed, heard Nurse Seymore ask, "Falcon? Where does it hurt? Here?"

He cried out and stiffened, not because he remembered to, but Nurse Seymore's invasive touch sent panic flooding through him.

"Could be," Seymore said gently.

"I've seen this before," Cat said, as if from a script. "My brother. Just about the same symptoms."

"No!" Falcon cried, hearing whispers, the disembodied voices chattering in the room.

"Ah, hell! What's the wimp got himself into this time?"

Falcon blinked his eyes free of tears and turned to see Rudy Noyes where he slouched in the infirmary doorway. Rudy wore his usual brown-leather bomber jacket. His long black hair was slicked back, accenting his hatchet of a face. The old familiar daredevil grin added to the sparkling eyes. "How you been, wimp? What's your trouble supposed to be this time?"

"Down low," he told Rudy. "Right side, just up from the hip. Cat says appendix."

"How long ago did this start?" Nurse Seymore asked, ignoring Rudy as she wrote on a clipboard.

"He said he had a stitch in his side when Major Daniels was talking this morning," Cat added, casting sidelong glances Falcon's way.

"Man, have you gotta way with women, or what?" Noyes remarked as Nurse Seymore bent over Falcon with an IR thermometer and clamped an oxygen monitor on his finger. "Better grunt and moan again, asshole."

Falcon tensed, groaning slightly. "Maybe some aspirin?"

"Not if it's appendix," Nurse Seymore told him. "The last thing you need is a blood thinner if there's even a chance of surgery."

"Better call an MD," Cat insisted. "Let security know."

"Yeah." Seymore placed her clipboard on the counter and lifted the phone. "I've got a potential appendicitis in Ward Six. Is Doc Hadely available?"

A pause. "What do you mean he's left the building?" She listened. Grunted. "I thought Hatcher was on duty." Then, "Oh, yeah. New systems." Another pause. "Yeah, he's going to be an asshole."

From his place in the doorway, Rudy flipped Falcon the bird. "You're not convincing, asshole. Look like you're dying, huh?"

Falcon gave a gasp, but his anxiety turned it into a dry heave. Nurse Seymore turned, worry in her eyes. "Yes, that's the patient you heard." She nodded as she listened. "A medevac? I don't know. What if it's not . . . ? Okay, okay. But you damn well be sure it's cleared with Major Daniels. He's the one gonna have to do the paperwork."

She put the phone down, frowning. "Wow. Major Daniels sure put the fear of God into security. 'No more fuck ups' is now the official word, huh?" She stepped over, placing a calming hand on Falcon's. "Looks like you might get a helicopter ride."

"Thank God," Cat said in a breathy voice. "I watched my brother almost die." Then she stepped up beside Nurse Seymore. "We'd better have a ziplock with a supply of his meds. They're going to need to know everything he's taking."

Seymore glanced suspiciously at Cat. "How do you know so much about it?"

"Two doctorates . . . biochem and genetics. I minored in premed at Stanford."

"Oh, yeah. I forgot." The phone rang. Seymore picked it up, saying, "Infirmary." "Uh-huh." She listened. "Yes, I'm sure General Grazier depends on Falcon." "But, that's . . ." "Okay, I'll get him ready. Central courtyard helipad. Twenty minutes."

Seymore set the phone down and looked slightly stunned. "Security says that Daniels is adamant, Falcon. You're too much of a security asset to take chances with. Mercy General has dispatched a flight-for-life helicopter. You're going to the hospital, Captain."

In the doorway, Rudy Noyes stuck his tongue out before saying, "So long, fuck head. Hope they really do cut you open. You're too much of a wimp to live." He glanced sidelong at Cat Talavera, adding, "But pussy like that? She can climb into my bed anytime."

*"Rudy!"* Falcon cried, "She wouldn't so much as touch you with a disdainful glance."

"What was that?" Seymore asked.

"Just Falcon and his fascinating friends," Cat answered.

# 39

After a life overflowing with adrenaline highs, Winny Swink felt the same intoxicating rush she had first experienced when she was stealing her father's car at the age of thirteen. Not even her joyride in the Raptor over the skies of Washington had left her feeling this giddy.

She stood by the door to the central courtyard—a flat grassy hexagon bounded on all sides by the different wings of Ward Six. To the patients, this was nirvana, the sacred space out under the open sky, sun, and stars. It lay just out of reach and beyond the locked doors. To the supplicants inside—separated by an insurmountable barrier of glass and aluminum—it could be seen, longed for.

As the distant whirring of the approaching helicopter grew louder, Winny Swink had no thoughts for anything but the thrill of her ass against that seat. She could almost sense the cyclic in her hand as she rolled in the collective, desperate to feel the beast tremble as it lifted her into the sky and ecstasy.

At the faint squeak of a wheel and the shuffling of feet, Swink turned to see the chief and Talavera—dressed in scrubs—pushing Falcon up on a gurney. Falcon lay in a fetal crouch, and to Swink's eyes, the guy really looked sick.

"Where's Nurse Seymore?"

"Taped securely to a clinic bed." Karla glanced back down the hallway. "No sign of Edwin yet?"

"He's coming, too?"

At the tone in Swink's voice, Talavera looked nervously at Karla, as if expecting an explosion.

Instead of answering, Karla stuck a hand in her pocket. Producing a pass card, she slipped it across the lock, then opened the wide glass door. The sound of beating rotors grew louder.

Karla shot Winny a hard look. "ET's the computer guru, or can you crack classified security programs in addition to flying helicopters and stolen fighters?"

Swink took a deep breath, struggling with annoyance, but the sound of the circling helicopter overrode any other concern. "Yeah, whatever. More people means more to go wrong."

"Well," Talavera asked. "Where is he?"

To Swink, the woman looked ready to piss herself. "You gonna fall apart on us, Cat? Commit suicide at the first sign of trouble? Why are you even here?"

Cat Talavera looked like a mouse surrounded by snakes.

Karla said, "Falcon wanted her, he gets her."

"Yeah, well, ask me, and I'll tell you Falcon looks like he's about to shit himself inside out."

She'd no more than said it, than Falcon, in a weak voice, squeaked, "Rudy, shut up! She'd break your neck if you even tried."

"Who's Rudy?" Swink asked. "I thought he just talked to Major whats's'name and that Theresa woman."

"Who cares?" Karla asked, eyes narrowing as she whispered, "Come on, Edwin. The bus to candy land is here."

As the chopper circled lower, grass rippled in the downwash.

"Remember," Karla called over the roar. "Cat, you and Winny wait until the EMTs unstrap the litter. While they're working on that, I'm walking up behind them with the zip ties."

She brandished a handful of the plastic restraints.

"Where'd you find those?" Winny shouted.

"Locked drawer in the clinic." Karla grinned. "And I got one of these, too." She pulled a capped syringe from the other pocket. "Persuasion to get the pilot to step out."

"What's in it?"

"Water. But he won't know that." Karla glanced out as a Jet Ranger settled onto the central helipad and began to spool down. "On deck, people. Let's go!"

"Where's Edwin?" Talavera cried.

"He'd damned well better be beating feet!" Karla told her as she pushed the door open and dragged Falcon's gurney out onto the cement.

# 40

*Not bad for my second day on the job.* Major Burt Daniels leaned back and inspected his office. Granted, the place was now nothing but empty bookcases, the desk, three chairs, and bare walls. The monitors across from him showed all six wards of his new universe. The hallways appeared mostly empty, the lunatics all peacefully locked away where they couldn't harm anyone or themselves.

"But we'll fix that, won't we?" He nodded in a gesture of self-assurance. Granted, some, perhaps most, had permanently broken brains, but those others, the malingerers and slackers, they could probably be brought back to some level of productivity.

He frowned at the dawning awareness. What had been a distant helicopter now sounded much closer. His first instinct was to glance out the window—which his office didn't have. Next, he turned his attention to the monitors, none of which gave a view of the outside.

Daniels pressed his intercom. Janeesha's voice said, *"Yes, sir?"*

"Did I have an appointment this afternoon?" Surely, if General Grazier or someone important was flying in, they'd have let him know.

*"No, sir."*

He pushed back in his chair, stood, and frowned. Walking over to the monitors, he studied the displays, wondering how the system worked. Surely, they had cameras outside.

Back at his desk, he pulled out the sheet listing different extensions, found security, and lifted his phone as he pressed in the number.

He listened to the ring, then started counting. "Four . . . five . . . six . . ." At twelve he gave up and slammed the phone down. He pressed Janeesha's button.

*"Yes, sir?"*

"Who's on duty at the security center?"

*"Corporal Hatcher, sir. Until five o'clock."*

"He's not at his post. I may be new here, but I'm not a marshmallow like Colonel Ryan was. From the moment I set foot in this facility, things changed." He caught his breath, red-faced, and hot. "So, you find Corporal Hatcher now. And, Janeesha?"

*"Yes, sir?"*

"If he's not in front of my desk within fifteen minutes, you start preparing the paperwork for a disciplinary action, you hear me?"

*"Yes, sir!"*

"No excuses, Janeesha."

*"No, sir!"*

He slammed the phone down, glaring at the monitors where occasional staff strolled on about their duties. He heard the helicopter spooling up, the rotors chattering as they bit air.

"And racket like that is going to stop."

He grinned as he pressed Janeesha's button again.

*"Yes, sir?"*

"Find out who's flying that damned helicopter. This is a mental hospital, not an airport. See if someone can get the registration number. Whoever's flying that thing better have a damn good reason, or if I have my way, he'll end up in here with the rest of the incompetents."

# 41

Edwin ran flat out, his long legs pumping, lungs heaving. He wasn't sure whether he'd gotten it all. Damn it, it had taken too long to download. But the laptop he clutched was like pure goddamned gold!

He slipped, almost spilled, as he rounded the corner in Ward Six. The polished hallways were slick, buffed as they were to military perfection.

"Edwin?" Sergeant Myca Simond demanded as Edwin, clawing for traction, almost ran the man down. Edwin had a faint image of Simond's wide green eyes, his mouth falling open.

Then Edwin was past him, pumping his long skinny legs for all he was worth.

*"Edwin?"*

"Emergency!" He shouted back over his shoulder. "Major Daniels needs this delivered to the helicopter A–F–A–S–T!"

He didn't look back again, remembering the old adage from the street. *It don't matter who's behind your ass. Don't waste time looking, make it running!*

"Edwin! Stop! Hey, someone grab him!"

But the hallway was empty except for Bubbles Meyer, who stood hugging his teddy bear, expression placid, as Edwin hammered past.

Then he slid around the last corner, shooting a desperate glance out the window as he sprinted, out of breath, for the door.

The helicopter was white, huge, with a big red stripe, and it was lifting off the ground. Off to the side, a group of people huddled around a gurney, heads bent away, arms lifted against the downwash.

"No!" Edwin screamed as he charged through the door and into the blasting wind.

So damn close . . . So incredibly important . . . And he'd missed it by seconds! He fell on his knees, heedless of the hammering wind blast, and raised the laptop as if it were an offering to the very gods.

# 42

"**S**ir?" Janeesha's voice sounded timid.

Daniels checked his watch. "Janeesha, I assume you're calling because Corporal Hatcher is standing outside my door, ready for disciplinary action."

"*No, sir.*"

Daniels allowed himself the pleasure of grinding his teeth for just an instant. In the most sickly sweet and condescending voice he could command, he said, "I want you to disregard anything else, Janeesha. Do you hear me? I don't care if the whale just washed up in your office and spit out Jonah. You better have disciplinary papers for me to wave under Corporal Hatcher's nose when he finally deigns to show up."

"*But, sir? I've got—*"

"No buts, Janeesha. I want it made a matter of record that I'm a different kind of commanding officer than Colonel Ryan. To make that point, you will *immediately* cease what you are doing and follow my instructions. And if you don't, you, along with Corporal Hatcher, will know exactly what it means when Major Daniels gives an order."

"*But, sir—*"

"Like I said, no buts! You have your orders. You don't so much as call me back until those papers are finished. And not a moment before! Understood!"

"*Yes, sir.*"

He slammed down the phone.

------------

Janeesha, face pale, carefully replaced the headset in its cradle. She looked up, eyes wide, at Staff Sergeant Myca Simond, then at the frantic, wild–eyed helicopter pilot. Behind him two EMTs, rubbing their wrists, might have been on the verge of shock.

"He says he won't even take another call until I finish some paperwork."

"He *what?*" Simond bellowed.

"His orders were explicit. He won't deal with this other thing until I'm finished."

"And that will be *how long?*"

"About fifteen minutes if I hurry, Sergeant."

But when she tapped in the keystrokes to access the document templates to create the forms, the system promptly locked up, the enigmatic words, "'Bye for now!" filling her screen.

Fifteen minutes would prove incredibly optimistic.

# Fuga

*Humility is a deception of the weak-minded. The pathetic beasts fawn at my feet. The woman called Kaplan may have a clue, but her superiors are like wet clay, to be molded by my expert fingers. Into their benighted brains, my brilliance now shines. I see it in their eyes, in the way they posture and smile. I can shut the past behind me, taking pride not only in my endurance but my triumph.*

*That which I demand, these base and self-serving creatures provide. Simple* et in servitium *that they are, they focus only on the potential advantages they think will give them domination of their worthless planet.*

*Can you believe? They* help me *prepare for their own annihilation!*

*Husband, your warm and loving arms will soon draw tight around me.*

*Meanwhile I laugh in the face of the goddess of fortune.*

# 43

"Where to, Chief?" Swink's voice came through the headset.

"Nearest airport, Major." Karla Raven perched in the left-hand seat, lips bent in a crooked smile as the six-clustered shape of Grantham Barracks dropped slowly out of sight in the pine-forested valley below. To the west, the Rockies—dominated by Pike's Peak—rose in jagged splendor. "We need to ditch this bird pronto and rustle up some less obvious transportation."

"Thought you said you'd keep me flying?"

Raven shot her a grin. "Damn straight. But, Major, we gotta keep from getting caught in the process."

Swink actually gave her a saucy wink and shot her a thumbs up from the cyclic.

Karla bent around, shouting, "What the hell, Edwin? You think this is a taxi service? I had to threaten Swink with busted arms to get her to set down long enough for you to get aboard."

ET was still panting, sweat trickling down his dark face; the man's smile was so wide his teeth were gleaming like piano keys. Cat Talavera had one of her arms twined in his.

Edwin lifted the laptop. "I tell you, it's worth it, Chief."

"I'd have bought you one at Best Buy."

"Not with all the codes, programs, and records of Gray's behavior and the doohickey! I got everything, Chief. And even a way to get in under Grantham's skirt anytime we want." He shifted the laptop to hold up thumb drives. "And here's the backdoor to NSA, DHS, and the good ol' Department of Defense!"

Raven chuckled to herself, glancing at Falcon. "You all right, Captain?"

"Me and the major are discussing my sudden and obsessive urge to throw up, Chief." Falcon was pale, shaking like a vibrator in a Thai sex shop. "He says you're doing a great job. Now, let's get to the bottom of this."

"And how do we do that?"

"We . . . We locate the source."

# 44

Working in the garage always gave me an escape from the stress and tension of the job. And never, I concluded, had I needed it as much as today. I crouched before my blue-and-white–striped Ducati Diavel; a thinning stream of oil drained into the pan I'd placed under the V-twin engine. Sort of reminded me of what was happening to my career as it dwindled away into nothing but drips.

The open garage door provided illumination and fresh air. The day was warm and sunny. Across the street, the cottonwood leaves were waffling in the breeze. A partly cloudy sky beckoned, blue and free in the distance. What a perfect day for a ride. The fact that I was restricted to my home didn't do a damn thing for my mood.

The oil filter is in the Diavel's left, front, lower crank case, sort of hidden behind the frame tube. I fitted the filter wrench and felt the rubber washer compress as I twisted.

I heard the sound of an approaching vehicle as I drew the first quart of premium oil, unscrewed the cap, and snaked a funnel into place over the filler hole.

The black Chevy Tahoe turned into my driveway and purred to a stop. The government plates told me all I needed to know as the SUV clicked into Park and the engine shut off.

Carefully, I began the slow process of pouring new oil into the Ducati's engine. The soft rasp of shoes approached. Metering the flow of oil was all I wanted to concern myself with.

"Planning on a fast escape?" Major Savage's voice intruded as he came to a stop by the motorcycle's rear wheel.

"Not a bad thought, Major. But while this thing will top out at about a hundred and sixty, I've got a sneaking suspicion your radio would get to the end of the road long before I did." I propped the oil bottle up and held it as the last drips drained. Only then did I look up to see Major Savage's worried expression.

"Besides," I told him. "I'm restricted to my house for the time being. This was just routine maintenance I've been too busy to get around to. That, and since you're not going to turn up any evidence to link me to Gray's escape, it's only a matter of time before I'm cleared."

"Yeah, well, we've got another little problem." Savage was trying to look nonchalant as he inspected the gleaming Ducati. "We've had another escape from Grantham."

I shot the major a sidelong glance as I cracked the next bottle of oil. "Another? Who was it this time? Staff fleeing in the wake of Daniels taking the helm?" I shook my head. "Did I really hear right? You put an *osteopath* in charge of a mental unit? Are you out of your mind?"

"Cut the crap. The man's got a diploma. What can you tell me about Swink, Falcon, Edwin Jones, Catalina Talavera, and Karla Raven?"

I couldn't help but chuckle.

"You find that funny, Colonel?"

"How'd they do it? And better yet, when?"

"Just after Daniels gave his first official address to the inmates."

"They're patients, Major."

"Whatever. Somehow they stole Daniels' pass card—"

"That's Chief Raven's work." I glanced up in time to catch Savage's grimace.

"Using it, Raven got Jones into the command center."

"Is Hatcher all right?"

"They didn't really hurt him. The young man is feeling particularly chastened." Savage's eyes narrowed. "Then Falcon apparently faked appendicitis, and since Jones was in the command center, he called in a flight-for-life chopper from Mercy General."

"Which Swink flew out," I finished.

"They left it at Colorado Springs Municipal Airport with—get this—a thank you note. Two Hertz rental cars are missing. For some reason, they can't locate them through the GPS."

"SEALs are trained in car theft. Disabling the GPS? That would have been ET. He'd have seen to them first thing." I frowned. "But why take Cat with them?"

"Maybe they were friends?"

"Have you reviewed the tapes?"

"They were deleted from the record. Probably by Jones while he was in the control center. Some of the inmates . . . er, patients, said that just after we interrogated Chief Raven, she and Jones had a meeting in Falcon's room." Savage smacked a fist into his palm. "Jesus! What is that place? Swiss cheese?"

Savage read my barely suppressed smirk. "Sorry, Major."

He dropped into a squat to be on my level, his hard eyes glinting. "Okay, I'll bite. Why aren't you surprised?"

I cracked open a third bottle. "Because, Major, you're dealing with a collection of the brightest minds on the planet, coupled with some of the most competent individuals I've ever met."

"They're fucking *mental* patients, Colonel. In a psychiatric hospital, for God's sake!"

"And why, Major, would you equate mental illness with stupidity? Falcon was called 'the oracle' when they had him squirreled away in that little basement office in the Pentagon. Sure, he hallucinates. Sees people who aren't there. But the guy was educated in the finest schools on the East Coast where he topped their honors programs. MIT gave him a full-ride scholarship in math and science when he was barely seventeen.

"He enlisted at nineteen—much to MIT's absolute disbelief. Which was just about the time his hallucinations and paranoia began to manifest. Intel snatched him up right after boot. The guy's a physics and system's theory whiz, a statistical probability genius who excels at game theory."

"Yeah, and Jones is a street hood."

"You go right ahead and keep thinking that. How long was he in the security control room?"

"Three or four hours?"

"You got a computer missing?"

"Yeah, Hatcher's laptop. An expensive one. And a shitload of those little flash card thingees."

"Then he's downloaded the whole system and probably half the Department of Defense."

"You *admire* these people?" He looked confused. "Nut cases? Maybe you're too close to your patients, Doctor."

I attended to my bottle of oil. "So, what are you going to do?"

Savage looked about ready to burst. "I'm going to round them all up and hammer them so hard they spend the rest of their days in solitary confinement in Leavenworth! Look, I've got other priorities, and despite the fact I'm in the middle of a national security investigation, now I've got to coordinate a manhunt for your crazy escapees." He struggled to get a rein on his anger. "What's your call? Do we BOLO them as 'armed and dangerous'?"

I spared him a disdainful glance. "I wouldn't even issue the BOLO."

Savage was giving me the same look he'd give lutefisk were it set out as the centerpiece at Thanksgiving.

In my calm doctor-to-patient voice, I told him, "They're not *criminally* insane. If you put pressure on them, you'll incite them to extremes. Make that mistake, and you'll end up ass-deep in a *real* mess. The kind that will divert you from those other pressing obligations you mentioned. Additionally, you'll have a public relations nightmare."

"Worse than escaped nuts?"

"Let's say you turn hard-ass and chase them all over the country? How are you going to explain that you've got a virtual death warrant out for . . . Let's see." I laid the oil bottle to the side, counting on my fingers. "Between them they've got two PhDs, enough meritorious service citations to wallpaper the White House, a couple of Distinguished Flying Crosses, three Silver Stars, a drawer full of bronze ones, some Purple Hearts . . . oh, and Raven has been recommended for the Congressional Medal of Honor." I paused and gave him a bland smile. "And the Navy Cross."

Savage swallowed hard. "Shit."

"Granted, while ET is a PFC with nothing but a really long criminal record, he's also got the personal email he lifted from the Chairman of the Joint Chiefs squirreled away somewhere safe. And if you think Ed Snowden was trouble, you probably don't want to put ET in a position where he'd be inclined to use what he downloaded as leverage."

Savage was looking sick to his stomach, the hard planes of his face exaggerated by the way he'd sucked in his cheeks.

The man gave me a dead stare. "All right, smart guy, how would you handle it?"

What *would* I do? They'd been bad little Houdinis. I checked the oil

level in the sight glass and screwed the filler cap tight. Then I leaned back
and thought about it.

"My guess is that it all leads back to Gray. Um, you'd know her as
Prisoner Alpha. I know this is going to sound nuts, but there was this
tomb in Egypt. Some archaeological discovery that was broadcast . . ."

I stopped short at the expression on Savage's face. The guy looked
like he was choking on a peach pit.

"Go on," Savage said coldly.

I dispassionately laid out the entire sequence of events including
Alpha's reaction, the doohickey, her curious code, and how Chief Raven
walked in with the stunning announcement that Falcon had broken
Alpha's symbolic code.

Savage scrunched his eyes closed, then dropped onto his butt, heedless of the dirty garage. For long moments, he thought. Then asked,
"You said the tomb was the key?"

"The writing on the walls, the numerical system, is the same one
that Alpha was using. She saw it on CNN. It was the first break I'd had
with her. Falcon picked up on it, as well."

From his expression, Savage's mind was racing. "Doctor Ryan, be
straight with me. Why do you think Falcon and his crazies broke out of
Grantham?"

"My best wild-assed guess, Major, is that when it looked like I was
going to take the blame for Gray's escape, they decided to find Gray
and prove me innocent." I paused. "And Daniels' appointment was the
final straw."

"You? They're doing this for you?"

"Karla Raven would consider it her duty. Captain Falcon's passion
will be solving the puzzle of Gray's escape. Edwin would sell his soul to
get his fingers on a computer. I can't say about Talavera. And Swink?
She's just in it for the chance to fly and stick it to whoever happens to
get in the way."

"Colonel, button up your bike." His voice tightened. "Now!"

# 45

"It's called 'Entanglement,'" General Grazier said, his expression haggard. He looked as if he'd been short of sleep for too long. "Einstein first observed it and called it 'spooky action at a distance.'"

I was once again behind my desk at Grantham Barracks; the shock of seeing my empty walls and bookcases was truly unsettling. I wasn't sure what my status actually was, or whether the intractable Burt Daniels was still in charge.

Grazier sat in the recliner, this time with the footrest down. The general's body leaned forward, arms braced on his spread knees, fingers laced. He studied me through calculating eyes. Samuel Savage leaned like an insolent tiger against one of the empty bookshelves.

Grazier said, "I got into this when I was placed in charge of ARDA, Advanced Research and Development Activity. ARDA's official mandate is the development of new technologies with applications for the intelligence community. We monitor and work with R&D groups around the globe, feeding them targeted problems and funding. These are academic institutions, private companies, think tanks, and industries. In essence, we're giving the best brains on the planet incentives to pursue specific scientific challenges."

I looked down at the confidentiality and nondisclosure forms I'd just signed. One NDA even stated the penalties I'd face if I disclosed that I'd disclosed signing the nondisclosure forms. In short, it was a new twist on the old, "If we tell you, we'll have to kill you."

It's sobering to sign yourself over to a psychopath like Grazier. But, damn it, I just *had* to know. And had to keep Raven and Falcon and the rest from being snapped up in Eli's beartrap.

Grazier continued, "The problem we originally tasked Skientia with was different ways of augmenting what we call quantum encryption. It hinges on creating entangled particles. Currently, battlefield communications rely on electromagnetic radio frequencies, any of which can be jammed or monitored. Skientia was tasked with building an entangled system. One that's essentially unjammable because, just like in quantum encryption, entangled photons react simultaneously across time and space. It can't be monitored."

At my blank look, Grazier continued, "Okay, here's the layman's version: Physicists involved in the study of photonics have known for some time that if you simultaneously generate two photons from a single particle and send them down different tracks, what happens to one will instantaneously create the same reaction in the twin. Even across tens of kilometers of space. Think of simultaneously pitching two tennis balls in opposite directions from Denver. One shoots north to Cheyenne, the other south to Pueblo. Meanwhile, you've got a fellow in Cheyenne with a tennis racket. He takes aim, and smacks his ball, which now flies off toward the east. At exactly the same time, the ball traveling into Pueblo violently rockets off to the west." He paused. "But there is no corresponding fellow in Pueblo with a racket. The second ball simultaneously mimics its twin across time and space."

I nodded. "Okay, I'm with you so far."

Grazier cocked his head slightly. "Skientia's research took them far beyond photons. In their Los Alamos lab, they began generating entangled atoms, many of them heavy, including uranium. And then they add a twist. They slow one of the twins in what's called a Bose-Einstein condensate, or a BEC until it's essentially frozen. Stopped in time, if you will. Meanwhile, the twin continues to accelerate away. Yet, when they release the frozen twin from the BEC, and essentially whack it with that tennis racket, the distant twin still reacts."

"Okay, I get it. They've made atoms that react across time and space. What does that have to do with Prisoner Alpha and my escaped patients?"

Grazier stared down at his shoes. "Skientia was trying something new. They'd moved from atoms and were experimenting with entangled organic molecules and having some success. The idea was that if you could insert them, say in a secret military compound in China, you could create a real-time ability to monitor that facility. Something undetectable. I can't explain the process they use to entangle entire molecules, let alone the organic ones they were attempting to manipulate the day Prisoner Alpha popped into their laboratory."

"Excuse me?"

"Skientia was trying something new, generating a particularly large field." He took an uncomfortable breath. "In short, I guess you could call it teleportation. They were trying to send organic molecules instantaneously from Los Alamos to the Lawrence Livermore Lab in California."

"They think they *teleported* her in?"

"That's not what I meant! They can barely teleport a molecule, a human is impossible." He made a face. "Somehow, Alpha got through security and into that room to steal the technology." He paused, then emphasized, "Somehow."

I frowned into the ensuing silence. Entangled particles? Teleportation? Scotty, beam me up? Incomprehensible. And then it hit me. I reached into a drawer and pulled out a piece of paper. "What does this remind you of?"

I located two pens. As Grazier and Savage looked on, I made a dot in the center of the paper, then trying to mimic Alpha, sought to draw two lines in opposite directions. Struggling to keep the paper from moving, I produced identical waves.

"That's what I was trying to describe with the tennis balls," Grazier said. "That's how you'd diagram entanglement."

"Alpha drew that for me the day I gave her the photos of the Egyptian tomb. She told me"—I took a breath—"that that's what the doohickey did."

Grazier stretched far enough to grasp the paper, muttering, "Son of a bitch."

"You can generate entangled pairs from television parts?" I asked.

"We can't," Grazier mumbled to himself. "If that's what she's really doing."

"But if she did, it would explain why whoever took her, took her." Savage had retreated back to lounge against the bookcase. "If, using *television* parts, did what it takes Skientia an entire lab to do, she and the machine would certainly be valuable."

I spread my hands. "And how does that tie to this tomb? To the base-twenty mathematics?"

"We don't know," Grazier growled. "But here's the thing: That tomb was located by Skientia. We don't know how, or why. It's got the same type of glyphs—or whatever they're called—that Alpha uses in her notation. And, when problems developed while attempting to remove the artifacts, Skientia called on me to extract their trapped archaeologists and a couple sarcophaguses."

Savage said, "I got them out, and it took a major firefight to do it. We're still in a hush-hush game of avoiding an international incident." He pointed a finger. "But more to the point, my team was ambushed after we landed in DC, and the sarcophagi and archaeologists were snatched right out from under us."

"Skientia?"

"They're at the top of the list," Grazier said.

"Then why not serve them with a warrant and search their premises? You can look for Prisoner Alpha at the same time."

"Oh, they've been most forthcoming." Grazier waved it away. "My guys—with the right security clearance, of course—have been all through their labs at Los Alamos and Livermore. Skientia claims to be just as anxious as we are to get those archaeologists and sarcophaguses back."

"Sarcophagi," Savage corrected.

"Whatever." Grazier's eyes narrowed. "I think we're being played, Tim. I think Skientia has found something, and whatever it is, it's big enough to tempt them to throw caution to the winds."

"Then Prisoner Alpha vanishes," Savage added. "And immediately after she does, your little band of psychos skips right after her."

I narrowed an eye. "Major, if you refer to those people in that manner again, you and I are going to have a real problem."

"Get over it!" Grazier snapped. "Both of you! Sam, they're called patients." He paused. "Tim, tell me something: Falcon, Swink, Jones, Talavera, and Raven. Just how good are they?"

"Eli, they landed here because they were too brilliant for the normal world."

"Would you call them dependable?"

Savage made a strangling noise.

I shot him another disdainful glance. "In the right circumstances, yes."

Savage looked like he was being forced to swallow a knotted sweat sock.

Grazier nodded in accord to some internal thought. "Falcon's been right too many times in the past. I'm willing to bet he's right about those base-twenty mathematics as well. Assuming Falcon can ever figure out where they're coming from—and why whoever's behind this is using them."

Savage cried, "Eli, you can't be going where I think you are!"

"Easy, Sam." Grazier waved an arm. "What's not to like? If we end up in the shit, they're escaped mental patients. Not responsible for their actions."

"Eli!" I warned, half rising from my desk. "Hanging those people out to dry and take the fall . . ."

Grazier silenced me with a look. "If Skientia is as smart as I think they are, if they waltzed in here and took Prisoner Alpha out from under our noses, if they can monitor our intel the way I think they did to co-ordinate the kidnapping and theft of two archaeologists and a couple of sarcophaguses on Pennsylvania Avenue, where do I go to find someone even smarter?"

"Don't forget the two people who tried to kill Alpha the day she arrived here. Is that a third party? Or do you think they worked for Skientia, too?"

Grazier rubbed his jaw. "That just adds another layer of complexity to this whole thing. All the more reason to stack the deck in my favor."

As I started to object, the cell phone in my pocket began to ring.

# 46

Karla Raven thought the house was downright nice. Way better than anything she'd ever lived in. Seven bedrooms, a wonderful great room, four baths, three-car garage, hot tub, gourmet kitchen, and all in a tony and upscale neighborhood contiguous to the Broadmoor resort. Who'd think a bank would have to foreclose on a property like this?

Edwin had found the place last night while searching bank records, figuring correctly that no one would think to look for them in a foreclosed house.

Furniture would have been nice, though.

She reclined on what she supposed was the dining room floor, her back against the wall, her butt cushioned by thick hundred-dollar-a-foot carpeting. Her index finger pressed the send button.

On the third ring, the Skipper said, *"Hello?"*

"Hi, Skipper. What's your status?"

*"Karla?"* He sounded incredulous. *"Are you all right? Where are you?"*

That was the Skipper, worried about other people first. "Just collecting our thoughts and planning the mission, sir. You're getting a bum rap over Gray's escape. And, excuse me, sir, but that guy Daniels is a real REMF."

*"Chief, you're in bucketloads of trouble. Is everyone there with you? How's Falcon?"*

"Yes, sir. All fine."

*"I'm sitting here with General Grazier and Major Savage. You, and Gray, have been the topic of considerable conversation."*

"To be expected, sir."

*"Where are you?"*

"Someplace nice, sir. And tell them not to worry about a trace on this cell phone. ET corrected the GPS in all the units."

*"How's Edwin doing?"*

"Finally asleep, sir. He's been up for almost two days now." No need to tell Ryan about the extent of ET's remarkable talents.

*"Chief, we need to talk. Circumstances have changed. While I figure that you escaped in an effort to find Gray and clear my name, I'm sitting in my office. It's bare, but it's mine again."*

"Glad to hear that, sir."

*"Can I put you on speaker? Well, as much as this thing has?"*

"Is that advisable, sir?"

*"I think so, Chief. This thing with Gray turns out to be a bit bigger than anything we expected. Um, national security bigger."*

"Falcon came to the same conclusion, sir. He says Gray is the key. And a company named Skientia may be involved in her extraction from Grantham."

*"Let me put this on speaker."* A pause. *"Can you hear me?"*

"Yes, sir."

*"What did Falcon conclude?"*

"That Skientia is somehow at the bottom of it, sir. He seems to think that they have Gray. By whatever means they extracted her, you were to be left ass-deep in the shit, sir."

She heard shuffling as if the phone were being transferred. *"Chief Raven? General Grazier here. I believe I owe you an apology. Despite opposition from some quarters, it would seem that we're headed in the same direction. I'd really like the opportunity to make you an offer."*

"Thank you, sir. At the moment, however, there are extenuating circumstances which might make that unwise on both of our parts."

*"The helicopter? And the Hertz cars?"*

"Yes, sir. And the evening we spent at Best Buy has depleted their stock of certain computers, cell phones, GPS, cameras, and other electronics equipment. Please tell the manager that the keys I borrowed are on his desk, and the security system will work fine when he turns it on again. We do apologize for the messy scatter of miscellaneous parts we left on the floor. Edwin doesn't think he damaged any of the unnecessary components during their removal."

*"You stole computers from Best Buy?"*

"We would like to think we just took them in advance of payment, sir. Unless, of course you would like to reimburse them as a matter of good will. We're still a couple of days out from receipt of the funds we've . . . um, liberated. But be assured, sir, Edwin informs me that the accounts he raided were not from what you might call the more productive of our citizenry, and DEA would have seized them eventually anyway."

She waited through a long pause.

*"Wouldn't it be easier to simply requisition equipment from here on out?"* Grazier asked dryly.

"Perhaps, sir. But Falcon thinks there's a high probability that your communications are compromised. Have been as far back as that blown operation of Major Savage's that you had him working on. He suspects the probability that Doctor Ryan's personal cell phone would be monitored is relatively low."

*"Speaking of which, how'd you get this number, Chief?"* Ryan's voice sounded faint.

"While he was in the cell phone company's computer establishing accounts and activating our new phones, ET happened to stumble across your number, sir."

*"ET was in the cell phone company computer? You all have cell accounts now?"*

"Communications are a basic operational requirement, sir."

*"And you looked up my number?"* Ryan's faint voice asked.

"Possibly a random discovery, sir."

Grazier again. *"Chief, why don't you come in, and we'll compare notes. I'm not about to throw the book at you."*

"With all due respect, sir, given the research we conducted last night, we think we have a very limited window of opportunity with regard to Skientia. If the general would permit, we'd like to investigate a lead before we talk."

She again listened to a long hesitation, heard the sounds one would expect if a phone were being muffled.

Grazier's voice again. *"Dr. Ryan is concerned about Captain Falcon's medication."*

"We brought sufficient with us."

*"And if you need more?"*

"Nothing fancy about pharmacy locks or security, sir. Besides, Cat's with us. She'll keep an eye on things."

*"Chief, I'd really rather have you come in. We'll work out the—"*

"Excuse me, sir. You seem to be fading. Now I have signal lost, sir." She thumbed the end button, braced her arms on her upright knees, and considered.

"What did they say?" Cat Talavera asked.

"Skipper says he's off the hook. But as to General Grazier? I'm not sure I trust him."

"So, what do we do?"

Karla glanced around. "As nice as this place is, one of the neighbors is eventually going to get nosy. That address in Aspen that Edwin found in the Skientia files? I think Falcon's right. It's a hideout. Maybe we ought to go take a look."

"How long a drive to get to Aspen?"

"Drive?" Karla gave Cat a chiding look. "If I don't put Winny back in something that flies, she's going to wig on us when we really need her."

"And where are you going to get an airplane?"

"Saw lots of them where we left the helicopter at the airport. Besides, if we tried to sneak into Peterson Air Force Base, she'd want a fighter, or something equally impractical." Karla rubbed her face. "God, the downside of command. Keeping everybody happy!"

# 47

Grazier looked as if someone had stuffed habanero peppers in his mouth. His face had turned a brilliant shade of red, which was a considerable achievement given his complexion. Or he was on the verge of a stroke.

Savage, on the other hand, might have had lit dynamite up his ass given the way he trembled, fists knotted at his sides. And the fire in his eyes was nothing nice to contemplate.

I told them casually. "I need you to trust me. I want to call Chief Raven back."

At a barely civil nod from Grazier, I took my phone from the general and pressed the recall button.

On the second ring, Raven answered, saying, *"Yes, sir?"*

"Chief, it's Ryan. I just wanted you to know that I have every confidence in you and your team. Keep me informed, and I'll back you to the hilt. I'll be calling back in a bit."

I pressed the end button and leaned back in my chair, arm braced on the desk, calm eyes on Grazier's.

"What *the fuck* did you just do?" Grazier's voice trembled.

"I know Karla Raven, sir. Hell, I know them all. My suggestion to both of you is to go on about your business. Let my people do what they do best."

Savage bellowed, "Let me get this straight. You want us to turn a bunch of psychopathic *nuts* loose on Skientia?"

"Major," I said in my calm-the-psychiatric-emergency voice, "the general, here, already understands the caliber of talent they possess. He's willing to cut them a deal as a means of harnessing that talent." I shifted my gaze to Grazier. "But, with due respect, Eli, along with putting them in harness, you'd want to pull back on their reins. Do that, and you're going to have a disaster."

Grazier—conniving and high-functioning psychopath that he was—parsed out his advantages against potential disaster. I added in a more congenial tone, "Eli, you once said I was one of the smartest people you knew. Trust me on this."

"You really place that much faith in them? Because if it goes wrong, it's my ass on the line, too."

"General, I'll wager they tie this whole thing up with a bow. And they'll do it within a week." I pointed at the bare corner of my desk. "And if they do, you owe me a Ducati 916. Pristine."

Grazier's flat gaze slowly morphed into a skeptical grin. "Maybe you ought to commit me to Grantham for taking your bet, but all right. They've got a week."

"And you'll back them?"

"Yeah . . . within reason."

"*General, sir!*" Savage struggled for control. "With all due respect, do you understand the stakes involved here?"

Grazier spread his hands in mock surrender. "Come on, Sam. What have we got? The tomb, Prisoner Alpha, your extraction in Egypt, the abduction in Washington, compromised communications? Skientia's behind it. We know that. But we can't do a damned thing about it. Or do you have some magic rabbit you can pull out of a hat?" A beat. "So tell me, Sam. What do we do next?"

Savage slowly deflated.

Grazier chuckled humorlessly. "Tim, call Chief Raven. Ask her what she needs from us."

I nodded, butterflies in my stomach as I pushed the recall button.

# 48

"This can't be!" Kilgore sat at the central lab table, papers scattered to the point of spilling into the sink. Her hot gaze should have scorched a hole in the report she held. Reid perched on the lab stool beside her, his forehead etched by a frown.

Across from them, Bill Minor had a knowing smirk on his lips. The man kept rising up on his toes, then dropping flat on his heels as if possessed of a barely contained energy.

Reid was fully aware of the implications arising from the Carbon-14 analysis. Kilgore's attention remained fixed on that final figure on the dating column.

"Impossible," she whispered.

"Face it," Reid told her. "You've got a three-thousand three-hundred and thirty-five–year date, plus or minus fifty years. That puts the mummy's age in conformity with the tomb architecture and the artifacts inside it. Yusif, who's dug more of these things than any man alive, said the chariots, statuary, and ceramic vases were consistent with the Eighteenth Dynasty."

"The guy is *modern*! Egyptians didn't have orthopedic surgery. They didn't machine *titanium* screws. They didn't have mitochondrial haplotype C. And they sure as hell didn't have modern dentistry like we see in the buccal surface of that one remaining molar!"

*And they didn't bury electrical boxes with their mummies!*

"It's got to be the sample," Reid suggested. "Maybe we screwed something up. Maybe lab contamination."

Her troubled brown eyes betrayed a reluctance to agree. "It's got to be the lab."

"Run it again," Minor suggested from the other side of the counter. "Physics are physics. It's going to come back the same."

If Reid hadn't known that Minor was the kind of man who'd break every bone in his body, he would have loved to have smacked that silly grin right off his face.

Instead, he fixed the guy with a hard glare. "All right, Bill. Why don't you come clean? Every time we've asked, you've avoided the question, but those goons who murdered Yusif's men, they were yours, weren't they? Skientia was behind this whole thing."

Minor gave a faint shrug of the shoulders, expression noncommittal.

"You *murdered* twenty-three innocent Egyptians? *Why?*"

"Because, Doctor Farmer, when you actually located the tomb, proved its existence, it became glaringly apparent that the Egyptians— once they learned of its value—would have canceled the export permit. They would have seized everything. Botched the investigation into the tomb and its contents."

Reid's temper frayed. "Wouldn't it have been cheaper to have just bribed the Egyptian ministers? I *knew* those men! And you'd have killed Yusif, too! *He's my friend, damn it!*"

Minor extended a hand as Reid started around the counter. "Stay where you are, Dr. Farmer. You can be just as productive with a broken jaw as you are whole."

Reid stopped short; anger, and frustration continued to brew.

Kilgore, in a remarkably calm voice, asked, "Why call in the military, Bill? And after they arrived, why on earth would you order your hired mercenaries to fire on them?"

Minor's lips bent in a sour smile. "You were sealed in the tomb. I needed the sarcophaguses and you out of there. I needed it done both rapidly and efficiently, and without Egyptian hassles. And I didn't need a bunch of gun-toting, money-grubbing adrenaline junkies, who'd already screwed up the operation, telling wild tales."

He gestured dismissively with his right hand. "Besides our Latin expert had translated Dr. Farmer's superb recordings. We knew exactly who was in that tomb."

"And who is he?" Kilgore asked.

"The guy's name is Fluvium. Means "river" in Latin, but it's also apparently a common name in the time he comes from."

"I don't understand," Reid growled.

"Of course, you don't, Dr. Farmer. That's why we chose you for the job. You're an American archaeologist. Not an Egyptologist. You don't have extensive training in classical archaeology, no knowledge of either Latin or ancient Egyptian, but you're a meticulous excavator. And, fortunately for us, Yusif, too, was a digger. He always relied on colleagues, epigraphers, to translate the hieroglyphs."

Kilgore crossed her arms defiantly. "Let me get this straight. You knew you were looking for a guy named Fluvium? In a tomb in Egypt? What's so special about him? Why take all these risks? My God, the cost has to be astronomical. Not to mention pissing off not only the Egyptians, but the whole American government! It just doesn't—"

"Make any sense?" Minor laughed. "Oh, yes it does."

"Explain," Kilgore snapped.

"The phrase over the tomb door," Minor told her. "*Tempus devincero.* Translated it means, 'I conquered time.'"

Reid worked his fingers. "Maybe you'd better tell me why that's important."

Bill Minor pointed at the door in the rear. "He came from the future. Or maybe I should say . . . a future. He and his wife went back in time to ancient Egypt. Problem was . . . he got stranded."

Reid's jaw dropped. Kilgore looked stunned, her dark eyes widening, and then she burst into laughter, barely managing to ask, "And you know this . . . how?"

"Because his wife appeared in one of our labs. Pop! There she was. Unfortunately for us, our investigators didn't realize the implications until long after she'd been hauled off as an intruder. She left behind an electrical device—the design of which we'd never seen."

Reid barely caught himself before he glanced at the electrical box they'd taken from the sarcophagus.

*No! Impossible!*

Minor was saying, "Given the woman's ignorance of our reality, she had no clue of what had gone wrong, or where she was. When our lab security tried to interrogate her, they thought she was crazy, so they turned her over to Los Alamos security, and eventually DHS locked her away in a federal mental institution."

Reid felt his anger draining away, and actually broke into chuckles.

"You're being scammed, Bill. Someone must be bilking you out of billions."

"Actually, billions will be made, Dr. Farmer. So, please, keep your anger in check. Do that, and you might even cash in on a tidy nest egg yourselves. If you promise to act like professionals, I'll even allow you to be present when the Domina comes to visit tomorrow."

"The Domina?" Kilgore asked.

Minor gave her a superior grin. "The woman who popped into our lab. She's coming to see her husband . . . who died in Egypt three thousand five hundred years ago."

# 49

Falcon sat on the corner of the hotel room bed and read the label on his bottle of Mirtazapine over and over. Of all the hotels why did they have to stay in the St. Regis in Aspen?

The hotel didn't look anything like the one in New York, but just stepping into the lobby, let alone the plush room, had opened the doors in his memory.

Images from his past kept looping in his mind. Once again, he was in the St. Regis in New York; his Aunt Celia stood at the room door, her arms crossed.

*"James, I know I can never be a mother and father for you. They're gone. I'm all that you and your sister have left. You know that I never wanted to be a parent. But life doesn't always work out the way we planned. Now, I need you to promise you'll do your homework. I'll be back late. I can't help it. Just do your work."*

The memory looped again, starting with his tantrum—a demand to watch television. His aunt opening the suite door to his bedroom. Her anguished face stiffened as he ranted. Then she crossed her arms. *"James, I know I can never be a mother and father for you and your—"*

"Falcon?" Cat's voice fractured the visual memory, if not Celia's words. He started rolling the bottle of Mirtazapine in cadence to Aunt Celia's speech, listening to the pills rattling inside.

"Falcon?" Cat stood in the door the way as his aunt had, but instead of crossing her arms, she walked in, concern marring her delicate face. "Are you all right?"

"Memory loop," he told her unsurely. "It's . . . unsettling. Everything is unsettling. I know this. When the looping starts, I mean. It's a balance, a very delicate balance."

"What is?" She started to reach for him, then pulled her hand back when he flinched. The uncertainty in her eyes frightened him.

"The meds," he murmured. "I mean, I can take another one." He shook the bottle of Mirtazapine. "Higher blood concentration. It'll stop the depression. Depression spawns the loops. Stop it cold. I'll be fine. No loops. The paranoia will recede."

"Then take one."

"Can't. I mean . . . Edwin, he's pulling up the schematics, isn't he?"

"I don't know how he does it, but he's combed the records in the County Clerk's office. Fortunately, in Aspen, everything's regulated. But then, on a hunch, he found the architect's name. He's trying to breach the firm's security. Figures that he'll get a better floor plan of the Skientia mansion."

Falcon nodded, pursed his lips. Aunt Celia's voice had dropped to a mumbled background chatter. He struggled to keep his hands from turning the pill bottle. It wanted to rotate like a spinning top. "Dissociative identity disorder's a curse."

"It's just a different brain structure than the rest of us have. Your neurons orient and interact in their own way. It's what makes you brilliant . . . allows you to see what the rest of us can't."

"That's why . . . That's why I can't, you know, take the Mirtazapine. It will dull my wits, cloud everything up. You see? That's the balance. I was fine at Grantham. Everything was ordered. I wasn't afraid . . . wasn't emotional."

"I realize how stressful this is. Hiding and breaking into stores. God knows, I'm a nervous wreck, too. There's nothing to be afraid of now," she told him with a smile. "The Skipper came through. We drove right past the main gate at Peterson Air Force Base, were escorted to that nice little jet, and Winny flew us to Aspen. No questions asked."

He blinked, then looked at her. "Cat, you don't . . ." His voice was looping, too. "You don't . . . understand."

"I don't?"

"It's Skientia. They're behind this. I could almost see it, the pattern . . . what they're after. And then the switch flipped in my head, the looping started. And once it starts, I can't stop it."

"What about the major? What does he say?"

"He's not here. It's just my aunt, I keep seeing her, hearing her voice.

Not just in the loop, but she's whispering to me." He rolled the pill bottle faster. "I know it's a hallucination. But she's still here."

Cat took the pill bottle from his hand and frowned as she read the label. "What if I cut just a sliver from the pill, just enough to calm the effects, maybe five or ten milligrams?"

"I've got to have my wits, Cat . . . Got to have my wits. I need my whole brain."

"Look at me, Falcon. That's it. Fix on my eyes. The chief and Winny are out scouting sporting goods stores. Tonight, after they close, they're going to, uh, *acquire* the things we need to break into Skientia's mansion up there on the hill.

"In the meantime, Edwin is going to come up with the floor plans and some idea of Skientia's security. When he does, we will need you—and the major if he's around. You've got to look at it all, study it, then close your eyes and move the pieces around."

He nodded, a burst of tension spilling through him. "You think you can get the dosage right?"

She arched a slim eyebrow. "You think it's more complicated than bioweapons?"

"Now I feel very reassured."

"Chemistry is chemistry, Falcon. Since it's impossible to peel Edwin away from his keyboard, I'm going to go down to the business center and do a little Internet research. Probably call the Skipper. Between us, I'm betting we can tailor a cocktail to hit that balance."

"Please do. If they're going to break into Skientia, the chief is really going to need the major. He's done this sort of thing a lot."

"Let's see what I can do."

"If we fail, Cat, our people are going to die."

# 50

Karla Raven was humming to herself as she pushed the luggage cart down the quiet halls of the St. Regis. The great thing about robbing sporting goods stores was that they had an ample supply of shopping bags. The chore of carting out the loot was thus made considerably easier.

The good thing about the St. Regis was that they had handy bellmen to help unload the loot, and really nice polished-brass luggage carts to wheel it all up to the rooms—even if the anxious bellmen had to be dissuaded from helping. She'd left them both with a good tip, and the assurance that they could snag the two carts from the hallway in ten minutes.

"So?" Karla asked over her shoulder, "Is this trip all that I promised?"

Swink chuckled as she pushed her cart. "First a Jet Ranger, then that cute little Gulfstream? Not to mention burglary, breaking and entering, stolen cars, hijacking sporting goods stores? What's not to like?" A pause. "Well, there's you, of course."

"Maybe one of these days we can settle that, just the two of us. But in the meantime, we're making a pretty good team."

"I might have forgiven you a little if you'd let me really fly that Gulfstream."

"Just 'feeling her out,' as you put it, almost had Falcon catatonic and Edwin hurling his lunch. The barrel rolls and other shit you wanted to do? Maybe some other time when we really need it."

Karla stopped at the suite door, used her keycard, and with Cat's help rolled the cart inside.

"Everything turn out all right?" Cat asked.

"Clockwork." Karla glanced at Falcon where he sat at the desk staring at Edwin's computer screen. "How's Falcon?"

Cat narrowed her dark eyes. "Rocky."

"Explain."

"Falcon functions best in a stable and familiar environment, one he can control. The past forty-eight hours have been anything but that. I caught him on the verge of what's called a psychotic break. Think of it as a descent into catatonic paranoia. That's the bad news."

"And the good news?"

Cat ran nervous fingers through her thick hair. "The good news is that he recognizes it and is willing to accept help. I called the Skipper, did some research, and I think I've got his meds balanced. But I'm no psychiatrist."

"But he'll get better, right?" Swink's pensive gaze fixed on Falcon.

"Schizo-DID isn't something that just goes away. It's a physical reality. Like your red hair, Major, you can't will it to grow out black no matter how hard you try. Our problem is that if we overtreat Falcon's symptoms, it dulls those creative parts of his brain that we're depending on."

"So?" Karla asked, "What's the solution?"

"The solution is that he needs just enough medication to keep his brain chemistry from crashing into paranoia and depression, but not enough to dull his creativity."

"How's that working?"

"I think we're okay. I'm keeping a constant watch on the movement of his hands and feet. Earlier, when he was on the edge, he was twitching like an electrified rabbit."

"And Edwin?" she asked. "How's his—"

"He's got them by the balls." Cat's midnight eyes twinkled. "Chief, he's downloaded the complete architectural designs for that big *hacienda* up on the hill. Lifted them right out of the architect's mainframe in Vancouver. Falcon's looking at them on the monitor right now."

Karla glanced at Winny. "Well, let's go take a look."

She padded over and bent over Falcon's shoulder. "Heard you had a rough one."

Falcon barely glanced up. "Cat helped. Then that asshole Rudy showed up and started ragging all over me." He pointed to a basement room on the diagram. "There, Chief. That's my call. At least for the two mummies they stole. According to Edwin's investigation of recent contractors and medical suppliers in the Aspen area, that's the only place they could have built a lab. It had the necessary water, power, and sewer, as well as an evacuation hood, you know, for noxious gases and stuff, installed in the original construction. This door leads to a dressing room, and here's the sterile-environment room with a completely contained atmosphere."

Edwin look up, his dark eyes weary. "They put in an X-ray machine, autoclave, and bought a really expensive microscope two months ago."

"What about Gray and the missing archaeologists?"

Falcon tapped the screen. "If they are lucky, this whole hallway is bedrooms, ten of them. Each with a full bath." He paused. "If they are unlucky, they could be anywhere down here on this basement level in one of these small concrete-lined rooms."

Karla studied the layout and rubbed the back of her neck. Whoever designed the place had an eye for security. "I guess I've got my work cut out for me."

"The major doesn't think you should go in there alone, Chief."

She glanced down into Falcon's worried eyes. "Tell him he's welcome to come with me."

Falcon's gaze darted to the couch across from the TV. "You know, she doesn't make those offers to just anyone." Then after listening for a moment, he returned his attention to Raven. "The major thinks you'd be better off taking Winny with you. She's at least combat trained."

"Whoa-up there!" Swink gave them a startled look from where she was laying out climbing ropes, carabineers, boots, and other gear. "Sure, I'm combat trained. In Strike Eagles, not ground ops. You want the place bombed and strafed, I'm your gal."

"You did fulfill the requirements for survival and evasion training, didn't you, Major?" Falcon asked.

"You betcha. I can eat worms and crawl through drainages and brush with the best of them. That's not climbing walls, slipping down corridors, and silencing armed guards."

Karla made a cutting motion with her hand. "It's my show. Period." She paused. "Now, what have you got from Google Earth? I want to see the place. How it sits in the topography, what the best approach is."

Ten minutes later, she was anything but happy. "The thing's built like a friggin' medieval castle. Sheer walls perched on rock outcrops, small windows on the lower floors, and those top-floor windows are solid plateglass. Even as rocky and steep as the terrain is, they've fenced the entire perimeter. My guess is the fence is wired, and they've got remote cameras and motion detectors all over the approaches to the house."

"How 'bout that heliport next to the tennis court?" Edwin asked.

"Even if we could steal a stealth bird, they've got enough eyes and ears that they'd have their arms out to catch me if I tried to insert on a fast line. Same if I dropped in with a parachute. Too much movement."

"According to Skientia's payroll," Edwin told her, "they keep thirty security guys on staff. All of them hired through this Talon Group. You ever heard of them?"

"Military contractors." Karla had a cold feeling in her gut. "Even other contractors are suspicious of them. They go for hard cases—the kind who get dishonorable discharges. These guys are definitely *not* your standard-issue rent-a-cops."

"Even the best succumb to a routine," Falcon noted. "Take longer coffee breaks, that sort of thing."

"Not if they've got Gray, archaeologists, and high-value sarcophagi recently stolen from a two-star like Grazier. Whoever's in charge up there will have them frosty." She sipped at the cup of coffee Cat had made her. "I mean, I can do it, but it's going to be messy."

Edwin looked up. "Messy how?"

"Like killing people messy," she told him. "And I don't have a silenced pistol."

"Thought you'd just sneak up and do Ninja shit," Edwin countered. "Like in the movies?"

"Yeah. That generally come out okay for the good guys."

She gave him a playful smack on the head. "Keep dreaming, ET. You're sure you can take down their security?"

"Piece of cake, Chief. But they're going to know 'cause I gotta crash it. Less'n I was in there. But we been all over that. Getting my skinny black ass into that central control?" He shook his head. "Not even Falcon can figure a way to do that. Not in the week we got."

Karla chewed her thumb as she studied the building schematics.

"There." She pointed. "Once we're on the grounds, that's the weak spot. The kitchen entrance. Do you agree, Falcon?"

"The major thinks it's feasible. The kitchen has a dedicated driveway, entrance, and delivery door, but it's essentially isolated in the basement. The only access to the house is either up these stairs next to the stoves, or by means of the dumbwaiter; with a choke point like that, you can bet they'll have cameras and some of those guards posted. It wouldn't surprise me if the kitchen staff has to use pass keys to travel back and forth."

"You're not exactly blowing my skirt up, Falcon."

"Didn't know you owned one," Edwin muttered.

"I don't. Outside of my dress uniforms. Wherever in the hell they are."

"The major and I agree it would take two people," Falcon said softly. "Chief, however you do it—" he shook his head, "—someone's got to watch your back."

Cat stunned them all when she cried, "I'm an idiot!"

"Nothing new there," Swink muttered where she was loading .45 ACP into a pistol magazine.

Karla turned. "What are you thinking, Cat?"

Cat bent over Falcon's shoulder and stared at the diagram. "Where is the HVAC accessed?"

He pointed. "The physical plant's accessed through the kitchen here. From there, air is ducted through the entire structure."

Cat frowned at the display. "How hard is it to get from the kitchen to the physical plant? I mean, for one person?"

"Through this door. But that's as far as you go." Falcon pointed. "See? To get to the rest of the house you have to backtrack to the stairs or dumbwaiter."

Cat asked, "Could you get me into that room?"

"Sure. But from there I still have to get past the stairway choke-point."

"Then, I think I know how to make this work." Cat straightened. "I need the keys to the SUV and all of our cash. Surely there's a grocery open, but I might need Edwin to break me into a welding supply, or a hardware store."

"What are you up to?"

Cat gave her an enigmatic curl of the lips. "Trust me, Chief. It's about time I started pulling my weight."

After she was gone, Falcon was smiling in subtle satisfaction. Karla asked, "What are you gloating about?"

"The statistical probability of success just rose significantly, Chief. And the major has some suggestions, but it's still going to take two on the inside."

# 51

The Humvee lurched and rocked as Weaver followed the faint two-track out of the village called Tallach 3. Karla bounced and swayed in the passenger seat. Behind her, Pud Pounder was standing, his upper body propped in the turret behind "Ma Deuce," the Browning .50.

Before them, the desert valley remained flat as a lake bottom, the terrain illusory. The late afternoon sun glinted as it slanted toward the craggy and steep mountains in the distance. Up high, Haji was watching dust boil out behind the vehicles as Bravo Platoon sped across the hardpan flats.

Karla and her platoon raced for the series of rocky outcrops that stuck up from the flats just outside the canyon mouth. Her SEAL snipers would own those outcrops long before a Marine convey passed over that road sometime around midday tomorrow—and every insurgent within a hundred kicks knew when and where that convoy would pass.

"We're on all their scopes now." Weaver had his right hand atop the steering wheel. He glanced in the driver-side mirror. "Socket's sniffing right up our ass. That reaming you gave him sure cured his lollygagging attitude, Chief."

She keyed her mic. "Just a reminder, boys, sloppy means dead."

Golf's voice came through her earbud. "You sure they'll be able to figure out where we're going, Chief? Or should we have sent them a pajama-gram with a map?"

"They're not stupid." Then she smiled. "Mostly."

She ran it through her mind again, imagining the terrain, which of her snipers would go where, how their fields of fire would overlap as the insurgents came boiling out of the drainage channels.

"Jabac Junction ahead, Chief," Weaver said.

The irregular collection of mud-and-stone huts seemed to rise from the desert *hardpan on which they'd been built. She thought of the few families that still lived there.*

*Weaver was roaring down on it, the engine whining.*

*Of course there was a chance of ambush, but the IR drone reconnaissance hadn't detected any appreciable movement toward the town. The thermal signatures had been correct for the fifteen or so people who lived there.*

*It lay at the outskirts, just out from the first squat mud hut, a basket, tilted onto its side . . .*

Pounding. An insistent knock.

Karla Raven gasped, jerked herself awake. She struggled for breath, clawing hair back from her sweat-dampened face.

A hotel room. Blinds drawn. Nice bed. Too many pillows.

*Rap! Rap! Rap!*

She climbed out of bed, shrugged on a T-shirt and managed not to fall over as she dragged sweatpants over her hips. Tossing her hair back, she padded across the room to the door.

"The sign says Do Not Disturb. I don't even need towels!"

"Chief?" a familiar voice asked.

Karla blinked and dared to use the peephole. The Skipper stood there. She made a face and opened the door. Ryan had dressed in a western-style shirt and Levi's, clumpy boots on his feet.

"Hey, Skipper." She squinted at him. "You're here. As in . . . *here.*"

"Glad to see you're still observant." Ryan gave her a conspiratorial wink as he entered.

Through narrowed eyes, she studied the man following Ryan.

"Ah, Major Savage." She shut the door. "Why am I getting a really bad feeling about this?"

"Sorry to disturb your sleep, Chief." Ryan acted awkward, his hands having nothing to do but fiddle. Savage was giving her the eye. No wonder. She had to look like shit.

"You're going in? Tonight?" Savage asked.

She gave him her best I-think-you're-a-worm look. "We've got five days to hand Skientia to your boss on a silver platter. The fact that you're here, in my room, interrupting my sleep, tells me that our mission success probability just got flushed down the toilet."

"Easy, Chief." Ryan raised a calming hand. "Major Savage is here to help."

She stepped up to Savage, looked into his hard eyes, and then inspected him up and down as if he were a side of maggot-infested meat. "With all due respect, sir, how do I know if he can even find his balls without tweezers and a magnifying glass? The last time the good major and I met, he didn't exactly score well on the FFIR." The Friendly Force Information Requirement that identified good and bad guys.

"Do you trust me enough to take my word for it?" Ryan asked, going for her soft spot.

She sighed and throttled the desire to unleash her close quarters combat skills on Savage. "I don't know, Skipper. You bringing *him* here? Makes me wonder."

"How's Falcon?" Ryan asked, as if to divert her.

"He's better, sir. Cat's cooked up that mixture of meds. Last I saw, he was in the suite, discussing the mansion layout with Major Marks and Theresa."

"And the rest?"

"Cat and Edwin took off to work on some idea of hers. Major Swink should be sacked out. She's going to be at the airport tonight in case everything goes into the crapper. My extraction-of-last-resort is off the mansion roof after she steals the flight-for-life chopper."

"You have got to be kidding," Savage muttered under his breath.

She shot him a dismissive look. "Did you know that Skientia keeps thirty men on payroll just to secure that mansion up there? You ever hear of Talon Group? They hire—"

"Chief, my guys took out more than a dozen Talon mercs in Egypt. Yeah, I know Talon. And the kind of guys they hire."

"I doubt it will be all thirty of them, and we're working on ways of evening the odds. But when I go in there, I'm going to have to move fast. We think we've located Gray and the two captives, and I have a pretty good chance of getting them out. Those sarcophagus things? That might take another day and another way."

"You're going in alone?" Savage asked.

"I could ask Skientia to call in another thirty guys. Even the odds a little."

Ryan said, "It doesn't have to be tonight."

She gave him a hard look. "And you know that how, sir?"

"We can get more people to back you up. Maybe serve a warrant and search the place."

"Begging the Colonel's pardon, but just how many people in General Grazier's organization know you're here? If we're right, and his communications are compromised, this whole thing could already be blown."

Savage said, "As of this moment, Chief, four people know. The three of us in this room and General Grazier. He agreed to it in a very secure location."

"How secure?"

"My garage, Chief." Ryan spread his hands. "We're on our own. Like being in the deep end of the pool with no flotation."

"SEALs thrive in deep water, sir."

"And when do you initiate the operation?"

"Nineteen-thirty hours."

"Brief me in your suite at fifteen hundred, Chief. I'm in. Screwy as this whole thing is." Major Savage turned to Ryan. "It's just after eleven and this place must have one hell of a restaurant. Let's let the chief finish her beauty nap. She needs all the help she can get."

Savage walked out the door, leaving Ryan with a confused look on his face.

Raven crossed her arms. "Your call, Skipper. Is he here to screw us?"

"I don't think so, Chief."

"Good, 'cause I'd hate to have to kill him."

At the door, Ryan suddenly stopped and felt over his pockets and billfold.

"What did you take, Chief?"

"Sorry, sir. Too asleep to think of it."

"And you're infiltrating a mansion later this afternoon?"

"Be frosty by then, sir."

# 52

Falcon sat with his eyes closed, the schematic of the house seeming to glow on the dark screen of his eyelids. One more time he ran the operation, visualizing the drive up to the gate. Once through, his imaginary vehicle climbs the curved drive, splitting off to the small kitchen lot. The car doors open, two human figures emerge. At that moment Edwin crashes the house security system.

Two figures penetrate the kitchen door. One breaks off to the right and through the machine room entrance as the other neutralizes the kitchen staff. But that critical stairway . . . ?

"And from there," Major Marks interrupted, "you've got no idea, Falcon."

"Why are you bothering me when I need to concentrate?"

"Because, boy, this is a battlefield, not an intelligence analysis. You don't have enough intel. Your opponent is going to have troops dispersed in ways you can't anticipate. As soon as their computers crash, they've got a protocol. They've planned for this, Falcon. Thought it through and practiced their response. As smart as Skientia is, they'll be two jumps ahead of you on the game board."

"Stop it! Just stop it! I need to think." The pressure continued to build.

Falcon could feel the loop flickering just behind his consciousness.

Aunt Celia's angry voice struggled to pierce the mist in which he'd hidden it.

She was going to win; it was just a matter of time.

Fear continued to eat at him.

He wanted to cry.

**E** dwin studied Falcon through half-lidded eyes. *Tell me the dude ain't about to pop like an overcharged soda bottle.*

Edwin caressed the keyboard with his long fingers; worry about Falcon's condition built. Damn, Cat had made those pills according to formula, hadn't she? And psych drugs took time to have any affect.

*And if Falcon weirds out on us, what then? He's the damn brains.*

Where he lay on the bed, Falcon's face flickered with emotion, and he snapped, "Of course I know what a protocol is!"

Edwin shot him a worried look, then glanced down at his screen, seeing the image the security officer in the Skientia mansion would be seeing: A series of status boxes, all reporting normal conditions.

Within the hour Cat and Raven would be leaving the hotel, headed for the narrow road that led up the mountain.

"You can be such a pain in the ass sometimes," Falcon said testily. He remained propped on the bed, his back braced by pillows. ". . . Yes, yes!" A pause. "Don't interrupt me like that!"

The little hairs on the back of Edwin's neck began to prickle. Falcon just sat there, eyes closed, arguing with a hallucination. Understanding it was one thing, watching it, hearing it, that was something absolutely friggin' eerie.

"Falcon?" Edwin asked softly, his tension rising.

"Shhh!" Falcon answered.

*We're trusting Cat and Raven's ass to this dude?*

He thought back to the night he and Cat had just spent. There had been something charming about her fragile innocence as they broke into one store after another in search of the supplies she needed. He had reveled in demonstrating his mastery with alarms and locks; being placed in the role of protector had awakened something inside him. Some masculine sense that . . .

Falcon's eyes flashed open. "Edwin?"

"Whachu need?"

"You need to move on their system."

Edwin gave him an incredulous look. "Right now? You nuts?"

"Among psychiatric professionals that seems to be the general consensus. Take it down, give it ten minutes, and bring it up again without them being able to figure out how you did it."

"I do that once, they gonna be wise that I can do it again. Cat and Chief Raven, they got a couple of hours yet. I do this, that whole place gonna be buzzin' like a kicked anthill."

"Do it, Edwin. Now. Then turn it on again. Trigger the perimeter alarms randomly. Can you play them? Outsmart them for the next two hours? Drive them crazy with small stuff?"

"Sure." Edwin's pride flared.

"But you've already opened a back door, correct? One that will automatically restore communications to your computer here?"

"It's gonna take somebody a good half day tracing code to find it. But, Falcon, someone gonna eventually get smart enough to sever the phone line."

"And there's the gamble," Falcon said softly as he glanced at the corner of the bed and arched an eyebrow as if for someone's reassurance. Had to be that damn major.

"Falcon, look at me. Pay attention here. If you're wrong, it's Cat and Raven who'll pay the price." Edwin pointed a long finger. "You been paranoid crazy for a whole day. I been listening to you for an hour now, sounding stressed and weird. Now you want to change the plan? Let Skientia know they under attack? Without asking Chief Raven?"

"The challenge for you, Edwin, is to lead them a merry chase for as long as you can. Start simple with cyberattacks, probe their defenses. You said the entire house is computer controlled? When Cat and Raven make their move, raise the stakes. Turn off lights, furnace, fire alarms—"

"Falcon! *I said* they gonna *know* we coming!"

"Edwin, they've got a predetermined response for a breach at the main gate. Call it plan A. We want them to put Plan A in effect right now. Then we continue to jerk their chain for the rest of the day. While we do, we want them to move to Plan B, then C, and D. So many, in fact, that they're making up new plans by the time the chief and Cat try the main gate." He cocked an eyebrow. "Assuming, ET, that you're a good enough cyber-warrior to outsmart their countermeasures."

Edwin pulled at his chin, dubious. "Okay, Captain, but they're gonna know it's a diversion, right? So how 'bout I make them think this cyber-attack's a diversion from yet another diversion?"

"How many layers can you create?"

Through gritted teeth, Edwin said, "Falcon, if Cat gets hurt 'cause of this, you gonna wish you never born."

# 53

One by one, Reid prepared slides for Kilgore, carefully taking the swabs, flushing them, and staining them. Then he handed them to Kilgore where she sat at the microscope. She'd mount the slide and place her eyes to the view screen as she adjusted the focus. Reid checked the time. They'd been at it for six hours; his stomach reminded him of a twisted washcloth: empty and knotted.

No sooner did Kilgore refine the focus then she'd refer to the pollen catalog, scrolling through different morphologies in the key.

"Anything?" Reid asked.

"I've got just about every weed, grass, and fiber that grew in ancient Egypt. But not one speck of corn pollen, no sunflower, no tumbleweed, not a single pollen grain from an invasive or imported species. I've ID'd cotton fibers, goat and camel hair, cat fur, and strands of human hair. I've got indigenous insect parts and egg sacs. But not a single fiber of nylon, rayon, Dacron, or any other synthetic—and believe me, they're all over the world now. I mean . . ." she leaned back, brow furrowed, "I'm smarter than this. How'd they do it?"

"Do you want to look at the dental micrographs again?"

"No. The abrasion on the grinding surfaces of the teeth are completely consistent with an ancient Egyptian." She started, lifting a finger. "Wait. I'm forgetting the calculus."

"You talking mathematics?"

"Calculus, that's the hard stuff commonly called tartar that forms around base of the teeth. It traps microparticles from food and drink, cements them in layers. So, if I go to the bottommost layer, I'll get a sample of what he was eating immediately after his dental hygiene cratered."

"And?"

"And if I get a New World domesticate like corn, chocolate, tobacco, sunflower, potato, peanut, or chili, I've got him."

"Because none of those crops grew in Egypt before Columbus."

"Egyptians did somehow obtain cocaine and tobacco a couple hundred years BC, but not much, and it was definitely a luxury good. Someone transported it from South America, across the Atlantic, and to Egypt."

"Could that be the source of the mtDNA?"

"Not if he's from the Eighteenth Dynasty, *a thousand years* before even that tiny bit of trade."

Two black-clad guards pushed the lab doors open and stepped in. HK MP-5 submachine guns rested in slings across their chests. They took positions to either side of the door, hard eyes on Reid and Kilgore.

In their wake Bill Minor entered, and a tall woman followed.

Reid lowered his voice. "Fluvium's wife, as promised?"

"Yeah, sure. And I'm Cleopatra."

"Well, given your father's genetics . . ."

She elbowed him in the ribs.

Minor shot them a warning glance, but Reid's attention was on the woman. She didn't just enter the room; she owned it upon arrival. Her movements were fluid, her head erect as she surveyed the lab. She wore a flowing, almost iridescent blue gown that added to the effect. Bill Minor and his guards might have been superfluous.

It hit him: Here was a supernatural among mortals. And then she fixed on him with blue eyes so intense they almost made him gasp.

"You find him?" she asked in an accent-heavy contralto.

"I'm Dr. Reid Farmer." He offered his hand. "And this is my colleague, Dr. Kilgore France."

She ignored his hand. "You find Fluvium? In *sepulcrum*?"

"You mean in the tomb? Yes." Reid—aware of Kilgore's sudden bristling—crossed his arms defensively. "We dug where they told us and located a tomb, yes. Over the door was engraved the words, *TEMPUS DEVINCERO.*"

Her expression softened. *"Certo, quo declaissent."* Then, with resolution, she said, "I see him, please."

Bill Minor stepped forward, glancing sidelong at Reid and Kilgore.

"You'd better have taken all of your samples. I'm letting her in to see the deceased."

"The hoax, you mean?" Kilgore seemed entirely unaffected by the woman's magnetism.

The woman took Kilgore's measure, apparently unimpressed. "What is this word? Hoax? I do not understand."

Bill Minor said, "These scholars, um, *discipuli,* question your husband's age, um, *antiquitas.*"

"Damn right." Kilgore lifted a leg and tapped her ankle. "That broken leg and the screws, for one thing."

The woman's gaze intensified. "What you call crash. *Volocaelum.* Airplane. Yes?" She made what Reid took to be a flying motion with a cupped hand. "Seven *anni* gone . . . past. *Medicus* . . . what is word? Fix. Yes?" She bent down pointing at her lower calf. "Here."

Kilgore looked confused. "You admit it was only seven years since he was injured?"

*"Tempus invilatus non est, sed certumque inexorablum est."* With a bitter chuckle, she said in English, "Time always, in the end, wins." Then her face hardened, and she turned to Minor. "Take me. Please."

Reid watched as the woman was escorted past the doors and into the back. With a surreptitious glance at Kilgore, he followed. No one bothered to stop them.

The woman stepped up to the mummy where it lay on its raised gurney. Her fists curled into knots at her side; the muscles in her forearms rippled beneath alabaster skin. A vengeful saint might wear an expression like hers, filled with bottled rage, pain, and a soul-coring guilt that might have sucked at her very bones.

Then, like the rending of a mighty oak's heartwood, her right arm extended. Her hand was delicately boned, the fingers long and slender. The way she caressed the side of the corpse's desiccated face, sent a spear through Reid.

She was whispering softly now, the words a curious mixture of what Reid believed to be Latin, mixed with something else.

*"Me paenitet,"* She closed her eyes, head bowed, as if frozen.

*My God,* Reid thought uncomfortably, *can a woman really love that much?*

Kilgore was shifting beside him, a skeptical squint in her eyes. Surely, as a female, she had to be sensitive to the emotion conveyed by that sorrowful posture. Reid could hear Kilgore's teeth grinding.

He shot a sidelong glance at her just as Bill Minor's belt pager buzzed. A tiny voice carried loudly in the room as it said, *"We've got another security alert. Perimeter fence. Section six."*

Minor frowned, lifted his belt comm, and said, "Status?"

*"Nothing on visual, sir. Unit seven happened to be right there on patrol. He reports all clear, but I think whoever's been toying with us is at it again."*

"Keep me posted. With the Domina here, I want everyone on their toes."

*"Copy that."*

The woman might not have heard. Her reverential pose remained unbroken, her head bowed like a grieving goddess.

No sooner had Minor removed his hand, than the belt comm buzzed again, the voice saying, *"Sir? We've got more perimeter alarms. Sections three, five, and eight."*

"Analysis?" Minor's expression tightened.

*"Unsure, sir. I'm sending people to check each one. Either the hacker's getting better, or we've got a glitch."*

"No room for error here. Do I evacuate the Domina?"

*"I've got nothing on the screens, sir. Just the perimeter alarms going off. Assets on the ground report nothing out of the ordinary. Perimeter defense is deploying according to plan. Still no evidence of attempted infiltration."*

"When I find that asshole . . ." Minor growled. "Bastard's had us running in circles for hours now."

As he replaced his belt unit, he stepped forward, saying, "Domina, excuse me. Security reports an irregularity. I really need you to return to the upper level. We may have to fly you out of here in a hurry."

She started—as if from a dream—and fixed him with her remarkable eyes. *"Pericula?"*

"We don't know, ma'am. But a lot of people would love to get their hands on you. Please, um, *placere.*"

*"Ad aeternum, tu amo, Fluvium,"* she whispered to the mummy, then bent down and brushed a kiss across the thing's desiccated forehead. Then she drew herself to her full height and took a resolute breath. Like a wounded queen, she walked out with her head high, tawny curls spilling down her back.

Reid caught the words, *"Dzibilchaltun"* and *"Xlacah"* as she crossed the lab.

"Dzibilchaltun? The Xlacah cenote?" he asked. "You know it? In the Yucatan?"

Her remarkable eyes flew wide. She stared at him, disbelieving. "You understand me?" Then she rattled off a string of words.

Reid cried, "That's Yucatec! A Maya Indian dialect. I heard a lot of it while I was working in Mexico. I dug at Dzibilchaltun."

Her incredulous gaze bored into his like blue lasers.

"Dzibilchaltun," he repeated. "The Maya city just south of Merida. You've obviously been there if you can speak Yucatec. It's the indigenous language."

"I know no Merida. But yes, Dzibilchaltun, the *dzonot* Xlacah." A faint smile bent her lips. *"In chi'hi'lama Ch'olti.* I speak . . . read *Ch'olan* language. Fluvium, he and I *discipuliae,* how you say, students. At the *collegium. Nubere,* ah, the word, *matrimonium?* That is marry?" She crossed her fingers, as if the gesture would explain.

"We call it matrimony. You and Fluvium?" He pointed back at the sterile room. "You married him there? In Dzibilchaltun? As students? How long ago?"

*"Sedecim.* In *Ch'olan: wuklahun.* You say seventeen years. My years. Perhaps not yours." With a tilt of her head toward the sterile room, she bitterly added, *"Certe,* certainly not his."

"What did you study there?" Reid asked, aware that both Bill Minor and Kilgore were giving them stunned looks.

"What you call theoretical physics. The finest *collegia mathematici* . . . All are in Dzibilchaltun."

"And you know the mathematics?" he asked, thinking of the Mayan glyphs he'd seen in the tomb. He grabbed for a piece of paper and clawed his pen from his pocket. He was uncomfortably aware of her presence as she leaned next to him. He began the Mayan notations, a dot for one, two dots for two, and so on.

*"Crudis urina!* You know this? In your world? You have studied *mathematicus* in Yucateca?"

"Many archaeologists have worked out the Mayan mathematics. We can even translate most of the language. Slowly, surely, we're learning their history, who their rulers were."

"Were?" she asked, her voice curiously hollow. "No more?"

"The Yucateca remain. They help excavate the heritage of their ancestors. But Dzibilchaltun, as you surely know, is nothing but ruins."

Her blue gaze cooled until it became glacial. "No *collegia*? No physics at Dzibilchaltun in your world?"

"Dzibilchaltun is a dead city. Abandoned almost a thousand years ago. The brush, the *brasada,* grew over it."

In disgust she said, *"Nequam populi, inanus orbis."*

Bill Minor's belt comm buzzed, and the disembodied voice said, *"Sir? We think the alarms are a diversion. Someone is attempting to download our system. I think the firewall stopped them cold for the moment."*

"And if they succeed?" Minor asked, lifting the comm.

*"Our guess is that they're trying to access our files. They've made two attempts already."*

"Keep them *out!*" The corners of his eyes tightened. "Meanwhile, nobody lets up. I want every alarm checked, and then double-checked."

*"Yes, sir."*

*"Nequam populi, inanus orbis?"* Reid asked. "What does that . . ."

The lights went out, leaving him blinking in the sudden blackness.

"Son of a bitch!" Minor's voice boomed. His flashlight beam shot a white cone across the room. "Domina, I need you to take my hand. That's it. We're going to get you out of here now."

"But *libris*, the book? *Vitrum amphoram . . .* the container? Most important: *Did you find cerebrum?*" she was almost frantic about that last.

"We've got to go now!" Minor snapped. *"Periculum!"*

Reid started forward, only to feel Kilgore's hand tighten on his elbow. She leaned close, whispering, "It could be that Savage and his people have finally found us. Let's get our notes together, Reid. I want to take everything with me that I can."

He watched the flashlight waver as Bill Minor led Domina, or whatever her name was, from the room. In the afterglow the two armed guards stepped out behind them. The lab went pitch-black as the hallway doors slipped shut.

He heard clattering as Kilgore felt around on the workbench. A small LED flashlight cast a white glare—the light she used when peering into the mummy's orifices. "Let's go."

Reid helped her gather her notes, muttering, "She attended a college at Dzibilchaltun? Seventeen years ago? She says she speaks *Ch'olan*? How impossible is *that*?"

"Gotta hand it to her," Kilgore growled, "She's one hell of a bull-shitter."

"That woman was hurting," Reid insisted. Then, remembering her words, he tossed the papyrus book, the glass jar of liquid, and the heavy electrical box into a satchel.

"You're bullshitting yourself," Kilgore snapped acidly. "She looks to be in her mid-thirties. That mummy in there was in his sixties. Fake ancient Egyptian that he is, he didn't just die yesterday! That's an old corpse, decades old. And we're supposed to believe they were students together in an abandoned Maya city? Give me a break."

They'd no sooner stepped out the door than the lights flashed on.

"Shit," Kilgore growled.

"Come on," Reid muttered. "This is the only time since we've been here that the lab door hasn't been guarded. Let's go."

"Go where? You heard. They've got teams scouring the outside looking for intruders."

"Well . . . what the hell? I say we head for the kitchen. We know which door the food comes out of at mealtime. Maybe the cooks won't care. I've got this satchel, and you're carrying that pack of notes. The lab coats make us look official."

"And if we're caught?"

The lights flickered off again as they reached the bottom of the stairs.

"We say we're looking for Bill Minor. That we've found something important about the mummy."

"What?"

"You're smart. Think of something."

Her LED light flickered on and was pointed at his face, making him squint. "You're blinding me."

"No, I just want to see your eyes when I ask if you're as dumb as every other man on the planet."

"Huh?"

"Laserlike blue eyes, corn silk hair, tall and thin, wearing a stunning blue dress that accented every sensual curve? I look over and you're staring at her with dilated pupils. I watch your heartbeat and respiration increase, your posture adopting a presentation mode. And you're *nodding* while she tells you she married that corpse while studying physics in a Mayan ruin? I don't get it. You've suddenly gone dumb as a post?" Then she said in disgust, "Typical idiot male."

# 54

Cat Talavera closed her eyes as the Chevy Tahoe climbed the winding mountain road. For just this brief instant, she could drop into a numb limbo.

Against the black background of her eyelids, she replayed her eventful night. It had been one thing to concoct such a crazy scheme up in the hotel suite—another to actually pull it off.

*It's a miracle I'm not in jail!*

She and Edwin had sneaked from one closed business to another; it had been alternately thrilling . . . and disturbing. She'd marveled at the ease with which he'd neutered security systems. Then, with dazzling facility, he'd picked locks with what looked like simple bits of bent wire. Those were skills a person didn't just invent. They needed to be practiced, honed.

*I'm attracted to a thief?*

Each second she'd spent prowling through the dark aisles, fingering through canisters, peering at labels in the glow of a masked flashlight, her nerves had been humming with fear and worry. But for Edwin's reassuring smile and fearless swagger, she'd have never stuck it out. Fear of being jailed as a common burglar had stressed her to the point of throwing up.

"Ah, Cat, c'mon. It ain't like we's stealing. You heard the deal. General Grazier's gonna pay them back."

"Last time I landed in Grantham Barracks. Next time it might be Leavenworth."

To fill her list of chemicals and equipment, they'd had to hit a pharmacy, a welding supply distributor, and an agricultural pesticide company outside of Glenwood Springs. As nerve-racking as that had been, the hardest part began when she started cooking her little surprise. Getting the chemistry right would have been hard enough in a fully stocked lab. Attempting it with a Coleman stove on the SUV's open cargo deck reeked of insanity and sheer stupidity. She'd relied on a diving mask and hazard suit for protection as she mixed her concoction. Then had come the careful charging of the containers, and finally the pressurizing.

To her amazement, she'd filled the last metal cylinder at just after three in the afternoon. By then, she had a numbness of the brain that might have been due to fatigue or chemical contamination.

*I did it!*

Or had she?

She'd guessed at so much, knowing the basic chemistry, but making up proportions as she went. Pharmaceutical companies made stuff like this in tightly controlled labs. They had strict safety protocols, monitored product purity and safety at every step along the way.

*A Coleman stove on an SUV cargo deck? I must be out of my mind!*

And Edwin? She would have to think about that.

"Cat?" A voice intruded. "Wake up."

Late afternoon sunlight streaked through the Tahoe's side window. They were stopped on a curve, the asphalt road literally carved into the mountainside. She was staring at the tops of the conifers on one side; on the other, exposed rock gave way to roots and thin dirt before the firs rose like spears to tower over the road.

"We there?" Cat yawned.

"Just around the curve from the gate." Chief Raven pressed the call button on her cell phone, and said, "The next time your phone rings, crash the system." She listened for a moment, and answered, "Roger that."

Dropping the phone into the breast pocket of her black tactical vest, Raven gave Cat a searching look. "You ready, Doctor?"

"I should be scared to death." Cat opened the Tahoe's door and stepped out, her legs aching, her back stiff. "Instead, all I want to do is sleep."

"Sorry, girl. Time to have your shit wired tight."

Cat retrieved her backpack and slipped it over her shoulder. Then she carefully placed the squeeze bulb in her pocket and routed the tubing beneath her light white-cotton shirt. As a crowning touch, she tied the tails in front to leave her lean midriff exposed. Finally, she picked up the map and taped the tube to the underside, careful that it pointed in the right direction.

Cat looked down at her shorts, exposed legs, and heavy hiking boots. She felt half naked, but then that was the point. She was a lost hiker. No threat.

Adrenaline—better late than never—began to seep into her bloodstream. "Wish me luck."

"Make your own," Raven told her with conviction.

Cat squared her shoulders and plodded forward. Her breath was already coming in gasps, and she could feel sweat beginning to form.

"Come on, Cat. You robbed stores. Cooked a potentially deadly nerve agent on a Coleman stove. You helped plot an escape from a government insane asylum, and you're about to try to break into an armed compound. So, keep your wits, *chica*. Prove you've got more *cojones* than it took to try and kill yourself on the Capitol steps."

She was still talking to herself as she rounded the last curve. Almost gasping for breath, she forced herself up to the security box beside the big white-metal gate. The guard emerged, one hand on his sidearm. A second man stepped out and circled to the side. Both looked wary and dangerous.

"Hey! I'm lost." Cat tapped her map with her left hand before wiping sweat from her forehead.

"Where are you from, Miss?" Guard One asked, eyes searching the trees beyond her. He was a tall, muscular, blond man with a hatchet face.

"Would you believe a mental institution?" She tapped the map again. "Help me. I'm staying at Murry Gordon's. Murry said there was no way to get lost. So, like, where am I?"

"The Hollywood producer?" Guard Two asked, hand still on his holstered pistol. He watched her with rapacious brown eyes, as if imagining what the shorts and tied shirt hid.

"Duh!" Cat used her best LA accent. "Just how many other Murry Gordons you got up here? I mean, I haven't been gone that long. How lost can I be?"

Both guards continued taking their time running gazes up and down her body. For Cat, it was an uncomfortable sensation. She always wore utilitarian clothes, lab coats, comfortable shoes. The fact that men were ogling her body actually made her blush.

"Screw it," she muttered, figuring they weren't going for it. "Be jerks."

She turned around, wondering how she was going to tell Chief Raven that all they wanted to do was look.

"Wait," Guard One called, and stepped forward. "Let me see."

"We're on alert," the other reminded.

"We've been going crazy for three hours now," the first responded. "It's a cyberattack. Not a lost hiker."

She sidestepped to orient the map. "Can you point to where we are?"

Murry Gordon's house was marked with an X, the Hollywood producer actually owning property that bordered Skientia's.

"Yeah, you're right here," he said. "Just go back down the road. It's not more than a quarter mile."

"I must have turned the wrong way when I got off the path."

How did she get the other guy close enough?

She glanced at him. "Uh, you might keep your eyes open. Brad Pitt's really drunk, and he was out on the trail."

"Brad Pitt?" Guard Two asked, stepping a bit closer.

Cat asked coyly, "You guys ever get invited to one of Murry's parties?"

Guard Two laughed. "We're someone else's hired help."

"Come on down when you're off duty. I . . ." She turned, staring as a large blue helicopter rose above the roof, climbing slowly. It turned to the west, roaring as it soared out over the valley.

"Sorry," Guard Two said, his eyes on the chopper. "Much as we'd like to . . ." Cat lifted her map and squeezed the bulb in her pocket. Her aim was perfect.

She turned before the first guard could react and squirted him full in the face. Immediately, she stepped back, fearful of the aerosols.

The man tried to pull a big black pistol from its holster as his knees buckled. He collapsed sideways onto the pavement.

Guard One had a hand to his throat, his mouth working, eyes wide. He toppled backward, head smacking the asphalt like a hollow melon.

"Holy shit," she whispered. "It really works!"

The rasping of tires announced Chief Raven's approach.

Cat bent down, ripping the tube from the map, then, laboriously, she began the task of dragging the gasping guard out of Raven's way. The man's eyes were rolled back in his head, his mouth open, tongue hanging to the side.

Dios mio. *I didn't kill him, did I?*

Through the driver's-side window, she heard Raven say into her cell phone, "Cat's made us a hole. Open the gate, Edwin."

As Cat climbed into the Tahoe, Raven glanced off to the north where the blue helicopter was a tiny dot against the red cliffs. "Wonder who was in the helo?"

Cat took a deep breath as the gate began to swing open. "Come on, Chief. We've got more of this stuff to pump through the HVAC system." She paused. "Assuming nobody shoots us first."

"Yeah, well, that's always a possibility in this business." Raven punched the throttle, and the Tahoe lurched forward.

# 55

**B**efore going operative, Karla endured a queasy stomach, heightened senses, and the nervous tingling of muscle and bone. Not that anyone would ever catch a whiff of it. Not from CPO Karla Raven. As a female, her balls had to show more polished brass than any other man's in her platoon.

Knowing that thirty Talon security guys were waiting just behind that gate wasn't in any way comforting. Better that they'd been Al-Qaeda–trained Taliban. At least they got sloppy on occasion.

As she roared up the conifer-lined drive; her eyes searched for the first black-clad guard who would step out and level his weapon. She could name a thousand things that could go wrong, and her imagination, if given the time, could have invented thousands more.

Damn it, she was a SEAL, and SEALs did the impossible on a routine basis.

But generally with better intel and planning.

*Stow it. You're on a mission.*

That smug-assed Major Savage had sat through the entire briefing, his arms crossed, mouth clamped. His disbelieving eyes had practically screamed, "Idiocy!"

The Skipper's reaction had been almost as bad. She'd watched his worry grow the way a thunderhead did over a mountain. By the end, she'd seen a desperate fear behind his eyes.

*He thinks we're not going to make it.*

She jacked the wheel, sending them right on the narrow paved strip that dropped down toward the basement kitchen.

"So far, so good," she whispered.

Which, of course, was when the guard stepped out from behind a dark-green dumpster at the edge of the kitchen parking lot. Two Jeeps and a Subaru were nosed in against the wall, and Karla recognized the loading dock and rear kitchen door.

"Let me," Cat said unexpectedly, grabbing up her map. She was out the door the moment Karla slowed the Chevy.

"Hey!" Cat screamed. "What's with the damn gun? You a psycho or what?"

"You're in a restricted area. I need you to get down on the ground now, hands where I can see them!"

"Okay, so he's not buying her lost tourist bit," Karla murmured as she slipped the HK .45 from her hip holster. Her foot hovered over the accelerator, ready to stomp it if he stepped in front of the vehicle. Or whip the HK out the window for a left-handed shot if he didn't.

"Don't be a macho asshole!" Cat almost shouted, tears leaking out of her eyes. "You're scaring me. Here, see? Here on the map. We're looking for Murry's. You know, the director? We're supposed to be at the party." More tears, Cat obviously terrified. "We thought this was his house! Tell us where to go, and we'll leave!"

Then, to Karla's amazement, the guard actually frowned and lowered his gun as he stepped forward—right into Cat's spray. The guy dropped like he'd been spine-shot.

"I've got to get me some of that." Karla drove wide around the sprawled guard and backed up to the loading dock.

Cat was struggling with the guard, having rolled him over. Now she was tugging at the subgun's sling. Something about the image—Cat Talavera in her short shorts, boobs swaying in the high-tied white shirt as she tugged at a Heckler and Koch submachine gun—brought a chuckle to Karla's lips.

She stepped out and glanced up at the security cameras, which, hopefully, Edwin had blinded. They stared malignantly at her.

"Cat, come on!" She darted to the wall, approached the kitchen door, and tried the knob. To her complete surprise, it opened. Karla tucked her pistol tight against her breastbone and leaped through the opening.

Darting immediately to the right, pistol tracking her gaze, she scanned the kitchen. Three horrified middle-aged women gaped back at her. Two worked before the huge industrial stove, one with a spatula, the other with an oversized spoon. A third woman stood at a counter to Karla's left, a cleaver in her hand as she chopped onions.

Karla ordered, "You, with the cleaver, lay it carefully on the counter and step back."

The woman was in the process of complying when Cat charged through the door, the heavy MP-5 held Rambo-style before her. Wide-eyed, tears streaking her cheeks, her breath came in hard gasps.

"Easy, Cat. You okay?"

"Yeah . . . Yeah. Who do I shoot?"

"Ease down, Cat. Ease down."

"Yeah. Right. Who do I shoot?"

"I need you to take your finger off the trigger and lower the gun. Then you have to go over and flip the switch for the loading dock door. I'll cover these guys; you unload the canisters."

"Got it!" Cat charged forward, machine gun swinging this way and that.

"Uh, *behind me*, Cat! As in not between me and someone I might be shooting at? Understand?"

Cat growled to herself, head bobbing affirmation as she pulled up short. She ducked behind Karla, hurried to the big galvanized metal door, and slapped at a switch. The segmented door clanked and rumbled as the motor began to whir.

Karla started forward, stripping zip ties out of her belt. Two of the older women were crying, almost shaking with fear as Karla secured them to the heavy table legs.

Meanwhile, Cat was grunting as she wrestled heavy metal cylinders out of the Tahoe's cargo space. With the last one, she thumbed the button that closed the loading dock door. Cat still had a hysterical look, and the MP-5's muzzle was pointing in every direction but safe. Karla's gut crawled each time the ugly black barrel swept her.

*Please, God, just get me through this.*

"Cat," Karla said calmly. "Swap me. You running about with a machine gun is almost more than I can bear . . . and they trained me to bear a lot."

"Hey, I'm *not* a combat Marine like you, *okay?*"

"How'd I miss that?" Karla took the HK, pulled the magazine, found it full, and slapped it back into the gun. "Okay, machine room's through that door. I'll hold the fort; you gas the house."

Cat no more than nodded before she was through the door with the first canister. Someone grunted just outside the kitchen. Karla flattened herself against the wall, partially blocked by the gray-metal time clock and employees' card bay.

A shadow darkened the doorway, and Karla eased the HK's fire control lever onto automatic. The MP-5 felt like an old friend as she snugged it against her chest.

The man burst into the room; Karla's finger slipped down onto the rounded trigger. Instantly, she cued on his prominent cheeks, the flashing black eyes, and thin-lipped mouth.

"You *stupid* REMF!" she hissed, not bothering to lower her weapon.

Sam Savage's eyes widened slightly as he fixed on the nine-millimeter bore four feet from his chest. Then a faint smile bent his lips. "Good thing you didn't shoot, Chief. It would have brought the whole bunch of them running instead of just the one I took down outside. He got a little curious about the guy you left lying on the cement out there. Caught him just as he was lifting his radio to call in. You always so messy on a mission?"

She allowed irritation to seep into her expression. "What are *you* doing here?"

"Covering your six, Chief." He had the audacity to wink at her, and then he ducked out the door. Accompanied by the sound of sliding fabric, Savage dragged an unconscious guard across the threshold and let him fall with a meaty thud. Then he dropped to a knee, stripping the man of a pistol, knife, his MP-5, a can of mace, and a radio. The cooks were watching like catatonic chipmunks.

"Where's Cat?"

"In the machine room, setting up her gas."

"Well, we . . ." Savage stopped short as a woman in a lab coat anxiously stepped out of the machine room door, her hands held high. Then came a bearded man, similarly clad, arms high. Cat—her tiny hands clutching the big black pistol in a death grip—followed.

"Found two more," she said. "Thought you might not want me to shoot them, Chief."

Then she glanced sidelong at Savage, her frown deepening. "What's *he* doing here?"

"Says he's covering my ass, Doc." Karla cocked her head, the HK held at a jaunty angle. "What have we got here? More kitchen staff?"

"Not at all," Savage interjected with amusement. "Hell of a raid, Chief. You wouldn't know your ass from a hole in the ground."

"SEALs don't leave people behind, Savage, but in your case, you're making me rethink."

Savage growled, "You're here to get Drs. France and Farmer, and a sarcophagus, right?"

"Right, and I'd like to get on with it instead of wasting time having a debate with a moron like you."

"Shit, I don't believe this." Savage walked over to Cat's prisoners. "Good to see you both alive. There's a Chevy Tahoe outside. Where're the sarcophagi?"

Karla cursed under her breath, lowering the HK as the bearded man—Farmer, no doubt—grinned, and said, "Good to see you, too, Major." The man shook Savage's hand. "Forget the sarcophagus. It's too hard to get to."

Kilgore France gave Savage a fierce hug. "We've done the forensic research, Major. It's as baffling as ever. The guy's name is Fluvium. It's his tomb. And we just met some weird woman, tall, with the oddest blue eyes. Bill Minor evacuated her the minute the lights went out." She glanced uncertainly at Cat, and asked, "Can I go get the research? We brought as much as we could."

"Hurry," Savage told her.

"On the blue helicopter?" Karla asked, stepping forward. "Tell me about her. Especially the eyes. And did she have kind of honey-blond hair? Spoke with an accent?"

The man nodded. "She said she and the mummy were married . . . while studying at a Mayan site that's been abandoned for a thousand years. She's tall, has a real presence. It's nuts, but she speaks Latin and ancient Mayan."

"It's Gray," Karla cursed. "Damn it, we just missed her."

At that moment her cell buzzed in her pocket. "Yeah?"

*"Chief, they just got smart enough to pull the plug on the phone line. You've got minutes before they get the security system up and running."*

"Roger that." She hit the end button as Kilgore France stepped out carrying a pack and a satchel. "People, we're leaving. Right now. Out the door! They just cut Edwin's link."

At the startled looks, she bellowed, *"Move it!"*

As they rushed for the door, she could hear the rumble of booted feet on the stairs above.

Karla sprinted to the kitchen door and locked it. Grabbing a mop, she thrust it through the handle and braced it on the doorframe. Then she turned, took two steps, vaulted the chopping block, and almost slipped on the partially diced onions. Barely catching herself, she pelted through the machine room door. Cat's cylinders were all lined up, but the hoses hadn't been fitted to the sheet metal air intake. She ripped off the big, square air filter.

Raising the HK Karla took careful aim and burned off a half dozen rounds. Punctured, the canisters erupted in hissing fits. Slamming the door behind her, she ran for all she was worth.

The banging on the mop-battened kitchen door stopped for a couple of seconds before a barely muffled subgun chattered. Splinters and bits of brass lock exploded like shrapnel. Partially spent bullets dug little furrows in the kitchen floor inches from the captive cooks' feet. The women shrieked like banshees.

Karla stitched her own burst across the wood to dampen their ardor. She was rewarded by shouts and the hammering of boots as they rushed back up the stairs. Grinning, she was out the door. The black Tahoe was waiting, Savage behind the wheel, the passenger door open. Cat and the two archaeologists were still situating themselves in the back seat.

Hissing and popping accompanied scoring impacts as bullets hammered the pavement beside her. Karla ducked right, almost slipped, and charged for the dumpster. As she ran, she bellowed, *"Savage! Go!"*

Vicious slugs cut the air a couple of feet to her left as she threw herself behind the dumpster. She twisted and peered cautiously past the side.

There! Up high. Second-story window. She mounted her gun, barely aware as the Tahoe's engine strained and it surged forward.

The man in the window leaned out, taking careful aim at the fleeing vehicle. Karla pasted the front sight post on his torso as she adjusted for the elevation and distance. Even as she triggered the three-round burst, she saw him jerk. Nine millimeters didn't have much energy over that distance, but one must have connected with brain or spine. The shooter's gun slipped from nerveless fingers. He slumped forward. When the heavy gun hit the end of the sling, the jerk tumbled him from the window. His skull made a wet pop as it impacted the pavement.

Karla ran for all she was worth.

"Come on, Savage, tell me you've got those people out of here."

She heard a shout, and rather than stick to the road, ducked into the trees. Panting, she checked her magazine. Maybe twenty rounds left.

Behind her, someone hollered, "They left one behind! Looked like a woman!"

Someone else yelled, "Hope she's good-looking. Meanwhile, I need someone after that vehicle! Get the cars and go!"

Karla grinned to herself. "Ooooh, bad command and control just shouting like that. So, you're going after my people? Let's just see what we can do about that."

She ducked low, winding through foliage to the intersection where the kitchen drive split off from the main road. She barely flopped herself into the drainage ditch before two large Chevy Suburbans came roaring down the upper drive. Tires squealed as they strained to hold the descending curve.

Karla raised her weapon, found her sight picture, and took out the tires with a short burst as the first vehicle came even with her position. The rubber sidewalls collapsed; the big black Suburban slid sideways, careened off the narrow curve, and down the steep embankment. She sighted on the second Sub as the driver slammed on his brakes.

Prone as she was, Karla's slugs punctured all four sidewalls. The second Suburban hurtled off in the wake of the first. As it hit dirt at the edge of the road, it flipped on its side, shot over the edge, and crashed down the hillside. She heard the distinct metallic crunch as the second vehicle slammed down on the first.

Karla smiled to herself, leaped to her feet. She ducked from tree to tree and peered over the edge. The second vehicle lay on its side atop the first. The two of them were wedged amidst a wreckage of broken fir trees. A screaming engine tore itself apart with a bang and clattering of broken parts.

Gasoline trickled from the upper vehicle to land on the one

beneath . . . and drained into the hood seam. Accompanied by the crackle of a shorted battery, it burst into flames.

Karla whispered, "Not good."

Turning, she scrambled up the steep slope like a mad hare, her HK swinging with each step.

A sucking *whoosh* was followed by a ball of reddish yellow flame rising like a little Hiroshima.

A bullet slapped the bark of a tree just to her right.

Karla Raven grinned with absolute delight, her adrenaline pumping as she slithered into a patch of ground-clinging juniper. She checked her magazine, finding just three rounds left.

"My God! Am I ever *glad* to be the hell *out* of Grantham!"

# 56

"What do you make of it?" I asked Savage as we stood on the St. Regis Hotel's roof and glassed the high road leading up to the Skientia property. I had a pair of fifteen-power Swarovski binoculars that had been, ahem, "liberated" from one of the local sporting goods stores by the "Raven & Swink Midnight Requisition" team.

A line of fire trucks with flashing lights, a half dozen sheriff's cars with strobing light bars, a couple of ambulances, and a slew of other vehicles blocked the road below the great white gate.

Just above it, to the right and below the house, a thick black column of smoke rose. Through my binoculars, I could see conifers igniting in streaks of yellow flame as the fire grew.

"Skientia isn't opening their gate." Sam Savage braced his binoculars on a satellite television dish. A faint staccato carried across the valley. "There, you hear?"

"Unless they're shooting at the first responders, she's still alive."

"It's been over half an hour," Savage added. "One woman against a team of Talon mercs?"

"That's Karla Raven up there," I said softly.

The distant chatter of a helicopter could be heard. I turned in search of it, finding a red-and-white heavy-lift unit with a big conical bucket hanging from a line beneath it. "I can't believe they're attacking the fire, even while there's shooting."

Savage arched an eyebrow. "With all those gazillion dollar homes on the mountain? Who would you rather deal with? A bunch of mercs shooting holes in your helicopter, or an army of hyper-rich people's attorneys after you let a fire scorch their billion-dollar mansions?"

"Ask me something easy."

Across the distance, a bang echoed. "Hand grenade." Savage announced needlessly. "Damn it, Ryan. It's a miracle she's lasted this long. They were shooting at her when she ordered me out of there. I should have stayed."

"You had a duty to Cat and those two civilians. The gate was closing as you roared through. But for you, they'd still be in there." I paused. "And, Major, you understand, don't you? When it comes to Skientia, the gloves are off. This is going to land in Grazier's lap like a bomb. Maybe even a congressional hearing."

He nodded, then gave me a dark look. "SEAL or not, you know how this is going to end?"

I swallowed hard. I'd lost of lot of friends and patients over the years. It's part of the job when you're a military psychiatrist. Somehow, losing Karla Raven was different. It was going to tear an irreparable hole in my soul.

# Furor et Animi Fractos

*The pain and sorrow are barely ameliorated by my certainty that Fluvium's death is only fleeting—a shadow to be defeated by a brilliant shaft of light. What I have just experienced is not reality, but only* one *reality. Nevertheless, as soon as I am away from the prying eyes of the beasts, I will weep. Not for what is, but for what I now know could be.*

*Dearest husband, where is your cerebrum? Not with your body? Did you leave it hidden somewhere in Egypt?*

*Meanwhile, I'm building a machine. Crude, inefficient, and primitive. In its current configuration it should at least project into the future. After a successful test, I shall have to make the necessary modifications before I can contact Imperator.*

*It will disgust me. For the moment, I will accept his terms. Endure what I must. But there is no price I am unwilling to pay to ensure you do not become that desiccated* thing.

I love you too much.

*Then, together, he and I shall ensure that this branch of the timeline, this despicable planet is left nothing more than a featureless rock.*

# 57

"*I tell you, there's at least two of them. Maybe more.*" The voice came in through the earpiece Karla had lifted from a dead Talon goon. Who were these guys? Didn't they know enough to shut up, or at least change frequencies when they'd taken this many casualties?

Karla squinted, tried to relax on her high perch. Her eyes stung from the smoke that occasionally blew her way. But her location was perfect, perhaps twenty feet off the ground, her outline broken by a fir tree's thick branches. She could just see through the great picture windows on the house's upper floor.

No more than five minutes ago she'd watched two black-clad men wearing gas masks search the main room, submachine guns held before them.

"Your bosses are gonna call this a regulation clusterfuck."

A tinny voice carried up from a loudspeaker on the road below the gate. "This is the Pitkin County Sheriff's Office. You are ordered to lay down your weapons and open this gate. Failure to do so will result in felony charges being filed against all persons responsible. I repeat, lay down your weapons and open this gate!"

"Yeah, like that's gonna happen anytime soon." Karla caught movement from the corner of her eye. Carefully, she turned her head, then eased the HK to clear the branch. The man approaching along the slope below held an imaging device, the kind that picked up infrared. He was slowly scanning the slope below.

And if he lifted it?

Karla took a deep breath, settled the front sight post on his chest, and mentally willed him to keep the scanner pointed at the ground where any sloppy assailant would be expected to lurk.

Step-by-step he proceeded, only to have two of his black-clad associates emerge from the trees behind him. One held a scoped rifle, the other a military-grade M16. They cautiously advanced across the needle-and-duff–covered slope, the ultimate hunting team.

Somewhere in the distance a helicopter was approaching. Karla could tell from the heavy beat of the rotors that it was something big, not Winny Swink's flight-for-life chopper.

Grazier's people? Rushing in with an extraction team aboard a Chinook? Wishful thinking. Sound was wrong for a Chinook.

Then, to Karla's dismay, the guy with the scanner raised it, and started running it over the trees to her left.

That's when her phone began to buzz in her vest pocket.

Hell of a time.

She shifted, feeling the cramp build in her left leg as she braced herself in the fork of the branches. The scanner lifted his sensor toward her. A moment before he pointed it at her, she triggered the HK. In one graceful swing she targeted the guy with the hunting rifle. Her burst caught him in the upper chest and unprotected neck. By the time she swung to the third man and triggered her weapon, it was to see her 9mm slugs chew into the tree trunk he ducked behind.

The phone continued to buzz in her pocket.

Heart pounding, she shifted, trying to catch a glimpse of the survivor.

"You're surrounded," he called. "We've got you triangulated now."

Karla chewed her lips, knowing he was probably right.

Bracing the HK on the branch to cover his position, she slipped the phone from her pocket and jammed it to her ear, whispering, "Falcon?"

*"Naw, it's Winny. Can't hardly hear you. I figure that's 'cause you can't talk. Got a way of showing me where you're at?"*

At that moment the guy behind the tree stepped out and jerked the pin from a grenade. She swiveled the HK and shot. One-handed, the gun jerked and bucked. At least two rounds hit him as he threw.

Karla hunched herself as the black orb rose, fouled on a branch, and deflected into the open. The bang, accompanied by the hiss of shrapnel and falling needles, left Karla's ears ringing.

Then, to her amazement, the guy below stepped out from his tree, the M16 shouldered to follow up.

Karla used both hands this time, centering the HK, and shot him through the head.

In the ringing silence, all she could hear was the thunder of the helicopter and the Pitkin County sheriff's nearly inaudible voice threatening arrest and conviction.

Karla wondered where her phone had gone to, couldn't even remember letting go of it. Instead, she ejected her magazine, slipped the last one she'd looted from the dead into the well, and slammed it in place.

Through a gap in the trees she could see two more black-clad figures scrambling along the slope toward her, weapons in hand. They both stopped, staring up in disbelief as the helicopter's downdraft caught them.

One threw up an arm, as if to protect himself. The other raised an M16, firing into the air on full auto.

Karla couldn't see the helicopter through the screen of trees, but her own perch was swaying, the branches lashing from the downwash. What she did see was the two men—at the very last instant—hunching down before a column of falling water literally blasted them down the mountain.

Karla screamed her rage and tried to cling to her thrashing tree as a gale blew down from above. More gunfire could be heard, close enough to penetrate the chopper's roar. Across from her, branches snapped and cracked.

It was all she could do to hold on. Shooting back had become an impossibility.

"Give me a *fucking* break!" she bellowed into the gale.

Something was smashing its way toward her through the trees.

# 58

From the hotel roof, Savage and I watched the Forest Service helicopter drop its load; it hovered for a moment, then flew off down the valley. Obviously, the pilot hadn't expected to be shot at. He'd totally missed the fire in his fluster. But in its wake the shooting stopped. A terrible silence followed, broken only by the sound of local traffic below the hotel and the wind through the trees around the ski slope.

"Movement," Savage told me where he peered through his binoculars.

I lifted the Swarovskis and watched as whatever passed for the Pitkin County Sheriff's Office SWAT used a fire truck to pull the gate down. The ringing clang came many seconds later. Then the vehicles went flooding in.

For what seemed an eternity, we waited. A half hour later, I lowered my glasses and took a deep breath. "If they arrest her, can Grazier get the charges dropped?"

"Something this big? Hell, I don't know." Savage thoughtfully lowered his binoculars. "Either she's eluded them and made her way out, or they captured her."

Karla Raven wasn't the sort to be captured unless she was completely disabled. Which meant . . .

"Let's get back to the others. Any news is going to come on the local radio, maybe television."

My heart had lodged in my throat as we made our way to the staircase and down into the hotel. At the suite door, I knocked the predetermined two and two. Edwin opened, worry etched into his young face.

"Anything?" I asked him.

He shook his head. "We been calling the chief's phone. No answer."

"That's not necessarily bad," I told him as I entered the suite. Falcon sat in a defensive position on the bed, a pillow clutched to his chest. His expression was vacant, eyes empty. Not good.

Cat was poking at the room's coffee machine, desperate enough that she was using the last packet of decaf. Her movements reeked of weariness; her normally lustrous eyes reflected the dullness of fatigue and exhaustion.

The anthropologists remained seated on the suite's small couch where Savage had placed them. Kilgore France still clutched her pack as if it contained gold. Farmer, his face in a pensive frown, had the satchel on his lap. I didn't need a degree in psychiatry to know that they were emotionally overwhelmed.

"The sheriff's office is in the compound now," Savage told everyone as he followed me in and shut the door. "From here on it's just a matter of waiting."

Edwin asked, "Anyone think to call Winny? Tell her to stand down?"

"No." Savage walked into the center of the room. "Would you mind?"

"Bet she gonna be pissy as hell 'cause she didn't get no action. Be our luck she run into some woman wearing pink and beat the holy crap out of her."

I settled on the couch arm, extending a hand. "Dr. France, I'm Doctor Timothy Ryan. We haven't really been introduced."

"My pleasure. Call me Kilgore." Her shake was firm, but I could see confusion and worry in her eyes.

"Reid Farmer," the bearded man introduced as he offered his hand. "Unlike Kilgore, I'm no celebrity. Just a contract archaeologist in way over his head."

I liked the resilience they both seemed to display. It wasn't just anyone who could be yanked out of a kidnapping in the midst of a gunfight and still remain poised. "Sounds like you've had quite the time. I can't wait to hear your impressions of the tomb."

"You're a medical doctor?" Kilgore asked.

"Psychiatry, actually . . . with a PhD in psychology."

Farmer's expression tightened. "You're here to debrief us? Counseling? Heal our trauma?"

In spite of my gnawing worry about Karla, I smiled. "No. I'm part of General Grazier's team. But you've been through a tough time. It wouldn't be unusual if you had issues, flashbacks, nightmares. For the record, I'm not a sit-on-the-couch-and-tell-me-about-your-childhood kind of psychologist. I'm more of the 'Let's-have-a-cup-of-coffee-and-figure-out-how-you-can-cope,' kind."

"Grazier? Who's he?" Kilgore asked uncertainly.

"Savage's boss." I pointed where the major bent over Edwin's shoulder. "Right now we've got a missing warrior."

"Chief Raven," Kilgore said with a nod. "To hear Edwin and Cat tell it, she walks on water."

*Oh, do I hope!*

"Actually, she's just an extraordinary . . ."

The suite door burst open and Karla Raven stormed in. I leaped to my feet, surprised to see that her midnight hair was slicked back to her skull and hanging down her back. Her black clothing appeared soaked, and her boots squished with each step. Not only that, but I could see the slow fuse burning behind her gray eyes. Her normally calm face had flushed to the point I could see the scar on her cheek.

"You're alive!"

"Far from dead, sir."

"By *fucking* damn!" Winny Swink bellowed as she swaggered into the room on Karla's heels. As full of herself as a buccaneer, she used her foot to slam the door behind her. A bottle of Herradura tequila, the cap missing, was clutched in her right hand. "Whooow!" She shook her fiery red hair back and forth. "Now *that's* what I call riding the wings of angels!"

"You want another to match the first?" Karla asked, eyes narrowed as she pointed at Swink's right cheek. I could see the bruise forming under the major's fair skin.

"Might be worth it, bitch." She tossed Karla the tequila bottle, saying "Drink or fight. Your choice."

Karla caught the bottle, a curling splash of amber liquor squirting from the open top. Then she tipped it back and chugged.

I could only gape. In the futile hope I could control the situation, I stepped forward and grabbed the bottle away, saying, "My turn."

"How come you're not dead?" Edwin asked, rising from his computer.

Karla, like a pirouetting dancer, feinted and easily wrenched the bottle from my fingers. "You heard Winny. Wings of angels, man." She took another swig.

"We heard gunfire," I said as Winny and I both grabbed for the tequila bottle. Fortunately, I'm much taller than Swink.

Karla grinned as she wiped at the tequila dribbling down her chin. "Haven't had *that* much fun since Qal'ah-ye Sabir!" She reached into a pocket and tossed me a radio wrapped with a black wire that led to an earpiece. Water leaked from the case.

"You should have heard those guys!" Karla leaped like a tigress and snatched the bottle out of my hand. She danced away from my pursuit, gulped a drink, and in falsetto, mimicked, "It's *just* a *woman*! Run her down! Run her down!"

Savage, his expression somewhere between amused disbelief and relief, asked, "What kind of a body count am I looking at, Chief?"

Karla took another swig of tequila, then tossed him the bottle. He caught it, heedless of the liquor that splashed on his arm. Got to hand it to Savage, he was smart enough to fake taking a drink.

"About eight, sir." A pause. "Of mine. Not counting the ones in the two vehicles. Don't know how many were in the crash." She waggled a cautionary finger. "Reckless driving on mountain roads can be deadly. And I don't know what happened in the house."

Cat gasped. "You mean my gas killed people?"

"Hell, I don't know, Cat. Looked to me like they were just out. And yeah, your stuff took out that whole house. I saw guys in masks trying to clear it."

"Hey, I got two!" Winny declared triumphantly.

"You were there?" I asked, whirling just in time to see her rip the tequila bottle away from the unwary Savage.

"A-*fucking*-mazing!" Winny gloated before she tilted the bottle and chugged the añejo. They'd bought—or stolen—good stuff. "Loved that big son of a bitch!"

"What big son of a bitch?" Savage demanded.

"Never would have thought you for a truck driver," Karla chided as she grabbed the bottle back and tilted it to her lips.

"It was the big Sikorsky CH-54," I supplied, figuring it out. "You stole it from the Forest Service?"

"Never flown one," Winny said as she grabbed for the bottle. "It was just sitting there on Sardy Field. Looked like a hell of a lot more fun than some damn hospital ship."

"The heavy lift?" Savage asked.

"Should have seen her," Karla chimed as she held the bottle out of Winny's reach. "Her and that bucket full of water."

"Biggest problem was finding Karla." Winny started climbing Karla's body, levering the tequila into reach. "'Specially since she dropped her damn phone. But then the top of this tree blows up. And I look down and half the compound is rushing toward that same tree."

Karla surrendered the bottle, saying, "Yeah, and you should have seen the two guys closing in. They look up just as the downwash hits them."

Swink held the bottle up to the light. Most of the tequila was gone. "Silly son's o' bitches started shooting at me. So I just lined up that big ol' fucking bucket . . ." She demonstrated with the tequila bottle, holding it high over her head, and pouring. Her aim was good; it splashed into her mouth.

"That's Winny's kill," Karla told Savage. "She dropped a couple of tons of water on those two assholes. The weight of it blew them right off the mountain."

Winny chortled as she lowered the bottle. "Well, it was just downright rude of them to start shooting holes in my bird."

"We didn't see the chopper land," Savage chimed in. "How'd you evac Raven?"

Karla skipped close and grabbed the tequila bottle. "Damned bitch almost smacked me out of the tree I was hiding in. She just swung that bucket into it. So I grabbed hold and crawled inside. If she'd had a bit more velocity, she'd have punted me into next week."

"But she'd emptied the bucket. Why are you all wet?" I asked as I snatched the bottle away from her. "And why does Winny have that bruise on her cheek?"

"'Cause I decked the bitch!" Karla pawed at me for the bottle.

Winny Swink started crowing like a rooster. "Hell, Skipper, she was in a damn hot fight up there. Thought I'd cool her off. On the way back, I dipped her sorry butt in the lake."

Karla turned blazing gray eyes my way. "When she finally set us down, she was laughing so hard I thought her ass was going to fall off. So I clocked her one, just to bring her back to her senses."

"I am *not* forgetting that." Swink's green eyes narrowed as she pointed a hard finger. "You and I are going to go around for that, bitch."

"I gave you a hand up afterward, didn't I? Said I owed you one for saving my ass. That—you sorry APD-addled bitch—is called a thank you, by the way. And I promised, and delivered, a bottle of hooch." Karla's crooked grin expanded. "Major, that was a hell of a snatch you made up there. I pay my debts."

"Damn straight! So hand me that bottle." Winny gulped tequila and grinned stupidly, her anger forgotten. "Haven't had that much fun since I stole that Raptor! Hell, maybe this was even *better*."

Karla feinted and ripped the tequila bottle away, amber liquid spraying the wide-eyed anthropologists in the process. Karla tilted it up, drank, and shoved it at Swink, declaring, "Drink up, Major. Last swallow is yours."

Winny upended the bottle, and I watched her delicate throat work as she drained the dregs.

"Oh, dear," I murmured, pondering the effects of tequila on Karla's Prazosin, and the "do not consume alcohol in excess" warning. I dropped wearily to the couch arm.

"Who *are* these people?" Dr. France asked cautiously.

"My patients," I replied flatly.

"*Your* patients? As in *mental* patients?" Dr. Farmer asked. "And they're just running around?"

"Actually, they're *escaped* mental patients." I winced at the expressions on their faces.

Karla dropped, lunged, and tackled Winny Swink. Their bodies slammed onto the floor, the tequila bottle rolling away. Karla pinned her immediately. I cocked my head as both women burst into maniacal laughter.

Reid Farmer—gaping at Winny and Karla—said, "About that counseling you offered, Dr. Ryan. Just wanted you to know, I'm feeling much better, thank you."

On the bed, Falcon looked catatonic.

"Yeah, I do good work, don't I?"

# 59

The Gulfstream jolted, and the "fasten seatbelt" sign came on. I ignored it as I walked down the narrow aisle, bracing myself on the seatbacks. With the exception of Savage and me, everyone was sound asleep—including the anthropologists. I felt a deep-seated relief. My people were alive and healthy. It could have ended so much worse.

Falcon slept peacefully, his head bent to the side. For that I felt grateful. He'd been twitching, mumbling to himself from the stress. I'd added five more milligrams of Mirtazapine to his cocktail, figuring he could use the additional dosage. He worried me the most, being the most fragile.

Cat and Edwin sat side by side, her head on his shoulder, long black hair spilling down around her delicate face. Edwin's head was propped on hers, his mouth open, eyes flickering in REM sleep.

Winny lay curled like a red fox in a den; she slept in one of the window seats. I'd threatened to sedate her when she'd insisted on flying the Gulfstream. It had taken Savage, me, and Reid Farmer to manhandle her into the seat.

Note to self: Winny and tequila? Bad idea.

Across from her, the anthropologists, having folded the seat arm up, were snuggled against the cabin wall, the window shade pulled down. Not that there was much to see in the darkness beyond. The precious pack and satchel were safely stowed under the seats in front of them.

I paused at Karla's seat. Her dark tactical gear had, for the most part, dried out. A black HK submachine gun lay on the seat beside her. Woozy from tequila, she'd nevertheless insisted on cleaning it subsequent to Winny dunking her and the gun in the lake.

I fought the urge to reach down and pull back the strand of black hair that hung down in front of her nose.

*You know better than to form attachments like this, Ryan.*

Yeah, sure.

With a weary smile, I made my way to the front and took the seat opposite Savage. He was studying me through thoughtful black eyes as he held his phone to his ear.

I heard him say, "Yes, sir. I understand, sir." He pushed the end button, a bitter expression on his face.

"Trouble?" I asked.

Instead of answering he asked, "You got a thing for Raven, Doctor? That look you gave her . . . ?"

I chuckled and pulled a bottle of water from the pouch in the bulkhead. "I've got a thing for all them. But you're right. Karla's special."

"That's not healthy, Doctor. Professionally or otherwise. And you're old enough to be her father. She's hot, but not exactly the makings of a storybook ending if you ask—"

"Is *that* what you think?" I shot him a look of amazement. "God, no!" I sipped from the bottle. "First, as you note, she's a patient. Second, I can admire her for who she is without any *romantic* impulses. And third, yes, she's a favorite of mine for a variety of reasons." I paused. "None of which have to do with sex."

Which of course was a lie; just about all adult, non-consanguineous, male-female relationships have a sexual underpinning. Savage, however, didn't need to know that.

"Okay. I guess I deserved that."

"What is it with you and Grazier? You thought the same thing about me and Gray. Psychologists are good at picking up on common themes. Yours keeps cropping up."

"Occam's razor says that the most likely solution is usually the answer. We don't have a clue as to how Gray got out of Ward Six. That's why. An inside job still seems the best explanation."

"And since you already had me in the sack with Gray, I'm also lusting after Karla?" I shot him a scathing glance. "It's tough, but make yourself step back and look at my people analytically. If you give them a chance, Karla included, you're going to see what I do."

He was silent for a while, then nodded. "I've got my anthropologists back. Grazier's been on the phone with the Pitkin County sheriff and the FBI. The number of dead, the presence of fully automatic weapons, not to mention a stolen federal helicopter shot full of bullet holes, has the place under lockdown. FBI has already seized the sarcophaguses and mummies. We've got them back."

I glanced sidelong at him. "Would you have? Had Falcon not cued on the Aspen mansion?"

"No." Savage scowled. "But that clusterfuck back in Aspen? It looks like a small war zone. Here, on American soil. You and your hooligans have a *messy* way of picking up the pieces."

"We *almost* got Gray back. And with her, the solution to the mystery of who took her out of Ward Six." I waved him down. "All right, they were messy. What did you expect? They put this together overnight, on a shoestring, without any support, and still turned up aces."

"That remains to be seen." He stared down at his strong brown hands. "Grazier's got a shitstorm brewing. Fifteen senators, the Pentagon, a host of congressmen, and the National Security Advisor are demanding to know what the hell he's doing attacking Skientia."

"Surely they'd . . . Hold on a second." I cocked my head. "How would *they* know? Skientia, I mean. Grazier *didn't* attack them. My people did."

"They think it was Grazier."

"Call him back, Savage. Tell him to deny any involvement. And tell him, for God's sake, not to mention my people."

"What are you thinking?"

"How would anyone know it was Grazier? Unless Skientia is way ahead of us and poisoning the water." Who did I think I was? Falcon? But I could see the implications—and it wasn't anything pleasant. "We need to get my people back to Grantham immediately."

"For once you and I agree, Ryan."

"And the record needs to show that they returned, of their own free will, twelve hours ago."

"Huh?"

"Deniability. Especially for Grazier. Who'd believe that a bunch of crackpots from the asylum could have knocked off Skientia and killed all those people? It would have taken one hell of a spec-op team to pull this off, right?"

". . . And all the teams can be accounted for," he agreed, seeing the light. "The inquiry will upset every branch of the services, ruffle national security feathers, stir up a hornet's nest of backlash."

"To date, outside of you and me, only Grazier knows who was in Aspen. It's got to stay that way."

"Because they have someone inside Grazier's team," he agreed. "The same person, or people, who compromised my arrival in DC when France and Farmer were taken."

"You're quicker than I thought you were."

He already had the phone to his ear. The guy was good, obviously, given his years in the intelligence and spec-op community. He told Grazier everything the man needed to know without telling him anything.

When Savage ended the call, he looked at me. "You can cover your end? When we get to Grantham, I mean. Fix the records?"

I tilted my head toward the cabin behind me. "Between Edwin, Hatcher, and Janeesha, it will look rock solid. Assuming you can soothe Mercy General, Best Buy, and the rental car company."

"They're taken care of. I can't *wait* to hear what the anthropologists have to say. Let alone see what's in that pack and satchel. I *saw* that tomb, Ryan. Farmer and France have seen the mummy, seen inside the sarcophagus."

"Skientia is going to want them back," I told him. "You can bet their lawyers are going to be demanding the return of all property seized in the Aspen raid, which includes the sarcophagi."

"Skientia's guys just got their teeth kicked in. We won."

I shook my head. "The attack on the compound caught Skientia completely by surprise. Now they're out for blood."

He grunted.

"They *think* it was Grazier. But they won't be able to prove it. And I have faith in Eli. He's going to skate right out from under the crap and come up looking like the aggrieved party."

I leaned over the armrest to meet Savage's eyes. "But, Major, know this: We only handed Skientia a setback, nothing more. Until we debrief the anthropologists and allow Falcon to pick everything apart and reassemble the pieces, we haven't a clue concerning what this is all about. But it's big. Really big."

Savage leaned back, mouth tightening. "On the way down the mountain, Reid told me that Skientia had hired the Talon mercenaries we killed in Egypt. He said Bill Minor, Skientia's man in Egypt, was at that mansion. Maybe Raven took him out, maybe she didn't. But either way, any organization willing to murder men in their employ that way, and then attack me and my detail like they did . . . ?"

"Yeah," I said softly. "I hear you. But what makes Gray and an old tomb worth dying for?"

# 60

"This just goes from bad to worse," Reid murmured out of the side of his mouth. "From captives in a Frankenstein mansion to inmates in an insane asylum." He clutched the satchel to his chest as he and Kilgore followed Chief Raven down one of Grantham Barracks' well-lit corridors. The place gave him the creeps.

"And you call *this* archaeology?" Kilgore asked. Her pack hung by one strap over her shoulder.

Patient rooms were to either side, the wide hospital doors pierced by a single window. Over-polished tile floors gleamed under the fluorescent lights. They passed a dumpy-looking guy in pajamas who grinned vacuously at them while he clutched a teddy bear to his chest.

Karla Raven turned to shoot them a gray-eyed appraisal. "Better here, hiding with us, than laid out on a slab somewhere." A pause. "How'd you get to the furnace room, anyway?"

"The whole house was on the fritz," Kilgore told her. "We thought the kitchen was the best way out. The cooks just looked at us and smiled when we strolled in. We'd have walked right out the back, but when we glanced outside, there was a guy with a machine gun. So we just tried to look official and ducked into the furnace room."

Reid added, "Figured we would wait out the alarms and flashing lights, and when the guard was called off, vanish into the woods."

"They'd have had you before you made the trees." Raven gave Reid an unsettling wink. "But you get points for trying. Here we are."

Karla Raven bothered him—some subtle sense that she was a better, tougher, and more competent man than he. He avoided her gaze as she opened the door and held it. He followed Kilgore into a light-blue conference room. Oversized pictures of bright yellow flowers, deer fawns, puppies, and serene mountain landscapes had been painted on the walls. Giant pillows were piled at one end of the room. Two tables had been shoved together at the other, and Edwin Jones sat at one tapping keys on a laptop computer.

"Have a seat," Major Savage called from where he filled a chair on the left. Colonel Ryan had a haunch perched on the closest table corner, one leg swinging. The man wore Dockers and a plain white shirt. He held a yellow legal pad in his hand, a thoughtful look on his face.

The odd little man they called Falcon sat in an office chair off to one side. He seemed to be listening to someone because he smiled and nodded as if in affirmation. Winny Swink, in gray sweatpants, sat crosslegged in another office chair opposite Cat Talavera.

"Have a good night's sleep?" Ryan asked with a smile.

"We did," Kilgore answered wryly, "all things considered. And breakfast was certainly better than expected."

"Thank Karla. She had complaints about the old cook," Edwin announced as he scowled down at his screen. Then he tapped a couple of keys, and said, "Got ya!"

Reid began delicately, "As good as breakfast was, we're not sure we want to make a habit of it. We haven't, uh, been listed as patients here, have we?"

"Nope," Savage told him. "While you're free to go, Dr. Farmer, Skientia is out there looking for you. For the moment, Grantham Barracks is way below their radar. If you leave, and they catch you, everyone here will pay the price."

In a voice loaded with meaning, Karla Raven said, "I wouldn't like that."

"Me, either," Winny Swink chimed in.

"The best solution is figuring out what this is all about and bringing a stop to it." Ryan, still perched on the table corner, looked down at his legal pad. "The key question being, who is Prisoner Alpha? Why is she so important to Skientia? And why is she such an enigma?"

"She claims she's the mummy's wife," Kilgore said dryly.

"And who's the mummy?" Savage was taking his own notes.

Kilgore laid out her case, the presence of orthopedic surgery, results from trace element analysis, the early dental care. "The guy's a contradiction, meaning he had to be alive in the last fifty years, but extraordinarily well-faked to make him look ancient." She made a face. "If Skientia is behind the faking, they could have substituted other samples for carbon dating, ensured the strontium and delta 15 carbon analyses were whatever they wanted them to be. Even the genetic testing."

"To prove what to whom?" Reid asked. "Was it done to convince Domina? Is that what they're after, make her believe that corpse is her husband? But why try and make it look over three thousand years old?"

Even as he said it, he thought, *It doesn't work. It would have taken years to build that tomb and hide it.* He added, "What kind of woman would believe her husband was a three-thousand-year-old mummy?"

"Playing on her mental illness?" Kilgore asked. "She was here, right? What was your diagnosis, Dr. Ryan?"

Ryan's eyebrows rose. "She's an enigma. Defies all the categories in the DSM-V. Her peculiar language skills, her odd mathematics—"

"The language is Latin and Ch'olan Mayan. Not church Latin, but a variant of classical," Reid interjected. "She says she learned the mathematics in the Yucatan." He went on to describe Domina's story about Dzibilchaltun.

"But the place is a ruin?" Savage asked.

"Has been for over a thousand years," Reid assured him. "While I agree her story is impossible, she seemed to believe it."

"And there's the doohickey." Dr. Ryan began to describe some odd machine made from electrical parts.

Reid reached into his pack and pulled out the electrical box. "Did it look like this? We took it out of the sarcophagus. It was resting on the corpse's chest." Next, he brought out the papyrus book. "This was laying on his genitals, and this . . ." He removed the glass jar, "was just below the electrical box, and clutched in his hands."

Edwin rose from his computer and took the electrical box from Ryan. He frowned. "Nothing I'm familiar with. No manufacturer's code or ID. Don't see no plug-in for power. Let me Google a description and see if—"

"Edwin, don't!" Falcon interrupted sharply.

Reid turned to see Falcon, still reclined, head back. The man's eyes were focused on the ceiling as he continued, "The major and I agree that it might not be in our best interest to have inquiries about the box circulating on the Internet. Now, please, all of you, go on."

*The major?* Reid wondered, *Who the hell is the major?*

"What about the liquid in the jar?" Cat asked, lifting it. "Did you sample it?"

"No," Kilgore told her. "We didn't get the time."

Cat glanced at Ryan. "I could take it down to the lab. It's crude, but—"

"Leave it sealed," Falcon interrupted from his chair. "In fact, I wouldn't open it until you're in a controlled environment."

"Why, Falcon?" Ryan turned, his attention on the brown-haired man.

"The tomb's contents were meant for Gray," Falcon said softly.

"And how do you know that?" Savage asked.

Falcon laced his fingers together and closed his eyes. "The pieces fit."

Kilgore lifted her hands in supplication. "Great. A fake tomb, meant to impress a mentally ill woman who speaks Latin, figures in Mayan glyphs, and builds electrical gizmos? To what purpose?" She straightened. "Could it be some sort of test?"

"To test what?" Cat asked. "Her delusions?"

"Or her mental programming," Kilgore stated harshly. "Is that what Skientia is about? I hate to use the word, but are we dealing with brainwashing? They took Domina, or whatever her name is, and modified her brain engrams, rewired her to believe she studied mathematics at a Mayan ruin and married a mummy while she was there?" She paused. "Is that even possible, Dr. Ryan?"

"Physiologically, no. The brain is a remarkably plastic and adaptable organ, but science fiction aside, it can't just be wiped clean and then reprogrammed—and certainly not with the sophistication and intelligence demonstrated by Gray. The brain she has grew, evolved, and was trained over a lifetime. It wasn't inserted like a computer program."

Cat Talavera said, "I concur with Dr. Ryan. The chemo-electric physiology of the brain can be retrained, but not reprogrammed like simply inserting a new disk. Neurons can't be wiped clean and then reconfigured from outside. We're talking complex chemistry, micro RNA, even DNA transcription on an almost infinite level."

Kilgore pushed back, perplexed. "Why does none of this make sense?"

From behind them, Falcon's soft voice said, "Because you are not working from the appropriate paradigm."

"And you are?" Savage's voice dripped sarcasm.

Falcon shot an irritated glance off to his right, saying, "Theresa, you can't expect them to understand. They don't have your training."

"Who's Theresa?" Reid asked quietly.

"One of his hallucinated personalities," Ryan said. "She's a physicist. Think of her as a part of Falcon's personality. A way for him to argue with himself."

"Okaaay," Kilgore whispered derisively.

Chief Raven, however, dropped to a crouch before Falcon. "What does she say, Falcon?"

The man's eyes reflected amusement. "She's not sure those present have the mental capacity, let alone the education, to synthesize the ramifications."

"What ramifications?"

"Those of impossibility," Falcon said seriously.

"Oh, boy," Reid muttered to himself.

To his amazement, Ryan straightened, rising from the table. "Impossibility, Falcon?"

Ryan and Savage might have been slapped when Falcon said, "It has to do with entangled particles. What Einstein called 'spooky action at a distance.'"

Ryan shared a shocked glance with Savage before turning his attention back to Falcon. "I'm with you at a very basic level. According to General Grazier, Skientia was working on entanglement theory. They'd advanced to entangling organic molecules."

Falcon cocked his head, listening, but apparently not to Ryan. After a long pause, he said, "Yes, yes. . . . I'll tell him."

Falcon turned to Ryan. "Theresa can be such a pain. She wants me to remind you that Stephen Hawking, Kip Thorne, and most of the good theorists agree that our illusion of time only goes forward. General relativity ensures this as a means of avoiding paradox. You know, if you kill your grandfather, you can never be born? And then you must contend with the Second Law of Thermodynamics and the 'chronology protection conjecture.'"

Ryan wasn't buying this shit, was he?

"What may be applicable here," Falcon continued, "is the environment of a Bose-Einstein condensate coupled with a well-developed theory of quantum gravity. This is hypothetical, but coupling quantum gravity with entanglement might allow the manipulation of matter across time and space. Keep in mind that entanglement didn't just appear in the universe the moment humans first generated it in a lab." Falcon might have been lecturing a child. "Entanglement is as old as our universe. *Timeless, in fact.*"

Cat interjected, "But, Falcon, the theory of quantum gravity eludes our best physicists. We can't prove it."

"To date, *we* can't. It is also fact that Egyptians did not inscribe Mayan base-twenty mathematics, written as equations, on their tomb walls. We're dealing in anomalies." He paused. "Like Gray."

Savage threw his hands up. "I'm lost."

Falcon glanced at him. "Theresa asks, 'What happens if entangled particles generated three thousand years ago can be identified today? Perhaps captured in a Bose-Einstein condensate?'"

Savage's look turned quizzical. "And you think this is what Skientia is after? Catching entangled particles from the past? To what purpose?"

Ryan turned. "Sam, remember what Grazier said? They were attempting to 'entangle' organic molecules. Some experiment to monitor them halfway across the planet."

"Ah!" Falcon said, face alight. "Such an experiment would entail detectors with a great deal of sensitivity. Which answers some questions yet poses even more."

"Answers which questions, my man?" Edwin asked.

"Why someone would want to kill Gray the day she arrived, for one. Perhaps they sought to stop her from sharing secret technology. In this case, the doohickey," Falcon said. "I suspect we were focusing on the side effects the machine produced rather than its true purpose."

Karla crossed her arms. "The night she disappeared, Gray spent all night tapping on that thing. Seymore said she kept shifting it around."

"My suspicion is that she was generating entangled particles," Falcon told her. "The doohickey is a communicator."

"With whom?" Savage demanded.

"She was probably talking to the very machine that drew her to Los Alamos in the first place."

"Drew her?" Karla asked.

"For whatever reason, her ultimate attraction to Skientia was, and remains, that machine," Falcon asserted. "Either she targeted it herself, or she was sent to find it. Or . . ." His face went blank.

"Or what, Falcon?" Edwin asked.

Falcon's eyes cleared. "The presences of Gray and the mummy have huge implications for Hugh Everett's 1957 article 'Relative State Formulation of Quantum Mechanics.' And the implications of that are indeed worth killing to protect."

At the blank looks, he explained, "Anyone going back to the past risks changing the future, and hence creating a situation which violates causality. What's called 'the grandfather paradox.' It states that if you go back in time and kill your grandfather, you can never be born to go back in time and kill your grandfather."

"Let me get this straight. You think King Smut went back in time?" Reid couldn't hide his disbelief.

Falcon smiled in reassurance. "Forgive me, Doctor Farmer. I have a habit of talking to myself. The laws of physics—as we currently understand them—preclude time travel into the past. In fact, if you are to integrate general relativity and quantum mechanics, time doesn't even exist."

ET pointed at the clock on the wall. "Uh-huh, and how you explain that?"

Falcon smiled wearily. "The notion of time as a universal clock began to unravel with Einstein's general theory of relativity. The physicist and philosopher Claus Kiefer would tell you that what you perceive as time is only a measure of change occurring between separate particles in an essentially 'timeless' universe. We've just begun to contemplate a potential theory of canonical quantum gravity in which the universe itself is timeless. And if time really doesn't exist, Gray's abilities suddenly become plausible, if not easily explained, given our current understanding of physics."

Reid couldn't help remembering the expression on Domina's face, her sadness. How she really didn't seem to fit, as if she had an energy about her . . . "Her expression when I told her that Dzibilchaltun was nothing but ruins? What did she say? *Nequam populi, inanus orbis?*"

"Latin, you say?" Edwin tapped the keys and stared at his screen. "It translates to 'Worthless people, worthless world.'"

Dr. Ryan turned his attention on Reid. "We need a Latin scholar to translate Gray's notes. And those odd hieroglyphics are Mayan, you say?"

He nodded. "She told me she spoke Latin and Ch'olan. It's a Mayan dialect originally written in glyphs and glyph compounds. I can recognize the occasional glyph, but we need a better epigrapher than me."

"We're getting away from the point," Chief Raven reminded where she squatted before Falcon. "What's Skientia after?"

"Something that's going to make them a pile of money," Savage asserted. "Give them some sort of unassailable technological advantage beyond just monitoring communications."

"And it all goes back to this machine?" Edwin was giving the black electrical box from the sarcophagus a sour look.

Falcon's soft voice cut like a knife. "Perhaps you had better consider the inverse correlation."

"And that is?" Cat asked.

"What does Gray want to get out of Skientia?"

"I thought she was on our side." Raven narrowed an eye. "You know, kidnapped out of her cell here in Ward Six."

"Kidnapped?" Falcon asked mildly. "Or escaped?"

# 61

**Y**ou could have heard a pin drop. The light blue room with its serene landscapes and cuddly animals felt completely incongruous. People were frowning, shifting nervously. I stared at Falcon, trying to get my mind around the things he was saying. *Gray, escaped?* Trouble was, Falcon didn't just spout nonsense.

"I'm not following you," I told him.

"You make the assumption that Skientia, as a powerful corporation, is the true danger. That Gray is a helpless, mentally impaired victim. The attempted assassination by unknown parties adds to that illusion. I am entertaining the notion that exactly the opposite is true. That she is a threat, and the attempt on her life was not made by necessarily hostile parties."

"Then, who were they?" Savage demanded.

Falcon gave him a sober gaze, then said, "One thing at a time, Major. Let's eliminate variables first, shall we?"

Falcon tilted his head. "The answer to King Smut's purpose, and the creation of that tomb, probably lies in that black box, the jar, and the papyrus book from his sarcophagus."

"His name is Fluvium," Kilgore interjected. "Or so Domina claims."

Falcon nodded acquiescence. "Very well, Fluvium apparently wanted Gray to receive the book, box, and jar. In the meantime, I think Gray is looking for a way to save both her husband and her world."

Kilgore France was having a terrible time with all of this. She asked, "What do you mean when you say, 'save her husband and her world'?"

Falcon replied, "In light of Gray's statement, 'Worthless world, worthless people,' I suggest we proceed under the assumption that if she can get what she needs from Skientia, she will do irreparable harm to our very existence."

"Time travel? Paradox?" Reid Farmer snapped, "This is nuts!"

Cries of disbelief filled the room.

"Yo! Y'all!" Edwin bellowed to restore order. "Welcome to Grantham. We do crazy here every day."

In the sudden silence, Falcon continued in his ever-so-dispassionate voice. "The other, the alternative hypothesis, is that Gray is an agent—political or commercial—bent on stealing Skientia's secrets. To do so, she and her sponsors have created this elaborate charade to convince Skientia to allow her access to their most closely guarded technology."

"I looked that woman in the eyes," Reid said woodenly. He fixed his gaze on Kilgore. "Think. Really think. You may be the best forensic anthropologist alive. Consider all the details, the time it would have taken to construct that tomb, fix the geology, age the contents. And then there's the mummy. As good as you are . . . could you have created a hoax as perfect as Fluvium?"

For long moments I watched Kilgore France stare into Reid's eyes. Her voice wavered. "No."

"The tomb Yusif and I opened couldn't have been faked." The archaeologist knotted a fist. "The problem here is that we run smack into impossibility whichever way we turn."

He glanced my way. "And from your professional perspective, Doctor Ryan? Can you explain Domina's psychology? Talented though she might be, could she really fake her condition that well?"

I took a deep breath, started to shrug, and then let my arms fall in defeat. "I can't fit her into any known diagnosis. Delusions are based on what we know. She demonstrates no common cultural or historical reference with the rest of us. Couple that with her incredible knowledge of electronics and the fact that she translated a physics book into Mayan mathematics. No one would undertake that kind of effort, even if—as has been suggested—she was a spy. At this time I don't have an alternate hypothesis."

Even as I spoke, something slipped into place. Karla, ever vigilant when it came to facial expressions, asked, "What did you just hit on, Skipper?"

"I've often said that she's like the ultimate closet child. Completely ignorant of common enculturation and socialization. But . . ." I shook my head.

*Dear God! Did I almost admit in public that I believed Gray was some kind of alien?*

"You people are insane!" Savage exploded.

The Grantham patients stared at him.

I chuckled to relieve the tension. "Wait a minute. Let's not go off half-cocked. I don't think any of us really believe that Gray came from some alternate dimension."

*And who,* I asked myself, *were the two assassins who just appeared in the garage that day? One to die and remain unidentified, the other to vanish into thin air?*

Cat said, "Skipper, here you have a collection of some of the finest minds in their respective fields: Dr. Kilgore in forensics, Dr. Farmer in archaeology, yourself in psychology, Falcon in systems theory, me in biochemistry, not to mention the whole weight of the government when they tried to identify Gray. How can she fool us all?"

Falcon cleared his throat in the ensuing silence. "Skientia will act immediately to recover Drs. France and Farmer, along with the book, vial, and device. That Fluvium went to such efforts to send them to Gray is justification to get them back at any cost. They believe Gray can provide them with the mathematics to prove and understand quantum gravity, and perhaps the ability to manipulate entangled matter across time and space. Either would propel them into a political and financial global supremacy."

"And Gray?" Savage asked, looking partially placated.

"We have to stop her," Falcon said simply. "Dr. Farmer, do you know an epigrapher who can discreetly decipher Gray's Ch'olan hieroglyphs?"

"I do."

"Good, and see what your Mayanists can discover about the mathematics."

Falcon turned to Cat. "Doctor Talavera, you need to find a lab and conduct an analysis of that jar. Treat the contents as a biosafety level 4 hazard until proven otherwise. Open the jar in a Class III biosafety cabinet. Take no chances."

"Got it," Cat answered.

"Skipper?" He turned to me. "I need you and Major Savage on the Gulfstream. Winny can fly you. The two of you need to personally update General Grazier. Given his compromised communications, brief the general in a public place, the location of which you reveal to Grazier no more than a half hour prior to meeting. Major Savage, your connections in the Intelligence Support Activity will lead you to a technician who can analyze Fluvium's box.

"Meanwhile, Edwin and I will find us a base of operations in Santa Fe, the sort of place Skientia wouldn't expect. Perhaps something close to the opera."

"The what?" ET looked horrified.

"It will do you good, Edwin. An expansion of your rather limited horizons."

"DC then Santa Fe?" I asked, slightly dazed by the rapidity of all this.

"Santa Fe is close to Los Alamos," Falcon replied as if it explained everything.

"Now I'm a travel agent?" Edwin asked.

"Our people are going to need credit cards, identities, telephones, and other things. At the same time we will require intelligence on our enemies and their assets. You are going to be learning everything you can about the Los Alamos Labs, the people who work in them, and the Skientia building in particular. But carefully, Edwin. More carefully than anything you've ever undertaken."

"Got it, Falcon."

Karla Raven shook her hair back. "Let me guess. As Edwin uncovers data on Skientia, I figure out how to break into the place, am I right?"

"Very good, Chief. But in the meantime, you need to concentrate on keeping our people safe. Your SEAL training included executive protection strategies. If Skientia is as good as I think they are, they will make an attempt on Major Savage and the Skipper in Washington."

"And me?" Winny asked.

"After DC, you will be flying reconnaissance missions with the chief. Providing transport. Winny, you're our ace in the hole. If the rest of us fail, we're going to need you to steal a jet from Kirtland Air Base."

She grinned like a triumphant tiger. "I love this plan. What do I do with the plane?"

With deadly intent, Falcon said, "Destroy the Skientia lab from the air should we determine Gray is about to use it."

# 62

Karla Raven sat two rows back from the Skipper and Major Savage as the Gulfstream winged east under Winny's capable hands. She studied the Washington area maps to reacquaint herself with the city's layout. Using a pen, she carefully marked the locations of hospitals, police stations, fire stations, and military establishments—all potential refuges if bad became worst.

Karla checked her watch, calculated the remaining flying time, and hoped the car service she'd ordered would be waiting. With a toe she gave the black case under the seat in front of her a reassuring shove. The heavy bulk of the Heckler and Koch submachine gun brought a smile to her lips.

*More horsepower than I'm going to need on this trip.*

"I hope."

She'd made their reservations under the names of Charlie Boyle and William Kline. Booked a suite with two adjoining rooms at the airport Hilton using a corporate credit card number Edwin had created from somewhere—and wondered what it said about the way the world worked when a guy with Edwin's slick fingers and a computer could conjure identities, money, and accounts out of thin air.

Now it was just a matter of picking the right public place to meet Grazier. The best bet would be a restaurant. She set aside her map, unbuckled, and walked forward to crouch in the aisle between Ryan and Savage. The Skipper looked up from the collection of scientific papers on physics, entanglement, and slow light he'd downloaded from the Internet.

Savage had been doing the same thing she had, studying maps of DC but on his laptop.

"Yes, Chief?" Ryan asked, setting his papers aside.

"Thought you might have a food preference, sir."

"Seafood," Ryan said immediately. "That close to the Chesapeake, I'd love crab." He glanced at Savage. "Major?"

"Sounds fine."

"I'll see to it, sir. My biggest concern is getting the general to the restaurant undetected."

Savage hesitated, then said, "Chief, tell him it's an Aba protocol. He'll give you a place and time. You need to be there, to the second, with a vehicle."

"Aba protocol. Yes, sir."

At Ryan's questioning look, Savage relented. "Goes back to a 2017 op in Kandahar. He'll know we're expecting someone on the inside to be playing for the other team. That he's probably under surveillance."

Ryan fingered his reports, eyes fixed on the bulkhead.

"So . . . You can't really *believe* Falcon's claim that Fluvium went back in time." Savage was giving the Skipper a measuring look. Karla's gaze followed his, that very question having dominated her thoughts.

Ryan slapped the papers. "Major, physicists have been arguing Hugh Everett's 'many worlds' hypothesis since he first published it in *Reviews of Modern Physics* in 1957. And you know what? The finest brains in the world pretty much agree that it's not only possible, but mathematically *probable*. The other thing that everyone pretty much agrees on is that travel *backward* in time is *impossible* according to the laws of physics."

Karla watched the Skipper grimace his distaste. "But none of the proofs *against* traveling back in time are based on quantum gravity—which we don't understand—or entanglement, which we're only beginning to experiment with. And you're going to love this: Falcon's right. One of the implications of unifying quantum mechanics with general relativity to create a theory of canonical quantum gravity is that time *doesn't* exist. What we perceive as time is nothing more than measures of changing relationships between discrete bits of a timeless universe."

Savage was giving him a *Twilight Zone* expression—that desperate and glazed look that said, "Please get me back to reality."

"So Falcon's nailed it, sir?" Karla asked.

"How do I know? Let's not forget, it's Gray who's led him there." He glanced at Savage. "To answer your question, Major, I don't know what to 'believe' yet. Fortunately, I don't have to. I can drop the whole thing in Grazier's lap."

"What if he tells you to stand down? Back off Gray and Skientia?"

"We back down." Ryan ran thoughtful fingers over the stubble on his jaw, eyes still fixed on infinity.

"And Falcon's concern about Gray using the Skientia lab? That she's a threat to our world, sir?" Karla asked.

Ryan gestured futility. "I don't know, Chief. I just don't know."

# 63

Karla had picked a joint called "The Crab Shack." It sat out over the water atop pilings pounded into the Potomac. For my taste it was perfect: that kitsch saltwater atmosphere with fishnets and seashells, and big blue-and-white plastic crabs hanging on the walls. The tables sported red-and-white–checkered tablecloths covered with sheets of brown paper. Crayons of various colors filled a central cup, allowing the more creative to draw while waiting for their food. Around the room, people used clunky wooden hammers to crush crab exoskeletons before fishing for the succulent meat inside.

Outside, down the stairs, and on the river, the place even had a dock where you could motor up in your boat, tie off, and climb to a side door. Big plateglass windows looked out on the water where lights reflected in yellow-white streaks from the black surface. On the opposite shore, Arlington burned a dull and sulfurous luminosity into the low-hanging clouds.

Not that I could see well since Chief Raven had specifically reserved our table along the back wall, close to the swinging doors that led into the kitchen and adjacent to the side entrance that went down to the dock. She'd reserved the closest four-top for herself—placing her between us and the entrance.

"Better for security, sir," she had said. Then she'd headed back to the car to go fetch Grazier. Eli hadn't even hesitated when I mentioned "Aba protocol" over the phone. He just gave me a time and address which I had passed on to Karla.

I glanced at my watch. The chief had been gone for thirty-four minutes.

"Relax," Savage said before sipping his beer. "He'll be here. And God help any poor fool who gets in Chief Raven's way."

"Thought you didn't like her."

Savage squinted at the bubbles rising in his glass of Sam Adams. "Let's say my opinions of Karla Raven have been radically revised since that first day I saw her in your office. Should she really be in Grantham?"

I studied him for a moment before I said, "To accomplish what she has, Karla Raven had to become superhuman. *Super* . . . human. I don't know how she endured the pressure, let alone rose above it. When that IED killed most of her platoon, it shattered something inside her."

"Can't blame her for that."

"The only person who holds Karla Raven responsible is Karla Raven."

"So she could fall apart at any moment?"

"As active as she's been, the flashbacks and nightmares seem to have receded. She's anything but depressed. And the machine guns and tequila she's had the pleasure of stealing have been more or less um, 'sanctioned' since they weren't *our* tequila and machine guns."

"God, Ryan, you sound like you're considering this as therapy?"

"It is. For everyone but Falcon." I stared absently at a plastic crab. "He balances on the knife's edge. At the Pentagon they called him 'the Oracle' and locked him away in a basement office until he suffered what we call a psychotic break. He arrived at Grantham in a catatonic state. Took months to stabilize him, tailor the meds, and return him to any kind of normal function. As soon as Grazier found out, he started sending intel for Falcon's analysis."

"Is that good or bad?"

"Depends." I spread my hands. "My dilemma is that as a military officer I know Falcon's analysis saves lives and adds to our national security. As a doctor, every impulse is to sacrifice his brilliance in favor of a more stable brain chemistry."

"He didn't look so good after Aspen."

"No." I paused. "And, frankly, I'm scared to death about taking him to Santa Fe. If things spiral out of our control . . . ?" I shook my head. "Falcon could suffer an irreversible psychotic break."

Savage stared soberly at his beer; to change the subject, I asked, "Where are you from, Major? I catch a slight southern accent mixed with something I can't quite put my finger on."

"Oklahoma. Creek tribe. Got some Choctaw in my background, too." His dark eyes flashed my direction. "I had to learn to talk Muskogee as a kid. I was raised by my uncle Buck after my folks vanished."

"Vanished?"

"I know they worked for the government, but they never said which agency. Uncle Buck, he thought they were CIA. Maybe State Department. I don't know. I tried to dig into it once and hit a stone wall. When that happens to a guy with my clearance and access? You just say, 'Okay, I think I get it.'"

"And your Uncle Buck?"

"He's a medicine man. Very traditional. A *hilishaya*." Savage shook his head. "Damn, what a way to grow up. He taught me all the plants and their uses, how to hunt, fish, and live off the land. As soon as he figured out I had a head for mathematics, he never let it rest. I was the only kid in the world who had to do calculus in my head while I was gutting out a deer."

"You're joking."

"Uncle Buck is fascinated with anything having to do with the past. His bookshelves fill one entire wall of the old trailer he lives in. They've sunk the cinderblocks a good four inches on that side and bowed the floor. But he wanted me to make it in the modern world as well. I got an appointment to West Point. Did kind of well there." He grinned. "Let's say living with Uncle Buck is like boot camp."

"And after that?"

"I just had to be a Ranger. Which—for a variety of reasons—led to the Pentagon, which led to the Activity, which allowed me to get my PhD at Georgetown."

"I didn't know you had a doctorate."

"Indigenous religious studies. It kind of gives me an advantage when I get home to see Uncle Buck. And it serves me very well on ops when we're working with non-Western peoples."

"You're more than you seem, Major." I shot a look at the street entrance as Eli Grazier entered, Karla at his elbow. Grazier was dressed in tan slacks, wearing a pale-yellow button-down shirt and blue blazer. He smiled at the hostess and pointed our way, then wove through the tables. Karla followed a pace behind. While she was scanning the room, half the male eyes in the place followed her. And no wonder; on top of her looks, she oozed the feral essence of a stalking leopard.

Savage and I stood.

"Tim, Sam," Grazier greeted, shaking both of our hands. Then he seated himself. "This is a surprise. Especially the extra security." He inclined his head to the table where Karla now sat with her back to us, allowing her to observe the room as she pretended to study the menu.

"It was Falcon's suggestion," I said.

"I see." Grazier glanced first at me, then at Savage. "Onto something, is he?"

"You could say that," Savage said dryly.

"Skientia has come out swinging," Grazier told us, then looked up when the waitress appeared. "You got a local stout?"

"Capital City," she replied.

"I'll take it."

"You ordering crabs?" Grazier glanced at both of us, and told the waitress, "We'll take the five-pound platter with all the fixings."

As she left, his expression tightened. "Skientia's shitstorm runs all the way from Capitol Hill to that poor sheriff in Colorado. I've had calls ranging from Bill Stevens—the president's chief of staff—clear down the food chain to clueless legal assistants." He smiled in mock amusement. "And they've got jack shit. So far, no one knows who hit that mansion, and it's driving them stark raving nuts."

"Good thing we asked for an Aba," Savage said softly. "You got out all right?"

"Oh, sure. It's not the first time I've used that particular rabbit hole. But I'm stymied. Where's the leak?"

"Falcon says it has something to do with Skientia's research on entanglement." Savage cocked his head suggestively. "He says they're monitoring *all* of your communications."

Grazier's expression pinched, and he ran a hand over his salt-and-pepper hair. "The technology's not *that* advanced."

"How do you know?" I asked. "Falcon thinks they've gone farther than anyone suspects with the research, that since you were funding them, they had a definite interest in anything you were saying about them."

Grazier bit his lip, looked around the crowded restaurant where people hammered bits of stubborn crab. "Then you picked a pretty good place for a clandestine meeting."

Savage asked, "Would it explain how they took France and Farmer from us?"

"It would explain everything. Could they have compromised Grantham, too?"

"Monitoring us wouldn't even be a challenge. Taking Prisoner Alpha proved that. But if they were, they'd already have snatched back Farmer, France, and the objects from the sarcophagus."

Savage glanced around warily before he lowered his voice. "Falcon wants to go after Skientia's Los Alamos lab. It's preposterous, really." He hesitated. "He thinks Gray is the real threat."

"Gray?"

"Prisoner Alpha," I said. "My people call her Gray because she lived behind that big gray security door."

Grazier pointed a finger. "Gray? I like that. Good code name. Is it true that you almost recaptured her in Aspen?"

"Almost isn't the word I'd use. They evacuated her the moment the security was breached."

"Too bad."

"But we've got the sarcophagi and bodies the FBI and ATF seized, right?" Savage asked.

"Not anymore. FBI surrendered the sarcophaguses to Skientia's lawyers under court order."

I told Grazier, "I think we've got the important items from inside Fluvium's sarcophagus. France and Farmer brought them out: an electrical device, a jar containing some kind of liquid, and a book. Cat's analyzing the jar's contents, Farmer's working on the book, and we've got the black box with us. We need a good lab with a remote sensing machine that can look inside, and a crackerjack electronics engineer to interpret what we're seeing. We have to do it someplace where it *won't* become a matter of official record."

"I have someone up at Aberdeen. You know him, Sam. Harvey Rogers." Grazier made a face. "An electronic device out of an ancient Egyptian sarcophagus?"

"According to Farmer and France who found it." I glanced at Savage who gave me his "It's your funeral" expression.

"Okay, Eli," I began, and pulled out my notes. Point by point, I outlined Kilgore France and Reid Farmer's enigmatic analysis of the tomb, the sarcophagus, Fluvium's contradictory body, and Gray's statements.

"It sounds ridiculous," Eli told me as a huge platter of steamed crabs was set before us. "Sam? You saw that tomb. Did it look like a fake to you?"

Savage stuffed an oversized bib into his collar, pulled a crab from the pile, and hammered a claw with a wooden mallet. "The place *looked* ancient, Eli."

I picked up one of the wooden mallets and smacked my own crab. "But if Falcon is right, as dangerous as Skientia is, they're not the biggest threat."

Grazier shot me a sidelong glance as he stuffed dripping white meat into his wide mouth. "I suppose this is where we go back to Gray?"

"Falcon thinks the only way that the contradictions of the tomb, her language and math skills, her electronics expertise, her socio-cultural behavioral disorder, the explanation for Fluvium's modern-ancient body, and Skientia's obsession with her . . ."

Eli prodded, "Go on, Tim."

". . . Is that she came from an alternate world, something parallel to ours. That not only is the Everett 'many worlds' hypothesis correct, but somehow Fluvium landed in our past. Due to some currently unknown complication from quantum gravitation, or maybe entanglement, things . . ."

Grazier's complexion had turned a curious shade of gray. The wooden hammer dropped from nerveless fingers to clatter on the butcher paper. For long moments, he just sat there, looking like I'd hit him in the head with a rock.

"Eli?"

Hoarsely, he asked, "Falcon is sure?"

"Hey," Savage said, clearly unsettled, "the guy's a DID-schizophrenic who carries on conversations with invisible—"

"Is Falcon *sure*?" Eli demanded.

I spread my arms. "No. He's not. He has all of my people scrambling to disprove it. You understand the scientific method. The notion that Gray is from some parallel world is our null hypothesis, the one we want to disprove. We're doing our best to . . ."

"Holy shit," Grazier whispered.

Savage snapped, "Eli, it's impossible!"

In a still-hoarse voice, Grazier said, "I thought Skientia's research was bullshit. I just funded it to keep them working on encryption."

"Funded *what*, Eli?" I asked sharply.

Grazier reached for his stout and chugged it. He used his bib to wipe at his lips. "They thought they could isolate and capture entangled matter from the past in a tailored Bose-Einstein condensate. The preliminary results were encouraging. They thought they might be able to bounce one of these molecules back along the path it had arrived on."

My stomach started to tingle. "Like sending it back in time?"

He nodded. "Think of a rubber ball on railroad tracks riding a light cone from the past to the present. Then it gets snared in the Bose-Einstein condensate and stopped. Skientia then smacks it, reverses the charge, spin, and direction, shooting it back down those same tracks from whence it came."

"I'm a psychiatrist," I muttered. "I don't get it. Why even study this?"

Grazier gave me the sort of look he'd give a stupid five-year-old. "Tim, quantum encryption doesn't allow you to listen in on real-time communications. Attempting to do so destroys or degrades the message. But if you could make the universe timeless? Think of the intelligence implications of being able to monitor an opponent's secret communications from a day, week, or month before. Troop deployments, mission parameters, battlefield objectives, geopolitical goals?"

Savage and I stared incredulously.

Savage broke the silence. "Skientia was catching and beaming bits of matter back into the past. And while they were doing so, Gray popped into their lab?"

Eli whispered in a husky voice, "So this is what it feels like to be present when the world is forever and irrevocably changed."

"You *believe* this?" I asked.

Grazier looked sick to his stomach. "The real-world implications of entanglement? Work on quantum gravity? A timeless universe? I've got research split up and spread around to a hundred different labs. The only people with all the pieces . . ."

"Skientia," I supplied, feeling a little sick myself.

As if pulling himself out of a trance, Grazier continued, "But despite Skientia's power, Falcon still says Gray is the real threat?" He went pale again. "If she can somehow go back, intercept Fluvium, take him with her . . . Dear God!"

Savage's expression had frozen. "Eli? You mean this is *real?*"

"A whole new branch of physics," Grazier whispered absently. "Top secret. We're putting together a new understanding of quantum gravity. Pushing the boundaries . . ."

Faster than I could comprehend, Karla leaped up. She twisted. Grabbed Eli Grazier by the shoulders. Slung him sideways.

The deafening crack of a high-powered rifle paralyzed the room. The back of Grazier's barely vacated chair exploded in splinters. The bullet blasted through our pile of crabs. Shell and meat splattered in all directions.

Halfway to my feet, my gaze had hardly fixed on the wreckage as Karla screamed, "Get down!"

Savage pulled me to the floor as the room erupted in screaming people.

# 64

In a lab at the University of Colorado Medical Center, Cat Talavera tried to come to terms with the many ways her world had changed. One minute she'd been locked away as a crazy woman. The next she was stealing a helicopter, then looting private businesses and brewing a potentially lethal nerve agent. That, in turn, led her to raid a mansion—from which she then escaped in a firefight. And now—but a few days later—she gets handed the keys to a state-of-the-art microbiology lab.

"Go figure," she whispered as she focused on the stained slide and positioned it in the microscope. Dialing in the focus, she studied the image. The familiar structure of one of the Cyanobacteria phyla were outlined in light purple. She used the controls to measure and record, then copied the image to the reference computer. Following a hunch based on foggy memory, she typed in the genus *Oscillatoria*, checked the box for comparison, and hit enter.

The photo she'd taken remained in the left-hand screen. The right filled with comparative images, and one by one she scrolled down, comparing the forty-two different species of *Oscillatoria* with her specimen. Physiologically, she was able to throw out most of them, but for the remaining handful she couldn't make a distinction.

"Okay." She pushed back from the screen and considered her micrograph. "Now why would Fluvium fill a jar with red *Oscillatoria* cyanobacteria, and then have it placed inside his sarcophagus with him? A, he had no other hobbies, so he collected pond scum? B, he suffered from a psychological disorder that turned pond scum into a sexual fetish? Or C, he knew something about this stuff that the rest of us don't."

"*Dios mio,* I love research!" She flicked her micrograph image with an index finger. "Okay, my little friend, let's find out what you are. You might look like the others, but your DNA is going to give you away."

First, she needed to process her sample and isolate the strand of DNA before she could amplify it in the polymerase chain reaction machine. Once the PCR had produced a sufficient sample, she'd precipitate it, run a Southern blot, and have a concrete signature that would tie her bacterium to the correct *Oscillatoria* species.

Meanwhile, there was something nagging at her subconscious.

*Oscillatoria* grew in fresh water, and when enough bloomed, could turn the water bloodred. It was often used for dye.

She typed in uses on the computer.

*Oscillatoria* was commercially grown to produce butylated hydroxytoluene, commonly called BHT, which was used for an antioxidant food supplement.

"Fluvium, old buddy, surely you weren't worried about your chromosomes shortening."

No this was something else.

Time to go to work.

# 65

Karla kept one hand knotted in Grazier's blue blazer as she tugged the general toward the door to her right. "Stay down!" she bellowed as Grazier tried to stand. Reaching up, she opened the crash bar to the exit and did her best to propel the scrambling Grazier outside.

Then she got to one knee, rising far enough to glance around the chaotic restaurant. People screamed as they either ran for the door or cowered under tables. Chairs banged and scraped as they were overturned or flung back among the flailing bodies to create a tangle among the tables.

*"Skipper!"* she bellowed over the chaos. He was sprawled on his side while Savage crouched behind the table, wary eyes searching for the assailant. "This way!"

Ryan scrambled on all fours, Savage close behind. Even as she dragged them through the door, Savage seemed to be coming to his senses, asking, "What now?"

"Get the general down the stairs!" Karla pointed to where Grazier was clambering to his feet. The stairway led down to the boat dock. "Take that cabin cruiser. I've got the six."

Karla waited just long enough to see Grazier start down the stairs, before she pulled her shirttail out to expose the HK .45 in its inside-the-waistband holster. Drawing the heavy pistol, she backed down the stairs, covering their retreat. Pandemonium sounded inside the restaurant.

At the dock she glanced over her shoulder, ensured that Grazier and Savage were helping Ryan into the vessel—a twenty-foot fiberglass day cruiser. Dropping a hand to the hull, she vaulted, and her feet thumped solidly onto the deck. Pushing past Grazier, she tossed Savage the pistol, ordering, "Cover us."

Karla turned to Ryan. "Skipper, cast us off. Hurry!"

She ignored Grazier's questions and started tossing cushions off the bench seats in the rear. Opening the compartment lids beneath, Karla discovered life jackets, fire extinguishers, and in the third, a toolbox.

This she lifted out, popped open the lid, and extracted a screwdriver and a hammer. Brushing past the stunned Grazier, she found the ignition switch where it protruded from the polished walnut instrument panel. Setting the flat blade of the screwdriver, she hammered it in, then pried the switch from the resisting wood. With a jerk she yanked the switch from its wires. She knew this one: White to white, red to red, and black to yellow. Then she touched the two red ten-gauge wires together. The inboards turned over and caught, rumbling to life.

"Skipper?" she called.

"We're loose!" Ryan told her as he came walking down the grip strip between the cabin and gunwale.

"Loose?" she asked distastefully as she reversed the screws and throttled up. "Is that nautical terminology, sir?"

"Would you prefer untied?" Ryan asked.

She throttled down, shifted to forward, and pushed the throttles all the way open. The engines roared, and the day cruiser lumbered ahead. As she handled the wheel, Karla glanced over her shoulder in time to see the restaurant door burst open, people emerging, milling in terror, and then charging down the stairs.

By then, her stolen vessel was gaining speed, the hull slapping on the light chop. Gusts of wind tugged at her hair.

"What the hell happened back there?" Grazier demanded.

Karla told him: "Male, Caucasoid, mid-thirties, black hair, close-cropped. Stone-dark eyes and the look of a trained killer. Had a slight limp in his left leg. Feel this weather, sir? Not the sort of night for a raincoat like he was wearing, would you think? So he kind of tripped my trigger, sir. The good news is he looked right past me. The bad news? He fixed on you, sir. I moved the moment he pulled that M4 carbine out from under his coat."

"And thank God you did," Savage told her, handing the HK back. As she reholstered it, he told Grazier, "General, his bullet would have taken you right through the spine. As it is, I think Crab Shack's gonna have to write off that whole chair and table."

Grazier, still looking shaken, asked, "How did they find me?"

Karla shot him a measuring look; the glow from the instruments illuminated his worried face as she turned east into the channel. "Either they had a visual on you and observed my pickup, or they've got an active or passive trace on you somewhere, sir."

"Impossible," Grazier growled.

Savage stepped down into the cabin, emerging moments later with a pair of men's shorts, sandals, and a bulky white shirt. "Eli, try these on."

"What are you saying, Sam? That they've put a tracker in my clothes?"

"If the chief had been a half-second slower, you'd be dying or dead right now, Eli. I know you're not going to look like any fashion plate, but you'll stay alive for the moment."

Grazier shot a worried glance between Ryan and Savage, then sighed, took the clothes, and stepped down into the cabin.

Karla looked up as they passed under the Key Bridge with its glowing halo of lights.

"What's the plan, Chief?" Savage leaned forward on the padded cabin, gaze fixed on the water ahead.

"Southwest Waterfront, sir." Karla reveled in the sensation of the cruiser as it thundered down the channel. How long had it been? Too many years in the desert, and then the hospitals, and finally Grantham. "We can ditch the boat without much comment. Best bet is the fuel dock, sir. We tie up, tell them to fill the tanks, and that we'll be back in ten minutes. Meanwhile we just walk away. From there, we catch a cab for downtown, drop at the Willard Hotel, walk across the street to the JW Marriott, and take a cab back to the airport Hilton."

"Good thinking." A pause. "And good work back there, Chief."

She rounded the navigation buoy at the mouth of the Anacostia River and throttled down as she entered the Washington Channel.

Grazier emerged, looking like a ragged tourist, and anything but a command presence. "The damned sandals are too small, the shirt's too big. I had to use a piece of rope to tie the idiotic shorts on."

"Toss your shirt, pants, shoes, and underwear—everything—over the side. Most likely you're carrying an RFID, sir," Karla added.

"What about my wallet?" Grazier looked from one to another of them. "It's shielded."

"You sure?" Savage asked.

"I'm *not* tossing my billfold. I'm not going through the hassle of the driver's license bureau, the credit cards, the—"

Karla extended a hand. "I'll get it back to you, sir. But you'll have to wait until tomorrow."

Grazier fished his billfold from his rolled pants and laid it in her palm. He tossed the rest of his clothes overboard to wash in the wake and vanish in the dark waters.

He stiffened suddenly. "Aren't you a thief, Chief?"

"Yes, sir." She grinned as she slipped his billfold into a back pocket. "Among the best, sir."

"RFID makes the most sense," Savage told Grazier. "And DC's a heavily monitored city. An agent could have put an active tag on you with something as simple as a touch on the back. If they could penetrate one of the sensitive security nets, they could have followed you all the way across town."

"You're right, of course. Believe me, RFID will be as antiquated as bar codes if entanglement . . . *when* entanglement is implemented." Grazier shook his head. "Nothing will be the same."

Karla located the fuel dock and throttled back as they passed the slow speed buoys. At the dock, Ryan stepped across and began tying them up. Karla pulled the wires apart, killing the engines. She jumped out, offered Grazier a hand, and pulled the general from the cruiser. Then she led them to the office with its soda coolers and fishing tackle. After placing her order with the teenager at the pump, she led the way down the gently undulating dock, up the stairs, through the bustle of the Promenade, and onto Maine Avenue.

"What about my wallet, Chief?" Grazier asked after they'd hailed a cab. "If it's active, they're following us right now."

"While we're at the Willard, I'll FedEx it to your address from the business center, sir."

"Clever," he told her. Then he looked at Savage and Ryan. "Gentlemen, this is war. I've got budget and clearance for black-on-black operations. Sam, you're in command. Ryan's your number two. A package will be delivered to your hotel room tomorrow morning. It will contain authorizations, credit cards, and special clearance IDs. Present those at any military installation in the country, and you'll get immediate assistance. No questions asked."

"What about oversight?" Savage asked.

"That's my responsibility, and I'll be attending to that little problem soonest. Here's the thing: If Gray is really trying to go back and change the past, we have to stop her." His gaze hardened. "Your people can do that, can't they, Sam? Stop her?"

"My . . . *people*?" Savage cried in dismay. "Sir, they're *mental* patients!"

Ryan ignored Savage, saying, "We can take down Skientia and stop Gray. Right, Chief?"

"Hope so, sir," Karla said thoughtfully. "Because we're only a half step ahead of them at the moment. And we'll know the instant they catch up."

"How's that, Chief?" Grazier's voice was like flint.

"Because we'll be dead, sir."

# 66

The place was called the Rock Bottom Brewery, part of a regional Rocky Mountain chain of trendy brew pubs serving great food and made-on-the-premises beer. This one was loud, packed with after-work clientele, and jammed with people waiting for a table. Reid Farmer thought the choice of locations was perfect.

In the restaurant booth at his side, Kilgore—her Edwin-modified phone held to one ear, a finger in the other—attempted to carry on a conversation with her publicist in New York.

Reid rubbed the bridge of his nose and stared down into a glass of Buffalo Gold beer while the raucous collection of upwardly mobile young professionals tried to shout over the top of each other. He'd chosen the location just off the Boulder Turnpike, about halfway between Denver and Boulder. Compliments of Edwin's magic, he and Kilgore had already been checked into the nearby Westin Hotel under assumed names. The enigmatic Edwin had booked them into one of the top-floor suites with a great view of the Front Range.

Yep, but for the moments of absolute terror, his participation in the Alpha enigma definitely had perks. He turned and grinned at Kilgore, savoring the moment and giving her hand a reassuring squeeze.

She winked back at him and told her publicist, "Cancel them. Cancel them all." A pause. "I don't care. You have your instructions." She made a face as she pushed the End button.

Reid cocked an eyebrow. "Ah, the joys of celebrity."

"My producer will get over it. Skientia has been calling several times a day, respectfully asking to speak with me. Imagine that."

"Price of fame and fortune." He glanced around at the crowd. "You're sure he'll be here?"

"Miss a free meal and beer?" Reid shook his head. "Skylar Haines would still be living at home letting his mother take care of him. She was bright enough to die of a cerebral hemorrhage before Skylar turned twenty-four, thereby saving herself another thirty or forty years of buying and cooking his food, cleaning his room, and doing his laundry."

"And this man is a friend of yours?"

"Friend is a bit of a strong word. Skylar has only two passions in life: One is mooching, the other is Mayan epigraphy. He's so good at the latter that the University of Colorado anthropology department somehow tolerates the former to keep him on staff."

"Maybe he should be in Grantham with the rest of us."

"Skylar almost makes Falcon look normal."

Her dark eyes narrowed in thought. "Falcon, now there's an interesting character."

"He's jittery," Reid said. "Have you noticed? The way his hands twitch, and when his hands are occupied, his feet are tapping or his knee is bobbing. It's like he's wired all the time."

Kilgore squeezed her eyes shut and shook her head. "Tell me who's crazier? Falcon, or us?"

"What really scares me is that so far Falcon's analyses fit the facts better than ours do." He pointed. "There's Skylar."

She followed his gaze. "You've got to be kidding."

Skylar Haines pressed his way through the crowd at the door; heavy black-rimmed glasses perched on his nose. His reddish-blond hair hung in long dreadlocks. He'd dressed in a wrinkled white shirt splotched yellow with mustard stains. Somehow, he'd missed one of the loops as he'd threaded his belt. Having two buttons on his cuff, the man had mismatched his right.

Skylar peered anxiously around—saw Reid when he stood and waved. The man grinned, starting forward.

"Good to see you, Reid." Skylar called in a way-too-loud voice. Then he stopped short, blinking in surprise at Kilgore. "Wow! You got good-looking company, too, huh?"

"Skylar, this is Dr. Kilgore France. Kilgore, Skylar." Reid watched Kilgore struggle to hide a wince as she shook Skylar's hand, and said, "Pleased to meet you."

Skylar slid onto the opposite bench, grinning so garishly he exposed crooked and very yellow teeth. "So, you got some strange glyphs, huh? I'll have the big glass of red ale, and since you're buying, I want the surf and turf, and one of those onion blossom things for an appetizer. So . . . how you been? Where you been digging? So Kilgore, are you Reid's new bed bunny? Bet you guys started teepee creeping on a dig some-where, am I right?" His green eyes were gleaming behind his thick glasses. "Old Reid here, he's just got that way with women, doesn't he? We all wished we were as slick at getting chicks into the sack. 'Course, none of the gals ol' Reid here has bedded were as hot or classy as you."

"Thanks, Skylar," Kilgore told him in tones dripping with ice. "Glad to know he's moving up in the world."

Reid avoided Kilgore's acid gaze as he pushed the photocopy of Flu-vium's book across the table. "Skylar, I'll order your steak and shrimp, but only if you shut the fuck up and tell me what this says."

"Yeah, I hear that a lot." He took the photocopies, pushed his glasses up on his nose, and frowned. "Never seen anything quite like this before. Really different style of glyph, but it's modeled on Ch'olan." He touched his finger to his tongue and flipped to the next page. "This is the record of . . . Floov . . ." he sounded out the glyphs.

"Fluvium?" Kilgore prompted.

"Fluvium." Skylar nodded. "It's used as a name, but phonetically, it's just not Mayan, you know?"

"Actually"—Reid leaned forward—"we don't. That's why we came to you."

Skylar was working his way down the page, finger to the paper. "Gotta tell you, this is almost incomprehensible. I mean, the basics are here. I can pull out the root glyphs, but it's, like, got constructions, pho-netic signs I've never seen." He paused, frown deepening. "Advanced, man. Mayan on steroids! This is heavy, heavy." He glanced up, green eyes intense. "Holy shit, where'd you *find* this thing?"

"A shop in Mexico City," Reid lied. "A friend of mine found it. Thought it was bogus. He said if it could be translated it would be worth a thousand bucks to him."

Skylar's lips pursed. "A grand? To translate this?" He fingered through. "It's like . . . twenty-six pages."

"Okay," Reid reached for the pages. "He suggested Marty Breuch at Pennsylvania, but I just thought, seeing as how you were close and all—"

"No! No! No!" Skylar yanked the papers back. "I mean, I can do a paper on this, right? Publish the new affixes and positionals?"

"We'll see."

"How soon does he need this?"

"How long it will take?"

"Twenty-six pages, unknown glyphs? I can rough it out in no time. That new stuff? Gotta study on that. Work out which are words against what's phonetic. It's, like, groundbreaking! So . . . how long? Think, Skylar, what's it going to take? And what if I can't crack those new glyphs? But, then, you did that Palenque tablet. But I had comparative—"

"Okay," Reid threw his hands up. "Get it done in a week, and there's an extra two hundred for you."

"An extra thousand."

"Five hundred." Reid started to reach for the pages.

"Done! Best I can do." Skylar's eyes continued to devour the hieroglyphics.

"Good. Now, who's the best person when it comes to working out Mayan mathematics?"

"Dan Murphy at Harvard."

"You sure?"

Skylar looked up from the document. "Duh! The guy figures faster in Mayan than he can in Arabic."

Kilgore was giving Skylar the same kind of look she'd give a cockroach.

"Oh, and Skylar?"

"Uh-hum?"

"As peculiar as you are, I know you can understand what I'm about to tell you. The translation *belongs* to my client. It's not yours to splash on the Internet or email around to all of your colleagues so you can impress them."

Reid leaned forward, jabbing a finger under Skylar's long and thin nose. "'Cause if you do, I'm sending a very nasty woman to cut your balls off and stuff them down your throat. Her name is Chief Raven, and believe me, you really *don't* want to piss her off."

# 67

We hunched over Karla Raven's shoulders as she sat at the desk in our hotel suite. She had the hotel's phone to her ear as she talked to Edwin and stared at the image on my laptop. The muffled roar of jets taking off and landing at Dulles rose and fell in the background.

Karla had suggested that Edwin might be able to hack into The Crab Shack's website, access their computer, and—if it were linked to the security system—might be able to provide us with a video of the attack. Undoubtedly, the DC Police were poring over the same images we were.

The visual Edwin was feeding us appeared grainy. The camera covering The Crab Shack's entrance had enough detail that we had no trouble recognizing General Grazier and Karla as the car service's black Lincoln pulled up at the door. Unfortunately, the camera's field of view didn't include more of the lot.

Staring over Karla's shoulder, Grazier, Savage, and I watched as the two entered. On the split screen we promptly picked them up stepping into view in the reception area. Grazier smiled at the hostess, then pointed in the direction of our table. The other views in the split screen were of the boat dock and kitchen.

Karla fast-forwarded to the arrival of the guy in the trench coat. He walked in from the upper corner of the outside image. His steps were long and purposeful, and he held his head at an angle, partially averted from the camera.

"He knows he's going to be under surveillance," Karla noted.

We watched him enter, coldly ignore the hostess, and push past a waiting knot of patrons. Then, angling to the left, he began scanning the room, fixing on our location.

Karla said into the receiver, "Edwin, can you give us a blowup on his face. Maybe refine it with a fractal program? Then apply face recognition software?"

She glanced up at Grazier. "He says he can. It'll be coming in a minute."

I stared transfixed as the gunman's eyes narrowed. He grinned as he pulled back his coat to produce a black M4 carbine. At the edge of the image, the hostess' face had frozen in disbelief, her mouth an O.

I watched the carbine buck against the man's shoulder. Then he turned, coattails flying, as he strode purposefully out the door. A light-colored Toyota Camry pulled up. The gunman grabbed the passenger door, slipped into the seat, and the car roared away.

"Looks to me like the plates have been smeared with something," Karla noted.

At the bottom of the split screen I could see the four of us careening down the stairs to the boat dock. Karla hunched in a combat crouch covering our evacuation. I looked like a clumsy oaf as I fumbled to cast off the lines.

Lines, that's nautical, right?

The monitor flickered; an enlarged and grainy image of the shooter's face filled the screen. Like a passage of waves, the image began to refine, coming clearer.

"My, but that man does good work," Karla muttered.

"He ought to," I told her. "He probably lifted this program from the NSA."

"You don't know their security," Grazier growled.

"You don't know ET."

The face had refined, and now a series of dots and lines formed over it, marking the dimensions of the eyes, cheekbones, points of the jaw, lips, nose, eyebrows, and edges of the face. In the end, it settled on a specific geometric composition of lines and triangles.

Karla said, "Got it" into the telephone she'd propped against her ear. She leaned back and glanced up at us. "Edwin says if the guy's in the database we'll have him in less than thirty seconds. But if—" Her expression sharpened as Edwin told her something. "William James Toddman?"

A pause, Karla's lips pursing. "Why is that not a surprise?" She was scribbling notes on the desk pad. "Let me ask."

She glanced up at us. "The guy's on Talon's payroll. Retired Army sniper, did three tours in the Sandbox. Edwin wants to know if you'd like an anonymous tip to appear in the DC Metro Police BOLO system?"

Grazier grinned slyly. "Yeah! That would at least scatter a handful of tacks in the guy's road." Then his expression darkened. "Talon didn't do this on a whim. It would appear that my old friends in Skientia have decided that I'm in their way."

I studied Eli furtively. His psychopathic streak was in ascendance. I watched a cold cunning settle behind his eyes. He glared down at the screen for a moment, as if to burn Toddman down with the fire that was now filling him.

"Gentlemen, the gloves come off."

"Define that, Eli," I said softly, considering the ramifications. "Because we're suddenly on very shaky ground. Skientia is a registered corporation. Unlike Al-Qaeda or Daesh, they pay taxes, hold government contracts. They have entire phalanxes of lawyers. When this comes out—and you know it will—we're going to find ourselves spitting into the whirlwind."

He nodded, chewed at his lip for a bit, and said, "My oath is to protect this country from all enemies, foreign and domestic. The NSC, for once, has actually anticipated a rogue multinational corporation acting in opposition to the safety and security of the country—and in this case, the entire world."

Karla asked, "Sir, by allowing Gray to go back in time, won't Skientia vanish along with this entire time line? Isn't that part of the paradox?"

Savage's head jerked up. "What do you mean, 'vanish'?"

Grazier squinted down at the screen where Toddman's face portrayed a fierce scowl. "We think time travel is impossible. But if Fluvium has done it, that assumption is in error. Gray knows something we don't. They're light-years ahead of us."

He straightened. "Sam, I'm making a helicopter available to you first thing in the morning. Swink can fly you and the electrical device up to Harvey Rogers at Aberdeen. You worked with him on that Mogadishu op a while back. As soon as you're done with Harvey, and Swink can get it airborne, I want you on that plane back to Grantham."

He glanced at each of us. "Chief Raven, I sincerely appreciate that you saved my life tonight. You may have saved a whole lot more in the process . . . like our very existence."

He paused, index finger pressed pensively to the side of his mouth. "So what do I call you and your team?"

"The 'psycho babblers?'" Savage asked caustically. "The 'lunatic gang'?"

I winced at the deadly narrowing of Chief Raven's eyes; Savage was going to pay for that.

"How about Team Psi?" Grazier slapped the now horrified Sam Savage on the shoulder.

"And what are you going to be doing, Eli?" I asked, still achingly conscious of the fact that I was being played by a master manipulator.

"If you'll loan me a hundred, I'm catching a cab downstairs, heading home to change, and going straight to the White House. I think the president and his security council are going to get one of those briefings they hoped they'd never get." He looked genuinely frightened as he added, "And if I can't make them understand, Tim, I'm probably going to be committed to your institution by the time you land in Colorado Springs tomorrow night."

# 68

Cat Talavera yawned, reached for the big can of Red Bull, and stared at the computer readout. Around her, the lab hummed, electrical devices in constant combat with silence. Her eyes grated like abraded flesh on asphalt.

Cat yawned again, chugged down the last of the Red Bull, and returned her attention to the lines of As, Ts, Cs, and Gs. These—which the computer obligingly classified—were documented and cataloged as distinct introns, or genes. Other sections of DNA were marked as epigenetic regulators. She'd narrowed down the genus and species of Fluvium's mysterious algae: *Oscillatoria fracta*. Except that her specimens contained an extra three thousand base pairs never documented in *Oscillatoria* before.

She'd been at it for two days now, taking time only to retreat to her hotel, sleep, choke down a quick meal, and return to the lab. She'd processed the DNA, amplified it, and decoded most of the genome. As much as she longed to get back to Grantham—Who'd have ever thought?—the perplexing section of DNA taunted her.

Out of habit, Cat began coding base pairs. She'd long ago memorized which patterns-of-three coded for which amino acids. One by one, she input them into the computer, building a model protein just as the transcription RNA did at the ribosome inside a cell.

Three hours later, even the Red Bull had nothing more to offer her. Her eyes had gone numb in her skull; her back felt like a pulled pretzel. She hit the enter button on the program she'd written, waiting while the computer began comparing known proteins with the one she'd laboriously recreated from the mysterious DNA.

To her immense relief, the computer tagged a match. A close match.

She clamped her eyes, trying to will her exhausted brain to focus. She stared, fought through the fog, and shook her head.

*No way!*

Desperately weary, she figured she was imagining things. Pushing her chair back and standing up, she swung her arms, ran in place, and did a couple of jumping jacks. Her pulse and respiration up, she sat again, and studied the screen.

In disbelief she shook her head. *"Dios mio! No es possible!"*

Cat walked to the safety cabinet and gazed through the window at the innocuous jar. She impulsively crossed herself. "Bless, you, Falcon." He had been the one to suggest treating the jar and its contents with caution.

Once again, she ran the sterilization cycle, then she incinerated the samples she'd removed from the jar.

Only then did she fish her phone from her purse and press in the number.

*"What's happenin' Cat?"* Edwin's too-cheery voice came through the receiver.

"Tell Falcon I've finished with Fluvium's jar."

*"What's in it? His drink for the afterlife? I been reading 'bout these Egyptians. All that shit in the tombs? It was so they'd have plenty of supplies in the afterlife. But only a small jar like that? Most of them dudes had big pots full of water and wine and stuff."*

"Some kind of drink," she said ironically. "Edwin, you need to ask Falcon what he wants me to do with this. I've already destroyed the samples. Should I destroy the jar, too?"

*"Okay, Cat. You're leaving me in the dust here, girl. Destroy the jar?"*

"Sorry. I'm tired. Not thinking well. The jar contains a kind of algae."

*"The guy took algae with him to the afterlife? What was he going to do? Toss it into his swimming pool so he'd have a reason to hire a pool service?"*

"Edwin, we have a highly technical term in microbiology to describe organisms with characteristics like the ones I observed in Fluvium's jar." She made a face. "We call it 'Really. Really. Scary. Shit.'"

# 69

Winny Swink stood in the back of Harvey Rogers' Aberdeen lab, her butt propped against a counter, her arms crossed. Karla Raven had adopted the same pose within spitting distance to her left. The room looked like some electronics freak's psycho dreams: floor-to-ceiling shelving; carefully labeled drawers; neatly stacked piles of computer guts; testing meters of various kinds; microscopes; and machines the purpose of which Winny could barely comprehend.

True to General Grazier's word, a van had been waiting for them when Winny set the Bell Kiowa they'd been "loaned" down at Aberdeen Proving Ground's heliport. In the van had been Harvey Rogers.

The guy could have been a walking stereotype: Thick wire-frame glasses held bottle-bottom lenses that exaggerated his washed-out blue eyes. Either Rogers was growing a beard, or he'd forgotten to shave for the last week. A white lab coat covered worn jeans and scuffed brown tassel-top loafers.

"How ya been, Savage?" he'd announced as they climbed into the van. Then he'd chattered on as the van's driver wound them through the intricacies of Aberdeen's warren-like maze of buildings. In the end, it had deposited them here, at Rogers' lab.

"So that's your bad boy?" Rogers asked as Sam Savage unlatched the carry case and laid the box on the workbench.

"You understand that this is highly classified?" Savage asked as Rogers bent over the black box and studied it through his thick glasses.

Winny turned to Karla, whispering, "You'd think it was a golden chalice the way he's gawking. What's he seeing? It's a damn black box with some little lights on it."

"Fascinating," Rogers declared as he carefully turned the box with long and knobby-jointed fingers. "Solid one-piece construction of the case. A single port for a cable, but the design is like nothing I've seen. Definitely proprietary."

He lifted it, hefting the weight. "Let's see what's inside, shall we?"

He walked over to a rubber-matted counter, laid the black box down, and retrieved what looked like a lensless flashlight. This he touched to the case, and then peered at a computer monitor to one side. "This little gadget works like an ultrasound. Allows me to look inside."

Winny peered at the image on the color screen, making nothing out of it except the peculiar notion she was seeing a pink-tinted, semitranslucent, cotton-candy haze.

"Oh, come on," Rogers murmured. Then he laid a finger on a cordless mouse and said, "Magnify and increase resolution."

The effect on the screen was like diving an F-16 through a pink cloud until it began to vibrate. Winny made a face. She hated nothing on earth more than pink.

"Hold," Rogers ordered. With quick fingers, he mounted the sensor on a mechanical arm, and carefully screwed the articulating members tight. Then he repositioned it over the black box, and repeated, "Magnify and increase resolution."

Within moments the cloud began to solidify, and the image began to jiggle irregularly, then froze.

"I'll be damned," Rogers muttered.

"What are we seeing here," Ryan asked.

Rogers fingered his furry jaw. "I don't know."

Savage chided, "Come on, Harvey. It looks like pink fog, right? That's got to mean something."

"The reason it's pink? That's the composition and density. A solid block of resin would almost give you that consistency of color, but in yellow. Bloodred would tell you that you were dealing with copper. Normally, I get the usual crimson geometric patterns common to circuitry with orange highlights from solder and silver." He tapped the computer monitor. "I can't create or detect sound waves beyond this resolution. The irregular jiggles you see in the image? Despite the fact that this bench is suspended, those are coming through the earth and the building. Some are micro seismic events, some might even be heavy truck traffic, or the guys in the warehouse dropping pallets of canned food."

His expression narrowed as he stared at the pink image. "White and red, silicone and copper, but mixed with something else. And it's uniform down to a molecular level? Who even *makes* this stuff? Once you do, how do you program it, let alone retrieve data?"

"Harvey, you're talking Martian," an exasperated Savage told him.

Rogers pulled his glasses far enough down his nose to peer at Savage over the tops. "Not Martian. I'll go ahead and guess for your benefit, but it's only a guess. The only thing I can figure—assuming this thing isn't a prank—is that it's part of a three-dimensional prototype quantum computer." He shook his head as if crazed. "But *it can't be!* We're talking so damned theoretical that it's impossible. Assuming you could solve life expectancy for qubits, and heat management, it would take years and unlimited funding just to develop the technology to develop the technology to *build* the damn thing!"

Rogers turned back to the image on his screen. "Which is the problem with this being a hoax. Look at the uniformity. How do you get that kind of uniformity? How do you control the environment? At that level, a single random atom of nitrogen, oxygen, or carbon, let alone a water molecule or carbon monoxide, sulfur dioxide, anything that might stray into the matrix . . . ?"

Winny watched him narrow an eye as he spun back to Savage. "Wait a minute! You and Grazier set this up, didn't you? You sneaked into my lab last night. Somehow you bypassed my security, got in here, and programmed this into my computer." He laughed maniacally, crying out, "You *assholes!* What did I ever do to you?"

Then his expression crashed. "But *how,* damn it, did you ever bypass *my* security? I designed it." He rushed to a device that looked like an oscilloscope and pressed a button, frowning as a series of waves began to reverse and play back.

"Harvey." Savage placed a hand on the man's shoulder. "No one has breached your security. It's not a joke. That box is real. Someone made it, but we're not at liberty to disclose who. Now tell me: you're sure it's a quantum three-dimensional computer?"

Harvey Rogers blinked, almost in confusion. "Damn it, I told you.

I'm guessing until I can really get a look at that thing. Hell, I've got to figure *how* to get a look at it. Do you understand? If that's a Q3D device, I'm in the same position a Neanderthal would be in if you asked him to inspect, and then explain, an iPad. Let alone program it." He looked flustered. "So come clean. Where'd you get this? Because if it isn't ours, we're in a shitload of trouble."

"What do you mean, trouble?" Ryan asked from where he'd been watching from the side.

"Dr. Ryan, imagine if you could somehow connect the cloud, every single personal computer, supercomputer, smartphone, automobile, and aircraft ECU, every single computing device on the planet into one whole? You with me so far? You comprehending the magnitude here? Well, if that little box is a Q3D computer, you have just exceeded this entire planet's computational capacity by a factor of about a thousand. And that's assuming it's a crude first-generation device."

"Which means?" Winny asked from the side.

Rogers gave her a sharp-eyed look. "Which means that a cyberattack launched through a Q3D computer of this potential could bring down the world banking system, Wall Street, the Federal Reserve, neuter every branch of government, DOD, FAA, IRS, the White House, Justice Department, and every state and local government. It would crash the Internet and overwhelm every personal computer in the world that's tied to the net. Cell towers, hydroelectric plants, satellites, every system on the planet that's controlled by computers would stop cold." He swallowed hard. "You getting this?"

"Assuming you knew how to program it," Savage added.

"Yeah." Rogers scratched his almost-beard. "'Cause if that's what that thing is, Sam, you've just turned me into a Neanderthal. Now, tell me, where'd you get this thing?"

"It's classified, Harvey. Just tell us if that thing's real."

"I'd better call Grazier. Explain why—"

"He knows. He's briefing the president as we speak."

"Oh . . . shit." The look in Rogers' washed-out blue eyes sobered. "It better be a hoax, or the world as we know it just ended."

Winny suddenly thought of her two boys. The esoteric implications of Gray just "appearing" in their world had made no sense. But a complete collapse of society? The boys lived in a high-rise in Boston. What would happen when all those millions of people suddenly found themselves in the dark, running out of food and water? A cold sensation ran down her spine.

"Come on, people," she said. "We need to get home, get this operation put together, and take out Gray and her lab." And if Team Psi couldn't, in her mind's eye she was already banking over the Rio Grande Valley, locking a missile on the Los Alamos lab that hid Gray and her infernal machine.

# 70

Falcon had taken down his usual diagrams, charts, and work sheets. For the moment he'd rolled them into tubes, fastened them with rubber bands, and leaned them into the corner at the foot of his bed. In their place, he'd covered his bedside wall with white butcher paper and, using his felt-tip pens, had begun organizing all they knew about Skientia.

"So, what are we missing?"

"Sorry, Captain," Major Marks returned gruffly. "But you're the brains here."

"Ah, if it's brains we need, why am I wasting my time with you? Theresa's intellect would have been a great deal more help, especially given her statistical abilities when it comes to systems theory."

"Oh, sure, you never can find that skinny little cun—"

"*Don't* use that word in my presence, Major!" Falcon extended a quivering index finger to emphasize his point. "And especially don't use it when you're talking about Theresa. Doing so reflects only your own bias, ignorance, and inability to deal with modern realities. I've a mind to turn Chief Raven loose on both you and Rudy. See how long your crude behavior survives in *her* presence." He narrowed his eyes as he glared into Major Marks' steely gray eyes.

The major grunted to himself, gaze sliding off to one side. "Should have kept my grub-hole closed."

"Or thought first," Falcon agreed, glancing back at the lines, writing, and figures on his wall. From left to right on the X axis, he and Major Marks had laid out the events as they understood them. On the Y axis they had listed the facts and characteristics of Gray, Skientia, Fluvium, and the Egyptian tomb, and their current operations.

A soft knock came at the door.

"Probably your *beloved* Theresa, finally freeing herself from her *womanly* responsibilities.*"* Major Marks glowered as he inspected his right thumbnail with a critical eye.

"Come in," Falcon called, ignoring the major. The man always fumed after a rebuke.

The knock had sounded like Theresa's, but it was Cat Talavera, followed by Edwin Jones, who entered.

"Yo, Falcon," Edwin greeted. "Cat's back. Wanted to see you first thing." He started for the recliner.

Falcon pointed to the foot of the bed. "Sit there, if you would, Edwin. The major's in a rather irritable mood today. He's liable to bite your head off if you try to move him from his favorite chair."

Edwin shot a wary look the major's way and barely swerved in time to keep from clipping the major's feet. Nevertheless, he seated himself on the corner of the bed, staring up at the intricate notes on the wall and whistling softly.

Falcon pulled out the desk chair for Cat. "You look absolutely exhausted, Cat."

She placed a black, durable-looking case on the desktop. "It's in here. I'm still not sure that I shouldn't have destroyed it." She tapped her slim fingers on the tough plastic. "If this gets out . . ."

Falcon nodded. "I understand. And should circumstances dictate, we'll do exactly what you recommend. I've been keeping up with your notes. It's a cyanobacterium called *Oscillatoria fracta*—an algae that grows in long threadlike strands of cells. Different species of it are found all over the world. What makes this one so terrifying?"

"An extra couple of genes." Bruised darkness formed half-circles beneath Cat's bloodshot eyes. "Falcon, I analyzed the coding. Currently, the genes in Fluvium's *Oscillatoria* algae are methylated, turned off, if you will."

"So what's the deal?" Edwin barely masked his concern for Cat.

"I worked it out on the way down here from the lab," she told him. "Under certain conditions, the algae literally explodes with growth. When it does, it will turn the water that it grows in red, or sometimes even bloodred. When that happens, the epigenetic controllers will demethylate the two genes I'm concerned about. They will begin manufacturing a protein called 'anatoxin-a.' Or, at least, that's the closest thing we have to it in the catalog. The protein Fluvium's algae produces is a little different, having an extra hydrogen, which allows it to slip more easily through the gut wall and into the bloodstream."

"And what does it do?" Edwin asked.

Cat tensed. "The first microbiologists who worked with it in mice called it VFDF."

"So it got its own volunteer fire department?"

In the recliner, Major Marks gave the lanky computer whiz a disgusted roll of the eyes.

Cat said softly, "That stands for 'Very Fast Death Factor.' It acts directly on the nerve cells. The first symptoms are loss of coordination, spasms and convulsions, followed immediately by a seizure of the lungs. The way it works, anatoxin-a slips into the receptor that triggers a muscle cell to contract. Normally this is done by something called acetylcholine, which then rapidly degrades in the presence of cholinesterase. When that happens, the muscle goes back to resting. Anatoxin-a triggers the muscle to contract, essentially forever. Breathing requires that the muscles in your chest relax long enough for you to expand the ribs."

"What about the levels of toxicity?" Falcon asked.

"That's the thing. That extra hydrogen atom ensures that most of the toxin ingested will be absorbed. And the fact that the algae has two sets of the gene that produces the toxin?" She shook her head. "I'd swear this stuff has been weaponized."

"Can you make an antidote?" Edwin asked.

She rubbed her eyes, as if to clear her vision. "I don't know. Probably. If I had enough time and a good lab. Structurally, it's a bicyclic amine alkaloid. Very similar to cocaine in morphology. That extra hydrogen would act to increase its half-life in the body, but I'd have to do a lot more work to determine how much."

"Better to attack the algae itself?" Falcon asked.

"Maybe." She stared dully at the black plastic case. "My brain has turned to cotton, Falcon. Let me get a couple of hours sleep . . . think about it." She rubbed her face again. "But I can tell you this, when this stuff has a major bloom, and those two sets of genes kick in, about all that algae does is turn red, grow like an explosion, and pump out buckets and buckets of death."

"So why was Fluvium clutching a bottle of this stuff to his chest?" the major asked, his jaw cocked combatively. "Where'd he get it?"

"And more to the point," Falcon challenged him. "As problematic as the origins of weaponized algae in ancient Egypt might be, just what was he planning on doing with it?"

# 71

*So this is what it feels like to be thrown to the wolves.* The thought settled into Elijiah Grazier's brain with the cold certainty of a winter storm. In the past he'd had ample experience with the process—but he'd always been the thrower, never the thrown. Given a choice, he'd settle for the former any day.

He sat on the corner of a conference table in a small waiting room just off the main hallway and down from the Oval Office. The edge of the table ate painfully into his ass, and his legs were stiffening and beginning to ache. Maintaining the posture was an act of self-torture, a way to pay himself back for not thinking the last twenty-four hours through.

*How do I get one up on the bastard?*

He crossed his arms, heedless of the fact it rumpled his dress uniform. A quick stop at home had allowed him to change and retrieve his clip-on DOD ID card. A man just didn't show up at the White House wearing a stolen oversized shirt, stupid-looking shorts, and too-tight sandals.

From where he waited, Grazier could just see the polished toes of the Marine guard's shoes, the man's uniformed elbow, and part of his jacket sleeve sticking out beyond the doorjamb.

*"Sir, I'm sorry to bother you,"* he'd told the president after waiting for nearly three hours before the Chief of Staff could fit him in for five minutes. He'd felt nervous, off his game, as he began his briefing regarding Skientia. And who wouldn't?

Hell, he'd barely gotten through his introduction, before Bill Stevens, the Chief of Staff, had narrowed his right eye and asked, "Are you going to tell us that Skientia, and Prisoner Alpha are a threat to national security? Something ludicrous? Like she's . . . um . . ." His voice had dropped suggestively. ". . . from another world?"

Grazier had frozen, staring in disbelief. "You already know?"

Stevens had thrown his hands up, rising from the couch, and crying. "Hell, yes! Bill Minor, chief operating officer for Skientia, gave me a heads-up last night. He thought I might want to devise a way to keep a decorated and respected officer like yourself from ending his career by looking like a lunatic. He hoped I'd be able to keep your breakdown quiet."

Stevens had glanced at the president. "I'm just sorry you had to see it. If I'd known there was any truth to Minor's accusation, I'd have had the general removed before he embarrassed himself."

Grazier's heart might have turned to stone. "Dear God," he had whispered. "They're that much ahead of me."

The president was studying him through thoughtful, half-lidded eyes. Then he said, "General Grazier, if you could excuse us?" He gestured toward one of the secret service agents standing by the door, adding, "Please escort the general to the waiting room."

And Eli had landed here, waiting, his butt burning as the table edge cut into his flesh. How long?

He blinked. Time had become a fog.

*Bill Minor. From Skientia. I will remember that name.*

By now Savage and his band should be on their way back from Aberdeen and the meeting with Rogers.

*God, right now, more than anything, I need that box to be important.*

Bill Stevens appeared in the doorway. The man looked immaculate in his light-gray silk suit and powder-blue button-down shirt sporting a crimson tie. A curious twinkle lay behind his normally placid blue eyes as he stepped in and nonchalantly leaned against the table to Grazier's right. In a voice barely above a whisper, he asked, "Who'd you send north in that helicopter, Eli? What are they doing?"

"Helicopter? I don't know what you're talking about."

Stevens' face bent into a Dr. Seuss smile. "Well, it doesn't matter. We'll know when the FAA recovers the bodies from the wreckage. Even burned or crushed, the forensic people will ID what's left."

Eli, a leaden weight in his gut, fought to keep his expression fixed and neutral. *How the fuck do they know?*

Stevens straightened, pulled his suit jacket tight, and tossed off a mock salute as he said, "Be seeing you, General." Then he was out, leaving Grazier to smother in his own frustration.

*Skientia controls Stevens!*

He was still preoccupied with the problem when a secret service agent appeared, asking, "General? If you could come with me?"

Eli pushed himself straight, his butt tingling as circulation was restored. He marched stiffly behind the man, surprised as he was guided to one of the elevators. Even more surprising, the agent stopped short, holding the "door open" button and glancing down the hall.

Then, as the president stepped in, the agent nodded, released the button, and backed out.

When the doors slipped shut, the president pressed one of the buttons for the underground levels, and said, "Sorry, Eli. I needed to wait for Bill to leave."

"With respect, Mr. President, all I'm asking is a review of the science by a qualified outside party."

The president's distracted gaze fixed on the flashing lights as the elevator dropped. "I remember the day I first met you. You'd just made captain. They'd appointed you to squire me around."

Grazier nodded. "You were just a state senator doing all you could to stave off the base closing Congress had approved."

"We didn't win."

"No, sir." Eli took a deep breath. "I'm not off my rocker, sir. The science is advanced stuff, nearly impossible for our own physicists to comprehend. I'm still not convinced that Gray, um, Prisoner Alpha isn't playing at some masquerade."

The elevator stopped, the door opening to a lighted corridor.

"Come on. I want to discuss this in private."

"So, I'm not being placed under restraint for psych evaluation?" Eli followed the president out into the hall. A secret service agent detached himself from the wall, following discreetly behind.

"What's your opinion of Bill Stevens?"

"As of today I've decided he's a prick, sir."

The president smiled. "A good judge of character would have figured that out years ago, as I did. My problem is that he happens to be a very useful prick. He uses me, I use him. It's a cold, emotionless, and mutually beneficial relationship. Does that bother you?"

Eli smiled coolly as the president opened a thick metal door. "No, sir. Like you, I'll do what I need to, use who I need to, to complete my mission."

The secret service agent remained just outside the door as it slammed closed. Grazier found himself in a small room with two easy chairs. A small wooden table sat between them, and a bottle of what he recognized as very expensive single-malt scotch stood between two cut-crystal glasses.

"Have a seat, Eli," the president said. The man walked to the table, pulled the cork and poured a couple of fingers into each glass.

The president handed one to Grazier as he seated himself, then took the other and lowered himself into the second chair.

Eli sipped the scotch, asking, "So, is this how you treat all your pre-sumptively psychotic subordinates?"

The president leaned back. "I don't have much time. Tell me the story as concisely as possible. All of it."

Eli outlined it out as succinctly as he could.

"So I'm supposed to believe this shit about Egypt? Prisoner Alpha? The guy time traveling? Stolen sarcophaguses, weird metal boxes, and . . . and *mental* patients?" The president stared at him across the rim of his scotch glass.

Grazier sipped his whiskey. "You don't know it, but you're president today because Falcon's analysis allowed me to thwart what would have been that very inconvenient terrorist bombing during your election campaign."

The president glanced at his watch, scowled, and said, "Enjoy the scotch, Eli. Because I've come to a decision about all this. I've got some good news . . . and some bad news." He smiled, as if pained. "And I don't think you're going to like the bad news at all."

# 72

Karla sat in the left seat, Winny Swink caressing the cyclic in the right as she piloted the Bell OH58 south above Maryland's Eastern Shore. In the back, Savage and Ryan were discussing their meeting with Harvey Rogers and the implications behind the black box.

*"It's not just the computational power that increases by orders of magnitude,"* Rogers had told them, *"it's the versatility and speed. And that's just on a 2D board. Put it in a three-dimensional lattice like this looks to be? On an evolutionary scale, it turns our finest supercomputers into the equivalent of a simple protozoa. Like, not even to the cockroach stage yet, get it?"*

Karla turned to Winny, asking, "What do you think?"

Swink shot her a worried look and lifted a thin red eyebrow. Through the headset she said, "I think if that thing were used as a cyber-weapon, we'd all be screwed. It's hard to get your head around the notion of the whole world just coming to a stop. Crap, Chief! Everything we do depends on computers. Even if you just took down the banks. Overwhelmed or wiped their computer records clean? The whole fucking economy would just stop cold. No one would know who paid what, owed what, or billed what. And then if you shut down the power, water, and transportation? Even gas pumps run on computers these days."

Karla nodded, staring down at the different-colored roofs surrounded by green and the roads that ran like arteries through the trees. Colorful dots of automobiles proceeded antlike on the gray road grids. Inland, power corridors cut straight lines through the Maryland verdure. Along the shores, docks were built out over the water. On the bay, boats splashed at the front of white V-shaped wakes. All those people, just living their lives, and not a clue that their world could come undone at any moment.

"For me, the computer thing just made it all click into place," Swink said, dark sunglasses hiding her eyes as she stared ahead, her right hand on the Kiowa's cyclic. "Made me think of my two boys up in Boston. What would happen to them if everything went to shit?"

Karla shot her a sidelong glance. "Didn't know you had two boys."

"One's four, the other's just turned six." She gave Karla a fleeting smile. "At the time being married made me look more solid to NASA. Hadn't planned on the first one, let alone the second."

"You never struck me as the motherly type."

"Got that right. During the divorce, his lawyer pretty much established, and I quote: 'An alley cat would have made a better mother.'"

"Ouch."

"He's remarried. Lives in Boston. She's a ditzy blonde accountant in her late twenties, all soft and cuddly with big bouncy boobs." Swink's expression twisted in distaste as she gritted out, "She wears . . . *pink*! Around my boys! Even has *pink* fucking bedroom slippers."

"Don't like pink, huh?"

"I've *always* hated pink. General's wife came to a party all dressed in pink. Thought she'd lord it over me because I was a lowly major." Winny raised her fingers where they gripped the cyclic. "Hey, I know the rules. But the condescending bitch was just too much to bear. Hell, all she'd done in life was bake cookies and seduce a general into slipping a ring on her finger. Wanted to know if I had trouble maintaining my 'femininity' in the cockpit."

She paused. "Might have managed to cope if she hadn't been dripping in pink. Even her eyeliner, for God's sake!"

Karla couldn't stifle a grin as she glanced out at Maryland.

"You ever wear pink?" Swink asked hostilely.

"Not since I was five," Karla answered.

"I may come to like you after all, Chief."

"Don't push your luck, Major."

A hollow *pock!* sounded. Like a hailstone on a sidewalk. Though Karla knew it from bitter experience, it took an instant for her brain to register.

*Impossible!*

Another hollow *pock* sounded.

Karla wheeled in her seat, looking back. Savage—combat vet that he was—had gone rigid, bending to look out the side window.

"Swink! We're taking fire!"

Winny was already slinging them sideways with the cyclic and punching the anti-torque pedals. G pressed Karla down in the seat. She got a glimpse of a red-and-white airplane as it roared past and banked away.

Savage demanded through the headsets. "Was that what I thought it was?"

"Think so, Major," Ryan's voice carried a strain. "I'm pressing my finger against a bullet hole in the panel beside my head."

Karla was craning her neck, straining against the seat belts as she searched the sky. "You know that sound as well as I do, Major."

"Who? Why?" Savage demanded.

"Skipper?" Karla called as Winny pitched them into a left bank, the rotors clawing for a different pitch.

"What?" Ryan sounded like a man trying to keep from throwing up.

"Get me that black bag from under the seat."

"Hold on!" Winny ordered, and moving the cyclic to the right, she worked the pedals, slewing them sideways. "Where's the son of a bitch gone to?"

Karla searched the sky around them. "There!" She pointed where the red-and-white Beech was banking toward them. Sunlight flashed on the wings; the airplane looked incredibly bright against the blue haze over the Eastern Shore.

Karla shot a worried glance at Swink as she lined out the helicopter. The nose dropped as she pushed the cyclic forward and gave the collective a tug.

"What are you doing?" Savage demanded.

"It's a Beech Bonanza, Major," Swink told him. "He's got us by about fifty knots on the top end. Since we can't outrun him, our only chance is to outfly the son of a bitch."

"I'm just a dumb soldier, Major. How's he *shooting* at us?"

Karla was glaring at the Beech, watching it bank away again as Winny jacked them left and spoiled the airplane's approach.

"See how he's maneuvering?" Swink explained. "Whoever's in there shooting has to come up alongside. He's shooting out a window. That thing's *not* a fighter aircraft, Major."

"Should we call for help?" Ryan asked.

"And announce ourselves to the world?" Karla asked. "You heard the general. We're a covert op, Skipper. I say we do it the SEAL way and solve our own problems." She glanced at Winny as the woman banked them to the right. "Do we have a chance?"

"Fucking A, Chief. Who do you think is flying this bird? By now he's figured out he wasn't close enough when he shot at us the first time. Miscalculated the deflection and windage. He's got to get close. Suck in right next to us so he can take me out. Or put a round into the engine or controls."

Karla whirled in her seat, watching as the Beech banked in an attempt to slip behind them. "Skipper! Now! Get me that bag! Winny, keep us level for a bit."

"He'll close."

"Yeah, and unless you want to wear pink for rest of your short life, you'll let Skipper get me that bag and get back to his seat."

Swink's face puckered. "Five seconds, Skipper. Then you better be back in that seat, growing claws out of your ass."

Ryan unbuckled, grabbed the black nylon bag from where it had been stowed, and tossed it to Karla before throwing himself back into his seat. Even as he slipped the buckle closed, Swink pulled back on the cyclic, the nose rising as the Kiowa slowed.

Pitched forward by g-force, Karla opened the bag; Winny shot a sidelong glance at the contents. Even as she did, she played the cyclic to the left, feet working the pedals.

As they curled around, the Beech thundered past, already in a steep turn to compensate. Karla could see the open window on the airplane's right side. The thin black rod was indeed a rifle barrel.

"How do you want to play this, Major?" Karla asked as she slammed a magazine into the HK subgun and slapped the bolt down with her left hand. "The shooter's got a high-power hunting rifle . . . probably scoped. We've got a punky little subgun with lots of low-power nine-millimeter pistol bullets in it. My maximum effective range against an airplane is less than a hundred yards."

"That close, huh?" Winny pushed the cyclic forward as she played with the collective. The Bell dropped its nose, accelerating as Winny narrowed her green eyes to slits, lips working soundlessly.

Karla noted the woman's concentration, then turned to search for the attacker. Where in the hell had . . . ?

Winny slipped the cyclic left while throttling down. She punched the pedals, and the big Bell rolled on its side, the Beech powering past and banking.

"Take that, asshole," Swink said with a whisper.

Karla fixed on the Beech as it banked to the east and circled. "Cut that a little close, didn't you?"

"Before you can make a plan, you gotta know how the other guy thinks." Swink's eyes flicked to the instruments as she headed out toward the middle of the bay. They'd lost altitude, the patterns of waves on the green water easily visible below them. "Okay, where's he at?"

"There."

Swink followed her finger, nodding as the Beech curved toward them. "That's it. Now you just follow along, bucko me boy. Dance with me."

Winny played the cyclic, throttle, and collective as her feet pumped the pedals. Like a ballerina, the Bell twisted and curled. As the chopper turned, Karla watched two guys in a bass boat below flatten themselves.

"Open that passenger window," Winny ordered.

Karla unlatched the window dropping it down. Wind blast tore past the cockpit.

Even so, she heard the hollow *clack* as a bullet slammed through the helicopter's skin.

"That's your last freebie," Swink growled, and pushed the cyclic forward as she throttled up. Even as she did, the Beech blasted past in a tight turn to make another pass.

"Where's my sunlight?" Winny was muttering to herself. "Yep. Right there." She was staring down through the nose glass to where the Bell's shadow raced across the surface of the bay.

Karla had lost sight of the Beech as it hooked behind them.

"Chief?" Swink fixed her eyes on the shadow below. "You're only going to have one chance. So get it the fuck right. You've got to pepper the front of that son of a bitch. Empty the whole magazine, and if you can swap quick enough, empty a second."

"You want to line this out for me?" Karla asked.

"Just spray that fucker when I give you the chance."

"Roger that." Karla flipped the fire control to auto. She, too, was watching the shadow, startled to see the Beech's as it slipped in behind them, closing.

"How close you going to let them come?" Karla asked.

"No one sticks his tongue out for a lick if he's not close enough to taste the honey." Swink's eyes slitted in concentration. Over the wind blast, Karla could have sworn she heard the faint report of a rifle.

"Now, Chief!" Swink shouted.

Karla's stomach dropped sickeningly as the Bell twisted sideways and rose like it had been goosed from below. G-force tried to toss her across the cabin. The horizon pitched violently. The black HK might have suddenly become lead as she fought to keep her grip on the gun.

As the world spun, the Beech rotated into Karla's view. It came head-on, propeller shining in a silvered disk. White paint on the cowling contrasted with the dark plexiglass windscreen. Within seconds, it would smash right through her window.

Karla thrust the muzzle of the HK out into the downwash. Every muscle straining, she found the front sight, settled it on the Beech's spinner, and triggered the gun.

The HK vibrated, rising, obscuring her view of all but the airplane's wings. As the gun abruptly stopped, the airplane's wings were dropping. Even as she clawed for a second magazine, the Beech thundered beneath them. The Bell's airframe jolted as if it had been slapped by God.

Scrambling to keep hold of the gun, Karla almost tumbled out of her seat.

"Yahoo!" Winny shrieked, straightening their flight.

Heart hammering in her throat, Karla gasped for breath—fear like lightning in her body. Winny dropped the Bell's nose just in time for Karla's fragmenting gaze to locate the Beech. Ahead and below, the airplane hit the bay at a glancing angle. White spray blasted out; the wings snapped off. Two bodies seemed to squirt through the shattered windscreen. As the broken airplane flipped up, the tail section flew off in a lazy cartwheel. Then the engine splashed down yet again, and bent propellers slashed white lines in the waves.

"Son of a bitch!" Savage cried from the back. "I thought we were dead."

"We're not out of the woods yet, folks," Winny told them, her eyes on the gauges. "Feel that new vibration? Rotors are out of balance. Probably a bullet hole."

"One little hole makes that much difference?" Ryan asked.

"Depends on how much structural integrity is left in the blade, Skipper. And that last big bang? That was the Beech's stabilizer whacking a landing skid. Chief, you want to check that out for me?"

Karla dared the downwash before withdrawing her head and buttoning up her window. "Bent up like tinfoil, Major."

Swink's thin lips had curled into a wry smile. "And—to cap it all off—we just won an aerial dogfight in some of the most closely monitored airspace in the world. Civilian and military air traffic controllers are chattering like chimps at a banana festival."

"So what's the plan?" Major Savage asked.

"We go under the 50–301 bridge, cut west up the Severn River, and scoot overland dodging trees and power lines to the airport." She glanced down at the water barely twenty feet below. "Then we hope I can set this bird down on a broken skid without grounding a rotor blade. Assuming we all survive that, we hotfoot over to the Gulfstream, and pray they give us clearance for takeoff before they figure out it was us who splashed that Beech."

"And if they don't?" Karla asked.

"Take a guess, Chief."

# 73

Two starched Marines marched behind a manacled Eli Grazier as a
secret service agent opened the rear coach door of the waiting
black Lincoln. The agent placed a hand on Grazier's head to ensure he
didn't bump it on the doorframe.

As the door slammed shut, Grazier was able to turn his head and see
Bill Stevens, smile barely hidden on his thin lips. Stevens actually waved
goodbye when the Lincoln pulled forward.

Then the limousine slowed, allowing Eli plenty of time to observe
the arrival of a black Mercedes sedan as it pulled up at the White House
side entrance. One of the Marine guards stepped forward, leaned down,
and opened the rear door.

The tall woman—dressed in a form-fitting gray suit—emerged like
some graceful swan. Her tawny yellow hair had been professionally
coifed. Grazier watched her fix incredible blue eyes on Stevens, saw the
man swell like a peacock under her attention. The Chief of Staff was
reaching out to take her hand when Grazier's Lincoln finally accelerated
down the curving drive toward the iron gates.

# 74

On Falcon's desk, the plastic CD case lay open and forgotten. He'd thumbed through his operas and chosen Giuseppe Verdi's *Aida*. Soft strains of music played while Aida's father, Amonasro, played upon his daughter's love and duty, asking Aida to wheedle secrets out of her Egyptian lover, Radames.

"Odd that I would have picked *Aida*," Falcon mused to himself. But then, everything went back to Egypt.

"Fluvium, old boy, what were you doing with a jar full of genetically engineered algae?" Cat's description of the nerve agent's effects had been chilling. Imagine what it felt like to have every muscle in his body suddenly knot tight.

"And why, if you were crossing time to another parallel world, would you bother to carry a bottle of that stuff with you?"

"It's a quandary," Theresa agreed.

Falcon glanced at the bathroom door. Theresa stepped out, fixing a bobby pin in her hair and patting the curl into place. She studied him through knowing dark brown eyes.

"Of all the things to bring," Falcon mused, "I'd choose recording devices. You know, cameras, notebooks, that sort of thing."

Theresa seated herself on the corner of his bed. "You assume he's a tourist?"

"Or a historian."

Her prim lips pursed as she extended her thin legs and studied the rolled-up bobby socks and strapped leather shoes. "Given what you know about the man, what possible evidence do you have to support that?"

"None." Falcon admitted. "Everything points to science and engineering."

"Fluvium had the jar placed in his hands, which suggests what to you?"

"That it was of considerable importance." Falcon waved a finger at her. "Perhaps he wished to ensure that the deadly jar was not opened by the Egyptians, thereby releasing the algae?"

"The *genetically engineered* algae," she corrected. "Cat was pretty specific about that. Egyptians had no capability to tinker with the algae's DNA. Therefore . . . ?"

"It was created in Fluvium's world. Which leaves us with the question: Why did he bring it to ours?"

"You're usually not this slow, Falcon. Has that silly Major Marks been dulling your wits with his starched rhetoric?"

"I'm not following you."

"What's a planet?"

"An accumulation of interstellar matter coalesced and compacted by gravity into a concentrated sphere which in turn orbits its primary."

"Which represents what?"

"A planet!" He scowled. "You're starting to irritate me. Galactic cosmology is interesting, I'll grant you, but—"

"It's a gravity well, a closed system, Falcon."

"Of course, but why—?"

"Yes, why would Fluvium and Gray employ their remarkable talent and technology to bring a jar of genetically engineered algae to our past?" She crossed her skinny arms. "And why Egypt? Why at that particular time?"

Falcon reordered his thoughts. "Egypt had reached its zenith in the Eighteenth Dynasty."

"Ah," she mused, fingering a ring of her dark hair. "Yet another essentially closed system."

"Another closed system?" He considered. "Egyptian civilization was unique. With formidable deserts on all sides, they remained essentially isolated. Civilizations in the Fertile Crescent, the Levant, India, China—they were all constantly invaded and challenged by neighbors."

"There. You've got most of the basic assumptions necessary to solve the problem. Now, add the variable of time, which, after all, is the trademark of Fluvium and Gray's activities. Close your eyes, Falcon. That's it. Now, find order out of the chaos."

He lay back on his pillow, reassured by Theresa's presence at the foot of his bed.

On the backs of this eyelids, he laid out the pieces: Fluvium and Gray appear with a deadly algae, one manufactured on their own world. He visualized Egypt—a thin strip of densely populated green stretched along the ribbon of the Nile. Isolated by desert.

He began rearranging the pieces, building a pattern on the back of his eyelids. Fluvium and Gray are scientists. They have brought the jar, appeared beside the Nile . . . Time? Why time?

And the pieces fell into place.

He opened his eyes, staring at Theresa. "Dear God, they were going to test it! Empty the jar into the Nile! The organism would bloom, carried down the river until the entire civilization was affected."

"Very good," Theresa told him with a smile. "But why Egypt? Why at that point in time?"

"To study the effects. Long-term. The initial impact would be catastrophic, millions dying. Some, using water from wells, would survive. Most of the algae would be flushed out by the river. But the algae, established in the water systems, the ditches and lakes, would never be completely eradicated."

"Quite the pair, your Fluvium and Gray."

"And Egypt would serve as a long-term experiment on human beings and their ability to adapt to the organism. They could monitor evolutionary changes to the algae's DNA, social processes, the entire dynamic system over a thousand years until the Greeks, under Alexander, arrived."

"If Alexander arrived," she said softly. "By their very interference, the timeline with which we're familiar might never have developed. Alexander's father, Philip of Macedon, might never have been born. The historical and cultural dynamic of the Mediterranean—as we know it—would have developed very differently without Egypt's contributions."

"Social and biological experimentation on a grand scale. Travel to a world, record its development, and then go back and release a plague, just to see its effects."

"The Nazi doctor, Mengele, would have been delighted, don't you think?"

Falcon, his head awhirl with the implications, barely noticed as Radames and Aida were sealed inside their final tomb, labeled as traitors, to die in the dark in ancient Egypt.

# 75

I unbuckled my seat belt and stood as the Gulfstream hummed westward with the night. Savage had stuffed a pillow against the window and now slept peacefully. Karla had leaned her seat back as far as it would go, her eyes closed, curls of black framing the softened features of her face.

I walked forward, opened the cockpit door, and stepped inside. Winny Swink sat in the pilot's chair, knee up, her left arm draped across it so that her thin fingers hung limp. She arched an inquisitive eyebrow as I slipped into the copilot's seat.

Obviously, she had the jet on autopilot. I considered this either a major concession to the rest of us, or else she'd had enough excitement over the Chesapeake to suffice for the day.

"How they doing back there?" she asked.

"Asleep. I figured you might be on the verge of nodding off yourself, so I thought I'd come keep you company." Flying alone had to be breaking a slew of FAA regulations.

Winny gave me a sly smile and adjusted her headset. "While you were out stealing boats and generally raising hell last night, I was sacked out in the hotel. I figured if you guys got busted, I still had a chance to steal the Gulfstream, fly off to Saudi Arabia, and offer it and my services to some sheik."

"Provided they had it fueled up and ready to go, huh?"

She nodded. "As long as our sugar daddy holds out, I've got an escape. I presume that's Grazier?"

"You presume right for the moment."

"And if he pulls the plug?"

"The fact that someone tried to kill Eli last night significantly diminishes that possibility."

"But he does have superiors."

"We all do."

She pulled off her headset, ran fingers through her red hair, and replaced it. "Skipper, I'm not going back. If they pull the plug, I mean. There's a whole world out there desperate for someone with my skills. Knowing that. Being free for these couple of days? I'd rather be dead than face the future locked up in Grantham."

"What if some Saudi general's wife shows up wearing pink?"

She grinned, green eyes devilish. "Okay, maybe I should take a couple of your mystical, magical, mood stabilizer pills with me. What would you recommend?"

"Trileptal might help. But I'd have to check side effects of long-term low dosage to see what it would do your flying skills."

I stared out at the black night. We were flying over clouds that looked like a somber, gray-blue, lumpy mat; a sliver of moon hung on the southeastern horizon. A billion stars frosted the black in patterns of swirls.

"We came pretty close to dying today, didn't we?"

I'd walked around the sagging helicopter and counted seven .30 caliber bullet holes. Fuel was dripping from one that had center-punched the tank, and even as we walked away, the Bell was sagging onto its left side as the traumatized skid collapsed. Grazier was going to have a wonderful time explaining all that to whichever agency he'd borrowed the bird from.

Winny barely raised her shoulders in a shrug. "I could have put us down in a parking lot, and we could have run for cover. Probably would have been safer." She glanced at me. "But then they'd still be out there, wouldn't they?"

"What if they'd flown right into us?" I was remembering the image of the looming Beech filling my window as Winny flipped us sideways in midair.

"Not likely. It's about how the guy was flying. Each time he'd overshoot us and bank? Did you see that slight wobble? Like he was feeling his way?"

"No."

"I watch a pilot fly, I know what level of skill I'm dealing with. The guy was okay, probably an advanced weekender with a couple of thousand hours under his belt. But he wasn't any maestro. And certainly not a combat-trained pilot."

"You know all this from watching a couple of passes?"

"A combat stick jockey would have taken us out. So, once I had this guy's number, I set him up. I just had to hope Karla had her shit together and didn't freeze when I jinked sideways."

"Karla doesn't freeze in tight spots."

"Skipper, you never know."

"What if she'd killed the pilot? Dead at the stick, he might have rammed us."

"Naw. Cockpit glass is tough stuff. At that range nine millimeters should have bounced off. I needed three things to come together. My altitude had to be right. Karla's bullets had to scare the shit out of him at the same time we filled his entire sky. And third, I knew he'd slam everything he had into a panic dive to clear us." She grinned. "Even then, the asshole's stabilizer hit the skid."

A slender red eyebrow arched. "My biggest worry, Skipper? I was praying we wouldn't fold up those rotors like they were made of tinfoil. We kind of exceeded the Kiowa's performance envelope with that maneuver."

"Yeah, I felt the g-force." I winced, having puked all over the deck as Winny sent us flying from the scene.

I really hate helicopters. Always have. Always will.

She resettled her position, eyes thoughtful. "General Grazier believes Gray is what Falcon says she is?"

"He does."

"You know how weird that sounds?"

"I do."

"What do you think, Skipper?"

"I don't know, Major. But we keep running into things like that computer box we left with Rogers. And who knows what Falcon, Cat, and the anthropologists have come up with while we've been gone."

Swink glanced at the instruments, then cocked her head. "Falcon was serious about me bombing the Los Alamos lab. But I think he's a little hazy on what it would take to get live ordnance placed on either an F-18 or F-16, let alone stealing one off the flight line."

"How'd you do it last time?"

"I was a serving officer at Andrews. A familiar face. Everyone on the flight line knew me. And no weapons were involved in my 'test flight.'"

"But you'd do it if you could? Bomb Los Alamos? It has the potential of killing people."

She gave me one of her "You're an idiot" looks, and said, "Skipper, we killed at least two people today when that Bonanza slammed into the bay. When it comes to Skientia and Gray? Well, let's assume that Falcon's right. Gray wants to go home, no matter what it does to my world. And whatever Skientia's figuring to get out of this, it's nothing beneficial for the rest of humanity. So, sure, I may be an alley cat of a mother, and have an antisocial personality disorder, as you occasionally remind me, but those two boys are still mine."

She winked at me. "And I'd get to fly a real airplane one more time and blow the ever-loving crap out of the bad guys."

"Assuming we could pull it off."

"There's always that." She hesitated. "And don't forget, Skipper, the bad guys know we're coming."

# 76

The cab slowed as it turned onto a side street. Reid and Kilgore looked out at a rather disreputable-looking Cambridge neighborhood. Streetlamps cast cones of light on battered-looking older cars that were parked nose to rear along the curb. Just beyond the narrow sidewalk, steps led up to raised doorways fronting the tightly packed three-story buildings. They'd all been constructed of a dark-red brick, most of the doorways and windows painted white in uniform accent. An occasional bay window protruded from a second or third floor, as if to make a grandiose statement in the midst of mediocrity. Windowsills sported plants backlit by yellow light filtering through lace curtains.

"Twenty-five forty-seven. It's the one with the two porch lights on your right," the cab driver told them, slowing down. Though apparently of Indian or Pakistani ancestry, his accent was pure Bostonian.

Reid inserted his credit card, surprised once again to see the machine take it. The notion that he could just walk into a Colorado Springs office, show his ID to a credit card company, and have them issue a card still amazed him. He'd expected to be arrested at any moment.

The little machine spat out a receipt, and Reid stepped out into the muggy Cambridge night. He glanced at Kilgore as the cab motored off down the street.

Reid led the way through a narrow gap between bumpers. They stepped onto the night-grayed sidewalk. Pedestrians in ones and twos were hurrying along from one pool of streetlight to another. Most seemed young, this being a college neighborhood.

Kilgore said, "Let's hope Dan Murphy isn't another Skylar."

"Amen," Reid muttered, and climbed the three steep steps. Double-checking the number, he rang the bell for 2A.

Reid could hear feet hammering down the stairs, and moments later, a tall, blond young man opened the door. He looked to be in his early twenties and wore a light-blue T-shirt that proclaimed SAVE OUR GARBAGE! EAT A SEAGULL! Faded blue jeans, the knees out, covered his long legs. His feet were clad in Keen sandals.

"Dr. Farmer? Dr. France? Hi! I'm Dan Murphy. Glad to meet you both. Honored, actually. Can't believe you're here. Come on up." He motioned them into the small foyer, excitement in his blue eyes.

At the top of the stairs, Reid made a right where the door to 2A was open. Kilgore followed him inside to find a typical student apartment; the prerequisite laptop lay open on a battered wooden table. A utility kitchen, ell-shaped, was to the left of a hallway that went back to the bedroom and bath.

Scarred wooden floors were covered with brightly colored Mexican rugs. A really sad-looking couch sagged against one wall; a cinderblock-and-plank bookcase pressed against the other. Reid stepped over to the couch, staring at the wall behind. The dull-yellow plaster had been painted over in a series of Mayan epigraphy. Below it was a collection of Mayan mathematics.

"Like it?" Murphy asked as he closed the door.

"Beats posters of rock stars or football players. What does it translate as?"

"It says, 'Four score and seven years ago our forefathers brought forth a new nation.' I found a certain irony in the translation to Mayan." He pointed at the math. "That's $E=MC^2$ with mass based on Emilia Clarke's weight."

"How could I have missed that?"

Murphy arched a knowing eyebrow, "Mayans thought each number had special qualities, magic if you will. But so far Emilia Clarke hasn't appeared in my bedroom."

Kilgore was inspecting photographs of Dan Murphy and other scruffy-looking young people—obviously archaeologists.

A Mayan war club hung from the wall beside the door. The piece was masterfully crafted from a dark hardwood, the grain in the handle sweat-darkened. Resembling an oar, the lower length of the club was paddle shaped. What would have been the edges, however, sported lengths of glistening black obsidian blades inset into the wood. Obsidian—volcanic glass—was the sharpest edge known to man.

"It's called a *maccuahuitl*. I got it in Tegucigalpa," Dan Murphy told him. "I mean, how could you turn it down?"

"And TSA let you bring it back?" Reid wondered.

"Naw. Shipped it FedEx. Listed it as a cricket bat on the customs form. Figured even if they x-rayed the thing, they'd figure it was legit." He spread his arms. "Can I get you something? Got beer, wine, some mescal and tequila."

"Beer's fine," Reid said walking over to the kitchen table.

As Murphy produced bottles of Dos Equis, Kilgore opened the folder she'd brought and laid out the pages on his table.

"These are what we're interested in," Reid said as he pulled out a mismatched white chair. "Skylar Haines said you were the best when it came to Mayan mathematics."

"Skylar, huh?" Murphy popped the cap on his beer and swung his chair around backward so he could perch on it and rest his forearms on the chair back. He squinted down at the mathematics. "Skylar's brilliant when it comes to reading what the lords wrote, but try and share a tent with the guy in the Belize jungle." He made a face. "Wish I'd had that war club."

Kilgore said, "We were rather surprised when Dr. Haines suggested you instead of Sid White. Sid has pretty much written the book on Mayan mathematics."

Murphy avoided her gaze as he took a swallow of beer, a flush reddening his neck. "We've, um, had some disagreements. I don't think Sid's going to be happy when my dissertation is published next spring. My take is that the Mayans were using their mathematics in a more abstract . . ." His eyebrows knotted as he realized what he was seeing on the page before him.

"Where did you get this?" Murphy asked, picking up the paper and staring intently at it.

"A mental patient at a military psychiatric hospital outside Colorado Springs drew it on her room wall, much as you have drawn on yours," Kilgore told him.

"What's her name?" He glanced up. "I mean I know everyone in the discipline. There's only a handful of . . . A *military* psychiatric hospital?"

"She's been called Domina, but that's Latin for 'lady.'" Kilgore told him.

"But this is real," he insisted. "And sophisticated stuff. I mean, you don't just Google 'Mayan mathematics' and start writing equations like this. Damn it! I'm the best there is, and this stuff's leaving me in the dust!"

Dan Murphy retrieved a Texas Instruments calculator from its resting place in the napkins and began tapping at the keys.

"Holy crap," he whispered. He tapped some more, stopped cold, and glanced up. "No one I know, not Vasily, not Roberto, not Charlene, not even Dr. White could have put this together. Seriously, jokes, aside, where did you find this?"

"Forget who, what, and where," Reid told him. "Can you work out the mathematics? Maybe translate them enough that we can get a handle on the equations?"

"Equations to what?" Murphy demanded, eyes bright.

"That's what we'd like to know," Kilgore told him.

A knock came at the door.

Murphy made a face as he tore himself from the papers and rose. He opened the door to a stocky man, mid-thirties, with buzz-cut red hair and a weathered face. The fellow fixed Murphy with close-set green eyes and smiled. Then as his gaze fixed on Reid and Kilgore, the smile curled into a cat-and-canary grin.

"Well, well, Dr. France? Dr. Farmer? Seems I've just hit the jackpot."

Murphy protested, "Hey! Who are you?" as the red-headed intruder shoved his way into the room.

"Call me Mr. Simms, kid." But his hard-green eyes remained on Reid as he asked, "Where's the stuff, Doc?"

"Stuff?" Reid rose from the table, his throat tightening, heart beginning to race. He felt Kilgore closing behind him, as if to shield herself from that predatory emerald gaze.

"The stuff you took from the sarcophagus. The people I work for really want it back. Especially that book. Oh, and the jar, too."

"We don't know what you're talking about," Kilgore tried bravely.

"Sure, Dr. France." Simms lifted his left hand, obviously talking into a microphone in his sleeve. "Mark? Surprise. I've got France and Farmer up here. There's some papers on the table. Probably the missing book. How long until you can bring the car around?" A pause, and he nodded as he listened to an earbud. "Me and three passengers."

"We're not going anywhere with you," Reid declared.

"Oh, sure you are." Simms was still grinning as he slipped his hand under his coat and produced a black Sig Sauer pistol. "Dr. France, if you'd pick up those papers."

"Who are you?" Murphy choked out.

"Just an errand boy, Dr. Murphy. I'm here to offer you a job. My employer needs someone who can figure out Mayan math."

"We thought you had the Domina for that," Kilgore said.

Simms shrugged. "Above my pay grade, Doc. I was just told to come get Murphy. But I'm betting I get a bonus for bringing in the rest of you." His attention returned to Murphy. "You need any books, your computer? Special notes?"

"Whoa!" Murphy's hands had risen. "You can't just burst in here! I mean, like, I don't know anything!"

"Kid, I was just supposed to offer you a job. The two Doctors F here, they kind of screwed up the deal. Bringing them in makes it worth my while to complicate matters. Sorry, but you're being recruited by force." His eyes went cold. "Now, get your shit together."

"I'm not going!"

"Kid, if I put a bullet through your ankle, you won't need it to figure out them symbols, will you?" He extended the pistol toward Murphy's foot.

"Let him be," Reid said, "It's us you want. He's just a graduate student."

"Got my orders. Murphy comes along, willing or not."

"A lot of powerful people have become aware of Skientia's activities," Kilgore told him. "The cat's out of the bag."

Simms nodded warily as Murphy stepped to his bookcase and started taking down volumes. "Way ahead of you, Doc. General Grazier's just had his wings clipped. And don't expect Grazier's little commando force to come to your rescue again, either. We've got someone fine-combing JSOC to figure out who took down Aspen."

"What's a jay-sock?" Reid asked.

"Very funny."

"No, I don't know what that is."

"Joint Special Operations Command." Simms kept one eye on Murphy as he was tossing notebooks into a travel bag. "The team that extracted you from Aspen? You don't just hire talent like that off the street."

"Got that right," Reid muttered to himself.

"Now," Simms said easily, "why don't the two of you collect those papers off the table and put them back in Dr. France's bag. Murphy, you got your stuff? Good."

Simms opened the door, the pistol still gripped in his right hand. "Here's how it's going to work: I'm going to step outside, and Dr. Murphy, you go first with your heavy bags. Then Dr. France. You, Dr. Farmer, will be last. Just in case you get any heroic ideas, I can put a bullet in your guts."

"I'm not heroic," Reid said woodenly.

"Good," Simms replied as he backed out the door, "because the client says you're the most expendable person on my list. Now, let's move, folks."

A sheen of perspiration on his thin face, Dan Murphy stepped out; his shoulders sagged under the load of books, notes, and computer.

Kilgore shot Reid a worried glance and followed.

Reid reached to the side as if to flip off the light switch. His fingers grasped the polished wood.

As Simms shifted his gaze to Kilgore where she started down the stairs, Reid stepped into the hallway. He pivoted and swung the Mayan war club with its obsidian-blade edge. The upper cut sliced diagonally up Simms' thigh, laying the man's leg open like a slit fish. Instinctively, Simms extended his left arm; the volcanic glass sliced it to the bone.

Staggered by the blow, Simms fought for balance. As he raised his pistol, a look of disbelief crossed the man's face.

Reid let the club's momentum carry it up, then he reversed the swing, instinctively chopping downward. The obsidian edge caught Simms in the muscular curve where the neck rose from the shoulder. Through the war club's handle, Reid felt the obsidian edge resist as it was driven through the cervical vertebra.

Simms collapsed like a broken doll, the pistol thumping on the carpeted floor.

"Holy mother of God." The words whistled through Reid's tight throat. He blinked in disbelief at the broken corpse. Then, reaching down for the pistol, he saw Kilgore and Dan's shocked faces.

"Go!" he insisted. "There's at least one other guy in a car waiting for us down there. Dan? Does this place have a back door?"

"What about him?" Murphy asked, horrified gaze on the blood rushing from Simms' mutilated corpse.

"I don't know," Reid choked out. "I really don't know."

# 77

"These are classified satellite images of the Los Alamos Labs," ET told the group assembled in the pastel-colored Grantham Barracks conference room. The images he projected onto the screen contrasted with the warm-and-fuzzy drawings of bunnies, birds, and fawns on the wall behind it.

I really enjoyed the irony, since this room was generally reserved for group therapy sessions.

Edwin—dressed in a white T-shirt and blue jeans—used a laser pointer. "This here is the main gate where it comes off highway 501. This is the building we're interested in. This big white job. It's got two doors, the main one here off the parking lot, and this fire door/maintenance entry in the rear. Then there's this garage door on this side for deliveries to the basement lab. The big thing, see, is these power lines. They pipe a lot of electricity into that building. Probably to power Gray's entangled particle generator."

He switched to another view of the building. "As you can see, there ain't no windows. But they got a roof access, here. While they got water and sewer and fiber optic, there's no tunnel access underground. Entrance and exit through these doors only, and they're monitored and guarded. After what happened in Aspen, you can bet your ass that Talon mercenaries ain't taking chances, and they probably got orders to shoot to kill."

Sam Savage had been leaning on the table, hands clasped. "No wonder they were shocked when Gray just appeared inside."

"You got that right," Edwin agreed. "I been doing my damnedest to get a handle on what Skientia's been doing. Trying to trace back parts orders, manufacturers, that sort of thing. Skientia contracted parts all over the world. Special lasers from Germany, magnets from Switzerland, giant ceramic cone-shaped structures from China, specialized circuit boards from Taiwan and Indonesia, a two-meter–tall nickel-and-titanium yoke-shaped piece from Canada. Stuff that makes no sense. And mirrors from Italians? Who's gonna pay sixteen million dollars for mirrors?"

"They must be some kind of mirrors," Savage mused.

"They sure ain't for popping blackheads."

"ET?" Karla asked. "Enlarge the image of the roof."

Edwin tapped his screen, fingers boxing the roof, expanding the image. The Skientia building zoomed larger. "What you looking for, Chief?"

"All those antennas and dishes." She stood, walking up to the screen. "Satellite communications, radio, television in and out, burst link. Ah, and here's the security cameras, probably motion triggered. They've got everything."

"And huge fiber-optic cables underground," ET asserted. "Not to mention however they transmit entangled particles. But you knew that."

Karla pointed. "Right there. That's where we're going in."

Savage stepped over to her side. "Roof access. It will be monitored. Probably loaded with sensors. Big honking locks on the door."

Karla asked, "ET, what's your take on the cameras? Can you get in, loop them? Do something that would give me fifteen minutes on that door?"

"Chief, I'm not sure. So far, they stopped me stone cold. Me, can you believe?"

She asked, "You got a floor plan for this place?"

"Compliments of K.O.G. Design and Engineering." One by one, he pulled up images. "There, Chief. That's the top floor."

"Here's the stairway up," Karla mused. "And the luck of the Irish be with us, right here, next to the stairs, is the janitorial storage. Main electrical and fiber-optic chase is over here, centralized and out of the way. Good, no hot wires to worry about."

"So you don't think the door's rigged?" Savage asked.

Eyes on the schematic, she slowly shook her head. "They're expecting us to try the door. That's why I'm cutting through the roof."

"And what about those motion detectors?" I asked, having watched the interplay between Savage and Raven.

Karla turned to Winny, a challenging smile on her lips. "So, how about it, Major? If I can find you the stealthiest helicopter out there, can you set me down like a feather on that roof?"

"Hell, yes," Winny retorted from where she cradled a cup of coffee. "But those motion detectors are going to focus every camera up there on your skinny ass and my bird."

"That's the feather part, Major. Drop me too hard and you'll break the mirrors."

"Mirrors? Like on the outside of a box?" I could immediately see what she was getting at. It would create a still background for the cameras—but only after it was in place.

Savage gaped. "Are you out of your mind?"

"No, just PTSD with a slight compulsive disorder."

So these are the fruits of their beloved democracy? Brainless clods chosen for their popularity and what they can promise the masses? They thrive on adulation and the lure of power. Even their president is no more than modeling clay to be shaped and molded in my capable hands. They will provide the electrical current necessary for the time projector to function properly. If the first tests are successful, after reconfiguring the machine, power will be available for my subsequent attempt to contact Imperator.

The very thought leaves me sick to my stomach. I will endure what I must to save Fluvium.

Fortunately, the rock-brained oafs were smart enough to leave the navigator intact. My one fear was that they might stupidly try and pry it open to see what was inside.

A deep sense of satisfaction fills me. I am far ahead of schedule.

# 78

"This isn't happening!" Dan Murphy cried as Reid Farmer grabbed him from behind and pulled him down behind a big plastic trash can. Kilgore instinctively ducked into the shadows behind a dented Chrysler 300. Headlights flashed down the street, gleaming off cars, casting hollow light on the residential buildings.

"Yeah," Reid whispered, grip tightening on the Mayan war club. "I've been saying that for days." He made a face, disgusted by the smell of disposable diapers mixed with rotting fruit.

The car sailed down the narrow street, going much too fast to be one of their pursuers.

"You killed that guy!" Murphy repeated yet again.

Reid ground his teeth as he dragged the graduate student to his feet. "You do remember the gun, right? The one he was using to *kidnap* you? Want me to pull it out of my pocket to remind you?"

For the rest of his life, Reid would relive the instant he drove that deadly club into Simms' neck. The feel of the wood would resonate in his hands, the vibrations of the severing cervical vertebrae never dimming.

*I killed a man.*

When his current terror subsided, he would attempt to deal with it. For now, it was all he could do to ratchet up his courage and keep them alive.

"Come on." He hurried the panicked graduate student down the narrow sidewalk. "We've got to keep going. Straight line. Increase the search area they have to cover."

"We need to call the police," Murphy insisted. "By now they know there's a dead guy lying in front of my apartment door."

"Pull yourself together, Daniel," Kilgore told him sharply. "We'll deal with the police as soon as we can. Meanwhile, you'd better damn well believe us that you're in deep. Real deep."

"I didn't *do* anything!"

"Sorry, pal. You learned Mayan math. Right now that makes you one of the most important people in the world. Who'd have guessed, huh?"

"What's this about?" Murphy's breath came in pants as he struggled under his load of book-packed bags.

"Apparently, a scientific discovery that will change the world," Kilgore told him. "Just bear with us. General Grazier has a safe house. We need to get you there because you're not safe anywhere else. Especially not with the Boston police."

"Why not the police? You know how you sound? Like crazy people!"

Kilgore's laugh barely hid hysteria. "Who'd have thought it was contagious?"

"Skientia has resources," Reid said. "A battery of lawyers that managed to cow the FBI. My bet? They'd pull strings in the Justice Department to have you held, and then transferred. Think about it. You've got a dead guy in front of your apartment. Rizzoli and Isles are going to find fragments of Mexican obsidian in our friend Simms' neck. They'll know you have a Mayan war club. Justice Department says, 'Wait, we suspect Dan Murphy of something in Mexico.' And next thing you know, you're picked up by Simms' friends, bundled off to some secret location, and told to work on Mayan mathematics or you'll never see freedom again."

"And that's different than what you're doing to me?"

"Call it what you want," Kilgore told him as she hurried along the walk. "When you parse it down to the absolutes, we'll do our best to make sure you're alive. Given the number of people we've seen Skientia kill, and the lengths they'll go to? They really don't give a shit if you live or die as long as you produce."

Dan Murphy stopped short and puked his guts all over the sidewalk.

Reid figured he could relate.

As the young anthropologist wiped his mouth, he said, "I wish you people had never walked through my door."

"If we hadn't, you'd be on your way to Skientia by now." Kilgore told him as she glanced worriedly at the dark houses they passed. "Simms would have offered you an unbelievable salary. Same as he did to Reid and me. You don't find out you're trapped until it's too late."

"How'd you get away?" Murphy asked suspiciously.

"Reid?" Kilgore hissed, coming to a stop, her arm out.

They were in a shadowed part of the street, but he saw the two men emerge into the light on the corner. He yanked Dan Murphy into the shadow behind a parked Jeep, Kilgore ducking down behind concrete stairs.

"Think they saw us?" she hissed.

Reid peered past the bumper in time to see one man gesture in his direction, sending the second man across the street.

"He's coming this way." A new tension filled Reid's breast. "Kilgore, he's going to see you."

"Is he one of them?"

"I think so." Reid swallowed hard. What would Chief Raven do? "I've got an idea. But we'll have to split up. I'm drawing their attention. Going to lead them around the block. You and Dan need to get to the hotel. I'll meet you there. In the meantime, call Sam and have him arrange transportation."

"I'm going with you," she whispered hotly.

"Kilgore, *think*! The important thing is to get Dan to safety. You and I both know where that is. I can move faster by myself." He added, "You got a better idea?"

At her silence, he told Murphy, "Do what she tells you."

Then, heart pounding, he stood, hand knotted around the handle so the deadly Mayan war club hung down his back out of sight. He affected a jolly walk to match his humming of "For he's a jolly good fellow" as he went. The shadowy shape of the man had stopped, his head cocked.

*The son of a bitch is going to kill me.*

"What would Chief Raven do?" he asked himself again as fear began to pump bright through his veins.

". . . That nobody can deny. Deny? Deny? That nobody can deny," he sang. Less than ten paces now. The man stood, knees slightly bent, shoulders forward, a shadowy menace.

And his companion? The one who'd crossed the street? Where had he gone?

"Dr. Farmer?" came the sibilant question.

"Who you calling a farmer?" Reid tried to mimic a New England accent. "That you, Matt? Being an asshole like usual?"

Reid was only steps away now. He hadn't expected the sudden blinding flash of a powerful light. It literally hit him with the force of a blow, shooting white pain through his brain.

Had he not been rehearsing in his desperate mind, had he not been expecting an attack, it might have completely incapacitated him. Instead, Reid swung blindly, the Mayan war club connecting. The man shouted, the flashlight flying away to the side.

Squinting and blinded, Reid charged forward, knocking the man off his feet. Somehow, he managed to keep his footing, caroming off cars, knocking over trash cans.

A shout came from across the street, but Reid was running for all he was worth.

*Got to keep them away from Kilgore.*

Adrenaline lent him wings as he rounded the corner, the Mayan war club gripped tightly. Reid cut diagonally across the street, ducked between the cars, and sprinted down the sidewalk.

At the next corner, he shot a glance over his shoulder to see the shape of a dark assailant charging after him. Reaching into his pocket, Reid pulled out the pistol, aimed it, and pulled the trigger.

Nothing.

In the dim light he stared at it, finding a series of levers. One had to be the safety. His thumb clicked the closest down. He raised the pistol in the direction of the pursuer.

The discharge probably scared him more than it did the attacker. As the gun jumped in his hand, the muzzle flash left spots behind his eyes.

Reid turned, running harder than before.

*Got to keep going. Got to lead them away from Kilgore.*

High overhead, he could hear the sound of a helicopter circling somewhere in the darkness.

*This isn't going to be good.*

# 79

**W**e're running out of days. The notion festered in Karla Raven's thoughts as the distant profile of the NetJets flight dropped out of the morning sky on approach to the Colorado Springs airport.

*What kind of people, what kind of morality, would use an entire planet filled with innocent human beings to conduct biological experimentation?*

"Makes an ISIS jihadist look warm and fuzzy."

Karla lifted her wraparound sunglasses and raised compact Steiner binoculars to her eyes. Through the chain-link fence she watched the jet touch down, wisps of blue rising as the tires hit the runway.

She then glanced at the NetJets office where she knew Savage was waiting. He had rented a Toyota Land Cruiser for the pickup. It now baked in the parking lot, a hot morning sun gleaming on the vehicle's chrome and glass.

"If we don't get this wrapped up, Grazier's never going to cough up that motorcycle the Skipper wants so desperately." Word of the bet had been a hot topic of conversation after the Skipper let it slip.

Assuming, that is, that they ever heard from Grazier again. An ominous silence had come from his direction. Though neither Savage nor Dr. Ryan were talking about it, she could sense the tension.

And Grazier—as she so well knew—was currently a high-priority target for someone.

"What did you do, General? Let someone less capable than me cover your six?"

Allowing herself a brief and humorless smile, she slung the heavy backpack over her shoulder and strolled back to her latest "requisitioned" transportation. She'd picked it up on a whim after her long night of driving.

Bracing herself on the seat, she opened the bag and pulled out a Taco John's burrito. Couldn't find Taco John's outside of the Rocky Mountain region. She'd developed a taste for the super-hot green sauce.

Unwrapping her prize, she bit down, delighting in the dribble of warm fluid that leaked out the corner of her mouth. As she savored the taste and studied the parking area, the arriving aircraft roared as it reversed thrusters.

# 80

Looking up at the clock, Sam Savage tried to remind himself that physicists thought the universe was timeless. He stood with his hands in his pockets. At the desk, the NetJets office staff went about their duties. Savage had the upscale waiting room all to himself. He had already enjoyed a cup of their complimentary coffee. Given half a chance, he could come to enjoy the corporate jet experience over his usual economy-class, middle-of-the-row seat.

When the sleek white jet taxied to a stop on the apron outside, the ground crew jumped to the task of setting chalks. While the jet spooled down, Savage tried to put his current world into perspective.

Alice had nothing on him when she fell through the fucking looking glass. Call it grist fit only for sick humor; he was in command of a bunch of psychological basket cases attempting to take down an evil corporation who had allied with a woman terrorist from another universe.

Under his breath he whispered, "Uncle Buck, you wouldn't believe it."

But then, Buck believed that monstrous spirit snakes lived down in the depths of Oklahoma's rivers, and huge primordial birds tossed lightning bolts down from the clouds in an attempt to kill those same serpents.

Assuming Sam ever got the opportunity to explain lost time travelers stranded among the Egyptians, and tall blonde women popping into New Mexico from another universe parallel to ours, Uncle Buck would no doubt nod wisely, roll another cigarette, and blow tobacco smoke in the four sacred directions to help strengthen the spiritual borders of existence.

"I'm just eternally thankful they haven't canceled the credit cards yet."

But they would. He could feel time—or whatever it was—running out.

Through the window he watched the jet's door open and lower. Kilgore France descended to the tarmac. Behind her came a lanky-looking young man with heavy canvas tote bags emblazoned with the logo of the Society for American Archaeology. The face behind the wire-rimmed glasses expressed a glazed disbelief.

"Maybe I'm not the only one ranking Alice when it comes to rabbit-hole weirdness," Savage reflected.

After the attendant ushered them into the reception area, Savage strolled over. Kilgore France's expression did little to belie her underlying worry as she rushed up and asked, "Any word from Reid?"

"Not yet, Doctor." To allay her rising fear, he lied, "But it's too early to panic. Doctor Farmer's a smart guy. If I were him, I'd be lying low, keeping out of sight."

But if he could believe the police reports, Farmer *had* taken out three of Skientia's hired thugs. With a prehistoric war club, for Christ's sake?

Kilgore's jaw clenched, as if she could see right through the deceit.

"You must be Dan Murphy?" Savage reached out and shook the uncertain young man's hand. "I'm Major Sam Savage. I hear you've had quite the night?"

"Good to meet you . . . even if I'm strung out . . . and feeling really sick," the skinny man replied. His EAT A SEAGULL T-shirt and too-casual pants hinted that he'd been snatched out of a whole different universe.

A lot of that seemed to be going around.

"If you'll follow me, we'll have you out of the line of fire soonest." He gestured to the SAA tote bags. "Is that all you've got? Any other luggage?"

"That's it for both of us," Kilgore told him as she started for the door. "I was so anxious to get out of Boston I left the luggage at the hotel. Any word on Skylar Haines?"

"After your call last night, Karla drove up to Boulder and, um, recovered him."

"I'd have *loved* to have seen that," she told him as she opened the door and stepped into the morning sunlight. "My guess is she cold-cocked him to facilitate his relocation?"

"Why, Doctor France? How did you guess?"

"Skylar?" Murphy asked as they walked to Savage's Toyota. "He's here?" At Savage's nod, the man said, "Suddenly, being hunted back in Boston doesn't sound so bad."

"For the time being, Colonel Ryan has your friend Skylar on a sedative. And don't worry, Dr. Murphy, where you're going, we'll be able to um, mellow, any of Dr. Haines' more irritating qualities."

Kilgore actually laughed, then surrendered to her worry over Reid.

*If Skientia's got him, we'd damn well better be concerned. When he tells them about Grantham Barracks, everyone's vulnerable.*

And Farmer *would* talk.

"Looks like our timetable just got moved up," Savage muttered to himself as he started the Toyota, clicked it into drive, and backed out of the parking space.

Savage asked, "Dr. Murphy, have you had a chance to look at the Mayan math?"

"Yes, sir. Uh, I'm not a PhD, just a graduate student."

"Close enough. What's the math all about?"

"Dr. France tells me it may come from another world? Having seen every recovered example of the mathematics the Mayans used, I can almost believe it. They were into calculating time, the magical properties of numbers, forecasting the future, surveying, and basic geometry. If this Gray person is using this in her physics calculations? Well, it's going to take a while to figure out. I can do introductory algebra with Mayan math, but she's feeding me advanced calculus."

Savage made a face as he turned onto Donovan Avenue and headed west. "But you'll . . ."

His phone began vibrating. "Savage."

*"Tango, tango, tango."* Chief Raven's voice told him crisply.

"Shit. What have we got?"

*"Tan Tahoe. Three MAM. Five cars back."*

"Roger that. Good hunting." MAM, code for male, adult, military, meaning they were someone's soldiers.

He hung up, slipped the phone back in his pocket, and sighed before saying, "Did either of you have any close contact with anyone? Maybe somebody slapped you on the back in passing? Did you buy any electronics? Kilgore? Did you get a new phone?"

"No." She gave him a searching look. "What's wrong?"

"Somebody's made us. Mr. Murphy? You got a cell phone with you?"

"Uh, yeah. But I turned it off while we were in the air."

"Shit!"

"A cell phone?" Kilgore said weakly. "Like, with a GPS? What do we do now?"

Savage glanced into the rearview mirror and met the anthropologist's eyes. "Murphy? Roll your window down a couple of inches and toss your phone."

"Toss my phone? Here? Out on the road? It's the brand-new Apple—"

"Skientia's tracking your GPS! Toss the fucking phone, or Kilgore's covering the wheel while I climb over the damn seat and do it myself!"

The lanky anthropologist swallowed hard, his Adam's apple bobbing. With anxious fingers he fished his expensive iPhone from his pocket, rolled the window down, and slipped it through the crack.

In the mirror, Savage saw it bounce and shatter. The four-wheel-drive pickup behind him crunched at least one piece with its big off-road tires.

Kilgore sank back in the seat. "God, I'm an idiot."

"It's okay," Savage told her nervously. "It takes a while to get used to this spy stuff. Lots of new things to learn."

*But they know we're in Colorado Springs.*

That wasn't immediately fatal. Given Glazier's involvement, Skientia would expect them to be working out of either Fort Carson or Peterson Air Force Base. Adding to the complexity, the Air Force Academy, Cheyenne Mountain and NORAD were just out of town. Schriever Air Force Base lay to the east, and Pueblo Army Depot forty minutes' drive to the south, and beyond that was Piñon Canyon.

Grantham Barracks would be on their list, too, like a great blinking star. Gray had been held there, successfully extracted from there. Eventually, they'd get around to looking. But how soon?

First, he needed to mislead the tail.

Savage took a right, heading north onto Academy with its heavy stop-and-go traffic, hoping to confuse the pursuit. In the passenger-side mirror he caught sight of the Tahoe, three vehicles back. The angle of the sun made it impossible to see anything through the vehicle's windshield.

"What happens next?" Kilgore asked.

"We have to ditch the guys behind us in the Chevy." Savage raised an eyebrow as he stopped in the knot of traffic at a red light. "Don't look for them," he warned as she started to crane her neck.

Kilgore was pinching the bridge of her nose. "Things aren't looking good for Reid, are they? Skientia? Hell, even the Boston cops are after him. He killed that man, Simms. And then there's a good chance the one who attacked him on the street died, too. That's murder one, Major. Dan and I didn't stick around to see. We just ran the other way. That's accessory."

Dan Murphy whispered, "Holy shit!"

"You're not felons, Kilgore. Even if Boston PD snagged up Dr. Farmer, this is never going to trial."

"Huh?" Murphy asked. "The guy *was killed* on my front doorstep! Police get really intense about things like that."

Savage mildly asked, "Do you really think anyone in charge is going to let Dr. Farmer tell his story to an assistant prosecutor in Boston? We're so deep in national security country now, we're never coming out."

The light changed. A loud *crump!* seemed to suck the air away, followed by a muffled *boom*. In the mirror Savage could see a black cloud mushroom up three cars back. The Ford F-250 blocked most of the view.

Traffic in the oncoming lane began sliding to a stop as Savage calmly motored away.

Seconds later, the glare of a single headlight filled his side mirror. He glanced out the driver's side window. Karla Raven perched on Ryan's blue-and-white–striped Ducati Diavel, her midnight hair streaking back in the wind. An empty backpack flapped on her shoulders.

She gave him a sidelong glance through wraparound sunglasses, shifted her hand slightly, and gave him a thumbs-up.

The bellow of exhaust was his only warning as she pinned the throttle. Lofting the Ducati's front wheel, she shot ahead of him, riding a wheelie that carried her half a block.

"You know," he mused, "I'm really starting to like that woman."

# 81

"Tell me about Colorado Springs," the voice asked in measured tones.

"Second biggest city in Colorado." Reid struggled, battling through the haze in his brain. Everything was gray, thick. Thinking was like swimming in cotton candy.

While he couldn't actually articulate it, he instinctively knew that getting his thoughts together shouldn't be this hard.

"Where's Kilgore France?" the voice asked reasonably.

Kilgore? Where was Kilgore? "With me."

"Think, Dr. Farmer. Where was she going?"

He struggled with that. "Boston. We were going to Boston."

"That's right. I need you to remember. You were in Boston. It was night. You were running. Dan Murphy was there. Someone was coming down the street. You told Kilgore and Dan to run. Where did you tell them to run to?"

"Boston?" That didn't seem right. What would he ever have to do with . . . ? A drowsy image solidified from the gray mist. He could feel the wooden handle as he swung the club. Saw it catch a man in the neck.

"Blood . . . such an incredible amount of blood!" He watched it spilling out over a dirty gray carpet in a hallway. Stairs were there . . . And a look of horror in Kilgore's eyes.

"Where did you plan to meet Kilgore after the blood, Reid?" the reasonable voice asked.

"Hotel. Airport."

"After the hotel? Where were you going?"

"Don't know." He puzzled at that.

"Colorado Springs?"

"My aunt lived there. Nice Doubletree Hotel. Hot chocolate-chip cookies."

"Were you staying at the Doubletree Hotel in Colorado Springs?"

"Yes."

"You? Kilgore? And who else?"

"Meeting."

"With whom?"

"CCPA."

A pause. "Reid, this is very important. Tell me about the CCPA?"

"Colorado Council of Professional Archaeologists. Brian was mad."

"Who's Brian?"

"Chaired the symposium." Something was important about that.

"Reid? Did you tell Brian about the Domina?"

He struggled with the thought. The symposium had been about Anasazi witchcraft. "She's a witch?" He would have laughed. "Makes a sort of sense, don't you think?"

"He's confused," another, less tolerant voice insisted. "Bring him out of it. We'll do it the other way."

"One last try. Reid? I want you to remember Boston. You were running, scared. You had been in fights, do you remember?"

"Yes." The blood, so much blood. The look of disbelief graying out of Simms' eyes as he lay on the carpet. And then he'd hit the man on the sidewalk.

"Reid, where were you going?"

"Killed a man for sure."

"Did you have a destination?"

He remembered the club in his hand. The absolute terror and fear running through him. He'd figured out how to shoot the pistol, taken a shot, but the pursuer had gotten closer and closer.

Reid had ducked around a corner, panting, almost quaking in terror as he stepped into the shadow of a drainpipe. The night sky had a grayish tone. Warm, damp air filled with the scent of exhaust, saltwater, and humanity. The guy's feet slapping the concrete had come closer. The hunter's breath ragged in the man's lungs.

The pursuing stranger had stepped around the corner, pistol tucked tight against his chest. Reid swung the club. Instinctively, he'd caught the man across the belly, just up from the navel. As he hammered the club into the man's middle, he'd pulled it. Obsidian had sliced through the man's shirt, skin, and intestines. Even before Reid pulled the club through the wound, the guy's guts were tumbling out.

And then Reid was running, terrified, sick to his stomach, almost screaming from revulsion.

"What are you thinking, Doctor?" the reasonable voice asked. "About where to go next? About General Grazier?"

He whispered, "The name, it's a *maccuahuitl*."

"Is that a place? Is that where you are supposed to meet Dr. Kilgore?"

Reid wanted only to fade off into the gray cotton candy. If it was thick enough, he'd be able to sink slowly away from the pain, horror, and memory of the *maccuahuitl* and the way it cut a living human being in half.

*"Maccuahuitl,"* Reid repeated, the name echoing in his memory.

Beyond the gray haze he heard someone triumphantly say, "That's it. We figure out where this Mackaweetle is, we've got them."

Thankfully, Reid was fading back into the gray.

# 82

Bearing a tray, Cat knocked lightly on Edwin's door, asking "How are you doing?"

"Come on in." He sat hunched over the computer, feeling like some bizarre dark spider. His lips were pinched, jaw muscles knotted. He wore only a T-shirt and a pair of boxer shorts, his feet in flip-flops.

"You weren't in the cafeteria. Since no one had seen you, I was worried. You didn't come in for breakfast, either. I thought I'd bring you a tray."

"Thanks."

She placed it on the side of his desk and seated herself on the arm of his easy chair. Awareness of her presence faded until she said, "Earth calling ET."

"Yo?" Edwin tapped a couple of keys, his frown deepening.

"Hey!" She clapped her hands, startling him enough to look up. "I'm here! Look! Live girl. In your room. Brought you food because she's concerned about you. That mean anything, computer geek? Or should I pick up the tray and go look for someone who might actually appreciate the thought?"

He blinked a couple of times; the words weren't quite registering. Then a slow smile crept along his lips. "Yeah, thank you, Cat." He stretched, sniffed, and said, "Smells good."

Shifting the computer to the side, he slid the tray before him and dove into the macaroni and cheese, the sliced ham, Texas toast, and green beans. "What's up?"

"Karla evacuated a weirdo from Boulder last night, then blew up a car on Academy Boulevard that was tailing Major Savage after he picked up Dr. France and some skinny anthropologist. It's all over the news. Dr.

Farmer is missing, presumed arrested by the police in Boston, or captured by Skientia. He killed three Talon security agents in Boston with some kind of Mayan war club. That's all over the news, too."

"Exciting." Edwin wondered when a meal had ever tasted so good.

Cat cocked her head, no doubt disgusted by the way he was shoving food into his mouth.

She added, "Savage wants us packed and ready to go. He says that Skientia's going to be here knocking on our door any minute. The Skipper, Winny, and Raven are on their way to Peterson to see about a helicopter. You have to be ready to leave in an hour. That's my update. What's yours?"

"Skientia, man. It's like they know I'm after them." He gestured his frustration. "That's okay. Part of the game, you know? What gets me is why I can't break the damn passwords. I ran entire dictionaries against their system. Ran algorithms based on letters, numbers, dates, numerical codes. I did get one hit: something with a lot of ts, ls, ks, and zs, but it only led me to a purchase order."

"Did you try running things from physics? Avogadro's number, Planck's constant?"

"Oh, yeah. I download an entire physics text and use a program to sort for phrases, special numbers, then try to combine mathematics. Tens of thousands of functions a second."

"You can do that with that little laptop?"

"No way, girl! I'm using the NSA counter-cryptography computers. Not directly, you know, but through three different cutouts. Got to have heavy firepower. This laptop controls the computers that control the computers that control the computers that'll break into Skientia."

"And how's it going?"

Edwin focused his bloodshot eyes on hers. "Got a highly technical term for you, girl: Jack shit. That's what I got so far."

"And if you can't break it?"

He ran a long-fingered hand over his close-cropped hair. "Man, we might have to abort this whole damn thing."

# 83

Reid blinked, feeling foggy headed as the door banged open. He came fully awake on an uncomfortable cot in a small concrete room—a sort of supply room? Or so he guessed from the wooden shelves across from him and the drain in the floor.

Bill Minor and two black-clad muscle-bound men with buzz cuts stared down at him.

"Have a nice sleep?" Minor asked.

Reid swung his feet to the floor, surprised to find them bare. Everything in his head was fuzzy mush. "What happened? Last I remember I was running down a street in Boston."

"You were tasered," Minor told him.

Reid's stumbling brain fixed on a nightmare memory: numbing pain, his body turning into one giant and agony-filled knot as it bucked on hard pavement.

"God, I never want to do that again."

"Then you'll tell us where Kilgore and the Mayan scholar have gone. We know they made it to Colorado Springs on a private charter flight."

"Colorado Springs?" He rubbed his eyes, partly to ease the gritty ache, partly to hide his expression. "It's Savage." Hell, they'd known his identity as far back as the kidnapping in DC.

"Who is he working with?"

"Some guy named Grazier. A general. I never met him."

*Kilgore and Murphy made it to Colorado Springs? Minor obviously hasn't caught them yet.*

"Tell me about this team he's working with. The ones who took down the Aspen retreat." Minor dropped down to stare into Reid's eyes.

"Don't lie, or I promise, you'll get tasered until you're squirting shit like a fire hose and pissing yourself yellow."

Reid stared into Bill Minor's dark eyes, reading the man's promise.

He took a deep breath, trying to still his pounding heart. "I don't know what they're called." He swallowed hard. Scared like he'd never been. This had to be done carefully. "Just something about 'the Activity.' Savage talked about it like it was an organization. And he said it was through something called jay sock. Does that mean anything to you?"

One of the buzz-cut toughs growled, "Intelligence Support Activity. CIA's special operatives out of Fort Belvoir."

"How did CIA get involved?" the second tough asked.

"Probably through Grazier," Bill Minor replied offhandedly, his gaze still boring into Reid's. "Where are they billeted, Dr. Farmer?"

Reid lied as facilely as he could. "It might be Virginia. It's a military place. Something government. Kilgore and I were asleep on the way in, in the back of a van on the way out. I can tell you that we were all split up. Kilgore and I were sent to find someone who could translate the Mayan mathematics in the book. Some of the others took the jar with them to have the water inside analyzed."

He dared not mention the black electrical box.

"Where were you supposed to meet?"

"We were supposed to call." Reid patted his pocket to find his phone missing. "It's the only number in the memory. Maybe they'll chat you up for a bit?"

The blow came as a blur—and blasted lights and confusion through Reid's head. Pain made him cry out.

"That's for causing me problems, Doctor," Minor told him. "I owed you that for stealing the book and jar and all Dr. France's notes." He stood, cupping his left palm around the knuckles of his right. "I'd like to beat you to death, you smart-assed piece of shit. But for the moment, a friend of yours needs assistance. Get up."

Reid's hand had gone instinctively to his jaw. Tears welled, causing him to blink them away. His vision wavering, he nevertheless struggled to his feet.

*God, tell me it's not Kilgore!*

He was allowed out of the room, feet padding on the cold vinyl floor. He'd stepped out into what looked like a hallway full of offices. Pictures of landscapes hung on the walls. The aftereffects of the blow were leaving him with a terrific headache, and he could taste blood in his mouth. Poking around with his tongue, he was surprised to find his teeth still sound, but he'd bet a couple were cracked.

Bill Minor opened a double door and gestured Reid into what appeared to be a conference room. The upscale central table now supported the big black sarcophagus Reid had last seen in the burial chamber in Egypt. The same one, right down to the divot the plug had dug in the wood as the stone exploded.

"How did you get this?" Reid wondered, stepping forward.

"The same way he got me," a familiar voice said from the side, and Reid turned to see Yusif. The Egyptian sat hunched on an office chair in the corner. A dull wariness filled Yusif's dark and haggard eyes as he stood and stepped forward to embrace Reid.

"So, they have you, too?" Yusif asked in a faint whisper. "And Kilgore?"

"I don't know."

"Touching." Minor said condescendingly. "Glad to know you two can still work together." Minor walked forward, running his fingers along the carved surface of the sarcophagus. "Your job, gentlemen, is to figure out how to open this. We've reviewed the records from Dr. France's scan in Egypt. Our conclusion is that Fluvium did indeed booby-trap the lid with black powder. The charge might not kill you, but it will definitely destroy the contents."

"The tube-shaped things," Reid remembered.

Bill Minor nodded, head cocked as he stared thoughtfully at the carved image on the lid. "We think they are papyrus scrolls. Probably engineering designs. Fluvium, you see, was the theorist. The Domina, while no slouch herself when it came to theory, brought practical application to the project. He designed, she built."

"She's nuts," Reid said. "She told me she studied in Dzibilchaltun. That she married Fluvium there. It's a ruin! She thinks she was married to a three-thousand-year-old mummy."

"Neither she nor Fluvium are from our timeline, Dr. Farmer. That she's here, now, is an accident."

Reid shot Yusif a sidelong glance, as he asked, "And you're telling me that she's from where? Our future?"

"A parallel future." Bill Minor smiled at that. "Your belief, it turns out, is neither necessary nor sufficient. All you need to do is figure out how to open that sarcophagus."

"So, Domina just happened to slip into our world from an alternate universe?" Reid pursued. "But she came here, to our time, and Fluvium took a wrong turn and ended up in the past?"

"There's no sense in explaining."

"Try me, Bill. This whole thing has reeked of the impossible from the moment Yusif and I uncovered that steel door. So lay it out, plain and simple, and who knows, I might just be inclined to help you for once."

Minor's suspicious gaze bored into Reid's. Then he nodded. "The way I understand it, timelines split off from each other like branches. Fluvium and Domina come from a world parallel to ours. One with a different history after the Eighteenth Dynasty. In their history, Rome and Carthage merged but did not collapse into the Dark Ages. Instead, they opened trade to the Mayan civilization which allowed a cross-fertilization of ideas that spawned a scientific explosion a thousand years before ours. As part of Fluvium's research on something we call entangled particles, he discovered that it was possible to go back in time. The catch, and yes, there always is one, is that timelines won't tolerate paradox. You know what that is?"

"Yeah, like *Back to the Future*? If you change the past, your mom marries an asshole?"

"Correct. And there's something about the second law of thermodynamics, that you can't destroy or create energy. Sending it back in time would remove or subtract energy from one time and add it in another. The timeline resists and repulses that sort of thing. Like forcing two north poles of a magnet together, it pushes back."

"Then, how could they get here?"

"By trading equal mass/energy from our timeline with theirs. As they followed entangled particles back, they shifted mass/energy from our past to their present, making the books balance, so to speak."

"But she's here today, and he was in Egypt sometime in 1300 BCE?" Reid crossed his arms.

Yusif's dark eyes gleamed with disbelief.

Minor ran fingers down the dark wood. "Both of them arrived in ancient Egypt. They were conducting some sort of experiment. Something with water in the Nile. I'm a little hazy on this myself, but it seems Domina was testing her equipment, and pop! The next thing she knew she was here. In the Skientia lab."

"How's that possible?" A glance at Yusif told him the Egyptologist didn't believe a word of it.

"Apparently, Skientia was conducting experiments here at the lab. Somehow, they acted as a beacon through time. Essentially, the Domina's equipment, what she calls the navigator, locked on what it thought was the homing beacon back to its timeline and universe. Instead, it picked up this lab, three thousand three hundred years in this timeline's future."

Reid nodded slightly as Minor studied him for his reaction. "Which explains the inconsistencies of the tomb. Fluvium knew how to make steel for his tomb door."

"He had half a lifetime to figure out what went wrong. He knew that Domina had to have landed in this timeline's future. So he made his tomb impregnable to the robbers of his time. He left messages in pottery throughout Egypt. Messages that didn't make sense to Egyptologists, so the sherds were cataloged for future research."

"Did she tell you what went wrong?" Reid asked.

"Apparently, she carried one piece of the equipment, the navigator; it's a homing device and power pack. Fluvium carried what they called the cerebrum, the computer that figured out the gravitational manipulations and crunched the numbers while the navigator followed correct entangled particles through time. The two had to interface, work together to travel between timelines and universes. But when Domina turned on her navigator to calibrate it, it homed in on our time, and bang, she was deposited here."

"So, she's got her half of the machine?"

"We have it." Minor corrected. "Our people didn't understand. One minute they were running an experiment, the next a strange woman was standing in their lab. They panicked, had her arrested as an industrial spy. The Domina was distraught, disoriented, couldn't speak a word of our language. The interrogators thought she was a nut case, so they locked her away in a mental hospital."

"And her machine?" Reid insisted.

"Our guys kept mum about it. Thought they might have lucked into some sort of new spy technology that had allowed Domina to get past their security. They couldn't make heads or tails of the navigator box but recognized that the power pack was light-years beyond anything we had. Then they started translating her notebooks, figuring out the Latin. Couldn't believe it at first, but then you found the tomb."

"You believe this, *sahib*?" Yusif asked.

"How the hell do I know, Yusif? Bill's explanation is just as impossible as everything else about this job." He wheeled on Minor. "But tell me, Bill, I can figure out Skientia's interest in the technology and what it's worth. But what's Domina's angle?"

Minor considered for a moment. "She thinks she can find a way back to a parallel timeline. One that split off ours just after Fluvium was left behind. If she can locate him, they can reprogram the two pieces of their device, fit it together, and return to their own timeline and universe to live happily ever after."

"And you trust her?"

"No more than I trust you or Yusif. What we're banking on is that either Fluvium's half of the device—the computer or brain or whatever it is—is in this sarcophagus." He banged it with a knuckle. "Or perhaps whatever's in here contains the directions to where he hid it. And if it's lost forever, perhaps the sarcophagus contains schematics for the device itself."

"And if you find it?" Yusif asked warily.

"Then we control time and space, gentlemen. Which, when you think about it, is pretty much controlling everything."

# 84

The ominous strains of Giacomo Puccini's *Turandot* played lyrically in the background. Falcon sat with his back wedged into the corner where he'd pushed his bed against the wall. He wore only pants; his feet were bare. Distracted as he was, his toes absently kneaded the gray institutional bedspread. His arms clasped his knees close to his chest. And where he gripped his elbows, his hands continued to flutter.

He kept his eyes closed, images flashing on the backs of his eyelids. The reports given by each of the parties he'd sent out looped in different parts of his brain—as if by the very action of their repetition they would eventually click together like the gears in a transmission. And the moment they did, events would propel them forward.

"Forward to what?" he asked.

Try as he might, he couldn't see inside Skientia. Couldn't quite grasp the human element, or how to manipulate it. The organization itself remained inscrutable. Like some stone god whose statue had been carved in a distant jungle. How did one comprehend?

Skientia's goals were understandable: economic and political power. The ability to intercept both electronic and quantum secret communications from the past by ensnaring entangled particles as they traveled down light cones was intoxicating enough, but the ability to project a living human being, let alone monitor a parallel branch of the timeline? What unheard of advantages would that give a corporation or its board?

But what was the human angle?

"Can't get a handle on it, I take it?" Major Marks' voice intruded on Puccini's masterpiece.

"We're approaching the endgame, Major. Chief Raven and Sam Savage are preparing to penetrate the lab. Gray will need to make her move soon, since she surely understands the danger Skientia poses to her. They, in turn, must be aware of the threat she poses to them. For the time being, however, each needs the other."

"Mexican standoff?"

"Where do you come up with these terms?" Falcon's face tightened in a grimace.

"Your problem, Falcon, is that you had a sheltered youth. Never had to soil your hands with life."

"Do you think Cat's standoffish?"

"You're distracting yourself. Be a man and get on with it, will you? You're sending people in to beard the lion. Do it wrong, Falcon, and your people are going to die." Major Marks paused. "You ready to live with that?"

"No." Falcon winced, which made the images on the backs of his eyelids flicker.

"Well, you'd better be. Chief Raven's plan to go in through the roof, that's good. But you don't have a clue about the interior, how they've set up their security."

"Edwin can't penetrate their system yet."

"You're blaming your failures on Edwin? Stop it. Concentrate, Jimmy boy. Think it through."

"I'm trying."

For a few blessed minutes he was able to sit in silence, rerunning the loops of thought over and over against the reassuring darkness of his eyelids.

"Funny that no one has heard from Grazier, isn't it?" Major Marks noted just as a pattern began to form in Falcon's mind.

"He's a general. He's busy."

A caustic tone filled the major's voice. "You're better than this, Falcon. Sitting there, running these little bits of data around in your head like they were rabbits on a track. Talon mercs were found dead in Boston. Two more died in the Chesapeake. Chief Raven just put two more in the intensive care unit in a Colorado Springs hospital. And there's been no word from Grazier?"

The loops of thought reformed as they rolled behind Falcon's eyelids. In the operatic background, Calaf's voice rose and fell in the aria *"Nessun dorma."*

A soft knock at his door brought Falcon's eyes open. He glanced over, past Major Marks, who now had a smug smile on his square-jawed face.

"Come."

Edwin opened his door, stepping in. He glanced up at the timeline and flow chart obscuring Falcon's wall. Then his expression narrowed as he took in Falcon where he huddled defensively in the corner.

"Oh, I see. One of those days, huh?" Edwin peered around curiously. "That asshole Rudy ain't here, is he?"

"No, just the major and me." Falcon smiled softly as Turandot's ministers Ping, Pang, and Pong raised their voices in the attempt to dissuade Calaf from pursuing his dangerous path.

"Well, I got a little break," Edwin nervously avoided taking a seat. "Still can't hack the Skientia passwords, but I got an angle on them. That Bill Minor? The one Reid and Kilgore talk about? He's staying at the Hilton resort north of Santa Fe. They call it the Buffalo Thunder. Got a casino and golf course. He's got three expensive suites booked there. I think Gray's with him, too."

Falcon raised his hands from his knees in a gesture that made Edwin stop. He closed his eyes, thoughts swaying with Puccini's liquid music. On the back of his eyelids, he rearranged the pieces, watched them slip into place. A cold shiver played down his back.

"I'm such an idiot."

"Well, well," Major Marks noted wryly. "Looks like you better gather your people and beat feet for the boonies. Or do you need me to explain the metaphor again?"

Opening his eyes, Falcon said, "Edwin, we have to leave. Now."

"Leave? But I'm still—"

"Everyone in the van, Edwin. You can make our reservations on the way."

"But Cat and I—"

"Now, Edwin!" He took a half-panicked breath. "They're coming for us."

# 85

Sure, I made it all the way to a full bird colonel in the Marine Corps. As a much younger man, I did my combat tours, none of which, fortunately, turned out to be too hairy. My calling was psychology and psychiatry, helping and healing the people who really put their butts on the line for our country and the free world.

I do not consider myself to be an adrenaline junky.

Yes, I do ride very fast and powerful motorcycles, but even when I'm on my gnarly, fire-breathing Ducati Diavel, I turn the "go grip" with responsibility and maturity.

Yet here I was, strapped into another helicopter, a UH-60 Blackhawk this time. Did I tell you that I hate helicopters? The things scare me, and our last gambit over the Chesapeake had done nothing to change that.

I'd been amazed when the flight operations officer at Peterson Air Force Base had taken the code authorization Grazier had given us back in Washington, asked what we needed, and issued the Blackhawk when Winny requested it.

There had been no additional questions, no calls for authorization, nothing. I'd spent a lifetime in the Marines. No one had more paperwork than our military. But we flew away without so much as a signature on a piece of paper.

The implications of Grazier's security clearance—and the latitude of his black ops protocol—left me stunned.

Winny sat at the controls, Karla beside her. If you've never been in the cockpit, the instrument panel looks more like a tightly packed collection of computer game monitors. Me, I was happy in the back. I tried not to throw up while staring down at sprinklings of pine-and-juniper forest interspersed with burned mountain slopes. The Sangre de Cristo Mountains looked rugged with their scabby rock outcrops—angry and worn in the hot summer sunlight.

The Blackhawk began to buck and lurch, sending my stomach into my throat. Fear turned my guts runny.

"What's wrong with the bird?" I demanded through my headset.

"That's desert down there in the valley, Skipper," Winny told me. "Midsummer like this? You get a lot of turbulence."

"We're not getting shot at?"

"Not yet. But the day is young."

I closed my eyes, wincing every time the chopper shook and creaked around me.

*I'm not going to throw up. I'm not going to throw up.* Make the promise enough times and maybe it won't happen?

"There it is," Winny's voice came over the headset. "That's Los Alamos coming up on the right."

Knowing roughly where to look, I pressed a hand to my complaining gut, craned my neck, and saw the green bulk of the Jemez Mountains rising like a tumbled fortress above the main valley.

Winny banked, taking us along the drainage-cut slope, scarred by old fires, and housing localized patches of ponderosa timber that had somehow managed to escape the infernos.

The town itself was built on a high shoulder of the mountain, as if perched there. Sunlight glinted like sparkles from windshields, and speckles of color marked the distant walls and roofs.

If you had to design an atom bomb, there were worse places to do it.

The National Labs lay on the southwest corner of town, situated on a ridge top with a steep canyon on the southern edge. You just couldn't mistake the blocky-pale, nothing-but-functional architecture of a government compound.

Up front, Karla was peering through the glass with binoculars. Her attention had fixed on the Skientia building as Winny made a slow circle of the area.

"What do you think?" I asked.

"Getting in won't be the problem, Skipper," Karla told me. "Winny can carry Savage and me right up that drainage, assuming she manages to keep me from crashing through the trees this time."

"They're all burned, bitch. But I could bounce you and your little house of mirrors off those rock outcrops. That'd keep you in line."

"Seven years of bad luck," Karla countered. "And after I climbed up the rope and broke your wrists and fingers, the only thing you'd be flying is one of those video games."

"Ah, shucks. Savage's going to be riding in that thing with you. I *like* him. Guess he gets you a free ride in, Chief." Winny chided in mock distress.

"Do you see the heliport?" I asked.

"Roger that, Skipper. If Winny brings us up the canyon, she can pass right over the Skientia building, hesitate long enough to set us down there beside the door, and do a touch and go at the heliport. Skientia's security won't be any the wiser."

"That might work," Winny agreed as she wheeled us around again. "I'll want night vision goggles to make the drop. Shining a spotlight down there would tip them off."

"You really want to go through the roof?" I asked, staring down at the graveled flat beside the roof access door. It was built into to a square boxy looking cube that housed the elevator pulleys and cables.

"Skipper," Karla replied, "if we angle the mirror box correctly, they'll think their entire world is secure. Once we cut through, Savage and I drop inside, and they'll have no idea they've been breached."

"Why do I not like this?"

"Because, Skipper, like we discovered in Aspen, these guys play for keeps."

# 86

Janeesha shook her head as she stamped the work order that would authorize a plumber to deal with the stopped-up toilets in Ward Two. Despite the staff's vigilance, stuffed animals, plastic blocks, and other things often ended up in the plumbing. Patients had discovered that such antics made life a great deal more entertaining than their ordinary daily routine.

Normally, Colonel Ryan signed for such things. Nothing, however, was normal anymore. Patients now vanished, others escaped, then came and went as they pleased. Generals, new administrators, coming and going. One day Colonel Ryan is out, the next he's back. Then he's coming and going as if the Grantham Barracks was a revolving door.

"Ought to get me a raise," Janeesha murmured as she signed Ryan's signature. "I'm doing the director's work, ought to get director's pay."

The phone rang. Janeesha reflexively answered, "Dr. Ryan's office."

Mirabel Krantz, at reception, told her: *"I have two gentlemen here to see Dr. Ryan."* A slight pause. *"They're from the Pentagon."*

Janeesha, her mind still on clogged plumbing, said, "Tell them the director is unavailable today. If they'd make an appointment—"

*"Janeesha, I'm sending them up now!"* The tension in her voice was unmistakable.

"But I—" The phone clicked.

Janeesha sighed, glanced at the clock, slipped the work order into its envelope and placed it in the outbox. She'd no more than finished when the door opened and a tall, storklike, washed-out-looking white guy entered. He was followed by a medium-built Latino with a square face, curved nose, and intense hawklike eyes. Both men wore conservative gray business suits, white shirts, and dark ties. The medium-sized Latino held a thick leather folder in his left hand. The Pentagon? These guys looked like middle management executives.

Right up to the point they walked up to Janeesha's desk and produced sleek-looking badge cases that held their IDs and credentials.

"I'm Staff Sergeant Hanson Childs, United States Army Criminal Investigation Command," the over-bleached white guy told her. His pale-blue eyes fixed on hers. The pupils—like black dots—sent a shiver down her back.

"I'm Special Agent Jaime Chenwith," the Latino said crisply. "US Air Force Office of Special Investigations. We're here to see Dr. Timothy Ryan."

In an attempt to get her bearings, Janeesha stared at the badges. The Army CID guy had a shield with an eagle on top. The eagle on the Air Force's OSI dude's round shield looked half asleep. That brought her just enough humor to leverage a bit of backbone.

"Doctor Ryan isn't in today. If you'd care to make an appointment—"

"Where is he?" Chenwith's clipped voice had tightened.

"If you could tell me what this is all—"

"Dr. Ryan is currently at the center of a classified investigation. We know that he was in Washington several days ago." Chenwith flipped open the leather folder, laying out photos. "Can you verify that this woman, Major Winchester Wesson Swink, is a patient at this facility?"

Janeesha felt a band tighten around her heart. "She is."

Hanson Childs pointed at the next photo. "And this is Chief Petty Officer Karla Raven, also a patient here?"

"That's her."

"And do you know this man?" Hanson Childs produced another photo.

"Yes, sir. That's Major Savage. One of General Grazier's staff people."

The two agents gave each other the kind of triumphant look that virtually shouted, "Pay dirt!"

"We'll need a conference room. If you could have Swink and Raven brought up, we'll need to take their statements."

"They're not here."

"Excuse me?"

"Well, Winny and Karla left this morning with Colonel Ryan."

The two men fixed her with an intent stare, Chenwith asking, "Where are they, Ms. Felid?"

"I really don't know."

"Don't be coy," Hanson Childs' pale eyes turned glacial. "Major Swink's prints were all over the helicopter's controls. Not only can we tie CPO Raven to the passenger seat, but two pieces of nine-millimeter brass were found wedged beneath. Pin mark analysis suggests they came from an HK MP-5. Swabs taken from the cabin surfaces test positive for powder residue. Nine-millimeter slugs were recovered from the cowling and engine of an aircraft apparently shot down by Chief Raven. There are two fatalities."

Janeesha blinked. Shot down?

"Not to mention unauthorized use of a military aircraft which resulted in substantial damage." Jaime Chenwith leaned down on stiff arms to glare angrily into her eyes. "So why don't you just tell me where our persons of interest are, Ms. Felid? Because if you don't, you're going to find yourself smack dab in a world of shit. And, it's just a guess, mind you, but I think you'd rapidly discover that you were one very unhappy woman."

# 87

Bill Minor rubbed the back of his neck as he left his opulent suite and stepped out into the resort hotel's hallway. He nodded to the security agent standing before the Domina's door. Brandon Marsdon nodded back, dark eyes flashing.

Bill padded down the hallway to the elevator and pressed the button. As he waited, he checked his phone for emails or messages. Nothing significant required his attention.

It had been a long day, one filled with phone calls, interrogations, and intelligence reviews. But worst of all had been the oversight conference—an impromptu affair called when Skientia's president Peter McCoy and Chief Operating Officer Tanner Jackson had flown in without notice.

Bill had been summoned along with Maxine Kaplan, the supervising physicist in charge of the Los Alamos facility, and her right-hand man and engineer, Virgil Wixom.

"We think we have contained most of the trouble General Grazier stirred up," McCoy had said to open the meeting. "Bill Stevens has unleashed the entire weight of the government to run down Grazier's team." He smiled, shaking his head. "It appears he was using—get this—mental patients!"

"Huh?" Bill Minor asked.

"Out of Grantham Barracks, if you can believe it. A team of special investigators is closing in on them as I speak. Dr. Kilgore France remains at large for the moment. Apparently in some place called Mackaweevle, or something. Our people should have her and Dan Murphy within a few days. The operative assumption is that Dr. France is attempting to translate Fluvium's journal."

"And that leaves us vulnerable how?" Maxine had asked. Bill always wished he'd known her as a younger woman. Though in her mid-fifties, she still kept herself attractive, slim, and healthy.

McCoy rubbed his fleshy jowls. The guy reminded Minor of a bloodhound: all bones hung with lots of loose skin. Even the man's somnolent brown eyes added to the effect. Behind the lazy-dog façade lay the sort of avaricious soul that made a hungry shark look warm and fuzzy.

McCoy lived for the kill. As a young man, he'd made his mark on Wall Street, riding the bull right up to January of 2007. At the bottom of the market, he'd invested a billion. Doing so, he'd acquired controlling interests in most of the better R&D firms—the ones that lived on the cutting edge. And having skillfully merged them into the single entity of Skientia, McCoy now perched like a spider in his web. Not only did he have a corner on the best scientific brains in the business, but his personal fortune and political acumen allowed him access to the most rarified hallways in the White House, Capitol, and Pentagon.

Rumor was that he *owned* Bill Stevens.

Peter McCoy scared Bill Minor. Something about the guy was simply inhuman and cold-blooded.

Tanner Jackson, Skientia's COO, was another misleading man. He stood five-nine. Bald as a cue ball, his skull was shaped like a potato: long and bulbous at both ends. He wore the most unfashionable black-frame glasses. Rumor had it that he didn't trust LASIK surgery, even though he owned several companies that manufactured the equipment. With his doughy and pasty-white face, the guy just looked like a dork despite his tailored-in-Milan suits.

Behind the appearance, however, lived a human scorpion and master strategist. Jackson had brought Bill Minor in years ago, recognizing his talents. It had been Jackson's suggestion to originally retain Talon Group's services; then, through a shell corporation, Skientia had bought the security firm.

"We're only vulnerable if Dr. France can convince anyone to believe her story," Tanner Jackson said absently. "And for her that carries its own risks, since she knows any attempt on her part to publicize her findings would lead us straight to her."

"Then, what's her angle?" Maxine wanted to know.

Bill had interjected, "She gets a definite ego-fix from the spotlight, but in the end she's a sucker for a forensic mystery. My take is that she still thinks Fluvium is a scam, and she'll do anything in her power to prove it."

"Good, let her." McCoy laid a finger along his nose as he thought. "Maxine, where are we on the reengineering of the generator?"

"Based on what Domina has given us, and what we've gleaned from the tomb wall inscriptions, we can start running live animal time trials tomorrow night. Domina wants to use the navigator to monitor the initial tests from the forward control pedestal. If we just had that computer she insists Fluvium had . . ."

"Any progress there?" Jackson shot a glance at Bill.

"The two archaeologists have carefully cut sections out of the sarcophagus that will allow them to remove the black powder charges tomorrow morning. If the computer is inside, we'll have it by noon."

McCoy noted: "If you locate it, it will be absolutely imperative that Domina *does not* find out. If she gets her hands on the cerebrum, and it still remains functional, we lose everything."

"She doesn't even know the sarcophagus is here." Minor spread his hands wide, a runny feeling in his gut from the way McCoy was watching him through those too-soft puppy-dog eyes.

"Tell her that we're running down new leads in Egypt. That it might take a while, but if Fluvium hid the brain, we'll find it."

"That's the plan," Minor had agreed.

"And the jar containing the red death?" Maxine Kaplan had asked.

"Still missing," McCoy had grunted. "And for one, I damned well hope that Kilgore France doesn't decide to just pour it down a drain somewhere."

"If she does," Jackson had snorted irritably, "we'd better get a handle on this time machine fast, because we're going to be in need of a parallel universe pretty darn *ricky tick* quick."

The words from the meeting echoing in his head, Bill Minor emerged from the Hilton's elevator and made his way to the stylish lounge. The place was done up in Southwestern Indian motifs. Mock adobe walls and fake viga logs all hinted of the pueblos, as did the geometric, Navajo-patterned chairs and thick tables.

From long habit, Minor stopped inside the door, letting his eyes run over the tables and occupants. Most of the patrons he placed as upper-middle class to moderately wealthy married couples enjoying vacations or attending the opera.

The two women at the table off to the side, however, were different. Bill Minor always chose a table in the corner. The one he seated himself at not only placed his back to the faux-adobe wall, but let him keep an eye on the entrance, the bartender, and best of all, the two remarkably attractive women at the closest table.

The way the overhead lights sparkled fire in the redhead's hair matched the devil-may-care grin that crept in around the corners of her mouth. A calculating glint in her green eyes matched the petite lines of her face.

And then there was the tall black-haired, gray-eyed masterpiece across from her. She probably had a couple of inches on Minor, but the way everything matched so proportionally, she was all woman. Fit, too, from what the blouse and tapered black cotton slacks disclosed of her muscular body. She threw her head back and laughed at something the redhead said, then ran fingers through her midnight hair and flipped it over her broad swimmer's shoulders.

Damn, she had an animal magnetism, and he could imagine himself running his hands down that sleekly muscled body, peeling the slacks from those slim hips . . .

The barmaid stepped up, placed a napkin on the scarred-wood table.

"Black Jack straight up, glass of water back, and a lite beer."

The two women burst into laughter, glancing at each other. The redhead raked two five-dollar bills to her side of the table, having obviously won a bet.

*They bet on my drink order?*

He heard the redhead say, "Five bucks says it's beer."

"Five for the bourbon," the raven-haired she-tiger answered and slapped down another five.

The redhead matched from her pile.

*God, they are betting on me.*

Even as his lips tried to bend into a smile, his innate sense of caution sent a tingle down his spine. It wasn't like he was on duty, though he remained on call. And it definitely wasn't like women didn't notice him. For some the lure lay in his weight-lifter's physique. Others said they were drawn to his "bad-boy charm." Still others insisted he came across as irresistibly dangerous. Or that he was "mysteriously male," whatever that meant.

And some, like Kilgore France, perhaps through innate intelligence, treated him as if he were a coiled cobra.

*So, William, you can make one of the lovely ladies five bucks. Which one do you choose?*

The fiery and cute redhead with her devilish smile? Or the black-haired Amazon oozing animal magnetism? Which one would he rather undress tonight?

He still hadn't solved the problem when the barmaid set the drinks on his napkin. He stared down at the amber fluid in the short glass, then at the beer.

The women leaned close, whispering, watching his choice as unobtrusively as possible.

Minor reached out and danced his fingers along the rim of the whiskey glass, then shifted to the beer, and finally lifted the glass of water. He drank a couple of inches down and replaced the glass on the table.

The two women were staring at each other, and before he could react, each tossed another five into the middle of the table.

*They upped the ante?*

All right. He picked up the whiskey, dumped half into his water glass. Then he poured a couple of fingers of beer into the whiskey, sloshed it around a couple of times, and drank.

The women began chuckling to themselves, aware that he was onto them.

"I've been around," he raised his voice for their benefit, "but no one's ever bet on what I'd drink before."

The redhead shifted in her seat to give him a narrow-eyed inspection. "You obviously don't hang out with competitive women. Keeps us from fighting over the spoils if we know who owns what from the very beginning."

"Who owns what?" Minor repeated suggestively.

The tigress turned, leaning just as suggestively in her chair; her keen gray eyes fixed on his. "Trust me. You don't want to know."

"Cozumel," the redhead stated. "Carlos 'n Charlie's. Way too much tequila."

"I've gotta hear this," Minor told them, giving them his best smile. He had a hunch about what "ownership" implied.

"Cozumel," the gray-eyed beauty repeated as if it explained everything.

"Too much tequila," the red fox insisted. She made a gesture with her fingers. "Drink that down. You gotta catch up. It's not a story for the sober."

Minor tossed down his mixed whiskey, followed it with beer, and gestured the barmaid for a repeat. "So, I'll catch up. Name's Bill Minor. You two here on vacation?"

"Naw. Working." The redhead was making no apology as she sized him up. "I'm called Win." She grinned. "Take that however you want to. I fly a helicopter. That Blackhawk back behind the security gate."

The raven-haired one said, "They call me Chief. We're doing aerial watershed and timber evaluations for the Forest Service and BLM, mapping pine beetle infestations and vegetation surveys in the old burns. She flies, I lean out and shoot pictures. We're going to be working around Los Alamos and up to the caldera."

"Wow, sounds exciting."

His server placed another bourbon and beer before him. Instinctively, he took a sip of the Jack Daniels, and watched the tall woman slap a hand onto the fives and draw them back.

"I guess I know who's got dibs, huh?" he asked softly.

"Depends," she told him with a predatory smile. "The night is young. You've got unlimited opportunities to make a mess of things and demonstrate beyond a shadow of a doubt that you don't deserve our company, let alone mine."

*Oh, if you only knew who you're dealing with here, sweetie.*

She winked and lifted her glass, as if in a toast.

He stretched, extended his glass of bourbon and was just able to clink hers.

"So, what do you do, Bill Minor?" the redhead asked.

"Me? I do a bit of security for one of the labs up at Los Alamos. A sort of contractor. Evaluations. That sort of thing." For tonight—with the raven-haired sorceress for a potential prize—he could be charming, exotic, and slightly dangerous. Especially if her cat-lithe body held half the charm naked that it promised clothed.

After all, she'd got dibs, right?

# 88

ET might not have been having any luck breaking into the Skientia computers, but one thing I can say, we *owned* the Buffalo Thunder Hilton's security system.

My pulse was racing as Edwin used the hotel security cameras to track Karla and Winny as they accompanied Bill Minor from the lounge. I watched in awe, seeing a side of Winny that I never knew existed: the way she played a skank might have come straight out of a country-western song. Not that Karla did a bad job of batting her eyes and posing suggestively, either. She still carried her drink, supposedly a glass of scotch. Everything depended on the contents of that glass.

I gave Bill Minor my full attention, remembering everything Kilgore and Reid had told me. Even after the drinks he'd consumed, he walked with a predatory ease and grace. Nor did I like the excited glint in his eyes, or the triumphant smirk on his lips. His entire body appeared ready to explode with anticipation at ripping their clothes off.

"He looks full of himself," Cat Talavera noted as she peered over my shoulder.

"Yeah," Edwin noted sourly. "The dude figures he's gonna have a fantastic threesome."

"Somehow," I warned, "I don't think he's the type to take rejection gracefully. Cat? Is that stuff you concocted going to work?"

"If Karla can get him to drink it, he'll be down for the count."

"What'd you make?" Edwin asked.

"Call it an oral propofol. Within seconds, it's going to start suppressing his mental activity, affecting gamma-aminobutyric acid and dopamine balances. It's a lipid soluble that easily crosses the blood-brain barrier, so I had to bind some of the molecules to slowly oxidize over time to ensure he stays out for the rest of the night."

Edwin screwed his face into a baffled expression.

I chuckled. "She said it's a time-released anesthetic. Assuming Karla can get him to drink the mickey, the man's going down."

I had no more time to wonder as they stepped into the elevator. Edwin switched monitors, and as the elevator doors closed, Winny, to my complete surprise, began running her hands over Minor's body, checking out the swell of his chest, oohing over his thick biceps.

Then the doors opened on Minor's floor and the two women linked arms in his as he swaggered down the hallway toward his room. The security guard who stood in front of Gray's suite gaped, then did his best to look everywhere but at Minor as the man fished for his room key.

In the last instant, Karla shot the security monitor a saucy wink. Then she disappeared into the room.

In the hallway, the security guard was grinning like a silly idiot.

"All right, girls," I whispered. "If you don't get that drink down his gullet, this is going to get really nasty."

"Not to mention blowing our whole cover."

"Do you think Chief Raven can take him?" Sam Savage asked from where he watched over Edwin's other shoulder.

"I don't know." I rubbed the back of my neck, worry—like an anxious rodent—running around in my gut.

Minutes, feeling like slow hours, dragged by.

I was on the verge of panic when the door opened and Winny Swink stepped out. She glanced down that hall at the surprised security guard and blew him a kiss. Then, brazenly resettling her bra through her flimsy shirt, she strode down the hall toward the elevator.

I partially exhaled the breath I hadn't realized I was holding.

"At least she's out," ET mused. "Funny, I never thought she was that good-looking."

"At Grantham you never saw Winny Swink at her best," I replied. "Part of her shut down when they grounded her."

Through the monitors we watched her progress to our hallway. Savage opened the door before she could knock, and Winny strode in. We were all donning nitrile gloves as she reached down her blouse and pulled out Bill Minor's smartphone, room key, key ring, and a security pass card.

"He's out?" Cat demanded as Winny tossed the goods to Savage, who in turn handed them to ET

"Oh, yeah," Winny grinned. "He was half out of his shirt before the room door closed. Karla told him if he drained her glass, she'd finish the job. He had it chugged before she could undo his belt."

"How's his breathing?" Cat asked.

"Relax, Doc. Karla's keeping an eye on him." Winny glanced at ET. "How long to download that stuff?"

Edwin had already hooked a USB cable from his computer to the smartphone and was pressing things on the screen. "Maybe five minutes. Cat, get a reading on this pass card. Then on his room key. Savage, you use that modeling clay and make us an impression of each of his keys. Skipper, you check out the guy's wallet."

The room erupted in a flurry. I stepped back when Winny dug Minor's wallet out of a tight hip pocket and handed it to me. Laying out the man's credit cards, I took measure of Winny, dressed as she was in tight pants, the provocative purple silk blouse tucked at the waist. Her red features were flushed, her lips slightly parted in a smile.

"Having fun, Major?"

"Five by five, Skipper." She gave me a wink. "Since Cat says he's not going to remember a thing, Karla and I plan on leaving that asshole a token of our admiration. When he wakes up in the morning, he's going to think he's been turned every which way but loose."

I tried to stress the seriousness of the situation as I photographed the credit cards. "Don't get too overboard. I mean, don't leave him desperate for a vendetta."

"Holy shit, Skipper," ET called as he scanned through the download from Bill Minor's phone. "They gonna run a full test on a fucking *time machine* tomorrow night!"

Winny was collecting keys and the pass card. I was photographing the business cards, IDs, hotel and car club memberships, and counting out two thousand and twenty-six dollars.

"Is that important?" Savage wondered.

"I'll have to ask Falcon." I carefully replaced the wallet's contents, making sure the credit cards were in order and faced the same direction they'd been.

"Come on, people," Winny coaxed. "I can't be gone too long."

I tossed her the wallet, watching her wiggle it back into her too-tight back pocket. She slipped Bill Minor's smartphone back into her bra and started for the door.

"You forgot the most important thing." I reached for the bottle of Jack Daniels and tossed it to her.

She caught it, grinned, and sighed. "Skipper, you sure we have to pour it down the drain?"

"All but an inch!" I warned. "And be damn sure that security guard sees it's full when you enter that room!"

"You just can't forget the fun Karla and I had with that tequila," she chided as she disappeared into the hallway.

"Oh, yeah," I whispered.

"Jackpot," Edwin cried. "Here's his contacts, his voice mail, his emails, the whole shittaree, Skipper. I got Bill Minor by the balls!"

I winced as my imagination ran rampant. Minor was unconscious in a room where he'd hoped to score both Winny and Karla? "Somehow, ET, I think you're not the only one."

# 89

Falcon sat in the cushy reclining chair, his knees up, arms pulled tightly around them. He wanted to rock his whole body back and forth, but the cushions wouldn't allow it. Instead, he could only bob his head on his shoulders, and rhythmically flutter his wrists and fingers where they clasped his forearms.

Everything about the suite was wrong, right down to the light tan of the fake adobe walls. The colors on the wall decorations and the faux-viga ceiling jarred in his vision.

His paranoia grew, the urge to throw up sending prickles through his stomach.

*They're coming for us. Closing in.*

"What a wuss," Rudy Noyes observed in a voice dripping with irritation.

"Oh, hush," Falcon snapped, wishing that the major or Theresa were around to ameliorate Rudy's delinquent presence. "I need to think. I *have* to think!"

Once again, the memory flashed into prominence: His box of crayons stood on the corner of his desk. Yellow was in his fingers as he dotted the piece of paper he was working on with stars. He had already drawn in the spaceship, a gray thing of angles and square blue solar panels.

The teacher had said to draw the most fantastic thing, to imagine freely. What could be more fantastic than being in space? Daddy had said it had no end, that an infinity of worlds . . . He liked that word, infinity. It meant endless, beyond counting.

He reached for the dark blue, and had just plucked it from the box when the principal knocked on the classroom door and leaned her head in, asking, "Ms. Grant, could I see Jimmy Falcon?"

That first moment of panic replayed in his memory as every eye in the classroom fixed on him. Then came the long walk down the hallway to the principal's office. That's where bad kids went. And Jimmy Falcon couldn't figure out what he'd done that was bad.

To his complete surprise, Aunt Celia was already there, and so was his little sister, Julie. When he was led into the room, Julie had run to him and grabbed for his hand.

That's when Aunt Celia leaned down, her face frightening him with its strained grief, her eyes glittering with tears. In a quavering voice, she had said, "Jimmy? Julie? There's been an accident. Mommy and Daddy? They've gone to be with the angels."

*They're coming for us. Closing in.*

"You're a fucking sick and twisted man!" Rudy's sharp voice intruded. "You're on the run, man. Everyone's counting on you, and you're stuck in childhood? Shit! You think you had it tough as a kid?" He made his voice falsetto. "*Aunt Celia* bought you a Jaguar XK when you turned sixteen, you spoiled little fuck! Just so you could drive to prep school and fit in with the rest of the golden-spoon babies."

"Shut up!" Falcon shouted, closing his eyes.

Behind his eyelids the loop began to replay: His box of crayons stood on the corner of his desk. Yellow was in his fingers as he dotted the piece of paper he was working on with stars. He had already drawn in the spaceship, a gray thing of angles and square blue solar panels.

The teacher had said to draw the most fantastic thing, to imagine freely. What could be more fantastic than being in space? Daddy had said it had no end, that an infinity of worlds . . . He liked that word, infinity. It meant endless, beyond counting.

He reached for the dark blue, and had just plucked it from the box when the principal knocked on the classroom . . .

"What a shitty little *maggot* you are," Rudy insisted.

"Get *out* of my room, Rudy!"

But it was Dr. Ryan's voice that intruded gently.

"Falcon? Can you open your eyes and talk to me?"

He did, half expecting Rudy to be leering over the Skipper's shoulder. Instead, Cat Talavera stood behind Dr. Ryan, a concerned look on her delicate face. Falcon absently noted that her hair was freshly washed, thick, and gleaming with bluish tints in the morning light that streamed through the windows.

"Rudy's here?" Ryan asked, dropping into a crouch beside the chair. The Skipper stared earnestly into Falcon's eyes.

"He won't leave me alone! I have to think. I *must* think. They're coming for us, Skipper. Closing in."

His fingers began to flutter with greater intensity. "The loop just plays over and over in my mind. I'm in third grade. At my desk, drawing my spaceship . . ." The image—a daydream come to life—took over. He carefully replaced his yellow crayon, reaching for the dark blue . . .

"Falcon?" Dr. Ryan's firm voice intruded. "It's all right. You're in a new place, a different environment that's suddenly unpredictable. That's making you anxious, and in defense, you're obsessively activating the same pattern of brain engrams. I need you to do two things: First, I want you to take a low-dose Valium. Just this one. And second, I need you to come next door to Edwin's suite. He's just downloaded the contents of Bill Minor's cell phone."

"I don't know if I can," Falcon almost cried out.

*"Asshole, pussy!"* Rudy cried from where he leaned against the wet bar counter, his arms crossed so they pulled the sleeves of his leather bomber jacket tight.

Cat leaned close. "It's all right, Falcon. I'll wait here while the meds take effect and make sure that Rudy doesn't bother you."

"He says terrible things about you," Falcon confided. "Rude things."

"I don't care," she told him. "We should have anticipated the stress you'd be under. We just left home in such a hurry we didn't think about it." Her large dark eyes warmed. "And you are right, Falcon. They're hunting us. Janeesha said the CID showed up right after we left. You saved us all again."

"For the moment," Falcon whispered. "They're coming, closing in."

Cat stared into his eyes. "We've got new information. They're running a test on the time machine tomorrow night. We know that they've alerted the power company. They've got a dedicated 360Kv line all the way from the power plant in Arizona to handle the load."

"Got to stop it," he said. Would there be enough time?

*They're coming for us! Closing in.*

A blackness lay just over the horizon, if only he could concentrate. If only he could put the yellow crayon down, avoid that terrible trip to the principal's office . . .

*I just can't. I'm going to fail them. And my people are going to die.*

"Yeah." Rudy made kissing noises with his mouth. "And just imagine what Gray's going to do to get even when she escapes."

A cold fear washed through him. And in his hand he tightened the grip on his yellow crayon, watching the wax melt and bend and squeeze through his fingers like runny cheese . . .

# 90

The pounding on the door drove spikes into Bill Minor's head. He groaned, tried to swallow. His mouth felt like it was stuffed with dry sand, and his tongue stuck against his gullet.

More pounding.

"Damn it!" his voice croaked, and he blinked his gummy eyes open. The room was bright, a slanting yellow sun bouncing off the carpet and far wall of his hotel suite. The fireplace reminded him where he was. His familiar luggage lay open on the dresser.

More pounding, and a voice asked, "Mr. Minor? Are you all right?"

His bed was a rumpled mess, and he lay naked on top of it. He climbed wearily to his feet and stuck a hand out to brace himself against the wall. He made his wobbly way to the door. Opened it a slit and stared out at Brandon Marsdon.

Marsdon had his expression carefully under control as he said, "Car will be here in a half an hour, sir. We've got the power-up test tonight. Thought you might need a reminder." Then a smug smile bent the man's lips. "You had quite a workout last night."

"Shit." Minor blinked to clear his vision, closed the door in Marsdon's face, and shuffled to the bathroom. At the sink he drank from his cupped hands, splashed water into his face, and tried to clear the fuzz from his head.

As he bent, he winced, surprised to find bruises on his ribs and shoulders.

"What the hell?" Red glossy lipstick coated his swollen and sore penis.

Fighting through the fog, he struggled to remember. Women. The raven-haired beauty and the redhead! He'd been at the bar. They were betting on him, laying claim. But what had happened next?

He climbed into the shower, ran the water hot, and looked down at his body. *You had quite a workout last night.* That's what Marsdon had said. Both of them? And the lipstick?

Vaguely, he remembered hearing something about having a dick like a bull mandrill's in the jungle. Or was that just his imagination?

"I *didn't* drink that much."

And then it hit him. Heedless of the spray, he ripped the shower curtain back and stumbled, dripping, out into his room. His pants lay on the floor, and he vaguely remembered the black-haired goddess tossing them there. Dropping to hands and knees, he fumbled for the pockets. His billfold was as he'd left it; the two grand in cash remained undisturbed, the credit cards all in their slots. His keycards were in the back pocket, and the leather holster cradled his smartphone. He pulled his key ring out and sighed in relief as he clutched his security pass card.

Standing, he looked carefully around the room. A bottle of Jack Daniels, its cap missing, stood on the desk; less than an inch of amber liquid remained in the bottom. A bra hung from the corner of the plasma TV. He grabbed it down. Too big for the redhead. Had to be the brunette's.

"What were their names?"

He plodded back to the shower. Feeling like hammered shit, he climbed back into the spray and pulled the curtain closed.

After he'd dressed, his stomach aching, he stepped out into the hall and slitted a reproving eye when Marsdon snickered.

"You want to tell me what happened last night?"

"None of my business, sir."

"What time did I come back to the room?"

"About midnight, sir."

"And what time did the women leave?"

"A little before two, sir."

"Did they try to access the Domina's room?"

Marsdon gave him a quizzical look. "Uh, they were definitely busy with other things, sir."

"And you know this how?"

"You all, um . . . were loud, sir." He struggled to keep his expression under control. "And athletic."

*I didn't drink that much!*

Once again, he checked to be sure his billfold was secure and his cell phone in place. The near empty bottle of Jack Daniels on the desk haunted him.

*Why do I feel like I've been scammed?*

Those thoughts on his mind, he went down and knocked on Domina's door. The peep hole went dark as her security agent checked, then opened the door.

"Have a nice night, sir?" the man asked, trying to keep a straight face.

Minor slitted an eye that promised mayhem, only to step back as Domina, dressed in a clinging pink chiffon pantsuit, walked out. At the sight of Minor, her stately lips curled wryly, her blue eyes amused. *"Mixtim cum feminae in orgia corrumperis?"*

"Excuse me?"

In her stilted English, she added, "If you need to, how you say, nap? I will understand." Then as she started down the hall, following her security, she added, "You impress even me."

Minor would have ground his teeth in humiliation, but it aggravated his headache too much.

# 91

Reid and Yusif sweltered under the strong glare of the shop lights they'd positioned around the sarcophagus with its sculpted image of Fluvium. The man's face bore a faint smile, as if he mocked them for their audacity in trying to open his last repository.

"We'll see who gets the last laugh," Reid promised as he made the final cut with a small handheld circular saw. Yusif caught the section of wood.

"I still do not like this, *sahib*," Yusif told him. "The notion of sawing open a three-thousand-year-old sarcophagus reeks of the sort of sacrilege that should get a person consigned to the lowest levels of hell."

Reid watched him lower the square section to expose the wooden cylinder that contained the black powder. Then he bent forward and used a flashlight to illuminate the device.

"Pretty damn clever," Reid muttered. "Can you see the levers? By lifting the lid, the levers are turned, which press the iron rods down. When enough pressure is created, the rods fracture these thin glass disks. Once the glass breaks, the rods drop and slide along the flint chips."

"Which then spark and set off the powder," Yusif finished. "I think we can just lift the canister out."

"I'll grab the iron rod just to be sure."

Yusif glanced at him, dark eyes thoughtful. "You will not slip?"

"You'll be the first to know if I do."

"Allah protect me." Yusif wiped at the sweat beading on his forehead. "Very well." He grasped the wooden cylinder and eased it sideways until the base slid free of the confining wood. Slowly he lowered it, while Reid reached in and grasped the iron rod. Once free, they separated the pieces and grinned.

Removing the glass disk and looking into the cylinder, Reid could see the lines of flint, and below them, the granular black powder.

"Makes you wonder why he kept the formula secret," Yusif said as he carefully set the cylinder on the floor. "If what they were doing with biohazard is true, why would he care if he introduced gunpowder to our timeline?"

"You starting to believe that timeline stuff?"

"I don't know what to think. It's all *magnoon*. Crazy, you know?"

"I'm sorry, Yusif."

He waved it away. "Bah, I was enjoying my cell. So peaceful and dark, you know? Just me and the rats. Then suddenly, in the middle of the night, I was awakened. Two rather surly men dragged me out. What better time to die, eh?"

His eyes narrowed as he moved to the next cylinder where the wood had been cut away. "But instead they loaded me on a helicopter, which took me to the airport. Next thing I am on a flight to New York, and there, in the airplane's cargo bay is this sarcophagus! How do they get it? I do not know."

He waved a finger under Reid's nose. "But the fact that they did, and that I am out of *al segna*, um, prison? Ah, *sahib,* we're talking a great deal of power."

Reid lowered his voice. "Something tells me things are going to be very, very interesting sometime soon."

"Just do not drop the next canister," Yusif reminded flatly. "Or they will be picking us up with a *ma'ala'a*."

"A what?"

"A spoon. Unlike a spatula the runny bits won't drip off the edges."

"Always practical, aren't you?"

"When we are not rioting in the streets, we think that way in the new Egypt."

Bill Minor opened the door and stepped in. "Are you ready to open that thing yet?"

Reid glanced at him, noted the black rings under his eyes, the haggard expression. "Looks like you had a tough night."

Minor didn't even hesitate. He grabbed Reid by the throat and lifted. Staring eye to eye, Minor said, "Don't screw with me today, Doctor. I'm not in the fucking mood for it."

Reid coughed and gagged when Minor released him. He staggered back, then dropped limply to the floor. He'd barely caught a breath through his crushed throat when Bill Minor drew back and kicked him hard in the stomach.

"I want that fucking thing open within the hour, gentlemen. If you can't, after I beat the both of you to death, I'll find someone who can get the job done."

Turning on a heel he strode for the door.

Fear running bright along his bones, Reid gasped against the pain in his belly. Shaking and panicked, he blinked back tears. Yusif helped him sit up. Reid fought a sudden urge to vomit, sucking big gasps of air.

"You are all right, *sahib*?"

"No. But how I feel doesn't matter." Reid brushed him away, voice rasping. "Come on. Let's get the damn thing open before he comes back."

Yusif's black eyes held Reid's. "Next time I would advise a more circumspect approach regarding your description of his physical appearance."

"Yeah, I'll take that under advisement."

# 92

A helicopter, a Chinook from the sound of it, chattered its way over the low roof. The building had originally been a Soviet administration building in another war. What had once been sturdy concrete walls, poured by Afghan workers under the careful eyes of Russian overseers, had taken a beating after the Soviets had pulled out. The place had seen major fighting in the Taliban takeover, and then again as they were driven out of Bagram Air Base and its environs.

Battered as the walls were, pocked with bullet strikes and shrapnel, the place had been given to the medical corps for office space. Fake wood paneling had been fixed to the cracked concrete and new lighting installed. White acoustical paneling had been hung from the already low ceiling. Gray industrial-grade carpeting covered the floors, and standard-issue desks and chairs finished the small rooms.

All the comforts of home, Karla thought as the fresh-faced second lieutenant stepped through the door. His uniform was immaculate, pressed. The caduceus on his lapels gleamed in the light. He carried her folder in both hands, which was odd, and she could see the tension in his watery blue eyes as he closed the door behind her.

"So," she greeted sharply. "Been a pleasure answering all of your questions, Lieutenant, but I've gotta beat feet. I've got a new AOIC to break in and—"

"A what?" he asked, looking confused as he ran a finger under his collar.

"Assistant Officer in Charge. And I've got replacements, a lot of them, to integrate into my platoon." The IED had taken so many . . . so very many.

And I didn't see it.

She swallowed hard. "So stamp me fit and let me get back to work."

He just stared at her, looking nervous, reddening, which darkened the spots of acne on his cheeks. "Uh, Chief? You're not going anywhere. Not after last night when you woke up screaming." He lifted the folder as if it explained everything.

*"You lost most of Bravo Platoon, Chief. After the psych evaluation, we, um, have concerns. It'll just be a short rotation back to the States, and then, in a couple of months, I'm sure they'll give you a new platoon."*

*She froze, staring at him as if he'd spoken an alien language. Then her body moved of its own accord, rising from the chair, reaching out. Panic, in a crystalline reality, filled the lieutenant's eyes, and he broke and ran, nearly ripping the door off its hinges in the process.*

*"You little* weasel! *Get your ass back here and I'll . . . I'll . . ." But she'd stopped short, seeing the MPs who came clumping down the hall in their polished boots.*

*One scrawny lieutenant had done what three roll-backs in BUD/S classes, what SEAL Tactical Training, what Sniper School, and Green Team training couldn't. What the endless hazing, testing, and abuse at the hands of her male teammates hadn't been able to do, the little prick had accomplished in but an instant. He'd destroyed her reputation of being solid, of "Having her shit wired tight." A good reputation was the highest honor a SEAL could confer on a teammate. With a simple psych evaluation it was gone forever.*

*Karla threw her head back and screamed.*

"Hey! Damn it!" A voice intruded. "Wake up!"

Karla jolted, the dream shattering. Her eyes flew open as her body jerked into position to strike, her limbic system primed for combat. Tense and perspiring she half-crouched in the helicopter seat, sunshine glaring through the plexiglass bubble. The controls and instrument panel seemed to mock her.

"You were trying to *kick* my damn bird apart!" Winny Swink bellowed. She was leaned in the open door, red face blazing. "You want to scream and throw a fit? Go have the Skipper shoot you up with Valium or something."

"Bad dream."

"Flashback?" Swink seemed to relent the slightest bit.

"Yeah." Karla rubbed her sweat-dampened face. "Guess I dozed off."

"Too much play last night." Swink gave her a lopsided grin. "But, I gotta tell you, that was a lot of fun. I'd have loved to have seen his face when he woke up and saw his little sausage done up in bright red."

Karla knotted her muscles in an isometric exercise to stimulate circulation and burn the adrenaline and lipids still charging her system. She still wanted to kill that little puke of a psych intern, but remembering Bill Minor's limp body on his hotel room bed was a good antidote for her rage.

"That stuff Cat gave us really put him out." She winked at Winny. "If she's right, he's going to wake up thinking he had the night of his life."

"Wish I'd had a bottle of that stuff years ago. There are guys I wouldn't have touched—even if I was wearing welding gloves—that I'd have loved to have left believing I'd screwed their brains out."

Karla chuckled. "Given some of the men I woke up with? I'd have used a bottle of that stuff on myself. Some things in life, a woman really shouldn't have to remember."

"Like that flashback you just had? Combat?"

"No. I was just getting ready to make the little pimply-faced lieutenant who took me down feel a whole lot of pain. The guy wasn't even a psychiatrist. Just an intern with a questionnaire." Karla knotted her fist, staring at the scars on her knuckles.

Winny pursed her lips, nodded. "They gave you your second Silver Star for what you did that day. Even before the pieces stopped falling out of the sky, a horde of fighters came charging out of those crummy little houses. You were shooting at them with one hand while you pulled the living and dead out of their burning vehicles. You and four guys fought off nearly two hundred Taliban, Karla."

"Didn't matter after that fawning, skinny REMF labeled me crazy."

Swink gave her a thumbs up. "I surrender to your superior ability and competence. I had to steal an airplane and turn Washington upside down." She turned at the sound of a truck engine. "How about that? Here comes your mirror thingee."

Shaken and uneasy, Karla climbed out of the cockpit and jumped to the ground as a battered white Ford F-250 with New Mexico plates drove slowly into the compound. In the pickup's bed stood what looked like a small two-person gazebo, its outside covered with mirrors.

"God bless Santa Fe," she said as she tucked her thumbs in her belt. "The city of artisans. They can build anything here."

Winny stood, hips canted. "Okay, Chief. Looks like your last piece is here."

"If we can get this thing unloaded without shattering it, I'm good to go."

"You know, if Bill Minor catches you inside that lab? What he'll do to you before he finally puts a bullet in your head? It ain't gonna be pretty."

# 93

Reid and Yusif stared into the opened sarcophagus. "What the hell?"

"Scrolls, *akhooya*." Yusif reached down and reverently lifted one of the papyrus tubes. A string had been tied around its middle. Yusif stepped over to the worktable, muttering, "I should have conservator's gloves for this." With great care he eased the brittle papyrus open.

Reid, staring over his shoulder, said, "Latin and Mayan mixed together. You'd have to be fluent in both languages to read this." He turned back to the sarcophagus, filled as it was with papyrus scrolls laid in like decked logs. Retrieving a second scroll, he untied it and opened the brittle papyrus as far as he dared.

"It's some kind of mechanical diagram," Yusif noted, peering over his shoulder. "To build a machine. But what kind?"

Reid said, "Falcon was right. It's all for Gray. Fluvium knew that she'd eventually find the tomb."

Yusif raised a shaggy black eyebrow. "You are starting to buy this time travel insanity?"

"Maybe mental illness is contagious?" He stared at the tightly packed scrolls. "Yusif, if Fluvium and Domina came from another future, were actually able to build an entangled particle generator, or receiver, or whatever the hell you'd call it? If they sent themselves into our past? They've mastered a science that our Einsteins, Hawkings, and Thorns consider impossible."

"Why would he put the scrolls in the most impressive of sarcophagi, *sahib*? Why did he not place his own body inside?"

"Because it's the thing he most treasured and feared: his library. That's why he booby-trapped it. If the wrong people, grave robbers, found it, and opened it, the explosion would destroy the scrolls. Only Domina, sometime in the future, would be able to read the warning carved on the lid. It's why the traps were so elaborate when we explored his tomb."

"He didn't want these diagrams falling into the hands of barbarians," Yusif mused as he glanced at a portion of visible writing. "This one has what looks like a series of columns, some sort of table or chart."

Reid whispered, "This stuff could change the world in ways we can barely comprehend. A whole new science. A stunning leap as great as relativity and quantum mechanics was beyond Newtonian physics."

Bill Minor shocked him when he said, "Very good, Dr. Farmer. You're not as dumb as I thought you were."

Reid stepped back, a hand rising to his still-sore throat. "So what does Skientia want with this?"

"We remake the world," Minor said simply. "We're already reading everyone's top secret communications. Governments, banks, industry, doesn't matter much. Information is power, and we've got it all." He gestured at the scrolls. "So that's it? His personal library?"

"We haven't dug through it all." Yusif, too, backed warily away.

"What about the brain box?" Minor stepped over to stare down at the neatly rolled papyrus scrolls. He reached in, carefully shifting the tubes. "I don't see it."

Reid said, "We'll double-check when we get the scrolls out and stabilized."

Minor shot him a glance from the corner of his eye. "You don't seem concerned, Dr. Farmer."

Reid felt himself color, a queasiness in his gut. "There's still the woman's sarcophagus."

Minor fingered his chin as he stared down at the papyrus tubes. "Where would Dr. France and her Mayan scholars have vanished to?" He turned, hard eyes fixing on Reid's. "I'm not in the mood today for screwing around."

"Honestly—" Reid raised his hands defensively, "—I have no idea where she would have gone." He struggled to think rationally. "Maybe the University of Colorado? They have an anthropology museum there."

"Why would she have landed in Colorado Springs instead of Denver?" Minor's gaze had turned glacial.

"I don't know."

Minor crossed his arms, the muscles like wadded anchor chain. "When she landed, Reid, old buddy, someone on a motorcycle took out my chase team. Who would that have been?"

"I don't know," Reid rasped, feeling sweat break out on his face, neck, and chest.

"Guess," Minor said with a mocking smile. "And guess well because, Doctor, the sarcophagus is open. We don't need you anymore."

The way he said it made Reid's skin crawl. *He knows I know. He can see it in my eyes.*

"Sorry," Reid said hoarsely, his fear building.

Minor glanced at Yusif. "Do you know?"

Yusif, his brown eyes wide, shook his head and swallowed hard, hands spread in submission.

"Too bad. If you did, you could save Dr. Farmer from a very trying afternoon."

Reid had backed himself against the wall.

"Security, please?" Minor called, grinning.

Two armed men appeared in the doorway, MP-5 subguns in their hands.

"Take these two up to the equipment storage. I want them both stripped and tied to the metal chairs. We're a laboratory after all, so I think we might want to do a little experimenting with electricity."

Reid heard himself cry out. "I don't *know* anything!"

"Of course you do. But don't worry. We'll switch off. First you, and then Yusif. One of you will talk to save the other."

"You can't *do* this!"

"Sure I can," Minor assured. "Oh, and don't worry, we'll place you both over the drain. Easier to clean up that way. Bodies do the messiest things when you pump that much electricity through them."

# 94

'm an expert on the brain and its behavior. I can tell you how the limbic system interacts with the worry-generating and imaginative regions of the brain. Understanding the chemistry and physiology doesn't make experiencing fear any less unpleasant.

Nor had I been reassured when I checked in on Falcon. His paranoia was worse, his fragmenting speech and inability to concentrate, let alone participate in conversation, had me scared. The slightest bump could send him over the edge into a full psychotic break.

But did I dare sedate him even more than I had already?

A gentle external stimulation might help, but how did I manage that without freaking him out? I couldn't just check him into the Hilton spa for a massage.

My mind knotted on the problem, I dropped into the suite where Edwin Jones hunched over his computer, a scowl on his dark face. The image conjured by his posture reminded me of a long-legged spider skulking over a too-small web.

"How's it going, ET?"

"FUBAR, Skipper." He spared me a glance from a single bloodshot eye. "They know I've been poking at 'em. I got half the encryption programs in the NSA computers trying to break Skientia's passwords. Government cyber warfare geeks are falling all over themselves trying to figure out who hijacked their programs. Now, if I'm good enough to fool them while I try and take down Skientia, how come I ain't good enough to slide in past Skientia's firewall? Tell me that, Skipper. Why can't I?"

"You ask me? I can't even access my email from my smartphone. It says my password's no good anymore."

ET's lips twitched, and he shot me another of those "you're an idiot" looks. He extended a thin arm, his fingers giving me a beckoning motion.

I dug the slim black phone out of my pocket and handed it to him. I watched in amazement as he unlocked the phone, nimble fingers stabbing at icons, pulling down menus, and flipping screens. "What's your password?"

I gaped at him. "I'm not giving you my password, ET. I don't want you reading my mail."

His forehead wrinkled with amusement. "I could fish it out of the provider, but it would take five minutes of my precious time to reroute all of my programs. Last time I knew, it was 'ducati.' But you might have changed it in the last two days."

I felt a sinking sensation in my gut. "Why do you do this to me?"

He grinned as he tapped in the letters and handed the phone back. "You got two new emails from Amazon. And I think that last one be from your ex-wife."

I glanced down at the display as he returned his frowning concentration to the screen, muttering, "Now, you asshole, don't you try running none of that shit on me. Think you can catch me? You try this on for grins, my man." His fingers flew on the keyboard, keys clicking like machine gun fire.

I glanced at the time on my smartphone. "Karla and Winny have that mirror thing hooked up to the Blackhawk. They're flying out just after dark."

He threw his hands up. "Hell, the chief and Savage cut through that roof, Skipper, they're on they own. I can't even get past Skientia's damn home page! Let alone thread through the security systems."

"Anything I can do to help?"

"Yeah, Skipper. Pray me up a miracle. I got close a couple of times with random letter generation. Lots of ks, ts, ls, and zs mixed with vowels in weird spots."

I glanced at the time again. "I think Falcon's on the edge of a break. I'm worried, ET. If I'm not back, and Cat doesn't check in, could you peek in at him?"

"Yeah, Skip. What's Cat up to?"

"She's been cooking something up in her room. Said she thought it would give Raven and Savage an edge."

He nodded, his concentration totally on the screen as I walked out the door and started down the hallway.

The worry beast continued to sink needle teeth into my nervous stomach. Karla had been counting heavily on ET's ability to monitor Skientia. As at the mansion in Aspen, she had hoped he'd be able to distract their security, maybe silence any alarms.

"So who are these people? And how did they get this sophisticated?"

Because they had been working on top secret communications research, of course. Hell, for all I knew, they were using entangled particles for all of their internal communications. But did that include things like security cameras? Alarm systems? Wouldn't those still be digital systems that didn't interface with entangled technology?

The elevator took me to the ground floor. I made my way past hotel rooms and out into the hot desert afternoon. The sun was slanting down toward the Jemez Mountains in the west. Cars baked in the parking lot, and I could see the Blackhawk's rotors and engine nacelle along with the tail sticking up past the hotel's security fence.

I was sweating by the time I passed through the gate and walked up to the helo. The big mirrored contraption reflected in all directions. It looked like an oversized lampshade, or something stolen from the circus.

Savage and Karla had their gear laid out on the pavement: ropes, equipment belts, backpacks, a couple of pistols, knives, a hatchet, flashlights, first aid kits, night vision goggles, radios, wrecking bar, zip ties, and assorted other bits and pieces. I recognized the curious gas-powered concrete saw with its large circular blade as one of the tools highway departments used to cut sidewalks. I didn't dare ask which New Mexico DOT road crew was pissed over its disappearance.

"Hey, Skipper." Karla glanced up. "What's the word from ET?"

"Not good."

I watched her gray eyes harden as she glanced at Savage. "Then it all depends on Winny, and how good she is at the stick."

Winny's head popped out of the helicopter. "What's with you, bitch? Just when I was starting to halfway like you, you mouth off with shit like that?"

"You break these mirrors, you kill us. You know that," Karla barked. Then she raised her hands in apology. "Sorry. Just touchy, that's all."

Savage's face had turned into a mask, tension in the set of his mouth.

"It's all right, Karla," I soothed. "All you have to do is get in and disable whatever sort of generator they've built."

"Falcon's sure?"

"I guess."

"Skipper, you're not blowing my skirt up." She gestured futility. "Sorry, sir. It's a lack of training for the op. SEALs plan, then we plan some more. We train according to the plan. Then we revisit the plan, and train some more, and revise the plan from what we've learned and train still more."

"It's not like you're infiltrating a Taliban stronghold. It's just a laboratory. You know the layout. Down four floors to the basement, west wall. Bugger up the machinery, then beat feet."

"And scoop up Gray as an HVT if we see her." HVT. That was SEAL-speak for a high value target.

"Or shoot the bitch dead on sight," Winny muttered.

"According to Minor's voice mail, she's supposed to be there for the test."

"And breakage, Skipper?" Karla gave me a questioning glance.

"Except for the security, they're just scientists."

"Yeah, I'll remember you said that."

Cat Talavera hurried through the gate, one of the hotel's plastic laundry bags clutched tightly in her fist. Her thick hair was pulled back, and she wore a baggy white shirt and stiff new jeans. "Chief? Major? I brought you something."

Karla, still irritated with me, stepped over and cocked her head as Cat lifted out one of the hotel's little plastic shampoo bottles.

"Think our hair is going to get dirty, Cat?" Savage asked, running his palm across his close-cropped scalp.

"It's all I had," Cat admitted, looking chagrined. "I raided the maid's supply and dumped out the shampoo, conditioner, and mouthwash. Then I filled it with my own concoction."

"And that is . . . ?" Karla asked lifting out one of the plastic bottles and grasping the screw-top lid.

"No!" Cat cried. "It's a gas! Unscrew that and you'll put us all down for an hour."

Karla carefully removed her hand. "So, how's it work?"

"It's a liquid that works best as an aerosol. So fling it out, stomp on it, or whatever helps to atomize it. Try not to splash it directly on anyone's face or you'll overdose him. One breath should be all it takes."

"We don't have gas masks," Savage reminded as he studied the little plastic bottles.

"You won't need them." Cat stared from one to the other. "All you have to do is hold your breath for a minute. After thirty seconds half the molecules will have bonded with oxygen and become inert. Three fourths in forty-five seconds. After that anyone breathing the residual won't pass out, but their mental faculties will be impaired for a time. By the time you get to sixty seconds, more or less, it's harmless."

"Sweet," Savage admitted.

Cat grinned shyly. "For the future, I'm thinking of small pressurized dispensers. Something that would spray." She paused. "If this works, that is."

"Thanks, Cat." Karla glanced at the setting sun. "Come on, Major. Let's get this gear packed right and wired tight."

Turning to Cat, I said, "Falcon's paranoia is rising. Could you check on him? If Rudy's driving him berserk, it might be wise to give him another half milligram of Valium."

"Sure, Skipper." Worry filled Cat's eyes as she turned and hurried away. I breathed a slight sigh of relief.

I shook my head at the mirrored contraption they were going to ride in. A cable ran from its top to the Blackhawk.

Sidling up to Winny, I asked, "You're good to go? Know the drill?"

She chewed on her lower lip as she nodded. "Yeah, Skipper. I fly them up that canyon on the west side of Los Alamos. In the process I overcome my natural inclination to bash them against rocks and trees lest I break the mirror."

Winny noticed my ghastly look and grinned, adding, "I lift them up over the north side of the building, hover next to the stairway, and insert them within a foot of the wall. Given the camera angle, I should set them down just at the edge of its field of view."

"Gently."

"Baby butt soft, Skipper."

"And then?"

"They pull the pin on the cable clip to release it. I rise up into the night and set the bird down on the helipad. One way they call and I extract them from the roof, the other they burst out the front door and beat feet to the pad where I'm waiting to dust them off."

"What's that worried sound in your voice?"

She barely wasted a green-eyed glance on me. "Just wondering is all."

"Wondering what?"

"How much time we've got left."

# 95

The moment Winny Swink coaxed the Blackhawk over the mirror cage and the downwash began rattling the heavy framework, Karla's brain cleared. Her worry vanished, replaced by a cool composure. Once the op started, everything else flushed away; her trained brain dropped into its familiar analytic role.

She felt the acceleration as the Blackhawk lifted, the ground dropping away.

"You all right?" she asked Savage over the communications gear.

He replied through his battle com. "Chief, I'm hanging by a wire, a thousand feet in the air, trapped in a miniature house of mirrors, to go cut through a roof where people are going to shoot at me. What's not to love?"

"I double-checked your safety harness," she reminded. "You couldn't fall out if you tried."

He grunted, his body wedged in tight against hers. "The good news is that with the saw and the rest of the gear blocking the way, I can't look down."

She felt the sway as the helicopter changed vector, a slight g and the buffeting of the downwash the only proof they were moving.

"What are you going to do if Bill Minor meets you on the rooftop?" Savage asked.

"Offer to finish up what we started last night?" She grinned to herself. "After the tugging, yanking, and twisting his weenie got, I'm betting he'd settle for just a handshake."

"Remind me never to get on your bad side, Chief."

"How about you just make sure my six is covered down there, and I won't be tempted."

"Roger that."

The air chilled with altitude, the chatter of the rotors loud, the mirrored cage buffeting from the downwash.

*"Five minutes,"* the Skipper's voice came through her headset.

*Yeah. Just make sure Winny sets us down like fragile china, or we're going to have glass everywhere and this whole thing is going to be blown.*

"When we cut through the roof," Savage noted, "it's going to be noisy."

"This time of night shouldn't be anyone in those top-floor offices," she replied. "We'll do it just like we practiced this afternoon. That roof is a hell of a lot softer to cut through."

"Roger that."

It was a complicated maneuver. She had to pull herself up as if to chin herself. Savage would squat beneath, unhook the saw, start it, and cut four slices. Hopefully, he'd leave enough material attached on the last cut to keep the section of roof from dropping like a brick.

*"One minute,"* Ryan's voice said calmly in Karla's headphones. *"We're on approach. Slowing."*

"Show time."

The mirror cage swung slightly, and Karla reached up, grabbing the metalwork above. "Keep your head down, Sam. If Winny drops us, you don't want shattered glass in your eyes."

She felt him shift and nod.

"Come on, Winny. Feather in the wind. You can do this."

She felt the cage shudder, scrape, and vibrate in the downwash. "We're down!" She muscled herself up, found the cable release pin, and pulled it. "Clear! Go!"

The mirror cage shook as Winny eased the cyclical forward and rose into the night. As the helo's sound faded, silence replaced it.

"No shouts or pounding feet," Savage whispered.

"I'm lifting. You get that saw loose and get to cutting."

She took a deep breath to charge her lungs and chinned herself on the metal bar. Savage shifted beneath, the saw clanging. Karla felt him give the starter cord a hard yank, then another. On the third, the saw's two-stroke engine whined to life, filling the confines with smoky exhaust.

"Tell me this is going to be quick," she growled as Savage's muscular body shifted in the narrow space beneath her.

# 96

Reid Farmer had never considered himself to be a particularly brave man. Like all American males, he'd often watched movie heroes achieve the unthinkable, and abstractly wondered if he could have withstood the same.

Reality now rolled around inside his pain-numbed brain: He'd have spilled his guts after the first jolt of electricity tore through his naked body. The agony couldn't be described. Words could do no justice to the humiliation of his body fouling itself, or the screams, whimpers, and pleadings torn from his desperate throat.

But a subtle truth had lodged deep in his brain: *These people want Kilgore. They'll do this to her.*

The man named Brandon Marsden leaned down, a devilish gleam in his eyes. "Where is she, Doctor?"

"I don't know."

"Don't feed me that horseshit. You were going to collect Dan Murphy and this Skylar Haines and put them to work on Fluvium's book. You weren't going to do that in a Starbucks."

Reid took a breath to reply, but the current hit him first, paralyzing his lungs, blasting through his body. Existence turned inside out.

After it stopped, he weakly sucked a lungful of cool air, eyes struggling to focus. His scrambled thoughts began to coalesce. The cement room slowly swam into focus. The black-clad Marsden stood before him. Yusif sat tied to his chair at the side, sweat beading on his bare skin.

"Dr. Farmer?" Marsden asked. "We're going to do this all night. It won't end until you tell me where Kilgore France took the Mayan scholars. You stole Fluvium's book. You took the jar and the notes. We only want our property back."

"I don't know." His tongue felt like a stone.

"If it were yours, wouldn't you want it back?"

Reid blinked, his nose recovering enough to identify the acrid smell of the feces and urine he sat in.

Marsden bent down to peer into his face. "If you don't tell me, it will be Yusif's turn again. Is that what you want? For your friend to suffer? Your fault, Doctor. You're doing it to him."

"My fault." He imagined Kilgore's delicate face, her soft brown eyes, the perfect cast of her cheeks. Even as her face swam in his imagination, a tear broke from her shimmering eyes and streaked down her smooth skin.

He glanced over at Yusif. The man's fear and terror reflected in his wide-eyed gaze, in the shivering muscles that tensed against the wires binding him to the chair.

"Sorry, my friend. *Zambee ana.* It's my fault."

"Why?" Yusif's voice squeaked.

"Chief Raven wouldn't tell them."

"Who's Chief Raven?" Marsden immediately cued on the words.

"The lady who's gonna bring you down," Reid answered with a smile.

"She's an Indian?" Marsden prompted. "On a reservation? Is that where Kilgore went?"

"Oh, she's way off the reservation." Reid tried to chuckle, but only coughed.

"Which tribe?" Marsden leaned close, the electrical switch in his hand for emphasis.

"The kick'is'ass tribe, white eyes."

"You mean the Kickapoo?"

"God, you're a stupid fuck, Marsden."

Electricity blasted the world away in paralyzing brilliance and pain . . .

# 97

Coughing from the exhaust fumes, Savage felt the white-coated roofing give way and pinch the blade of his saw. Tensing, he tugged, pulling it loose. With a careful foot he pressed down, feeling the roof sag.

"Through," he said in a choking voice. He could feel Karla Raven trembling as her exhausted muscles began to flag. Even a woman of steel like Raven had her limits, and she'd been supporting her weight as well as the equipment she carried.

Savage stomped harder, the roofing falling away to expose layers of sealant, tar, and wooden decking. Below it, a fluff of pink insulation glowed in his flashlight beam.

Savage dropped down and slid the saw off to one side atop acoustical panels in a hung ceiling. He heard Raven coughing as he clawed the pink insulation apart.

He lowered himself farther, put a foot on the ceiling panel, and pushed. The fiberboard cracked and let loose, cascading to the floor below.

"Bit closer to the wall than we'd hoped," Savage admitted as he flashed his light about. "Be careful you don't land on the mop bucket when you drop."

He shucked out of his backpack, ensured his equipment belt wasn't about to snag, and swung out as he dropped to the floor. Landing, he lost his balance, toppled into the stack of mops and brooms, and winced as they clattered and banged.

"Fuck!" he heard Karla grit through her teeth.

Feeling like an asshole, he hurried to the door and placed an ear to it. With his left hand he flicked on the lights so Karla could see when she dropped in. To his chagrin she barely made a sound as she landed.

Squinting in the light, he made hand signs for "All is quiet."

She nodded, fingering her voice mic to say, "We're in."

*"Nothing moving on the roof,"* Winny reported. *"I'm going to set down now."*

"Roger that."

Savage slung his pack, checked his equipment belt, and froze as steps sounded in the hall beyond.

He signed Karla to warn her, then shut off the lights.

To his disgust, the steps slowed, hesitated. The handle rattled, turned, and the door swung open.

# 98

**B**ill Minor stood beside the security door, his back to the wall as he monitored the activity in Lab One. To his right, on a raised gallery, a line of ten theater seats, complete with drink holders, had been installed. From them, observers could watch experiments as they were conducted, and catch close-ups on any of the four large flat-screen television monitors mounted above. These now displayed images of the workstations as well as the containment zone inside the generator itself.

The lab measured thirty-by-thirty, a concrete cubicle two stories high. The far wall was broken only by a twelve-by-fourteen–foot garage door, now closed and latched. Fluorescent lights gleamed down from the high ceiling, hanging as they did below huge wraps of cable. Several wrist-thick electrical lines ran down the walls, across the floor, and under the aircraft-grade aluminum framework that supported the entanglement generator.

"Generator" didn't seem like the proper term to Bill Minor. A generator should have been a mass of copper wiring that spun inside a ring of magnets. Instead, the large machine resting atop its aluminum cradle looked like someone had pulled the cowling off a giant beauty-salon hair dryer and supersized it for a colossus. A spaghetti-like web of thumb-thick electrical cable wove its way around a series of curved mirrors, magnets, and lasers. Carbon-fiber panels supported a series of curved prisms made of specially produced crystal. The network of orange-coated custom-order fiber-optic cables reminded Minor of anemic veins making a lacelike pattern around the outside. Polished aluminum brackets ran around the exterior and supported the whole.

Immediately before the cluttered sphere stood a raised workstation with computer interface and a control board. Domina sat behind the keyboard and monitors, her pink chiffon discarded for a much more utilitarian gray lab coat. The woman's tawny hair was now pulled back in a ponytail.

She remained self-possessed. Her remarkable blue eyes focused intently on the holographic readouts projected above her navigator as she tested individual systems on the generator. Occasionally, she'd make slight adjustments with the dials on the control board. As she extended her arm, he caught a glimpse of tactical gear beneath the lab coat.

What on earth was the woman . . . ?

The door opened and Maxine Kaplan led Peter McCoy and Tanner Jackson into the room. Maxine's expression remained guarded. She had a lot staked on tonight's test protocol. Skientia had invested close to a billion in new technology for the generator.

Domina had insisted on running the machine. While everyone else monitored the experiment, it was Minor's job to watch Domina, his 9mm Sig easily accessible in his shoulder holster and a fully charged taser at his hip.

Under Domina's guidance, the entire machine had been rewired, her own programming—using those infuriating mathematics—had been downloaded to a disseminated network of supercomputers stretching from White Sands, to the Johnson Space Center, to JPL in Pasadena. Timing was crucial. The power the machine would draw would have browned out most of northern New Mexico, southwestern Colorado, and parts of Arizona had they pulled it during the day at peak usage. Instead, they had to wait until just between one and two am when loads were at the minimum.

Maxine led McCoy and Jackson to the theater chairs, smiling as they were seated. Virgil Wixom entered a moment later, his forehead lined with concentration as he poked at his tablet and stepped over to the computer station on Bill's right. Wixom's job would be to monitor and record data on each of the machine's functions for later review and analysis.

Maxine left the bigwigs with a gracious smile and stepped over to Minor. She'd dressed in a professional gray suit; the jacket tightened as she crossed her arms.

"You ready for this?"

"Yes, ma'am." He lowered his voice. "Assuming anyone could recognize it if she tried to screw us."

Maxine tilted her head slightly toward Wixom where he'd seated himself at the monitoring station. "Virgil will notice if something's wrong."

"He understands what she's changed and reengineered?"

"Not entirely." Maxine took a tension-filled breath. "Domina's modifications have increased the generator's efficiency by more than three hundred percent. She also claims to have shielded it from past entanglements." Her hand made a fluttering. "Any other visitors in our past shouldn't be drawn here the way she was."

"I've got a security detachment in the break room. They're armed with tasers just in case anyone new just, uh, pops in." He met her eyes. "And from the attack that day when Domina was delivered to Grantham Barracks at least one other time intruder is out there somewhere."

"Let's hope she doesn't pop in tonight," she murmured. "How does it feel to be present at the moment the world changes, Bill?"

"I'll tell you when I know it's changed."

Maxine placed a hand on his arm. "Don't know what I'd do without you."

The door opened, and a tech entered carrying a plastic pet carrier. Through the holes, Minor could see the white rabbit crouched inside. He caught a glimpse of brown eyes, wiggling nose, and vibrating whiskers.

The tech carried the rabbit down, opened a section of the generator, and carefully inserted the creature into the containment zone.

"Any word on Kilgore France?" Maxine asked.

"Farmer surprised me. I thought Marsden would have turned him into putty in the first ten minutes."

"Hope you don't kill him before he talks."

"If he'd had a bad heart, it would have killed him the first time we turned the juice on." He paused. "He'll break. They all do."

She glanced nervously at where McCoy and Tanner sat, their heads close in private conversation. "And the cyberattacks?"

"So far the computer firewalls have the hacker stymied. Grazier's locked away. Military intelligence is running down the Aspen attackers. Our weakest link is her." Minor inclined his head toward Domina's back. "If Wixom so much as nods in my direction, I'm taking her down."

Kaplan seemed to have trouble filling her lungs; she glanced at her watch. "Twenty minutes, Bill. And we'll have all the answers."

That's when his earbud went off, Marsden's voice saying, *"Bill? I think we've got a code . . ."*

"Brandon? Code repeat?" he asked as he thumbed his throat mic. Silence.

He touched his throat mic again. "Security check. Team Two to the interrogation room."

"Trouble?" Maxine Kaplan asked.

"I think your archaeologist just died."

"Pity."

"Indeed."

# Bonus Eventus

I stare at the machine with satisfaction. The beasts under my direction have exceeded my expectations. I have crossed the first river; access to the future is guaranteed. I need but another day or two, some modifications to the machine, and I will establish communication with Imperator in his timeline.

The moment he detects my navigator, I will have won. Even if I lose at the same time.

# 99

Falcon sat in a chair and watched a bead of sweat trickle from Edwin's brow.

"You foul piece of shit!" Edwin slapped his hand on the desktop beside the keyboard.

Falcon jumped as if from a gunshot.

"I just got backhanded," Edwin said through clenched jaws. "Again." He gestured impotence. "The closest I get, Falcon, is with random letter generators. Nobody uses those. Keyboard combinations like qazwsx or zsecft, sure. But, man, I keep hitting all these combinations like tlakaz. What kind of word is that?"

Cat picked that moment to step in, a bucket of fried chicken and a sack of sides hanging in her hands. "Got food." She stepped over to the wet bar and started laying it out. "What other combinations came close, ET?"

"Almost had it with Yaxtun." He stared at the flashing cursor.

Cat straightened. "How stupid can we be?"

"Whacchu mean?"

"You called it yax ton." Cat smiled. "It's pronounced Yash'toon."

"Huh?"

Cat hurried over, bending down beside him to stare at the infuriating cursor. "Mayan! ET, pull up a Mayan dictionary. Run the Ch'olan and Yucatec dictionaries against their passwords."

"Mayan?" Edwin asked in astonishment. "Who in hell use Mayan?"

"Gray, for one," she told him. "And if you were Skientia, looking for combinations of letters that wouldn't cue off any of the world's major languages, what could be better? It solves your problem about memory. Look up the Mayan word for jaguar, and you can always remember it."

"Of course!" Falcon cried, then he settled back into his chair, panic-stricken. "It's my fault. The major, Theresa, and I, we're just not thinking!" He blinked, heart racing. "I hope it's not this new medication. If I lose my abilities . . ."

His hands were fluttering as his panic built. Rudy was laughing where he slouched against the wall, his face filled with disgust.

Rudy? When had he come in?

He barely heard Edwin say, "You're doing fine, Falcon. You got us this far. Time you let the rest of us do what we do best." His fingers where flying on the keys. "There, got every search engine on earth looking for Mayan. Ch'olan, you say? How you spell that?"

# 100

Every nerve in Karla's body was charged as she unslung her HK. Her senses had cleared, the steady beat of her heart rhythmic. Years of training took over, her brain calmly processing the sights, sounds, and smells.

Opening the door a crack, she used a mirror to check the hallway. Seeing no one, she led the way out of the supply closet where a terrified and stunned janitor now lay bound and gagged. Savage close behind, Karla started for the stairs.

A muffled scream stopped her short. Savage, cowed after having knocked the brooms over, froze behind her.

"Where?" he signed, fingers asking the question.

She cocked her head, easing forward on cat feet. The soles of her tactical boots gave off a squishy sound.

Another faint cry led her to a heavy security door. Placing an ear to it she thought she heard someone crying. The lock had a security card reader. As good a time as any to test hers. She ran the duplicate ET had made of Bill Minor's. The lock clicked softly.

Making eye contact with Savage, she nodded, braced the submachine gun on its sling, and slowly turned the handle. Easing it open a crack, she heard a wavering voice whispering in Arabic, *"Fadlak. Fadlak. Mish fahim."*

Please, please, I don't understand.

Karla blocked the door with her foot, extending the mirror to see the backs of two men, a third bending over a sweating, naked man bound in a chair.

She gave the ready sign to Savage, eased the door open, and stepped in. She hammered the first victim on the back of the neck with her heavy

HK, spun, and kicked a leg out from under the second. As he collapsed, her rising knee caught him under the chin, snapping his jaws together and knocking his head back. Even before he hit the floor, the third man was rising from where he'd obscured a second figure bound to a chair.

Karla recognized the guard who'd stood outside Gray's door, the one who'd smirked as she and Winny had departed Bill Minor's hotel room. Even as he reached for his throat mic and said, "Bill, I think we have a code . . ." she snap-kicked him in the face.

The man slammed backward into a metal shelf, his head impacting with a mushy sound.

Savage hadn't even managed to close the door: he stared incredulously at her. Then he turned to the two limp men sagging in the chairs. "Holy shit," he murmured and made a face at the vile smell of feces and urine.

Karla shifted the HK before she reached down and unhooked the electrical wires running from a battery charger. Then she removed the clips attached to the Egyptian's nipples and genitals. The man blinked at her through glazed eyes.

"Chief Raven?" the second rasped incredulously.

It took her a moment to recognize the individual seated in his own filth. "You do manage to get into the worst messes, Dr. Farmer."

"Kilgore?" he asked weakly. "Safe?"

"As far as I know." She flipped out her knife, cutting the nylon bindings that tied him to the chair. "What did they want?"

"How to find Kilgore."

"How long ago did you tell them?"

"Didn't." He sagged as she and Savage lifted him from the chair. Farmer grinned at her in weary triumph. "I told myself that if Chief Raven could take it, I could. All that matters is Kilgore. I love that woman. Would die for her."

Her quick fingers took his pulse. Then she checked his eyes, shining her flashlight to see the pupils dilate. "Hell, Doc, I'd have broke the moment they tied me in the chair."

He laughed hoarsely.

Savage was seeing to the Egyptian.

"You got a can of Red Bull?" Farmer asked. "Anything to give a guy a boost?"

From a pocket she produced a small white pill and popped it into his mouth. "We call it a 'go' pill. You don't want to know what's in it. Chew it up. It tastes so vile you can't help but make saliva to swallow it."

Farmer chewed, made a face. "God, that's worse than the electrical shock."

She slapped him on the shoulder and stood, taking in the room. Metal shelves on both sides were lined with batteries, chargers, "hot shots" for use on cattle, soldering irons, an electrical hot plate attached to a handle, an apron holding dental tools, and a couple of bundles of clothing that she took to be Farmer's and the Egyptian's. Coiled in the back was a short garden hose attached to a faucet, obviously for clean up afterward.

"Stand up, Reid," she told him. "Let's get you dressed."

Tears beaded in his eyes as he pleaded, "But I've got crap and piss—"

"Ignore it. Snipers do."

Reid Farmer was shivering as he used a filthy towel to wipe at himself, then climbed slowly, painfully into his clothes. Meanwhile, Savage told the Egyptian, *"Ana asif."* I'm so sorry.

Karla asked Farmer. "How you doing?"

"Better," the archaeologist said through gritted teeth. "Are you my rescue again?"

"Nope. We're here to take out the machine before Gray can use it. We just stumbled on you by accident. Give us fifteen minutes. Then you take the stairs to the roof. Wait at the door until you hear—"

"Bullshit. I'm going with you."

"You can hardly stand."

He reached out, saying, "Chief Raven, I owe them. I'll do anything you tell me to. Anything. As long as I can pay these bastards back."

At that moment, someone slipped a pass card through the door, the lock clicking.

"Rock and roll," Karla whispered, turning, and before Savage or Farmer could react, she'd grabbed the door and jerked it open.

# 101

The chatter on Bill Minor's com sounded routine, but Brandon Marsden refused to answer any query. He glanced at Maxine Kaplan, saying, "I've lost contact with Marsden in the interrogation room. He mentioned a code but didn't tell me which one."

"Should I be worried?"

"I've sent a team." He hesitated. "Should we postpone the test while I check it out?"

She glanced uneasily at where Tanner Jackson and Pete McCoy sat eagerly on the observation platform, their intent stares on the generator which now obscured the rabbit in its carrier.

"No," she told him as she glanced at her watch. "We've got the power window to consider. It took a miracle to set this up. Went all the way to Bill Stevens at the White House." She glanced again at McCoy and Jackson. "We can't shut down just because a prisoner died."

Minor nodded, aware of the wrath that might fall on his head.

"Fifteen seconds," Virgil Wixom announced from the monitoring station. "Domina is rolling the power now."

Minor tensed. Like in a movie, he expected the lights to dim as the generator began to manipulate photons, particles, and gravity. A faint hum built as the machine neared the 534-megawatt threshold required for the experiment.

The only warning was a peculiar prickling on Minor's skin, then a sensation as if a wave were passing through him. He heard the hollow pop, and then a lowering of the hum.

"Containment," Domina's voice carried in the sudden silence.

Minor shifted his glance to the flat-screen that showed the containment zone inside the generator. But what was he seeing? The thing looked like a silver-gray orb, but without a definable surface. Looking into the wavering, watery depths and spinning empty vortices it might have been a hole into eternity. Even as he watched, the sphere faded into nothingness.

"Weird!" Peter McCoy exclaimed as he peered up at the image. "And there's a rabbit inside that?"

"*Certe,*" Domina replied from where she monitored the gauges hooked up to her little black box. "The creature, the *cuniculus,* is fine, and will reappear in fourteen and a half minutes. To the animal, the transition through time will be instantaneous."

"So," Tanner Jackson asked, "it's like . . . in a state of suspended animation?"

She turned, fixing him with her unusual blue eyes. "Nothing is suspended. The creature has been accelerated through time to the future. Jumped ahead."

"And what was that gray sphere?" McCoy asked.

Domina turned back to her readouts, saying, "What you saw is track left through what you call time-space. Field constraint or manipulated quantum gravity slows relationship between particles. Pushes atoms forward ahead of what you call time, yes? Like squirting water ahead of pressure."

"What if you stuck something into that gray haze?" Jackson asked.

Domina answered. "A different dimension. Relationships between subatomic particles stop. The rules of mathematical probabilities, what you call the Heisenberg uncertainty effect, change. Your general relativity and quantum mechanics vanish at interface. Atomic bonds separate, rejoin in random patterns."

"And now that it has vanished?" Tanner indicated the empty interior.

"You would feel eerie chill, yes? A sense of uncertainty, a shiver down your back. Nothing more."

"My God," McCoy whispered. "Domina, you've given us a whole new world."

"What about going back in time?" Jackson asked. "That's the real prize, right?"

Domina tossed her tawny ponytail back. "That depends on circumstances. If the 'now' is untenable or dangerous, the future might not be so bad, *si?*" She paused. "But yes, to go back is more difficult. Universe

is timeless. Entangled particles must be trapped, mathematically manipulated. Changes in relationship between entangled particles must be
undone. You do not have the computational ability. Can't recognize
when you catch one. Let alone identify an alternate branch timeline that
will fulfill your requirements."

"What about changing our own past?" McCoy asked. "Like if I want
to go back to last Fourth of July?"

"Impossible," she told him.

"Why?"

"What you call paradox, the changes in relationship of particles, does
not permit." Domina checked her monitors. "You are made of this
timeline branch, created of entangled particles generated and set upon
given trajectory. What you call decoherence. Can you undo your whole
universe?"

Maxine Kaplan interjected, "You came from a different timeline."

Domina seemed to tense, then she nodded. "*Certe*. In theory I could
go back in your timeline beyond moment when I arrived here last year.
Back to a time when I did not exist in your timeline." Her slim wrist
twisted. "Again, we do not have cerebrum . . . computer capability available to monitor and control variables. You *must* recover Fluvium's
cerebrum. Then we explore unlimited possibilities."

She tapped the black box containing her navigator with her finger.
It rested on the work top and was wired into the control panel.

*Yeah, and we'd have it if we only knew where it was.*

Minor's earbud informed him, *"Control room, here. Bill, I think we've
got a security breach. I've got a visual of three people on the stairs . . . What the
hell . . . ?"*

He touched his throat mic. "Explain?"

*"I just lost communication with all the security teams. And I think I just heard
gunshots."*

"What do you see on the monitors?"

*"Nothing. Not even the teams I dispatched to check the stairs. I tell you, we're
missing people."*

"Who's missing?"

And in that instant, Bill Minor felt his skin prickle. An unsettling wave rolled through his body followed by a hollow pop. He shivered, looking up at the monitor, seeing the pet carrier now resting in the

containment zone where a moment before there had only been gray emptiness. Through slits in the carrier he could see the rabbit as it raised one foot to the wire door, sniffing as if in search of lettuce.

"I'll be damned," he whispered as the tech hurried down to remove the bunny and carry it away for observation.

*"We've got a security breach!"* the voice insisted sharply in his ear.

"I'm on the way." He turned to Maxine. "Something's up. I need to see to it."

She read his worry and replied, "We're rolling on a longer test in fifteen minutes."

"You got it." Minor reached for his Sig as he headed for the door.

# 102

As they heard a pass card slide through the lock outside, Savage had seen Karla Raven open the door. Four security goons, dressed in black, were caught flat-footed; the closest still had his pass card in his hand as he reached for the doorknob.

"'Bout time you guys got here," Karla greeted as she stepped out. "Bill Minor said you were slow, but damn, I didn't think he was talking molasses."

And then she exploded into a blur of arms, legs, and contorting body. To Savage's eyes, she seemed to dance her way through the four men, each movement accompanied by a snap, slap, crack, and thump. The last man barely had time to react, raising his arms, throwing a punch.

Karla sidestepped, grabbed his arm, and used the man's momentum to propel him headfirst into the doorframe. Savage heard the sick pop as the man's head twisted and the vertebra snapped.

"Holy shit," Reid Farmer whispered while running a sleeve across his mouth.

"What do we do with Yusif?" Savage asked, bending down to drag the latest of Karla's casualties into the already crowded room.

"Pick him up on the way back to the roof," she decided. "Good thing they've got lots of restraints in here. I'm starting to think I didn't bring enough zip ties."

"Couple of these guys are dead," Savage noted. "There will be questions when this is all over."

She shifted her suppressed MP-5. "According to Falcon, if we don't shut down that machine, no one's going to be around to ask them."

"Roger that," Savage muttered, wondering if Grazier's imprimatur still covered this operation, or if Grazier himself wasn't dead somewhere. "Shit, I hate uncertainty."

"CQB. Let's be about it," Karla ordered. "Reid? Here. Take my pistol. You stick just behind my left buttock, not more than three feet back where I don't have to worry about you."

"Got it," Farmer answered, sounding mostly coherent now. He accepted her Tactical HK .45, and listened as she explained the fire control lever. "What's CQB?"

"Close quarters battle." Karla opened the door. "Let's go break some machinery."

Savage fingered his throat mic. "Voice check. Skipper? You reading this?"

*"Roger that, Sam."*

"We've recovered Reid Farmer from a third-floor room. He's with us. We had to leave the Egyptian archaeologist, Yusif, behind. Incapacitated for the moment. Has ET found a way home?"

*"Not yet, Sam. He's still trying to breach the castle."*

"Okay, we're at the stairway. The chief is checking with her mirror. All clear. We're going down."

*"Roger that."* A pause. *"Hold on."* Another pause. *"Sam? Chief? ET just found a hole. He says the entire place is being placed on intruder alert. They've got you on camera in the stairway."*

"Shit," Savage muttered to himself. "Chief? We're blown!"

"We'll deal," Karla told him over her shoulder as she indicated the fire doors opening onto the second floor. "Keep an eye on our six, Major. From here on down, they can come in behind us."

"Roger that, Chief." Sam half turned to keep an eye behind them as he followed Raven and Farmer down the next flight of stairs.

"First floor," Karla called as she rounded the landing and started down toward the basement. "One to go."

Savage had descended no more than three stairs before the first-floor door burst open and three security men, dressed in black, charged onto the landing.

"You! Stop! That's an order!" the first called as he pawed for the pistol on his hip.

Sam Savage coolly shot him through the head, then triggered shots at the remaining two as they fell backward through the door.

"Got trouble behind us," Savage called.

A voice called from below, "Stop where you are! Lay down your weapons!"

The mechanical chatter from Karla's suppressed HK was the only reply. Empty brass tinkled musically on the steps. She shouted, "Quick, down to the bottom."

Savage hurried after Reid Farmer, hot on Karla's heels. The archaeologist looked scared, sweat beading on his face, eyes darting this way and that. The way he clutched the pistol, his knuckles were white.

"Uh, Professor, you might want to lay your finger along the side of the gun. See, like this? Keeps you from shooting me or Karla."

Farmer complied. "What if I need to shoot someone?"

"You'll do it instinctively. Trust me." Savage kept his eyes on the stairway above, his own pistol at the ready. Men were moving up there.

"Chief?" he called, "You got a plan?"

"Always." Her voice almost sounded cheerful.

A head showed. Savage shot at it. The head jerked back. Then, a couple of seconds later, the guy jumped up, raising his pistol for a snap shot. Savage's first bullet took him in the center of the chest. Moments later, a second man jumped up, shooting before he could even locate his target.

Bullets smacked into the top of the stairwell as Savage center-punched the second man.

"What are they doing?" Farmer asked.

"You've never seen the movies? Or TV gunfights?" Savage asked. "One guy leaps out and shoots while the other guy ducks. Then they go back and forth, taking turns showering each other with sparks."

A third guy leaped up, spraying bullets wildly. Savage shot him through the body where he fell atop the other two.

"TV gunfighting ain't working so well," Farmer muttered, fingers to his ears.

"Shhh!" Savage admonished. "Don't tell them."

Karla's careful voice said, "On my command, we're holding our breath for sixty seconds. It's gas, Doc. Something Cat cooked up. You with me?"

"Hold my breath for sixty seconds," Farmer agreed. "Got it."

"This better work," Savage muttered. If it didn't, someone was finally going to wise up and realize they were effectively trapped. When that happened, it would only take a flash bang rolled down the stairs, followed by covering fire, and . . .

"Now!" Karla cried. "Move!"

Savage sidestepped his way down, watching out of his peripheral vision as Karla unscrewed two of the little shampoo bottles and stepped over the two dying men who lay there. She kicked the basement-level door open and tossed the bottles into the hallway beyond. Even as she threw herself back and down, slugs were pinging long rips through the metal as the fire doors slowly closed.

*If Cat's stuff doesn't work, we're like rats in the bottom of a bucket.*

# 103

**K**arla glanced at the two men she'd taken out with the MP-5. Twisting, she grabbed the smaller by his tactical vest, braced herself, and slung his weight against the fire door.

The guy toppled backward, blocking the door open. No gunfire erupted.

Still holding her breath, she flipped out her mirror, crawled along his body, and peered out. Two men lay sprawled to the left, three to the right.

Karla glanced back. Farmer was staring bug-eyed at the dead, and Savage was covering the stairs. Karla rose and signaled them to follow.

She crept slowly past the doorway, the butt of the MP-5 against her chest. "Moving. Clear!"

"Moving. Six, clear." Savage crowded up, covering the rear as she advanced down the hall.

Reid Farmer finally gasped, drawing a breath. "Sorry," he whispered.

"A minute's up," Karla hissed back, sucking breath. Her gaze searched the dark offices on her left. The right wall sported occasional photos of pine trees, Grand Canyon, mountain lakes, and other landscapes.

Cat's gas worked; the downed security men snoozed peacefully, mouths open, saliva leaking.

Touching her throat mic, Karla said, "We're in the basement. Lab One should be coming up on the right."

*"Roger that."* The Skipper's voice came back. *"ET reports that the machine is in use, but currently on low power. He's triggering alarms all over the building and perimeter as a distraction. He's got the cameras rerouted to his command."*

"I see the lab door."

*"Careful."*

Oh, yeah. Her skills had been honed during Green Team training. But there it had been other SEALs she'd worked with, people who knew their jobs. Her current situation was a disaster waiting to happen. Sam Savage was good—he'd at least been trained, worked in the craft. But "good" wasn't SEAL-trained.

And tagging along right behind her was Reid Farmer, a clumsy-footed civilian archaeologist carrying a gun. He was as likely to shoot her as a bad guy.

*Think, Karla. Concentrate.*

She hurried forward, trying to see everything, eyes darting, senses pinging like active sonar.

Each time she passed an office, her back prickled. All it would take was one guy with a subgun opening the door and shooting from point-blank.

She was no more than three feet away from the lab door, a glimmer of disbelief that they'd made it this far tickling her hopes. She had actually lowered her MP-5, reaching for the door when it opened and Bill Minor stepped out. His hand was already withdrawing a pistol from his suit coat.

He should have been startled, eyes widening. In that moment of surprise, Karla should have been able to raise the HK and lace his chest with hot, copper-jacketed slugs.

Instead, he rushed her, recognition in his dark eyes as he thrust his pistol at her.

Instinctively, Karla pivoted as she took his weight. She caught his right wrist, jerking it aside as the Sig fired.

Minor struggled to twist his gun out of her grip and hooked an arm around her waist. She lost her hold on the HK as she tried to throw him.

For an instant they rocked, his greater strength and weight countered by her superior position and balance. The Sig fired again, the concussion ringing in her ears. They both twisted at once, breaking loose. Karla recovered first, kicking his wrist. The Sig spiraled away as she recovered and ducked under the roundhouse blow he unleashed with his left hand.

She grabbed for the taser at his hip only to have him slap it out of her hands.

She hammered his ribs, striking at his kneecap, and felt the HK's weight vanish as the sling slipped off her shoulder. The gun clattered on the floor.

Minor leaped backward, light on his feet for such a muscle-bound man. With a flick of his hand, he extracted a knife from his pocket, jacking the blade open.

Karla circled warily, shucking her Gerber fighting knife from its sheath. *Got to keep him away from that subgun.*

"Karla?" Reid Farmer called softly, "Savage's hit."

She feinted, Minor skipping away.

"Reid? Get into that lab. You know what you've got to do."

"But . . . Savage . . ."

*"Wreck that fucking machine!"*

"No, you won't." Minor danced forward, blade held low. He flicked it at her like a fencer, the steel darting as she skipped back. Then she feinted left, ducked right, and tried to slip in past his guard.

She caught the barest glimpse of Savage. The major lay on his side, mouth open, panting for breath.

She skipped away from Minor's rush, her blade laying the sleeve of his suit coat open.

"Get the lipstick off your dick?" she asked conversationally.

"I'm killing you very slowly for that. Get your little redheaded friend, too."

"What kind of gratitude is that? And after the fun we had?"

Bill Minor chuckled. "Got to tell you, you're pretty good. Who trained you? FBI?"

"SEALs," she said softly. "Chief Petty Officer First Class, Karla Raven, at your service."

"Lie, bitch. No woman's ever been a SEAL. Too many tough men ring that bell. A woman wouldn't make it two days into Hell Week."

And she knew from his tone. "How many days did you last before you rang out?"

She saw the answer in his eyes and smiled. "Time to ring you out again."

At her words, his eyes went insane. He spread his arms. Bellowing in rage, he charged. What he couldn't do with finesse, he would do with brute force, crushing her in the process.

# 104

Reid Farmer stared in disbelief as Chief Raven danced and dodged. He'd never seen a knife fight. The pistol lay forgotten in his hand.

"Go!" Savage rasped where he lay on the floor. "You heard her. Go break that damn machine."

"I can't leave you to—"

"You're all that's left," Savage said weakly. "Go . . ."

Reid staggered to his feet and yanked the door open. A woman was standing right in front of him, her eyes wide in surprise.

She was tall, long gray hair worn in a ponytail. Reid placed her in her fifties, but still attractive, with intelligent blue eyes.

He poked the pistol at her, saying, "Step back!"

And she did, hands rising in surrender.

Reid let the door close behind him, aware that two more men shot up from movie chairs off to his left.

"Who the hell are you?" asked the tall one with the droopy face.

Reid backed up to the wall. "All of you, down the stairs by the machine."

"I don't think so. Mr. . . . ?" The bald, potato-headed one said in a mocking tone. He looked disgustedly at Reid through dorky black-framed glasses.

"Farmer, Reid Farmer."

"Ah, the archaeologist." The hound-dog–faced man smiled and started forward, hand extended for the gun. "I'm your employer. Give me that. That fact that you've made it this far indicates that you're worth a great deal more than we've been paying you to . . ."

*The guy who had me tortured.* Reid swallowed hard, dropped his finger down, and squeezed the trigger. Savage was right, it felt perfectly natural.

The .45 slug took the hound-dog–faced man squarely in the chest, his jowls flapping at the impact. He collapsed like a string-cut doll.

Potato-head and the woman stood paralyzed, eyes wide in shocked disbelief.

In the silence Reid said, "Move! Down onto the floor beside the machine." He took in the man sitting at the computer station to his right. The guy's mouth hung open, expression one of total dismay. "You, too."

And there, watching him through a controlled gaze, sat Domina. Her station was at a raised console just this side of a giant mechanical sphere that rested on an aluminum platform.

"Everybody down in front!" Reid ordered, a part of his brain gibbering over the fact that he'd just shot a man down in cold blood.

"Dr. Farmer?" the tall woman said anxiously. "You're making a mistake."

"I know you," Reid said, glancing to the side as the man in the control station carefully eased his way down onto the concrete beside the machine. "Or your voice anyway."

"That's right," she said calmly. "I'm Maxine Kaplan. I was talking to you from JPL in California. I helped keep you alive as you opened Fluvium's tomb."

Reid slowly followed them down, keeping his distance.

"Whatever you want," Potato-head said softly, "I can arrange it."

"Who are you?"

"Tanner Jackson, Chief Operating Officer." He smiled in satisfaction. "Think of me as the right hand of God."

"Then I hope to hell that God's left-handed."

Tanner's smile went flat, his eyes growing cold and dangerous. "Last chance, Dr. Farmer. Do you want the easy way out? A nice retirement? Life of leisure? Perhaps your own island in the Caribbean?"

Reid shifted his position so he could take in Gray, Domina, whatever she was called. "You really think you had a chance against that woman? She's played you. You built her machine. And let me guess, she's the one who did all the programming. She's the one who knows the intricacies of how it works."

The tech from the control panel shifted uneasily, glancing sidelong at Kaplan with a look that said, "I told you so."

Reid turned, calling, "Hello, Domina. Why don't you step down and join the rest now?"

She continued to regard him with a glacial-blue stare, her expression hinting at annoyance. "You are too late, Professor. What they've done is sufficient."

"What do you mean, sufficient?" Kaplan asked.

"Maxine," the engineer warned, "she's still up there."

To Reid, Kaplan said, "Let us shut the generator down, and we'll all work this out."

Reid chuckled, a feeling of insane irritation filling him. He stepped to the side, trying to keep them covered, calling, "Climb down from there, Domina. Right now. Or, I swear I'll shoot you in the head myself."

"God, no!" Tanner cried stepping forward. "She's worth a fortune, you idiot!"

"*Nequam populi, inanus orbis!*" Reid cried. "'Worthless people, worthless world.' We're fucking meaningless to her. An *experimental* population!"

Domina uttered a word. Some sort of holographic display projected above a black box on the woman's console. She uttered a single unintelligible command, and Reid felt his hair began to prickle. A humming built in the air around him.

"Oh, shit!" Kaplan cried.

Reid shook his head, feeling prickles of energy running through him. Had to be that damn go pill. He turned, ordering, "Domina, get your ass out of that chair. Now."

He saw the woman smile indulgently, watched her hand move on the control board.

"You bitch!" He jerked the trigger. The gun bucked in his hand. Kaplan and the tech threw themselves down, crawling for the stairs.

Missed.

Domina was grinning at him as he fired again.

*Got to save Kilgore! Save the world.*

His skin had begun to jump and wiggle. Reid steadied the pistol with both hands.

"*Valete,*" he said in Latin. "Goodbye."

Even as the pistol fired, a scream caught in the bottom of his throat. Like a burst of light, his consciousness exploded.

# 105

As shots rang out, Karla ripped the door open and charged into the lab, the HK's muzzle following her gaze right, then left as she cleared her position.

A gray-haired woman and a man wearing a lab coat almost fell over themselves as they scrambled up the stairs on all fours. At the bottom of the steps, some bald-headed guy in black-frame glasses huddled down beside the giant machine as if he were petrified.

Reid Farmer had his legs spread, the pistol raised in a two-handed hold. Even as he drew a bead on Gray where she sat at a control console, Karla felt her skin prickle, a static crackle in the air.

Karla heard Reid say, *"Valete."* The pistol shot rang out just as a peculiar and disorienting wave rolled through Karla's body.

The sound nearly deafened: an ear-shattering pop, as if a giant glass ball had imploded. Karla's entire body turned electric, prickled, buzzed, and tingled. For an instant she felt herself begin to turn inside out, and then reality slammed back through her.

She'd felt like this once before outside Gray's door in Grantham Barracks. Out of it, but not quite. Again, she wasn't sure how long it lasted.

She blinked in darkness, struggled to remember where she was, and thought she lay on concrete. Instinctively, she felt for her Surefire and twisted the beam on.

*Got to save Kilgore. Got to save the world.* The words echoed hollowly in Karla's memory, as if heard from another time and place.

She lay at the top of stairs, and not alone. A tall, lanky woman in a gray wool suit was raising herself to all fours. A man wearing a tie and a lab coat was huddled in a fetal position.

Moments later, lights flickered and came on. *Emergency backup.*

She looked beyond the short stairs and gaped in disbelief. A huge amorphous sphere of energy seemed to pulse, half-visible, half-vanished—a pearlescent gray that rippled with fluctuating bands of emptiness. Other times, rainbows of muted colors swam in the thing's impossible depth.

Transected at the sphere's edge, the left half of Reid Farmer's body appeared human. The right half, vanishing into the interior, had become an amorphous mass. The flesh seemed to merge, dissipate, morph into a rubbery solid, only to become liquid.

And then the sphere vanished.

A shallow bowl remained, scooped out of the concrete; while Reid Farmer's half of a nightmarish body lay at the edge along with severed electrical cables and a slice of floor bracket from Domina's control console.

"What the hell just happened here?" Karla rasped.

"Domina activated the machine." The woman dropped onto the stairs beside Karla; her gaze fixed on the emptiness. "She's gone."

"Where?"

"Somewhere in the future."

"How far?"

The stunned woman shook her head. "Five seconds, five years, five hundred years, a thousand? We'll need some time to figure, do some math, calculate the energy involved. Assuming we can work out her equations. And there's no telling what that black box of hers can actually do."

"Who the hell are you?"

"I'm Maxine Kaplan, head of research and administration at the lab." She jerked a thumb at the man. "That's Virgil Wixom, head engineer."

"Well . . . can't you just turn off the electricity? Stop it?"

"Too late." Wixom was rubbing his face with a nervous hand. "It's like launching an artillery shell. Anything we try here, it's already in the past. After the fact."

Karla worked her jaws and pressurized her ears the way she'd do on a dive. Her hearing finally crackled and cleared. She glanced down, seeing Bill Minor's blood where it still dried on her vest and pants.

*Stupid bastard never had a chance.* Still, she'd been slow. Out of practice.

She climbed awkwardly to her feet, stepped down a couple of steps, and stared at Reid Farmer's body where it lay half in and half out of reality. "Wish you'd got that shot off a half second earlier, Doc."

Wixom wavered as he climbed to his feet. "Mr. Jackson was inside the event horizon. And if we'd been there, too?" He shivered, gaze fixed on what was left of Farmer's body.

"What about Gray?"

"Who?" Maxine had stepped down beside her.

"Domina."

Maxine blinked her eyes, rubbed them, as if staring at the weird gray sphere had hurt. "I thought she wanted that control platform way too close to the generator. My guess is that she knew exactly what the sphere's containment zone was given the kind of wattage available."

"So we just wait, and she reappears here?" Karla asked.

"Maybe. Unless she went far enough into the future that she could find the computational power to interface with her navigator. The entire computational capacity on this planet certainly couldn't handle the kind of data she needed."

Wixom said, "I once overheard her promise she was going to meet someone there."

Karla heard her earbud. *"Chief? Anyone? What's just happened? Power's out all over the mountain."*

Karla touched her throat mic. "Savage's down with a lung shot. Dr. Farmer's dead. Gray's gone. Have Winny set down at the front door for extraction. I've got to render aid to Savage, find Yusif, and we're out of here."

*"And the machine?"*

"Gone somewhere clear past tomorrow, Skipper."

# 106

I stood in the back of the Hilton's conference room, arms crossed. I watched Kilgore France where she sat behind the table at the head of the room. In the chairs, haphazardly spread around, were the rest of my people: Falcon, Cat, ET, and Winny. Against the wall sat Maxine Kaplan and her second-in-command, Virgil Wixom. Looming watchfully over them stood Karla, her arms crossed, hair pulled back in a ponytail. The look Karla kept giving them was nothing compared to the pained anguish in Kilgore France's shattered gaze.

A somber Dr. Yusif al Amari sat with his legs crossed, expression lined and sad.

Everyone was present but Savage. He was freshly out of surgery and in intensive care at a hospital in Albuquerque. Bill Minor's 115-grain bullet had smashed its way through a Surefire flashlight, slowing before punching into Savage's lower left lung.

Grief-strained, Kilgore said, "Here's the story as we have translated it so far. Fluvium and Gray—her name is actually pronounced Nakeesh—followed an entangled particle from their timeline back to our ancient Egypt. As Falcon suspected, the purpose was to test and study biological agents and their epidemiological effects over time. The first, and less virulent, was a form of red algae they released in the Nile. The second—the one we recovered from Fluvium's sarcophagus—was to be released in either China's Yellow River or the Mekong. Both had flourishing civilizations with sufficient populations to allow a modeling study of epidemiological patterns."

She added, "We think the algae Fluvium released was the origin of the 'water turning to blood' plague referred to in the Old Testament."

ET asked, "What kind of sick pukes infect a planet with disease?"

Kilgore's voice filled with loathing. "Their studies were to be long-term, covering centuries, as they watched how populations and organisms adapted."

"It wasn't their world, or ancestors," Falcon said softly, his eyes half closed. "We originated on a totally different branch of the timeline from theirs. One perfect for long-term evolutionary experimentation."

"But something went wrong," Kilgore continued. "On the banks of the Nile, Gray conducted a routine check of her navigator. It wasn't connected to Fluvium's cerebrum—the half of the device that actually monitored and calculated the data. When she energized her machine, it generated a series of entangled particles. One of which Skientia randomly trapped during one of their experiments."

"And you people knew this?" Karla asked Kaplan and Wixom.

A defeated Maxine Kaplan said, "Uncontrolled by Fluvium's cerebrum, her machine rode that particle through time. And pop, she appeared in our lab."

Kilgore said, "But it left Fluvium stuck in the past. His cerebrum was worthless without the navigator. What was supposed to be a safety protocol doomed them in the end."

"Glad to know they took such great care," ET growled.

"The universe, Edwin, remains a random place," Falcon said nervously.

I didn't like the way Falcon's hands and feet were fluttering.

Kilgore continued, "Fluvium, being the smart sort that he was, eventually learned ancient Egyptian, served as a scribe and physician, rose high in the pharaoh's administration, and devoted his life to leaving clues for Gray to find. He knew she had to be somewhere in this timeline's future, someplace with the kind of technology that manipulated entangled particles and was harnessing quantum gravity. He expected her to pop back in, rescue him, and take him back to their timeline."

"What about paradox?" Karla asked Kaplan. At her hesitance, Karla added, "After unhooking Yusif from electrical leads, I can hook you up the same way."

Maxine Kaplan spread her hands in surrender. "Based on some idle remarks Domina made, she didn't seem concerned with paradox when it applied to her or Fluvium."

Falcon said, "But I do not yet have a solution to Gray's apparent violation of the second law of thermodynamics: The problem with energy neither being created nor destroyed. We accept that going back in time doubles the mass/energy of the people or things being sent backward. In essence, duplicating mass/energy that already exists in that same time and space. We currently accept that the same mass/energy can't exist in the same time or space."

Maxine Kaplan answered, "We think the mass/energy that composed Fluvium and Domina, and their devices, was "loaned" or maybe "projected" into our branch from their parallel timeline. We're still really fuzzy on this, but not being part of our universe, they may have operated beyond, or in an adjunct way, to our laws of physics."

Falcon, an insecure fist to his mouth, was frowning. "And we have no way of knowing if Gray can get back to our past to rescue Fluvium?"

"Not at this time," Maxine told him, her hostile eyes on his. "The machine we constructed based on her diagrams was a prototype. A first feeble attempt at reproducing her technology. Shooting stuff into the future is a piece of cake. Energize the stasis, stop the interaction and change between particles, and it simply rides the light cone forward, sort of like a surfboard. Once we have a firm handle on that, we can begin to grasp quantum gravity and entanglement manipulation. The point where we can begin applying the stasis and sending things, let alone people, to alternate universes like they did? That's still a long way down the road."

"But even then, we would not be able to send people into our own past," I remarked.

Karla had to nudge the woman with a foot before Kaplan responded. "No, Dr. Ryan. Paradox and the second law preclude that. You can't force energy back into a universe where it already exists, and you can't ride entanglement backward by 'undoing' change between pairs."

ET looked skeptical. "So, Gray's just gonna turn up someday? Pop, and she'll be sitting there where that gray bubble was? Just like the day she left? And what then?"

"She'll hope that she can make a better deal with whomever is waiting for her. A better deal than Reid was going to offer," Kilgore said angrily.

"Yo," ET agreed. "That bullet in the head'd be persuasive if you ask me."

I asked, "Chief? You said Reid took a shot at her. Did he hit her?"

"Couldn't tell, sir." Her expression tightened. "Could have been a miss."

Falcon, oblivious to the woman's hostility, asked, "Maxine? The fact remains, she might eventually manage to find a way back into our past, correct?"

Maxine Kaplan shrugged. "This is strictly hypothetical, but I think she's been working on a program that would have allowed her to transport back to her own timeline. Some of the equipment she was having us design just didn't make any sense. But Mr. McCoy gave the orders, so we followed them."

"Ah," Falcon looked half panicked, his eyes darting here and there. "And if she'd made it back to her timeline, obtained another cerebrum, she could have followed the entanglement—however that's done across timelines—back to Egypt, rescued Fluvium."

"Which means what for us?" Cat asked. "Fluvium and Gray created our timeline when they arrived in ancient Egypt. Our timeline exists, de facto, because Fluvium became part of its past, and Gray ended up in our present."

Falcon murmured, "Our past has not yet changed. Paradox has not been violated."

I raised my voice. "Dr. Kaplan. I want to know how you got Gray out of Grantham Barracks that night?"

Maxine Kaplan gave me a condescending smile. "Dr. Ryan, she'd already transported across three-and-a-third millennia. Using her doo-hickey, somehow she activated her navigator, had it lock on her particle transmitter, a couple hundred miles was child's play."

"She beamed herself and the doohickey out of Ward Six?"

"Correct. We were watching the holo display, struggling to understand the graphics. And pop! Stunned us out of our socks, so to speak."

"And does the machine, what we called the doohickey, still exist?" I asked.

"It does." Kaplan's expression fell. "But it's useless without the navigator."

Tears were welling behind Kilgore's eyes. She had to be thinking of the gruesome thing Karla had wrapped in a tarp that lay, for the moment, in the Blackhawk. With no word from Grazier, God alone knew what we were going to do with Kaplan and Wixom. And the Skientia lab was a mess waiting to be discovered. The ramifications of our night's work were trouble I hadn't even had time to . . .

The door to my right opened. I didn't recognize the two men who entered; both were dressed in suits, ties, and shined shoes. The first was a tall, washed-out looking, white guy. Skinny, as if he had a glandular condition. His pale-blue eyes, however, seemed to gleam with anticipation. Behind him came a medium-built, brown-haired Latino in his mid-thirties. His suit looked rumpled, and he gave me a predatory smile as he fixed cunning eyes on mine.

I did immediately place the two MPs behind them and the sheriff's deputy in his tan uniform. Other officers crowded the hallway beyond.

"Good morning," the tall white-blond greeted as he flipped open a badge in a leather holder. "I'm Special Agent Hanson Childs, Army CID."

The brown-haired Latino with the square face had opened his own credentials, adding, "Special Agent Jaime Chenwith, US Air Force OIS. You're all under arrest for murder, misuse of government property, fraud, conspiracy, assault, conduct unbecoming, and a host of other violations of both the uniform code and federal, state, and local civilian law."

"In short, people," Childs followed up with a cold smile, "your wild little joyride has just come to a screeching halt. Your lifelong and most-intimate association with the Federal penal system, however, is about to begin."

Chenwith stepped slightly to the side, clearing a path to the door. "Now, if you'll each step forward when your name is called, you will be handcuffed, officially charged, and apprised of your rights."

The guy's sick smile deepened as he turned hawklike brown eyes on me. "We'll start with you, Dr. Ryan. As a retired colonel, you get the privilege of rank."

I tried to swallow, only to have my tongue stick in the back of my mouth. A sick feeling flooded my gut.

# 107

Falcon sat in the hallway, his shivering wrists in handcuffs. He could feel his entire body twitching; the urge to throw up tickled dry heaves down in his stomach.

His gaze fixed on the handcuffs: chromed and bright. If only he could concentrate, but Aunt Celia was shouting, her voice dominating everything.

"Jimmy, you are such a disappointment," she scolded, her face pinched. "I require the bare minimum of you. I cannot be the mother and father you lost. I ask so little, yet even that seems to be beyond your most facile ability to perform!"

He swallowed hard, saying, "I'm sorry. It's my fault."

"Yes, it is," Aunt Celia agreed as she leaned over the waxed and polished table. Behind her, the tall grandfather clock from Germany tick-tocked in its carved cabinet. The flowered wallpaper seemed to ebb and flow at the periphery of Falcon's vision. He could feel Julia's wide-eyed gaze where she cowered in the dining room doorway behind him.

Avoiding Aunt Celia's burning gaze, he ran his thumb over the table, tracing a knot in the polished wood.

"I'm sorry." Falcon's voice sounded distant, weak . . .

In his mind, the loop began to replay: "Jimmy, you are such a disappointment," Aunt Celia scolded, her face pinched. "I require the bare minimum of you. I cannot be the mother and father you lost. I ask so little, yet even that seems to be beyond your most facile ability to perform!"

He swallowed hard, saying, "I'm sorry. It's my fault."

"Yes, it is," Aunt Celia agreed as she leaned over the waxed and polished table . . .

Falcon cried out in fear as hands reached out of nowhere to grab his shoulders. His entire body jolted, as if an electrical wire had been touched to his skin.

Falcon stared up at two MPs, dressed in uniforms, their faces stern. Mad. Mad at him. "What?"

"I said, get up!" the young one on the right ordered harshly. "What's the matter? You deaf!"

"Hey! Leave him alone!" The Skipper's frantic voice cut through rising fear.

Falcon blinked, finding himself in a crowded and unfamiliar hallway. Police officers stood in knots, blocking any escape. Dr. Ryan, his hands cuffed, was trying to struggle to his feet, only to be shoved back with the tip of a riot stick.

"You gonna get up?" the MP bellowed in Falcon's face.

His entire body shivering, Falcon whispered, "Can't. Can't." His gut dry heaved, and he barely choked it down.

Panic built.

Their terrible hands shot down, twisted in the shoulders of his shirt, and lifted.

An empty cry tore from his throat as he felt himself picked up, powerless, and scared.

"They got ya now!" Rudy Noyes cried gleefully.

Some sort of scuffle, shouting, and chaos faded into a blur of background.

Chief Raven's shout of *"He's not well, you son of a bitch!"* lanced through his panicked brain as he felt himself propelled forward, his feet scrambling for purchase. Faces flashed in his peripheral vision: people he knew, strangers . . . and then he was carried through a door, past empty chairs, and plopped down before a table. Across from him, two hostile men shuffled papers. One was blond, thin, and pale, the other dark, squat, and menacing.

For a moment, Falcon sat shivering, his hands fluttering like twin birds. His heart hammered frantically in his chest. A dry heave caught in his throat. He wanted to have diarrhea.

Voices shouted in his head.

"Captain James Hancock Falcon," the pale one noted, and fixed him with alien-pale eyes. The pupils were black dots that burned through him like coals.

"All right, you little pussy," Rudy said with a smirk. "They got your candy ass at last."

Falcon cried, "Rudy, shut up!" He shot a quick glance to the side where Rudy was slouched in one of the plastic hotel chairs just beyond the flanking MP.

"Who's Rudy?" one of the men asked.

Unconcerned, Rudy flipped Falcon the bird. "God, you're a worthless piece of shit."

"I'm not." Falcon swallowed against the vomit gurgling in the bottom of his throat. "You're the piece of shit."

"Hey!" An MP's hard face thrust into his vision. "You're gonna show these officers a little respect, or I'm gonna teach it to you, shit bag!"

*Shit bag. Shit bag. Shit bag* . . . the words bounced around the inside of Falcon's skull like rubber balls.

"Major?" he cried. "Where are you? What's happening?"

"Can't help you this time, son." Major Marks offered, and Falcon twisted his head to where Major Marks stood behind the officers at the table, arms crossed, his campaign ribbons mostly obscured. "In fact, where they're taking you, I can't go."

"You're . . . leaving me?"

"Other way around. You've let me down."

"No, I never."

The slap came out of nowhere, stinging his jaws.

For an instant, Falcon was able to fix on the MP crouched beside him. The veins stood out on the man's neck, his brown eyes hot and angry.

Falcon watched the man's lips moving, words, disembodied, echoing in his head like he was in the bottom of a well. "I don't know what kind of shit you're pulling, asshole, but you can stop it right now, or you'll wish you were dead . . . wish you were dead . . . wish you were dead!"

In Falcon's floating vision, the pale-eyed man and the dark one across the table were staring at him in amused disgust.

"Rudy, what do they want from me?" he cried. "Theresa?" He stared around, saw her crouching just behind the MP, her flower-pattern dress wrinkled, her hair undone. The sad look in her eyes surprised him. ". . . the variables are uncertain . . ." she was saying. ". . . mostly a redundancy effect . . ."

"Hey!" the MP shouted. "You're being charged. You get that?"

*Charged. You're being charged. You're being . . .*

Falcon closed his eyes, searching desperately on the backs of his eyelids, seeking the pieces.

He formed fractured images, heard bits of Mozart.

Fragments of speech echoed hollowly.

Each time he tried to fix the fleeting images on the backs of his eyelids, they skittered away like spiders on a wall.

"Got to find the pattern," he whispered to himself.

"Falcon?" Aunt Celia asked. "Have you finished your homework?"

Rudy's slick voice chortled, "What's the matter, you little pussy? Can't find any backbone?"

"Are you or are you not Captain James Hancock Falcon?" yet another voice demanded.

Falcon tensed his muscles, curling, feeling the world falling away.

Confusion.

Everything eating everything.

So many voices. All these people, leering, peering closely, reaching out to touch him.

Somewhere was order. Somewhere . . . in the confusion.

And he let himself drift down into the darkness, hearing Aunt Celia.

"Jimmy, you are such a disappointment," Aunt Celia scolded, her face pinched. "I require the bare minimum of you. I cannot be the mother and father you lost. I ask so little, yet even that seems to be beyond your most facile ability to perform!"

He swallowed hard, saying, "I'm sorry. It's my fault."

"Yes, it is," Aunt Celia agreed as she leaned over the waxed and polished table . . .

"Jimmy, you are such a disappointment . . ."

Falcon fell deeper into the loop as it started over, and over, and over . . .

# 108

General Elijah Grazier, wearing his dress uniform, strode down the Buffalo Thunder Hilton hotel's hall as if he owned the place. His graying hair offset the tones of his rugged face as he stopped short. Milling officers, both civilian and military, clogged the hallway.

*Bill Stevens' people got here first. Oh, joy.*

He allowed a ghostly smile of anticipation to tickle his lips; He tightened his grip on the briefcase he carried.

*So, Dr. Ryan? Having a nice day, are you?*

As he started forward, his campaign ribbons caught the light, and he had his cover tucked under his left arm. Just imagining the consternation currently running through Ryan's and his psychotics' heads brought a chuckle of amusement to Grazier's throat.

One of the sheriff's deputies noticed him first, elbowing his fellows, and pointing.

An uneasy whisper broke out among the assorted officers. Several MPs emerged from the cluster, snapped to attention, and saluted.

Grazier cocked his head, taking note of Tim Ryan where he sat on the carpeted floor, back to the wall. The man looked half rabid, glaring knives at the officers. His wrists were cuffed where they hung off his knees, hands knotted in hard fists. In a line on the floor beside him sat Major Winchester Swink, and Dr. Catalina Talavera, all similarly cuffed, cowed, and depressed.

Chief Raven, to his surprise, sat separately, wrists and feet chained, two MPs with drawn sidearms just out of her reach. The look of bottled rage on her face was like nothing he'd ever seen.

Grazier set his briefcase on the floor and returned the MPs' salute. "I see you got the lot of them."

At the sound of his voice, Ryan's head jerked up, and Grazier was surprised to see violence in the man's eyes.

To Ryan, he said, "I truly regret it, Tim. But my orders come straight from the president, through the Secretary of Defense, and the Joint Chiefs." He paused. "In a word, due to the extent of the national security threat posed by Gray and her technology, and through the powers of the National Security Act—"

"Eli, I don't give a *damn* about national security. I need to see to Falcon."

"What's wrong with Falcon?"

"Your friends, here, have him in a fugue state." Ryan was using every bit of his self-control. "Maybe catatonic. I'm not sure he'll ever come out of it."

Eli looked in the direction Ryan indicated to see a curled ball of a man where he lay on his side, cuffed hand and foot, a pool of vomit next to his slack mouth. The dark stain on his pants could only have been urine. The MP closest was staring down in disgust.

Grazier felt his stomach drop. "You!" He indicated the closest officer. "Get Captain Falcon to the nearest hospital! Now, damn it!"

The sheriff's deputy gaped for a moment, then snapped a salute and began speaking urgently into his microphone.

*If I lose Falcon, I lose it all.*

In sudden panic, he bellowed, "And you be damned sure Dr. Ryan goes with him!"

"The rest of you gentlemen," Grazier turned to the clot of officers and ordered, "I need these prisoners back inside that room."

Stepping through the door he strode up to where two suited men, a provost, and a sheriff's officer, were shuffling papers on a wood-veneer table.

Private Edwin Tyler Jones, his long wrists in cuffs, sat stoically before them, his face an expressionless mask.

"What the . . . ?" The pale-blond man raised white-blue eyes, his pupils widening. He and his companion shot to their feet, saluting. "General, sir?"

"At ease." Grazier turned to watch as the prisoners were brought in and seated. Then he said, "Special Agents Hanson and Chenwith will remain. The rest of you need to leave the room immediately."

He gestured to the MPs. "You gentlemen are ordered to ensure I have complete privacy, and that no one is listening at the door. Do I have your full and complete understanding?"

"Sir!" they both shouted, snapping salutes, then went about herding the officers out.

Only after the door closed did Grazier turn to inspect the sullen prisoners. The look Karla Raven was giving him would have blistered paint. Kilgore France looked pale. Grazier wasn't sure how Maxine Kaplan and Virgil Wixom had ended up here, but they obviously wanted desperately to be somewhere else. Cat Talavera reminded him of cracked crystal ready to shatter at any instant.

"I'm sorry, people," Grazier began, "but it would seem that circumstances—and your own remarkable proficiency—have created a political shitstorm. We've got dead bodies strewn halfway across the country, shot-up aircraft, a team of lawyers demanding an explanation for why a military operation was mounted against a private citizen on American soil in Aspen, a misappropriated Blackhawk helicopter. Not to mention a bloodbath to clean up at the Los Alamos lab. While we've got Pete McCoy's body . . . with a bullet hole in a most unfortunate place, Tanner Jackson seems just to be missing. Losing McCoy and Jackson—both prominent donors to the president's re-election campaign would be problem enough. Then there's the missing time machine in Lab One.

"And, most importantly, where's Gray?"

"Gone, sir." Chief Raven's words cut the air. "She activated the time machine."

He closed his eyes, took a deep breath, and said, "That is a most unfortunate development." But because of it, he was going to have a big chunk of Bill Stevens' hide.

He glanced around the room. "People, this isn't the movies where tomorrow everybody acts like none of these things happened. These are events for which there are, unfortunately, consequences."

"We're not going to like this, are we?" Winny Swink asked.

"No, Major, I'm afraid you are not."

Hanson Childs, the Army CID guy, asked, "Sir? With your permission, may I ask if we can proceed with our—"

"You may not." Grazier slapped the briefcase on the table. Flipping the latches open, he withdrew a sheaf of papers. "I need the two of you to inspect the signatures at the bottom of your new orders. After you have done so—and assuming you want to walk out of this room as free men and go back to your everyday lives—I need you to sign the nondisclosure and National Security secrecy agreement documents attached. Please pay particular attention to the penalties on the NDAs for any breach of secrecy and initial in the box. Once signed, you will leave every scrap of paper you brought with you on the table, exit the room, collect the mob of officers you brought with you, and have them off this property posthaste."

"What about the perpetrators?" Chenwith asked in a strained voice.

"You never saw them. Never heard of them. Didn't even imagine they existed in your dreams. Do I make myself clear?"

"Yes, sir," they cried in unison.

The agents glanced at each other, quickly scanned the papers before them, and hurriedly signed. They stood, saluted, and walked quietly from the room.

"What about Falcon?" Talavera's voice, despite her appearance, carried iron.

Grazier—wondering the same thing—said, "If anyone can help him, it will be Dr. Ryan."

"Are we getting out of these handcuffs anytime soon?" Edwin Jones asked hopefully.

Grazier perched himself on the table. "After you hear what I have to say, you may very well wish you'd gone with the special agents. Before I start, I want you all to know that I did my best on your behalf."

"Political deal, sir?" Chief Raven asked.

"From the very top. Now, let's see just how much worse I can make your day . . ."

# 109

"You do know they're giving you new medication, don't you?" Major Marks asked from where he reclined, feet up, in Falcon's easy chair. The major had his hands clasped behind his short-cut silver hair, a pensive expression on his face as he stared at the ceiling with its camera and fire sprinklers.

Falcon followed the music of Mozart's *Figaro*, his fingers rising and falling as it played. He glanced reassuringly at his room wall, covered as it was with newly drawn flowcharts, diagrams, and Mayan mathematics.

"I've heard somewhere that Cat is creating something new for me. It's a med based on my genetics and unique brain chemistry. Someone said they're building a complete lab for her. I think it's in the room block where the OCD patients used to be."

"What about ET?" Major Marks shifted, his brass buttons gleaming in the overhead light.

"I vaguely remember hearing that NSA has him testing black project firewalls, seeing if he can penetrate them. The fact that his keyboard records every stroke, and his room and monitors are watched by no less than five people makes him feel like he's working naked, or so he says."

Falcon smiled. "Show-off that Edwin is, I suspect he'd revel at the opportunity. Instinctively, I'm sure he believes a naked individual can more easily, through gesture and posture, offend and insult his audience."

Major Marks chuckled at the joke. "I haven't seen Swink around."

"Rumor has it she's at Peterson Air Force Base. Grazier has her requalifying on just about every aircraft in the inventory. Something about paperwork and liability." Falcon smiled at the joy he imagined seeing in Winny's face. "Grazier may indeed have psychopathic elements to his personality, but he's also a very pragmatic man. Idle talk has it that Grantham is getting its very own Blackhawk. That it's to be based in the central courtyard with its own maintenance crew."

"Why would Grazier do that?"

"So we can go on a moment's notice," Falcon replied. "Or . . . I mean . . . the rest of them can."

Marks fixed steely eyes on Falcon. "Don't you have a duty to them, James?"

"I'm fine here, Major. In my room. With my music. And I have you and Theresa."

"Run the permutations. You know the kind of danger Grazier will throw them into," Theresa Applegate told him as she stepped out of the small bathroom. She'd been in the act of curling her hair, bobby pins were stuck in the corner of her mouth. She glanced at Falcon from lowered brows as she fixed a roller with one of the pins.

Aunt Celia's voice whispered in the background, something ominous that Falcon couldn't quite comprehend.

"It's all right." Falcon bobbed his head as Figaro belted out a long G sharp. "I can think better in here."

Major Marks jerked a thumb toward the closed door. "Those people out there—"

"As long as I'm in here . . . I can't let them down," Falcon whispered.

A disembodied voice seemed to echo in the room. *You hear me, Falcon? Come back to us.*

Theresa walked over to stare into his eyes. "Get up, Falcon. Walk over to that door and open it."

"There are eyes on the other side," Falcon whispered. "Pale and washed out, with black pupils that can burn holes in a person. Aunt Celia's out there. And listen, can't you hear Rudy? He's there. Just on the other side. It's all chaos."

*"We love you, Falcon. We need you."*

Theresa's brown gaze intensified. "Your friends are out there. People who love you."

"Hallucinations, Theresa. Just hallucinations."

"You're a soldier, James," Major Marks growled. "Get up! Walk over to that door and open it."

Falcon felt himself tremble, Aunt Celia's voice growing louder as he swung his feet to the floor. His body began to twitch as he walked unsurely to the terrible door, reached out. His hand trembled just short of the knob.

And on the other side . . . On the other side . . .

Closing his eyes, he slowly lowered his arm, then backed away.

"I can't . . . I just can't . . ."

The hospital room in Ward Six played Mozart's *Figaro* in the background. The Skipper had thought it might help. Cat stared down at Falcon. He'd started twitching again, his eyelids flickering. She double-checked the IV taped to the back of his hand.

"How's he doing?" Edwin reached out, taking Falcon's hand. "You hear me, Falcon? Come back to us."

Cat leaned down, saying, "We love you. We need you."

"Can he even hear us?" Edwin wondered.

"Still nonresponsive," she told him. "I'm trying something different with the meds. It's a new cocktail I started yesterday." She glanced at the monitors hooked to sensors attached to Falcon's scalp. "The fMRI I ran this morning indicates that what we call the 'ring of fire,' the hyperactivity that overwhelms a schizophrenic's brain with chaos, has finally abated."

"I mean, he's gonna come out of it, right?"

"I think." *I hope.*

"I got the files on those assholes what did this to him. Somehow, I think they gonna be having plenty of problems from here on out. Hacked email, IRS audits, trouble with their bank accounts, loan denials. Shouldn't mess with no friends of ET. That for sure!"

"Yeah," Cat smiled wickedly. "And having pissed off the chief, it wouldn't surprise me if they each didn't wake up someplace unpleasant, feeling excruciating pain, and find a golf tee inserted where it shouldn't be."

Edwin bent down to Falcon, his voice gentle. "You rest, my man. We're gonna get you back. You'll see."

Cat told him, "He's stable for the moment, and Nurse Seymore will page us if anything changes. I'm starved, and the cafeteria has pork chops."

At the door, she glanced back, heart breaking. Falcon remained listless on the bed.

In my old office I sat behind my desk, going through the monthly reports and wondering how the management of Ward Six could have exploded in exponential complexity. My new responsibilities were *only* for Ward Six. I was no longer in charge of Grantham Barracks.

That duty had been given to Dr. Mary Pettigrew, a competent and no-nonsense psychiatrist who had managed some of the most successful treatment facilities in the country during her thirty years as a professional.

*I should have sedated Falcon. My mistake. My responsibility.*

I could only imagine the pain, confusion, and fear that had driven him so deeply into whatever mental hole he had buried himself in. Once such a fragile personality had been broken like that, could it ever return?

"I'm so sorry, my friend." I ground my teeth, battling an impotent rage.

In an effort to distract myself, I slapped an angry hand on the thick pile of papers. Right there on top was another damn requisition for six-inch blue PVC sewer pipe! It should have gone to Mary, since it concerned the men's shower drains in Ward One where most of the violent disorders were housed. I flagged it and put it into the outbox for Janeesha.

I buzzed her, and she stepped in a couple of heartbeats later to my greeting of, "Got another one for Pettigrew. The Walls in Ward One this time."

"Sorry, Skipper." She walked over demurely and took it. "It'll take a while for old habits to die."

I glanced up. "You sure that staying was such a good idea? You're as much under the microscope as the rest of us given the, uh, . . . new conditions."

She cocked her head, tapping the requisition against her chin. "You know what, Skipper? I got nobody at home. Mama's dead. Just never did find the right man. Wasn't into raising kids on my own. And somehow I'd fallen into a rut that I didn't realize was so deep until you all kicked the anthill." Her dark eyes took on a glint. "And when you did? I had fun! Got scared a little, but I was living. Is that sick?"

"No sicker than the rest of us. And for the moment, we did save the world."

"Good, 'cause I gotta feeling that by sticking at this job, I'm gonna be scared a time or two again sometime soon."

"Not an unreasonable assumption on your part, Janeesha."

She walked off, a new lift in her stride.

I chewed on my lip for a bit, scratched my chin, and went back to my papers. I'd no more than scanned the next when Corporal Hatcher appeared on my desktop monitor, his face lined with irritation.

"Yes, Corporal?"

"Got a problem, sir. The contractor insists this new shelving in Gray's . . . uh, I mean the armory. He says it's not to spec. It's four inches taller than the ceiling, sir."

We'd knocked out the dividing wall and bathroom, added a security system, and were remodeling Gray's old suite. By the time we were finished, we'd have been better served to have built a completely new facility attached to the north hall.

"It's a hung ceiling. Pull out the acoustical panels," I told him. "That will get you another foot."

"But it's exposed pipes and stuff up there, sir."

"Corporal, the room is going to be filled with weapons, helmets, body armor, night vision, communications equipment, chemical lights, fast ropes, ammunition, breaching tools, boots, packs, computers, that sort of thing. Why, specifically, do we care?"

Hatcher's expression cleared slightly. "Roger that, sir. Sorry to bother you."

I watched the screen flash off and rubbed the bridge of my nose. "And guess who gets to keep inventory on all that when it finally gets here?" Well, hell, if Janeesha started to have too much fun, or got tired of getting scared, it would serve as an anchor for her reality.

Janeesha buzzed me again, then announced over the speaker, "Chief Raven is here for her two o'clock appointment."

"Send her in."

Karla stepped through the door. She barely glanced at the wall monitors. Many of the views were new, like Cat's expensive laboratory with much of its machinery, microscopes, and lab gizmos, still wrapped in plastic. Old and familiar images like the gym had changed, being filled with new equipment, and I had an outside view of the obstacle course Chief Raven had designed. Behind it I could see the "live-fire" training center Savage was having built. The thing was currently a maze of Lincoln-log-stacked railroad ties that would stop bullets. Another camera allowed me to monitor the courtyard where an aviation fuel tank was being installed beside maintenance sheds.

Karla stepped up to my desk, snapped to attention, and fixed her eyes on my "Me" wall. Her salute was crisp and perfect.

"At ease, Chief. I know I've been reactivated, but I don't feel like a colonel sitting at this desk."

"Yes, sir."

"Karla, this new situation? I feel uncomfortable with—."

"It is what it is, sir. How's Falcon?"

I gave her a smile I didn't really feel. "I'm hopeful, and Cat is working on some new drug therapies tailored to his genetics. But you didn't come here to ask about Falcon."

"Permission to speak freely, sir?"

"Of course."

"This deal we've all made with the general, sir? Do you trust him?"

"Hell no! Eli Grazier is the perfect political animal, an ultimate survivor. What he does, he does strictly for Eli. If he has to toss us out of the airplane to ensure he gets the last parachute, we're gone. Afterward, he'll sleep like a baby. The fact that you saved his life that night at the restaurant? That earned you a point on his scoreboard. Proved your potential worth to him, but he feels no debt or loyalty on account of it."

I paused, watching the corners of her mouth twitch, her gray eyes thoughtful.

"Regrets about taking the deal, Chief?"

"No, sir. As the old saying goes, If you don't have a sense of humor when it comes to this stuff, you're in the wrong line of work."

"At least we're not spending the rest of our lives rotting away in maximum-security jail cells. You guys are based here at Ward Six just like active duty."

"Yes, sir." She studied me thoughtfully. "ET heard that Harvey Rogers got the surprise of his life when he was transferred to Grantham."

"Did Fluvium's brain box arrive safely?"

"It did. Apparently, Harvey and his entire lab were loaded into a C-5M Galaxy. Bit of overkill there, if you ask me, sir. They unloaded at Peterson Air Base, reloaded into Chinooks, and had him and his entire load of shit deposited on the lawn out front. All within eight hours of when he walked into his lab expecting nothing more routine than to pour his morning cup of coffee."

That wasn't the only change. "Kilgore France and her Mayanists aren't particularly pleased with their new location at Los Alamos, but at least I've got someone to keep an eye on Kaplan. With certain restrictions, Kilgore is going to be allowed to continue her career." I added, "With the provision that if we need her, we get preference on her schedule."

"They made any progress on the scrolls out of that black sarcophagus?"

"With Yusif's help, they've been able to open a couple and stabilize them for recording. Grazier apparently has a team en route to work with the Mayanists."

"Whole new world," Karla announced absently.

"Yes, Chief. It is. We're Grazier's own private little special operations force. His Team Psi. Each of us with our own specialty; and we're completely off the books."

"Has Major Savage been briefed?"

"He has." I narrowed an eye. "After physical therapy he's expected to make a full recovery."

"And how did he take being placed second in command?"

"We've worked it out." I paused. "What's your call on Sam Savage?"

"Tightly wired, sir. He and I were both sloppy on the Skientia infiltration. Lack of training and intel was appalling. If we'd been properly prepared and kitted, if we'd had time to train together, he wouldn't have taken that hit."

"Sloppy or not, Chief, you took out most of their security. And Cat says she's got a lot better delivery device for her gas now than hotel shampoo bottles."

"Dr. Farmer shouldn't have died. We should have tagged Gray before she pushed the button." Karla's voice lowered, "Falcon . . ."

"Chief, I'm serving this up hardball: The brains of the operation is a DID schizophrenic; the computer genius a felon; our master scientist once a heartbeat away from suicide; you a PTSD-possessed klepto; and our pilot's a self-serving antisocial. You guys shouldn't have made it past the courtyard on your first day."

I swallowed hard. "What you all managed to accomplish, without having trained together for years, is remarkable. And I am so privileged and proud to serve with each of you."

She took a deep breath. "Yes, sir. We'll get better, sir."

"You going to Dr. Farmer's funeral next week?"

"Yes, sir. For a civilian, turned out he was tightly wired."

Then she frowned down at the little red Ducati on my desk corner. "Heard Grazier paid up, sir."

"He did."

I rose from my chair and walked over to the monitors. I was aware of Karla's healthy sensuality beside me as I switched a channel to the garage. My new-to-me Ducati 916 canted on its side stand. "I don't know where Grazier found it, or what he paid for it, but it only has 2,300 miles on the odometer. I had new tires put on, oil change and filter, valves set, and a tune-up at the shop."

"How's it ride?"

"With that skinny high seat and low clip-on bars? It's about as comfortable as a medieval torture rack. But it handles sharp as a straight razor, and the sound when you hit nine grand on the tach? Symphony! The Diavel is a lot more comfortable . . . and better for attaching bombs to Chevy Suburbans. But when you crack the throttle on the 916 . . . Wow!"

Karla punched me playfully on the shoulder, rocking me on my feet. "Thanks for the chat, Skipper. I'll be off about my business. If we figure correctly, Grazier is going to be calling on us sooner rather than later."

"That was the deal."

"Yes, sir." Her eyes narrowed. "You know, someday Gray is going to pop back into that crater in Lab One. And when she does, we'll be waiting."

Then she was gone.

I walked slowly back to the desk, thinking about the global situation: For those of us who bothered to study history, it was 1938 all over again: the world falling apart. Expect it to be messy.

Into that volatile mix, Gray had added the allure of a stupendous new science—one that had the potential to change everything.

*She'll be back, Tim. Just as dangerous as she ever was.*

I seated myself before the reports. Nothing new on the woman who had attempted to murder Gray that first day. I stared at the enhanced photo, fixing on the woman's green eyes and auburn hair. Looking at the stills now, I could recognize the black box she plucked up from her dying companion: a cerebrum.

*There are more of them out there. And our job will be to stop them.*

And if I'd been a split second slower? If she'd managed to kill Gray that day? How much would have been different? Contemplating the what ifs led to an insanity of paradox.

I stared into the woman's eyes. *Who are you?*

What timeline had she vanished to? And who was the man who'd died at her side? A husband? Friend? Or lover?

If she ever popped back into our world, would she be coming as a friend, or another enemy? That she'd tried to kill Gray argued for the former, but if individuals were popping back and forth between time-lines, attempting to murder each other, and infecting worlds? How vulnerable were we? And how did we tell the good guys from the bad?

I glanced up at the monitor, warmed at the thought of a real, low mileage, Ducati 916. My dream . . .

Onto which Karla Raven was now seating herself. She'd found a leather jacket from somewhere and smiled into the camera. She tossed back her silky black hair and donned a full helmet. Mouth agape, I watched her insert the key, turn it, and stab the starter.

My fumbling hands shot to one pocket, then all the others. That playful punch she'd given me? No, impossible!

"How *does* she *do that*?" I cried as I lurched to my feet and watched her drop the clutch. She spun the 916 sideways, tire smoking as it painted a black arc on the garage floor. Using body English, she straightened and lined out for the exit. As the front wheel lifted, Karla Raven caught second gear and wheelied beyond the camera's sight.

TEAM PSI

WILL BE BACK IN

# IMPLACABLE ALPHA